WILGA CREEK

a Novel by Arthur Rowe.

Rowe, Arthur Joseph, 1938 ---

This book is dedicated to the memories of my late son and grandson, David Bruce Rowe and David Aaron Rowe.

1

The soft light of a half-moon revealed a sea of Mitchell grass rippling in a gentle breeze. Resembling a low island, the clump of gidgee rose out of this wide expanse. The shadowy, rock-like forms breaking the surface nearby were, in fact, hobbled horses grazing contentedly.

A small shining lagoon, however, was real. It was made by an artesian bore, discharging its almost boiling underground water to cool. From the lagoon, plain as an exposed reef, a recently delved bore drain ran its well-maintained course for miles; such water not dissipated enroute would reach a distant chain of waterholes that passed for a creek.

Close to the thicket, like a boat riding at anchor in the lee of a windward shore, stood a wagonette. A lighted hurricane lamp within combined eerily with the moonlight and the dying campfire to produce flickering phantoms of light and shadow.

As he kneeled on the floor of the wagonette beside his straining young wife in labour, the drover had now to act as midwife at the birth of his second child. A competent stockman in an age when such men were of necessity their own veterinarians, he nonetheless found this a traumatic, nerve-wracking experience he would never wish to repeat.

More precious than some foaling mare or calving cow, she was the brave young bush girl he loved and cherished more than his life itself. He dared not contemplate the thought of anything going wrong in this remote area, so far from any assistance. A calm jewel of a lass, she assured him that everything was completely normal and going to plan.

He smiled ironically, as he mused over her definition of 'normal and going to plan'. The baby should not have been due until more than two weeks away. They were headed towards her parents' home at Charleville, still three days distant.

Driving the wagonette, accompanied by their infant daughter, and with a saddle horse and a packhorse running behind, the idea had been that Kathleen and little Ellen would remain with his in-laws for the birth of the new baby, and for some time afterwards.

He would then return home, and with the rest of his plant of horses, cook and overlanders, leave immediately for a station on the Georgina, 500 miles northwest of Charleville. There he would take charge of three hundred and fifty quality shorthorn bulls which he had contracted to deliver to two big runs beyond Katherine in the Northern Territory. It could well be two years, depending on seasonal conditions and other work, before he could expect to join his family again.

Kathleen, with the children, had accepted her parents' offer to stay with them and she would help them out by serving in their shop when able.

Tom and Kathleen always missed each other very much during these long absences, but stoical acceptance of such hardships was an inevitable part of life, although Kathleen frequently argued to accompany her husband on his droves. At times, Tom had been persuaded to take his wife and daughter along, on shorter routes through easier country of Southern Queensland and Northern New South Wales with quiet cattle. But despite Kathleen's protestations to the contrary, the isolated, unforgiving droves through much of the Channel Country, the Territory, or the country from Bedourie and Birdsville to Hergott Springs (now Maree) were no places for women and kids; particularly as big, half-wild bullocks were prone to rush when unsettled by lightning, thirst or any other factor.

Frequently, more than local knowledge and recent word-of-mouth reports were necessary for survival of herds. He often had to be able to follow a sequence of thunderstorms for enough green pick and claypan water to get through as the seasons dried up, just as native animals and brumbies instinctively do. Aboriginals learned such lessons from childhood. White men, too: explorers, drovers and prospectors either had observed and learnt, or had paid for their ignorance with their lives in such country. Barely 36 years before, Bourke and Wills had died battling such country. Many other white men had succumbed since.

Real bushmen, such as A.C. Gregory the surveyor, and others like him, had opened the door to this wide land. Men like Landsborough, McKinlay and Howitt had searched for ill fated, less competent, though more widely known explorers who had sought fame in a harsh environment. It was bushmen, so little remembered who had provided the real impetus to settlement of the inland.

Tom looked forward to again challenging the vast interior with the confidence of one born and bred to it; one who loved and understood it. When the rivers ran, the feed grew lush, the birdlife abounded and the wildflowers bloomed, one could almost dismiss from one's mind the dusty, arid, waterless hell that would inevitably return as part of the seasonal cycle.

Rabbit plagues, he knew, were becoming the critical factor that could eventually destroy much of the inland in a way that seasonal variations alone, never had! In huge areas the mulga and saltbush had already disappeared, tender young regrowth eaten out to the roots or ringbarked; all pasture destroyed, the soil eroded by the wind, the sandhills crept in. Could it ever be reversed? Could the country ever come back?

2

The young wife's confident assurances of a safe, straightforward birth proved correct. Their prayers were answered! In the small hours of an 1898 autumn morning, Joseph Thomas Merriton came into this world. A few days later, his wife and babies safely delivered to his in-laws' address, Tom Merriton set off in charge of a competent overlanding team on a journey that would take them across half the breadth of a continent.

At age thirty-one, he was well regarded throughout the Inland as a sober, courageous man whose word could be taken as a steadfast guarantee. Tom was an excellent cattleman who could be trusted to deliver any mob in his charge with minimal or no losses, and in the finest condition that was humanly possible. Accordingly, his services were eagerly sought and therefore he, like any other master craftsman, was able to amply provide for his family.

The two following years passed with good seasons. Several times the western river channels broke their banks and inundated the adjacent flatlands for miles around, intensively enough to even check the exploding population of rabbits to a noticeable degree.

It was a full two and a half years before Tom eventually returned to his family from the wild, exiting Victoria River region by way of Anthony's Lagoon and the prime Barkly Tableland with a mob of Territory store bullocks which he contracted to deliver to the railhead of Hughenden on the line snaking out from Townsville.

When his long-awaited reunion with Kathleen, little Ellen and baby Joe finally came, Tom was dramatically reminded of just how much family life he was missing. Ellen had grown from a toddler to a little girl with the best part of one year's schooling. The baby boy at whose birth Tom had assisted, was now a sturdy infant, friendly but shy in the company of

8

a father who was a complete stranger to him.

The young family had not long arrived home from Charleville when a telegram arrived offering another droving job.

"My word," Merriton told his wife, "no wonder that fellow has made a fortune! He must have the sixth sense of an old blackfellow! We've been gone nearly three years, yet he wires me barely days after I get back here."

"Really top drovers are worth keeping track of!" was Kathleen's reply. She was proud of her man and his reputation. It was true that a large measure of the success of men like Tyson, Kidman and others was attributable to their ability to quickly locate and hire master drovers in whatever localities they were needed.

Tom had already decided that one more overlanding trip would be his last, and then they would move to some place where he could still make a decent living yet spend more time with his wife and family. Perhaps he could become a carrier with a team-based at some good little railway town with a school for the kids, and more female company for Kathleen.

"Don't be too hasty," she told him, "I knew you were a drover when I married you. Whatever you decide will be fine with me!"

"No, this next job will definitely be the end of it," he told her firmly.

He would sorely miss the hard, nomadic way of life, Kathleen knew. But having decided his course, he would not renege on that decision. As Tom saddled a horse and rode away towards town to wire acceptance of what would be his last such contract, both he and Kathleen were reflecting on the hold it had always had over both their lives. Often boring, always worrying; a gnawing dread of the next waterhole being dry, or of little feed along the track; the eagerness with which he would update his information from any traveller who chanced to pass from the other direction. Those dangerous but exhilarating, wild dashes through the gidgee in the blackness of a stormy night, lit only by flashes of lightning, as men rode full gallop for miles to catch and steady the lead; to finally ring the snorting, terrified, weary mob. And the excitement of seeing new horizons! How his eyes had lit up as he had regaled the family with tales of the wild north, of buffalo, crocodiles, deep wild rivers and even wilder blacks!

His own personal safety had always been irrelevant to him, and even his wife now had come to accept, as he did, that he was virtually indestructible. But how he would miss the adventurous life! Kathleen was thankful for his determination to take a less nomadic role as husband and father, yet she would never have pressed him to do so.

Kathleen's father, Ellen's and Joe's beloved Grandpa, was a lovable but irresponsible rogue, always a source of worry to her devoted mother, whose ever-watchful eye and firm common sense were all that had kept their small business solvent. A born gambler and instigator of hare-brained schemes, Kathleen's father been cashiered from one of England's most illustrious cavalry regiments, had disgraced his family's name in a couple of scandals, and was banished to the Colonies. He was, in short, a "Remittance Man", the second son of an Earl, who had bought him a Queensland sheep station, and had sent him a regular allowance on the condition that he would remain in Australia, never again to return and darken the old ancestral doorstep.

Less than two years after his arrival in Queensland, the "Remittance Man" had lost the sheep station in a card game, and had won or lost several other wagers with his daring but often plainly stupid feats of horsemanship, which had managed to cripple a couple of good horses. Eventually, he had then found employment as a police trooper. It was then he began to direct all of his not inconsiderable charm at a young Irish hotel maid.

"You must have kissed the Blarney Stone," she had at first dismissed him, yet he'd persevered. She'd proved a steadying influence. They'd married, and she had managed to keep him more or less in line through the ensuing years. They were a devoted couple, and though the hardships of the Queensland bush took the lives of three of their infants, they still had managed to raise to maturity four fine young offspring, of which Kathleen was the youngest. All were baptised as Roman Catholics, yet raised and confirmed as Anglicans, in another of those mutual compromises with which Kathleen's mother never had felt entirely at ease.

Unlike her mother, Kathleen did not need to be such a repository of combined diplomacy and common sense in her marriage. She felt very secure in the love and stability of her honest hard-working husband. Eagerly, she looked forward to his return from South Australia, and the start of a new chapter of their life together.

Tom left with the mob of 1200 fats from the western Channel country for the railhead at Hergott Springs, buoyed with the satisfaction of a bushman seeing a bureaucratic impost disappear forever.

For Australia had become a federation and all customs duties between the states were abolished under the Constitution, from 1st January 1901. This mob would be one of the first to pass through the old Birdsville gate without having to pay the previous exorbitant dues of one pound ($2) per head. At a time when store bullocks frequently sold for three or four pounds in the paddock, and "fats" for ten or twelve pounds on a good Adelaide market, such Colonial Governments' tariff charges proved an extreme burden on producers.

It was not an easy drove. There was no shortage of water, but feed was more of a problem, there having been several other big mobs in a short space of time to have taxed the limited resources. Tom made several deviations from the route and sometimes camped for a few days at favourable locations to allow the cattle to maintain their condition. But by the time they reached their destination, the big bullocks had quietened, even fattened, under the care of good, steady men and the easy pace. Vendor and buyer alike had cause for satisfaction.

When the boss drover finally rode back towards the Queensland side, it became obvious that his timing was none too soon. The country was drying up, rapidly deteriorating, accelerated by the ravages of rabbit hordes. Unless heavy rains fell soon, either here or far to the north in the headwaters of the big river system, a major drought was a certainty. But drought was always a threat, a fact of life here. The occupations of overlander and pastoralist had never been for the faint-hearted!

None the less, Tom's instincts now shouted to him that he should be glad in the knowledge that he would no longer have to move cattle down the stock routes of the Cooper, the Diamantina and the Georgina.

3

The small settlement of Wilga Creek lay beside the Western Railway line in southern Queensland, several hours east by train from Kathleen's parents' home but still a night and half a day's travel west of Brisbane.

A pretty little oasis to break the monotony of an almost flat landscape, the tiny town boasted a post office, a police station, a general store, two hotels and, most importantly of all, a school! A two-teacher school at that!

On the opposite side of the rail line to the town, perched on a slight rise overlooking the little creek that had lent its name to the settlement, stood a tidy but humble sawn timber house. Its outbuildings, (a slab barn, a hayshed, a windmill and a small set of yards) nestled among a few scattered wilgas and belahs. The modest 320-acre selection was now home to the Merriton family. The year was 1905; Ellen was ten years old and Joe seven. Tom had become a general carrier, with a bullock team and a big flat-topped wagon. He delivered supplies from town and the rail siding to those orderly, well-managed sheep stations of the prime country to the south as well as to the much larger runs, mostly cattle runs but a few with sheep, in the more hilly country to the north of the line. His return trips to Wilga Creek usually brought the wagon home laden high and heavily with bales of wool for railing to Brisbane. Those first couple of years were difficult financially. The Merritons were feted to establish their new enterprise during the great drought of 1902/03 but they counted themselves as fortunate. Tom's longest absences were now in the order of a few weeks, compared to the several months or even years, of his droving days. The little family had grown by two; daughters Leah and Jennifer were born in 1903 and 1905 respectively.

Ellen and Joe were happy, contented and hard-working children who cheerfully carried out their allotted tasks before and after school each day. They tended the vegetable garden, fed the fowls, collected the eggs and milked the two nanny goats, which, together with the two horses and sixteen working bullocks, constituted the family's total livestock assets.

With childish fervour, they also conscientiously attacked with a hoe any prickly pear that they discovered on the small holding. Fortunately, for them, the pear was nowhere near as prolific in the district as it had become in the rich, ringbarked brigalow lands further east. The siblings were told of the "pear-menace" by their grandfather when he had drawn to their attention the millions of acres of infested land visible from the train windows during a trip they had taken with their grandparents to Toowoomba and Brisbane. Grandpa had explained the significance of the problem to them.

Just as surely as the introduction of the European rabbit had done, so too, other introduced species of fauna and flora had exposed the fragility and vulnerability of the seemingly harsh Australian landscape and its unique native vegetation and wildlife. Throughout the country, transplanted pests such as the fox, the feral pig, feral goat, Southeast Asian water buffalo, cattle tick, lantana, groundsel bush, scotch thistle, the dreadful prickly pear and many others, were all to have a devastating effect on whatever localities to which they acclimatised. This was always to the detriment of the native ecology and usually also to the commercially useful introduced domesticated species.

Yet not even educated, intelligent Grandpa could begin to envisage the extent of the encroachment and land degradation that would ultimately accrue. Nor could he imagine that Australians generally would be so tardy to heed the lessons already so clearly evident.

In the fields of interest that were being urgently and earnestly addressed, many years were to pass before science could bring even a few of these pests under viable means of control. The cactoblastis bug introduced in the 1930s and the myxomatosis virus of the 1950s would greatly reduce, and in some regions almost eliminate the respective problems of prickly pear and rabbit. For the culling of feral livestock, it would take the enormous expense of the Brucellosis and Tuberculosis Eradication Campaign of the nineteen-eighties before substantial inroads could be made against feral buffaloes, cattle, pigs, donkeys and brumbies. Many other introduced pests would remain virtually unscathed indefinitely. Apart from rabbits, erosion was also contributed to by compaction and overgrazing by hard hooved domestic animals. Even in tilling the soil, a long history of trial and error in adapting the farming practices of cool temperate Europe and North America to this tropical and subtropical land of climes ranging from rainforest to desert would ensure that the ecological and agricultural deterioration of Australia's rural areas would be enormous by the time of our Bicentennial of European settlement.

Few, if any, Australians of the early twentieth century could have visualised the enormity of such an impact beyond the problems of their own regional areas, any more than they could have comprehended the massive technological changes that would transform the fields of transportation, communication, medicine, social attitudes and leisure. So it was in a physically demanding but morally uplifting, God-fearing world of woodstoves, kerosene lanterns, cold showers and bush remedies, that young Joe grew to adolescence, his character moulded in righteousness; his strong young body having survived accidents, fever and childhood illnesses without the help of analgesics or antibiotics, but his psyche untrammelled by those insecurities of a modern child, the threats of nuclear holocaust, and the undermining of family life and community values.

By the end of 1911, at the age of thirteen and a half, Joe had completed primary schooling. He was a lively, intelligent lad with a strong urge to broaden his horizons, to earn his independence and to become a proficient cattleman. Tom and Kathleen had hoped their son might learn a trade. The local blacksmith had expressed a willingness to apprentice the likeable boy, but Joe's heart was not inclined to such a steady occupation. By way of compromise with his parents, Joe went to work on a nearby station under a fair and competent manager. Though he toiled industriously, and the employer was satisfied with his efforts, Joe's restlessness did not abate.

Twelve months passed. Tom recognised the stultifying effect a year of sheep husbandry had made on the boy, who had always yearned to follow the stock routes with cattle. He relented and allowed Joe to start out on the droving game under an old family friend, a tough but fair man.

The lad thrived on the life, as his father had done before him. His cheerful optimism returned, and no long hot day in the saddle was too arduous; no night watch too cold or boring to dull his alertness, no chore too menial. The few years of Joe's droving career filled him with a sense of satisfaction and self-confidence he would always treasure in retrospect.

4

Following Turkey's entry into the Great War on November 5th, 1914, the forces of Jamal Pasha and his very able Chief of Staff, the Bavarian General Kress von Kressenstein, advanced across the Sinai Desert Peninsula in three columns totalling some 15, 000 men. Their objective was to seize the Suez Canal, but although some of their units briefly managed to broach the great arterial waterway, these were immediately repulsed by the British 42nd Territorial Division. In the wake of the ill-advised and wasteful Gallipoli landings which tied up Australian, New Zealand and British infantry as well as dismounted Anzac Light Horsemen fighting as infantrymen, (with universally horrendous casualties until the final, brilliant Dardanelles evacuation of December 1915 and January 1916) the spotlight swung away from the Canal Defence, which remained more or less a holding operation until early 1916.

The end of the Gallipoli campaign released British, Australian and New Zealand Infantry for the campaigns in France, as well as some British Infantry, Yeomanry and the Australian and New Zealand Light Horse Divisions for operations in Egypt and the Sinai. Seven British and Commonwealth divisions under the command of General Sir Archibald Murray now garrisoned Egypt. A line was formed to the east of the Suez Canal to counter an expected new Turkish assault under Von Kressenstein, while other units including the Australian 1st Light Horse Brigade were dispatched south and west to put down the marauding Senoussi Arabs" Backed by the Turks, these had come out of the Libyan desert, it was said, to start their own Holy war. The real reason these tribesmen had entered southwest Egypt, and one conveniently overlooked at the time, was that the Senoussi were merely continuing their resistance to the colonisation of their country, Libya, by Britain's ally, Italy, since 1912. But now, it was feared, they would foment rebellion and sabotage in Egypt.

To the east of the Canal, Anzac and Yeomanry mounted men, and sturdy British infantry who held the outposts and oases of the Sinai, fought many a bloody battle as they sought to protect their positions and the railway supply line now snaking out into the desert from the canal base of Kantara. Not only had isolated, small garrisons to contend with the attacks of strong Turkish units, but also each had to be vigilant against Bedouin raiders, who could pose as neutral civilian nomads by day, yet creep stealthily into small sleeping outposts under cover of darkness to knife and garrotte the defenders as they slept in their blankets.

Hundreds of British Yeomanry from one mounted brigade were wiped out in surprise attacks by 5000 Turks at Romani, Katia and Oghratina Oases. They had fought valiantly but were overwhelmed in late April 1916. Many of their wounded later were murdered and their corpses robbed, by Bedouin who followed up like jackals before again melting away into the desert. At Bir el Duidar a detachment of less than one hundred Scots Fusiliers fought like tigers to successfully repel six or seven times their number in Turks and Bedouin under cover of fog. The Scots had lost only 23 men, killing more than three times that number of raiders, before being relieved by the Australian 5th Light Horse Regiment.

But the tide gradually turned against the Turks. By the end of April, Australian Light Horsemen and New Zealand Mounted Riflemen were camped in every oasis in the area; had fortified surrounding redoubts and had manned outposts securing the surrounding high ground. Mounted patrols ranged far to the north, harassing the Turks with the confidence of well-mounted bushmen whose horses easily ran down, or out-ran the tough little grey ponies of the Turkish Cavalry.

There were still setbacks, particularly from ambushes and from accurate bombing by low flying Turkish aircraft, but by June it had become possible to release small numbers of men to enjoy forty-eight hours of leave in Port Said, a brief respite from the dirty, louse-infested existence of desert life.

Hidebound thinking of British Military tradition, however, made no allowance for Australian reluctance to wear ragged, uncomfortably hot, desert-dirty, regulation tunics on leave. Anzacs preferred to buy clean new khaki cotton shirts to wear instead. Casual attitudes to saluting officers and various other failings led to a marked degree of hostility between British officers and military police on the one hand and Anzac troopers on the other. The preponderance of charges brought by Port Said Military Police against Light Horsemen on leave sorely tried the patience of Anzac officers, until a typically Aussie solution presented itself when one Light Horse regimental commanding officer discovered that the British commander at Port Said did not have jurisdiction to hear the charges. He insisted that all such cases be tried by the troopers' C.O. back at regimental H.Q. and that the M.P.s laying such charges must come out to the camp to give their testimony.

On the very first occasion that British military justice was to be so tested, the Queensland unit judiciously selected their worst rogue horses and provided these to meet the train as mounts for the visiting M.P.s. The resultant outcome was to produce a refreshing change of attitude by the largely city-bred police. British M.P.s thereafter showed a marked lack of further interest in antipodean misdeeds following the humiliating experiences of having been either bucked off or taken by their mounts on terrifying, out of control, jaunts into the desert.

And so, it was to this tough, competent, hard riding and proud, but far from "pukka" Light Horse Regiment that the young reinforcement, Private J.T. Merriton, arrived in the Northern Hemisphere Summer of 1916, just in time to be blooded in a battle against renewed Turkish attacks. Anzac "Listening Posts silently reconnoitred and melted back into the night to warn of any enemy advance, " Cossack Posts", lay in wait to pour a withering fusillade of fire into oncoming Turks, after which the "Cossacks" would dash back to mount up and retreat towards their Regiments and safety. It was in these sorts of situations that the young trooper's excellent night vision, honed by three years of night watch keeping on Queensland cattle camps, stood Joe in good stead. For the enemy were skilled in night manoeuvres too, capable of arising in large numbers from the shadows of bushes or sand ridges to surprise and bayonet the handful of men of any unwary outpost before they could mount their horses. Young Merriton's unfailing alertness and ability to sort out the shadows under the brilliant desert starlight, soon earned for the lad, the respect of his section mates.

Holding the great Romani Oasis and surrounding wells, the Australian general, Chauvel, lured a mighty Turkish army into a desperate trap. The Battle of Romani was a close-run thing, a bloody, brilliant, gamble that paid off.

Together with the 1st Light Horse Brigade, now reunited after the Sennousi Campaign, the 2nd Light Horse Brigade, the New Zealanders, Yeomanry Brigades, and various batteries of Royal Horse Artillery were all hard-pressed to stem the advance and sustained heavy casualties as a huge Turkish army swept down on Romani, supported by aircraft and Austrian artillery. The En Zeds, with the Yeomanry, broke the Turkish left flank while the Australians held fast in a furious night battle on the 4th of August. This Anzac Mounted Division, now reinforced by the addition of the 3rd Light Horse Brigade, forced the enemy to retreat, still fighting hard, back towards El Katia on the 5th of August. In a matter of a few weeks, the young bush lad had become a battle-hardened trooper in the nucleus of an army destined to become one of the greatest mounted corps in all of history.

To them, the remainder of 1916 became a mixture of boredom, skirmishes, and isolated sections or troops confronting sudden death in remote outposts, interspersed with long night rides such as that by the 1st and 3rd Light Horse Brigades and New Zealand Mounted Brigade, British Artillery Batteries and the Imperial Camel Brigade, to occupy El Arish. A further thirty-mile ride to pursue the evacuated Turkish garrison, and the subsequent bloody victory of Maghdada. Joe, as part of the 2nd Brigade, missed this bigger action. They guarded the right flank.

Then, on the night of the 8th January 1917, came another thirty-mile night ride, which preceded a bloody fight for the Palestinian border town of Rafa. The successful conclusion of this battle saw the Desert Column enter the Holy Land on 9th January.

"Whacko! In the land of milk and honey at last!" Joe observed appreciatively. "We're not home and dry yet lad," the Sergeant cautioned, "so just remember to keep your wits about you!"

Close to the coast, in the northwest Sinai and southern Palestine, were pretty villages, cultivation, even green grass! But treachery lurked among the mosques, the churches and the orchards, in the forms of snipers With the En Zeds, the 2nd Brigade probed and tested Jacko's cavalry patrols and isolated infantry positions, but as March rolled on, the expected Turkish counter-attacks failed to materialise. The railway continued unimpeded, to reach out along the old caravan route, bringing supplies and infantry reinforcements from the Canal. The huge British Imperial Divisions were now massing for the first Battle for Gaza.

In late March, under cover of darkness followed by morning fog, a great wave of Infantry, Artillery, Yeomanry, Light Horse, N.Z.M.R. and Camel Corps advance against Gaza and its redoubtable fortifications of Ali Muntar which overlooked the city. By the time the fog lifted in mid-morning, Joe's regiment was already positioned as part of a semicircle flanking the battlefield to cut off any likely Turkish reinforcements, yet under orders not to attack the town itself. The British General Staff had decreed that to be the lot of an Infantry Division!

Those brave lads of the British Infantry, no longer protected by fog, advanced across open ground under withering fire to take Ali Muntar with bayonet, only to lose it again under a strong Turkish counter-attack; then to re-take it, and so on, until some positions were taken four times, and lost three. Finally, Anzac mounted men were turned loose against the city itself, to gallop with fixed bayonets against redoubts protected by walls of stone or walls of cactus.

Dismounting to engage in fierce bayonet fighting with Jacko and his Austrian gunners, Joe and his mates fought like madmen. The Turks broke and ran when the two Australian and New Zealand Mounted Brigades swarmed into Gaza itself. On the heights above, the magnificent British 53rd Infantry Division, at tremendous cost, had secured Ali Muntar. Yet later, to the protesting disbelief of General Chauvel, the New Zealand General Chaytor, and all ranks down to the youngest trooper, came the order from the British General Staff, "Retire!" Give the place back to Jacko!

With other Light Horse and Yeomanry brigades capably repelling Turkish reinforcements, the decision to retire seemed a shameful idiotic waste of life and purpose.

"What sort of idiot is running this campaign?" Joe wondered aloud.

"Some chinless inbred sort, I shouldn't wonder," An older trooper replied laconically, with the air of one who'd seen it all before, at Gallipoli and elsewhere.

The great army pulled back to sit and wait, to be bombarded by Turkish shells and aeroplanes. Young Joe Merriton was disgusted! Youthful, patriotic exuberance was beginning to be replaced by a dawning awareness of the futility and obscenity of war.

Less than one month later, the whole debacle was repeated at the Second Battle for Gaza, but by this time a great Turkish line of defence was drawn across Palestine, from the sea inland to Beersheba. Again, some mule-headed British General had decreed that the Gaza/Ali Muntar objective would be taken by the courageous but slow-moving infantry, so once again the losses were horrendous and the result was another negative one; British Imperial losses for the two Gaza battles totalled more than twenty thousand men. Accordingly, for the following few months, the progress of the war returned to a stalemate once more.

For Joe, this translated to a series of patrols and minor raids, reconnoitring and harassment, broken by a weeklong spell for the Regiment at a beach camp on a stretch of coastline many miles southwest of the front. For an even more fortunate few, one in thirty, this was an opportunity to be rostered for five days of leave away from the Regiment.

Although two days were taken up in train travel to and from Cairo, there remained three days of leave in the Egyptian capital. Joe was one of those fortunate few.

5

Sister Ellen Merriton of the Australian Military General Hospital, Cairo, was surprised and pleased when her brother sought her out on his first day's leave. Almost three years had passed since they last had seen each other" and Ellen was determined to make the most of the opportunity.

"Never mind the flesh-pots of Cairo" O Wild Man of the Desert," she told him, "we have three days in which to return you to a civilised state of mind and behaviour!"

Joe happily acceded to his sister's fussing over him. Both were home-sick for Australia and their parents' unpretentious home at Wilga Creek. In her company, he found himself adapting cheerfully to some very un-Light Horseman-like practices such as saluting British officers and being as well-groomed yet regimentally dressed as was possible given the basic limitations of army kit. Twice he dined with her at one of the more fashionable restaurants and was surprised to find that he enjoyed the experience.

For his final day of leave before entraining back to the Regiment, Ellen managed to organise for herself both a full day off duty and a borrowed Model T Ford car so that she could share some sightseeing of the pyramids and other points of interest with him. There was another agreeable surprise in store for Joe as well. Ellen was accompanied by a fellow nurse, a young New Zealander whose initially demure demeanour could not disguise her laughing brown eyes and dry sense of humour. Both young women wore civilian garb and Joe thought they looked quite like a couple of well-bred English ladies.

Diana Smithfield, at twenty-one, was two years older than Joe, yet the strong masculine presence, quiet self-confidence and desert-toughened, whipcord physique of her friend's attractive younger brother served to bring out in Diana an uncharacteristic, girlish bashfulness that she had not felt in years! Had Joe suspected for one moment that his sister might be attempting the gentle art of matchmaking, he too might have been a little less self-assured. He saw this strikingly good-looking girl as merely Ellen's friend, probably of the same age as his sister, but pleasant company though a little reserved. At this stage, her potential as a romantic prospect did not enter his mind, although she did have a soft, attractive femininity about her that her brusque, somewhat defensive witticisms could not entirely conceal. He felt particularly drawn to her as he observed the genuine concern in her eyes for some ragged little urchins who eked out a living selling souvenirs and trinkets. Noting this soft centre to an apparent hard case, he was naïve enough to comment on it, expressing surprise that such a gentle soul could cope with the horrors of assisting with drastic surgery and patching up a constant stream of wounded, sometimes mutilated soldiers.

Defensively, Diana retaliated, "Oh, we manage, don't we, Ellen? But then, you great callous brutes are scarcely innocent little children, are you?"

Playfully, she made a face at Joe, lightly covering her embarrassment at his having articulated her obvious vulnerability.

"Sorry if I've put my foot in it!" Joe apologised, "I didn't mean to sound patronizing. I think it's great that you girls haven't been hardened by all the slaughter. I'm not proud of the fact that I'm getting far too used to it!"

Ellen stared innocently ahead, hiding a smug smirk at her brother's discomfort. Now Diana had him on the back foot! Serve him right, he'd been a little too full of himself!

"You're forgiven!" Diana told him, mischievously leaning across to give him a maternal kiss on the cheek. Ellen giggled aloud.

Joe blushed like a schoolboy. This girl had his measure, but he silently promised himself he'd be ready for her the next time they met. Even so, he'd need to watch his P's and Q's; like Ellen, she held Officer rank. He'd bear that in mind, too!

It was a refreshed, rested and rejuvenated young Trooper Merriton who returned to Palestine, only to be brutally jolted back to reality a few evenings later when a "Taube" bombed the camp. The terrified screams of injured and dying horses and the shouts and moans of wounded men rent the late afternoon air. Riding as part of the detailed escort that accompanied the wounded back to the Red Cross camp near the railhead, with the screams and cries of agony still fresh in his mind, Joe found himself reflecting on the countless tribes and armies through history who had probably fought and died for possession of those same wells that the Regiment now held and defended against even aerial bombing.

Warring bands of Bedouin, armies of Napoleon, of the Saracens, the Crusaders, of Alexander, of the Roman Empire, of Philistines and Israelites, must have all passed this way. Perhaps even Joseph and Mary may have camped by these very wells as they fled with the infant Christ to Egypt to escape the wrath of Herod!

6

The south east of Palestine in Mid-October, 1917 saw the Turks still entrenched at Beersheba Australian and New Zealand units a dozen miles south-west and twenty-five miles south-east, laboured to dig out the big wells of Esani and Asluj, blown in by German and Austrian engineers to deny water to the occupying Anzacs and Camel Corps.

Strong Turkish patrols continued to ride out from Beersheba to harass Anzac outposts but showed a marked reluctance to engage large units. Such was not the case further west towards Gaza, however. In late October, some engagements in that area were briefly fought at Brigade strength.

Riding from Asluj, through the moonlit night of the 30th October, Joe and the rest of the Anzac Mounted Division positioned themselves for the attack on Beersheba, as did units of the Australian Mounted Division from Khalasa and Esani, with two British Infantry divisions from Esani.

Beersheba! Where Hagar was banished into the desert: where her child, Ishmael, was rescued by God's intervention. Where Abraham had made a treaty with Abimelech, the Philistine. Beersheba, a prosperous Roman garrison town in the infancy of Christianity. It was now an important Turkish garrison town.

Beersheba! The name was about to signify a proud day of glory that would remain enshrined; a legend, in the memories of horsemen from two infant sister-nations of the South-West Pacific.

For, while to scholars the ancient Hebrew name meant "Well of the Seven" or "Well of the Oath", and while its Arabic name, Bir-es-Seba meant, "Well of the Lion", to the Desert Mounted Corps, it merely meant water and plenty of it! Whatever the cost, Beersheba must be taken by nightfall!

In the early morning sunlight, battle commenced. Smaller Turkish outposts on the way were swiftly eliminated. The mounted men broke from the cover of the Judean ranges for a five-mile dash across the plain and between the low hills flanking the saucer-like location of the town.

First at a fast canter, then at a gallop, riding to cut off a surprised Turkish Cavalry regiment; pursuing them right to their sanctuary beyond defending redoubts, Joe's regiment dashed wildly through an Arab village, across a wadi, then left their horses with holders in the shelter of its bank, as they stormed up and over to tackle the heavily defended redoubts of Bir es Sqati. Beersheba was still five miles distant. British Artillery wheeled their guns from the gallop to a dusty standstill and engaged the defenders' mountain guns at almost point-blank range. Rifle, machine gun, artillery shell and bayonet in a frantic crescendo, was capped by aircraft and bombing as Turkish planes heavily bombed some of the attacking units. Other Light Horse regiments galloped through the red haze attacking the other strong point of Tel es Sabe. Joe's rifle barrel was hot, and his bayonet bloodied before their first objective fell halfway through the day.

Remounted, the 2nd Brigade then raced away to hold the Hebron road against Mechanised Infantry reinforcements. Every man of the Desert Mounted Corps was aware they must take the town that first day.

Without the wells, there was no water closer than Esani or Asluj for the horses. The infantry divisions right along the front would be in a hopeless position without mounted support. British and Australian airmen were doing their best in support and reconnaissance, but still, a few Turkish aircraft continued to bomb and machine-gun the attacking horsemen. The situation remained desperate late into the afternoon. Nightfall was fast approaching.

Then, with the sun low on the horizon, an unbroken line of men and horses emerged from the direction of H.Q. The 4th Brigade, "Grant's Mob," trotted out of the swirling red dust, a grim, relentless wave, breaking into a canter, then a gallop for the final charge. Their casualties were relatively light, audacity their friend as Light Horse now closing too swiftly for the defending artillery left many shells exploding harmlessly behind them. Most of the rifle and machine-gun fire also passed harmlessly overhead as the now rattled defenders forgot to lower their sights against the fast-moving wall of horsemen. The mounted regiments galloped up the slopes and leaped the redoubt trenches as Turkish bayonets thrust upwards seeking the underbellies of fast-moving horses. Whole squadrons briefly dismounted to jump into the trenches and silence the defenders with bayonets. Remounting, they poured into the city. The tough Australian and New Zealand horses of all Desert Mounted Corps brigades themselves that day, the right to drink from the ancient wells of Beersheba.

The following day the big push began against all fortifications east to Gaza, while the 2nd L.H. Brigade patrolled the Hebron Valley to guard against any renewed Turkish advances against Beersheba. The 2nd's three-component regiments had some encounters with Turkish outposts and patrols, not to mention some nasty surprises when distant enemy gunners accurately found their range with the efficient Austrian howitzers, ably assisted by Bedouin spotters in the hills.

To the west, Gaza fell in the third and final great battle of that name. After an intensive bombardment by the Royal Navy, the Light Horse, Yeomanry and Infantry Divisions had driven the Turks out of the city in disarray. Now the Anzac Mounted Division moved north at a furious pace in pursuit of the retreating garrisons, killing hundreds of the rear-guard, taking a couple of thousand prisoners and many heavy guns, although at great hardship to the Anzac horses. These had to endure up to three days without a drink. But a new spirit of optimism had swept over the Desert Mounted Corps. It had awakened even before Beersheba, when the new British Commander in Egypt and Palestine, General Allenby, himself an old Cavalry man, had heralded a refreshing change in outlook.

In their wild sweeps against the retreating enemy, the Anzacs, essentially mounted infantry, envied the long cavalry sabres of their Yeomanry friends. Joe had always found exhilaration in wild gallops under fire, the desperate kill-or-be-killed rushes with fixed bayonet into the enemy territory, but sabres would have made the pursuits easier and more efficient.

With the supreme self-confidence of youth, his mind rejected any fleeting thoughts about his own personal safety. Indeed, he was very fortunate. The sadness of seeing many of his mates killed or badly wounded, over a long period of time left many a dull ache. Joe was one of a mere handful of men in his regiment who had not yet become a casualty. Most of them were wounded at least once. He could still feel compassion for maimed and dying horses, and even for a brave adversary whose lifeblood drained out upon the bare ground; though these things always touched him, somehow he had managed not to dwell on them. He was a survivor, yet, in his reflective moments, he would wonder, in a strangely detached way, if he was losing his humanity and degenerating into a heartlessly efficient fighting machine who thrived on frequent short bursts of danger and excitement which enlivened an otherwise harsh, boring, louse-ridden existence. Immediately before an action, excitement and anticipation submerged fear; during battle, adrenalin extinguished it for man and horse alike. Only in the reflective aftermath were the risks and sacrifices consciously apparent.

The latter weeks of November 1917 saw the Desert Mounted Corps in pursuit of retreating Turkish, Austrian and German units right across the whole breadth of Palestine. The Anzac Mounted Division, to which Joe's brigade belonged, supported by the British Yeomanry Mounted Division, accounted for the western section to the sea. They swept towards Jaffa. Their right flank joined the Australian Mounted Division, supported by the Camel Corps, as those divisions pursued Jacko back towards Bethlehem and Jerusalem. Hundreds upon hundreds of Turkish motor trucks, mules, oxen, horses and wagons littered the roads north, shattered or abandoned as the Anzacs and their artillery accounted for thousands of the enemy killed or taken prisoner.

Returning down the road between Jaffa and Gaza with his troop to meet and reinforce the escort of an Anzac Supply Column following in support of the Brigade, Joe felt sickened by one such sight. They rode through the remains of a battered, broken and deserted Turkish Transport Company, overtaken and shelled the previous morning when breaking camp. Dead and dying animals were still yoked to wrecked wagons; others unscathed, but perishing of thirst or exhaustion, were still trapped by their yokes and traces, while dead men littered the roadside. One elderly, aristocratic-looking Turk lying on his back, sightless eyes staring upwards in death, reminded Joe uncannily of his own grandfather.

More revolting yet, a horde of human vultures, Palestinian civilians, were greedily looting the wagons and the camp, with callous disregard for the agony of the wounded or thirsty beasts still trapped in harness to the wrecked vehicles.

Under orders to make their rendezvous, the Australians could only spare a few minutes to release some oxen and mules or to despatch the more pitifully mutilated beasts. At least, the surviving animals, once freed, would find water in the wadi, some little distance back from the road. Joe liberated a couple of oxen from a wrecked wagon being looted by an Arab family, man, wife and children. The man looked at Joe with hatred and contempt. Nearby, the dead wagon driver, a fine-looking young soldier, lay naked in the indignity of his corpse having been stripped by looters.

Something snapped! A hot flush of anger and disgust seized Joe when the Arab sneered. Joe decided that he would sooner shoot one of these protected jackals than an honest Turk anytime! He calmly and deliberately raised his rifle. The looter's countenance changed firstly to a look of disbelief, then to one of snivelling fear.

"Meriton! Leave it be!" baked the troop Sergeant. Joe lowered his rifle, as Lieutenant Creyton, some distance away, looked around in surprise at his Sergeant's sudden outburst. He'd missed it all! Only Joe and the Sergeant knew just how close he had come to shooting an unarmed civilian!

Sergeant Quinlan was a man whose basic decency and concern had somehow always seemed at odds with his undeniable power of command. Right from the start, the understanding old bushman had looked on this war not as an adventure, but as an unpleasant chore which Christian duty and Empire loyalty demanded be accomplished as competently, yet humanely as possible. Through nearly three years of bloody warfare, neither his strength of character nor his sense of compassion had altered one iota.

He reined in alongside the lad. There was no recrimination, only sadness in his voice, as he said in his quiet, fatherly way, "Don't harbour bitterness to these people, Joe. They may not share our sensibilities, but they don't have much else, either! They've had to live under foreign Armies for centuries, but they still have their families to feed and clothe, in a countryside laid waste. Who knows what we would do in a similar situation? To them, the Turk is just another invader, the same as we are, and you're too fine a lad to carry the murder of an unarmed man on your conscience through life!"

The Sergeant's words were for Joe's ears only. The lad realised it would go no further, and, so far as the older man was concerned, it was now ancient history.

Joe nodded. He returned Quinlan's earnest gaze.

"Thanks, Sarge," he replied humbly and sincerely.

"B" Troop re-formed and trotted off down the road to find the Anzac Transport column. A still shaken Hassan and his kinfolk wondered at the unpredictability of these strange Australian horse-soldiers.

7

Far to the east, Feisal's Bedouin force, coordinated and directed by Colonel T.E. Lawrence, was making a name for itself, wrecking railway trains and tying up a large Turkish force.

To the northwest, the New Zealand Mounted Rifles had taken Jaffa after some of the most bitterly contested fighting of the war, following the cutting of the Jaffa-Jerusalem railway by the Australian 4th Light Horse Brigade near Ludd. The 1st Brigade took Ludd and Ramleh, the Yeomanry, supported by the Camel Brigade, took El Mughar, and assisted the Infantry in the El Katra battle. Further inland, Hebron, Bethlehem and, finally, Jerusalem had fallen to the Australian Mounted Division by 9th December.

Heavy fighting continued into the New Year, with sniper fire also a continuing problem amongst the pretty northern towns, villages, and surrounding orchards. Much of this area was, effectively, a German colony, and the settlers remained fiercely loyal to the Fatherland, regarding the British occupation as a temporary setback only.

After a three-day battle, Jericho was added to the Desert Corps' laurels on 21st February 1918, and a long halt was called to the advance. The Mounted and Infantry divisions consolidated their gains, which had ended Ottoman rule over Jerusalem and most of the Holy Land for the first time in seven centuries.

Light Horsemen again found themselves living a more orderly existence, camped in neat, regimented rows of tents, sometimes between groves of orange trees, olive trees, or even transplanted Australian eucalypts. The latter appeared to have thrived among Jewish settlements, whose inhabitants prized them greatly.

The enemy had continued to test the northern defences with artillery, infantry and cavalry incursions, together with air raids, but the British and Australian airmen had finally established ascendancy in the air.

Along the coastal areas, "Jaffa fever," malaria and other insect-borne diseases took some toll of the health of the troops, but Joe had been fortunate and was not affected.

Mechanised infantry travelling in motor trucks with motor ambulances, and more sophisticated aeroplanes were beginning to appear in larger numbers, giving a foretaste of a future when stout-hearted horses and hard riding troopers would eventually become anachronisms, but not yet! Not in this war! Motorcycle despatch riders and self-important staff officers in their imposing-looking motor cars all took on a faintly ridiculous air when caught out by all-too-frequent mechanical breakdowns, even on the good roads of the more developed areas.

Whenever a staff car flashed by, Joe would remember, with a mixture of amusement and pride, his sister and the borrowed "Tin Lizzie" in Cairo. Fancy Ellen being able to drive a motor car! Inevitably, his thoughts would also dwell on Diana, Ellen's dark-eyed En Zed girlfriend. She was a darned good sort! No doubt about that! He often wished he'd paid her more attention.

Finally, the Desert Mounted Corps was again advancing. There were a few more desperate affrays for which Joe had lost much of his enthusiasm since the incident with the plunderers of the shattered convoy on the road north from Gaza. Then came the culmination of the Palestinian campaign with General Chetwode's brilliant outflanking of the enemy at Meggido, and the allies swept north and west. The 3rd and 5th Brigades raced ahead to beat the Hedjaz Bedouin under Feisal and Lawrence, to Damascus. The 10th Regiment, 3rd Light Horse Brigade were to claim the honour of being the first into that historic city.

Only a few weeks before the closing stages of the war, Corporal Joe Merriton, one of the few veterans of the regiment who, so far, had come through unscathed, finally saw his luck change. His troop was galloping along a winding track, just emerging from between two hills in pursuit of a Turkish patrol.

Suddenly, two deafening explosions to the right! Joe didn't know whether they were shells or bombs! A split second later, he knew! A roar and a shadow flashed past, struggling for altitude to clear the hills to the left, and simultaneously a third bomb blew a crater in the road ahead. As Joe sailed through the air with burning stinging sensations in his left arm and thigh, his game little mare, her near-front cannon bone severed and blood gushing from her throat, came down in a dying somersault.

Joe was thrown clear but landed with a shattering thud at the roadside. The following horses somehow managed to avoid crashing over or stepping on the fallen.

Concussed and semi-conscious, he did not remember much until the next morning when he awoke weak from loss of blood, in a casualty clearing station. Two of his mates and four horses had died, whilst he, 'Bluey' Thompson and Lieut. Creyton was wounded.

A long, painful trip by motor ambulance was followed by the relatively comfortable and orderly hospital trains; finally, the luxury of a spacious, non-moving bed in a hospital ward. Exhausted, and still weak from loss of blood, Joe fell into a long, sound, restful sleep.

He awoke, feeling refreshed, to the sound of voices. Bluey, in the next bed, was talking with a pretty, brown-eyed Sister.

Joe could scarcely believe the coincidence! She hadn't noticed yet, that Joe was awake, and as she turned away to leave, he said to Bluey, with a conspiratorial grin, "Hey, Blue, tell that slashing good sort I get jealous when she talks to other blokes!"

Blushing in spite of herself, Diana wheeled around. She smiled at his cheeky familiarity.

"Well, well, well! If it isn't Ellen's baby brother! O-Oh-h-h! Did we fall off our horsie and hurt ourself?" She playfully responded in a mock maternal tone.

"Kiss me and I'll tell. Or are you going to pull rank on me?" came Joe's nonchalant reply.

Another girlish blush showed briefly in Diana's cheeks, as an amused chuckle floated across from Bluey's bed. He was enjoying their repartee.

Slightly flustered, Diana tried to change the subject. "I suppose I'd better let Ellen know that Sleeping Beauty has finally awoken," she surmised aloud.

"Need help to handle me, eh?" was the mischievous response.

"Not at all!" she shot back, "I doubt you'll be quite so chirpy when I give you a sponge bath, later!"

"You wouldn't!" He was shocked.

"I would," she told him, "personally!"

And she did!

8

Ellen dropped in for a chat that evening, and Joe introduced her to Bluey, who told her, "This young larrikin brother of yours has been giving Sister Smithfield plenty of curry!"

"Yes, so I've heard!" Ellen smiled as she wagged a reproving finger at Joe.

"Diana is quite capable of looking after herself," Joe said ruefully, then brightened as he continued, "but, crikey, she's still real easy on the eyes, though!"

"Too right!" agreed Bluey, "if I wasn't a married man, I'd do a line for her myself!"

"Sis, how come Diana is not in an En Zed outfit instead of an Aussie one?" Joe asked.

"Simple. Her father was transferred by his company to Brisbane for a few years, and she did her nursing training there. Then, just after she graduated, a group of us all joined up together. Anyway, if you're so interested, why didn't you ask her yourself?" Ellen's eyes twinkled mischievously.

"Oh, I just wondered," Joe averted his gaze, "I'm not all that…"

"Not much!" chorused Bluey and Ellen.

As shrapnel wounds and broken bones gradually healed, the war ended. Both Joe and Bluey completed their convalescence on board ship returning to Australia. Diana and Joe had developed their mutual attraction into a growing friendship and respect, but the nurses remained overseas. They corresponded, as often as the erratic mail services would allow, but Joe, who after his discharge had become overseer on a cattle property thirty miles north of Wilga Creek, did not hold out much hope. He felt sure that some more polished fellow, an army officer or doctor, would sweep her off her feet, just as Ellen had become engaged to a young army surgeon who was a G.P. in a southeast Queensland town. After all, what could a simple bushman offer a girl like Diana? Dare he hope?

1919 rolled on, with the emotional relief, yet unsettling trauma of re-adjustment, mingled with an optimistic hope for a better world for the returning warriors and their families. Inevitably, and sadly, this tumultuous time also served to renew the pain and to deepen the aching voids in the hearts of the many whose beloved young men could never return. Nor did Australia escape the post-war outbreak of the deadly Spanish influenza.

Ellen came home to Wilga Creek, to revel in the love of her family, and to prepare for her planned wedding, whilst Diana had sailed on to Wellington, to where her parents had returned. Joe's spirits soared when he heard that, not only was she still unattached, but she would also be coming to Wilga Creek a couple of weeks before the wedding and would be Ellen's chief bridesmaid.

Two days before Diana's arrival, the young overseer was pleasantly surprised to receive an offer that, he felt, would greatly boost his prospects. Joe had always been a keen, intelligent pupil as he had learned about livestock, particularly cattle husbandry. He had absorbed everything his father, then his first employer, and then his old droving boss, Dave Simpson, was able to teach him. Whether it had concerned property improvements, land and pasture management, livestock handling or veterinary treatment, Joe was the sort of lad who had only to be shown a thing once, and his interested mind retained the knowledge. The past nine months as overseer of Mt Chillingham station, under the experienced old Manager, Dan Longford, had also broadened Joe's knowledge immensely. Mr. Longford had even familiarised Joe with the station's well-kept ledgers and journals.

The older man was very impressed with his protégé's keenness to learn and his ready grasp of the essential principles. Unbeknown to Joe, Dan Longford was grooming the lad to take over as Manager with the full agreement of the station's absentee owners" He and Mrs. Longford, in their gracious, unassuming way, had put the offer more as a request.

"Joe," Dan Longford had said, "my wife and I had hoped to retire several years ago and to move to a bayside suburb of Brisbane to be near our daughters and our grandchildren. Then the war came along. Most young men worth their salt enlisted and went overseas, so we stayed on here. When you came along earlier this year, with your common sense, your ability, and your ambition to make a future for yourself, we hoped that you might be the sort of young man who could eventually replace me as manager. You have exceeded our most optimistic expectations, and the owners have agreed with my recommendation. We'd like you to take over as manager early in the New Year. What do you say, lad?"

Joe was flabbergasted, "Mr. Longford, I don't know what to say! I'm not yet twenty-two and hadn't dared hope to find such a position much this side of thirty. I'm grateful, but I really haven't thought it through yet!"

"If I didn't think you were up to it, I wouldn't have recommended you, Joe. I know you can handle it! Look," Longford went on, "you don't have to give your answer straight away. Without wanting to appear an old stickybeak, I gather this young lady who'll be your sister's bridesmaid, might figure prominently in your future plans?"

"Yes, I'd like to know her views, or even if she'll have me," Joe answered.

"She's a darned fool if she won't!" was Mrs. Longford's firm opinion.

The manager was thoughtful. Finally, he said, "We don't have anything urgent, workwise, at the moment, Joe. You can have the next week off if you'd like. Just spend some time together and see what you can sort out."

"Yes, you bring her out here, and show her around," Mrs. Longford suggested, "I'm sure she'd like the place, and we'd love to meet her!"

9

Wearing his Sunday best, tingling with both nervousness and thrilled anticipation, Joe stood with Ellen on the Wilga Creek station platform as the Mail train coasted to a halt. The well-maintained little PB15 locomotive with its polished brass boiler bands headed a travelling post office, five end platform coaches and a luggage/brake van.

Eagerly, brother and sister scanned the length of the train.

"There she is!" cried Ellen, as a tall girl in a well-cut grey suit waved happily from a carriage window, and Joe sprinted onto the train to help with her suitcases. He had only the briefest glance at Diana's radiant smile and sparkling eyes before she was in his arms and her lips on his. Not a word had passed between them.

Dimly, he became aware of an audience as Ellen chuckled, "Come on, you two, or we'll all be carried onto the next stop!" Ellen and several of the passengers were grinning with benevolent amusement.

Diana indicated which suitcase was hers, and picked up her hatbox. They stepped back onto the station platform. As they walked towards the exit gate, Ellen laughingly declared, "Diana, you really are shameless!"

"Yes, I know," she happily agreed, "and your brother's no shrinking violet, either!"

For the short drive back to the Merriton household, the two immaculately groomed bay geldings in polished harness pulled the shining royal blue wagonette buggy under Joe's capable hands. Tom and Kathleen hadn't seen their family transport in such pristine glory for years. Diana was certainly getting the red carpet treatment from their son! The two teenagers, Leah and Jenny had also noticed and had good-naturedly teased their brother as he had prepared the turnout early that morning.

"Must be a pretty special occasion! I've never noticed you going to that much trouble for us," was Leah's amused reaction.

"Perhaps he's just practising for Ellen's wedding day," Jenny had impishly suggested. Both brats had then departed in a fit of girlish giggles.

It was a different story as the buggy swept up to the house, which had grown with extensions over the years. As the beautiful, well-dressed young stranger alighted from the vehicle with their brother's gallant assistance; for once, the precocious pair maintained a brief, awestruck silence. Tom and Kathleen warmly welcomed their visitor, and Diana's unaffected, natural charm soon relaxed the captivated Leah and Jenny.

Ellen was careful not to monopolise her friend's company over the next week of her brother's leave and discreetly organised her family to allow Joe and Diana quite a lot of time together. Very early on the Friday, Joe and Diana borrowed the wagonette for the long drive out to Mt Chillingham station.

Again, it was obvious that the Longfords also approved of Diana. Mrs. Longford showed her around the homestead, and fussed over her like a doting mother, but was careful not to give any hint of their own hopes, or Joe's intentions. The manager and his wife were the very souls of discretion!

On the way back to Wilga Creek, Joe observed, "I'm glad you liked the place."

"Oh yes, they're a lovely couple, Joe," Diana replied.

"What did you think of the homestead?" he asked.

"It seemed very comfortable," she told him.

Joe told her of the Longford's plans to retire in the New Year, and that he was offered the manager's job.

"Well, go on," she prompted, "you are going to accept, aren't you?"

"It's such a great opportunity," he said, then blurted out, "Diana, will you marry me?"

"Just try and get away from me, and I'll skin you alive!" she responded happily.

"Er – does that mean yes?"

"Of course it means yes, my darling! I thought you'd never ask," She kissed him, then continued, "Joseph Thomas Merriton, I'd even marry you if you could only offer me a slab hut! Didn't you know that?"

She snuggled closer to him as he drove on in elated relief. After a short silence, he said, "I'll have to meet your parents and ask your father's formal permission, of course!"

Diana shook her head, "We'll tell them by cable. They've been warned to expect it! Could we have the wedding in Wellington around mid-December? By the way, Ellen has agreed to be Matron of Honour"

"It seems I have been the last to know," Joe grinned, but won't a short, six-week engagement seem a bit rushed to some people?"

"Let them wonder! It's a practical date, given that Longfords would like to hand over the managership early in the New Year. If the cynics want to count the months afterward, let them! They'll be disappointed," she told him in her usual matter-of-fact voice.

The following day, Ellen married her doctor. An earnest but friendly young man, Robert and she seemed well suited to each other and were very much in love.

Then, a little over five weeks and a trans-Tasman crossing later, Joe met his intended in-laws for the first time. They made him feel very welcome, and Joe found them a very likeable family. They must have had some reservations about their only daughter having to start her married life so far away, on an Australian outback cattle property, Joe felt. But, if they did have, they were decent enough to keep such doubts to themselves. Diana certainly had no qualms. As they made their solemn vows in the picturesque little church, it seemed that no lovelier, more radiant bride had ever graced the altar steps. Joe would not have been surprised had his heart actually burst with the overwhelming mixture of love, tenderness, pride and unbelievable good fortune he felt, as he placed the little gold band on Diana's finger, and the minister pronounced them "man and wife".

The young newlyweds returned to take over stewardship of Mt Chillingham in the first week of January 1920. Despite the unfamiliarity of her new surroundings, Diana took to her role like a duck to water. There were a few clashes of temperament during the adjustment period, but those were easily overcome by their love, and their concern for each other.

As Diana had predicted, the gossips and cynics were duly confounded (but not by long) when, at Wilga Creek, on 10 October 1920, Rosemary Ann Merriton was born.

10

Rosie's birth was followed, fifteen months later, in January 1922, by the arrival of Michael Thomas Merriton. As she held the newborn baby boy to her breast, Diana in her usual direct nurse's manner, cheerfully informed the proud father, "You're just too darned potent, Boyo! Either you'll learn some self-control, or I'll have to tie a knot in a certain appendage to your person!"

Joe grinned, "That's right! Blame me! It takes two, and I've never had cause to complain of reluctance on your part, my darling."

Diana chuckled at his response. "I'm certainly not claiming rape, oh husband mine! But, seriously, Love, I'm going to have to figure out some system, or we'll soon have a whole tribe of little people running about the homestead, at this rate!"

Beneath the good-natured banter and unabated sensuality they shared, their love was maturing into a deeper and more spiritual union. It was a bonding of their very souls, one that was to sustain them through the droughts, the good times, the tragedies and the triumphs they would share for the rest of their lives together. So rare, and so wonderful, that Joe would never have eyes for another woman nor Diana for another man, not even for the most fleeting of instants, right to the end of their days.

Under Joe's capable stewardship, Mt Chillingham continued to prosper, through the difficult years of the twenties and into the thirties. There were setbacks, droughts, the Depression, during which Joe and Diana were very thankful for their good fortune, as a long procession of weary battlers came and went, carrying their swags and seeking work, which wasn't available. The best that Joe could offer at most times was a few hours of menial chores, in return for a meal and replenished rations. He and Diana felt sympathy for the poor wretches, struggling to find the dignity of labour in a crashed economy that was none of their making. Already, the workforce was pared to Joe and one ringer. Until times improved, only essential maintenance and station work was affordable, and the hours long and hard.

The absentee owners and their agent continued to be well pleased with their manager, and Joe found himself with very minimal outside direction. Apart from brief, twice-yearly visits, the owners' representatives were content to devote their time to their other investments.

Diana had become a most capable wife and mother and had also proven herself as an able teacher and supervisor of the children's correspondence lessons.

Whether by good luck or good management, it would appear she had also mastered the art of birth control, for it was not until April 1934 that their third child, Robert Lawrence Merriton, was born.

In the meantime, Rosie, a lively little imp of mischief who had inherited her mother's dark hair and brown eyes, had become the apple of her father's eye, and, indeed, was also somewhat pampered by her grandparents at Wilga Creek.

Michael, blue-eyed and fair-haired, was a quiet, undemanding child, as second children often are. He was friendly and intelligent but showed promise of becoming something of a bookworm. He would attempt to read anything he could lay his hands on, and he was his mother's pride and joy.

Robert, the youngest, was another dark-eyed imp. Even as a toddler, he was a handful, like his sister. Just the sort of child whose abundant energy and wilful self-confidence threatened perpetual mischief.

11

The year 1935 drew to a close. Joe's younger sisters, Leah and Jenny, both now married, had infants of their own. Leah's husband, Fred, was an engine driver with the Queensland Government Railways. They lived in Toowoomba, where Fred was based.

Jenny still lived at Wilga Creek, where her husband, George, was the local policeman, but things had not gone well for Jenny and George of late! There were persistent rumours around town that George had succumbed to the charms of Mrs. Lily Lonnigan, proprietress and licensee of the Railway Hotel, and locally nicknamed "Jersey Lil", after the notorious Lily Langtrey.

Lily Lonnigan was a strikingly handsome woman, a widow of around the same age as Joe, who had known her since childhood. She had started work as a waitress, then, later, a barmaid; had married the late publican, Jim Lonnigan, many years her senior, and had inherited the hotel after his death. She had two daughters at boarding school in Brisbane where they seemed to prefer to spend most of their time, learning how to be young ladies. This suited Lily just fine, allowing her to pursue the many amorous adventures, which had earned her nickname. Though quite amoral, the buxom blonde was a generous, good-natured woman who did not seem to be aware of the marital discord she sometimes caused in the district. "But I don't steal other women's husbands! I just borrow them occasionally!" she had often been heard to disclaim. Now, it was Joe's brother-in-law, George, who was making a fool of himself over Lil. It had long been Lil's custom to retire to her bedroom around 2 p.m. for an afternoon nap, leaving the maids to clear away the dining room, and the elderly barman to cope alone with a quiet couple of hours following; but of late, George also seemed to vanish into the first floor of the Railway Hotel most afternoons around that time. Lil's matinee performance, rumour had it!

Joe, Diana and family called in at Tom and Kathleen's home on their way through by train to Sydney, where Joe would put his family on board a trans-Tasman liner for a summer holiday with Diana's parents in New Zealand. Joe would return to Wilga Creek and Mt Chillingham alone the following week.

As Kathleen unburdened herself to her son, Joe told her, "I'd no idea of such goings-on!"

"No," said Kathleen, "and your father still hasn't! I'm afraid of what he'll do when he finally hears of it! I do wish George would come to his senses. It's the talk of the town, and your sister is terribly unhappy!"

Joe grimly determined to put things right, somehow, as soon as he returned from Sydney. Once again, fate was to take a hand.

'Old Andy' had been quite a ladies' man in his day. A 'gun' shearer, with a ton of presence and pride, the dapper little fellow was now sixty, and considerable mellowed, yet had retained his quick wit and cheeky humour. Lil still had a soft spot for the old bachelor, who was her clandestine lover fifteen years earlier, not long after her marriage to Jim Lonnigan. In fact, it was common gossip around town that Andy had fathered her second child.

Typical of Andy's risqué humour, and of Lil's good nature, was one scenario when there were half a dozen patrons in the bar. Lil was at one end, talking quietly and charmingly with a good-looking commercial traveller who had taken her fancy. Andy was breasting the centre of the bar, with an empty glass. Then, in a loud voice, Andy exclaimed, "Hey, Lil, Love! Bring us another beer or I'll tell your flash you're not wearing any underwear!"

Lil was in front of him in a couple of bounds, blushing hotly and unaccustomedly, "Andy, you're terrible! I am wearing underwear!"

Andy eyed her innocently. "Didn't say you weren't, Love. Just said I'd tell him you weren't!"

The mail train rolled into Wilga Creek in the midday heat of a fine December day, several hours late. Joe stepped onto the platform with his baggage. Doug Gray, the Mt Chillingham overseer, was to have driven the Ford in, the previous evening. Doug would have stayed at the Railway Hotel, across the road. It was now 1.20 p.m. The Station Master approached him, "Joe since the train was running late, Doug went back to the Pub for dinner."

"Thanks, Don," Joe said, and crossed the road to the Hotel. He stuck his head around the dining room door. There were only a couple of patrons apart from Doug, who was finishing his meal. "No hurry," Joe told him, "I'll just throw my swag in the car, and join you in the Public Bar." Doug had parked the Ford around the side near the stables.

"Righto, Boss! Have you eaten yet?" Doug asked.

"Yes," Joe told him, "on the train! Bought some sandwiches at a refreshment rooms stop this morning."

Joe walked past the stables to the parked Model A and dumped his swag. Nearby, in an open stall of the long shed, on a pile of clean straw, sprawled a small human form.

"Bit early in the day for anyone to be dead drunk," he thought. He went over. It was old Andy. Not dead drunk, just dead! But neat, and clean-shaven. Poor old chap must have been taking the shortcut from his shack across the paddock at the back, and 'had a turn' this very morning! He'd only been dead an hour or two, Joe guessed. Then a flash of inspiration hit him, with a recklessness he had not felt since his army days. He recalled the gossip of George and Lil's daily afternoon liaisons.

Old Andy wouldn't mind! He'd been a born larrikin, the poor old bloke, for all the years Joe had known him. He'd have enjoyed the joke of what Joe had in mind, and it might kill two birds with the one stone, so to speak!

Joe hurried back, around to the front of the hotel. Doug was just crossing into the Public Bar. Joe caught his eye and beckoned him outside.

"Which one is Lil's bedroom?" Joe asked. Doug often stayed at the Railway. Doug told him, and then asked why?

"You don't want to know! Not yet, anyway! Look, here's half a crown.

46

Set up the drinks and I'll be back in a few minutes."

Doug shrugged his shoulders, "Good-oh, Boss," he said.

Joe returned to the stables, quickly picked up the body of the little shearer, and carried him up the back stairs. He pulled back the bed-clothes, quickly undressed the corpse, and placed it naked between the sheets. Quietly, and unobserved, he returned down the back steps, walked around to the front of the pub, and entered the Public Bar.

When they'd finished their beers, Doug prepared to go.

"Hang about, son! Plenty of time," Joe caught Lil's eye, then called, "Good day, Lil. Same again, thanks."

Lil refilled the two glasses. "G'day, Joe," she remarked, "letting your head go, aren't you?" It was very unusual for Joe to spend a lot of time in a barroom. Pity, though. She'd fancied him ever since school! Those penetrating blue eyes that bored right through to a woman's soul, without giving anything away. Quite unnerving, really, but she doubted he'd ever so much as glanced sideways at another woman since he'd met that vivacious wife of his.

"Yair, well, the train was late. And hot! Be too late to do anything much by the time we get home, so we might dawdle a bit," he answered her. Lil stayed close, making small talk.

Doug looked at his manager curiously. Something was afoot! It was quite unlike Joe Merriton! First, the furtive query as to where Lil's room was; now this unusual reluctance to leave the pub, yet he wasn't exactly falling over himself with attempts to make scintillating conversation! Hot-pants Lil was certainly making the effort, though! Doug wished she'd put that amount of work into him sometime! He wouldn't knock her back!

They had nearly finished their third beer when Joe caught a movement in the corner of his eye. George, trying to be unobtrusive, glanced from the hallway. Lil's nod was almost imperceptible, then George disappeared along the hallway towards the internal staircase.

Lil excused herself, "Well, it's time for my afternoon nap!"

"Oh, must you go?" Joe asked, feigning disappointment.

" 'fraid so! Need my beauty sleep before the evening rush," she told him. Encouraged, she placed her hand on his, "but it would be nice to see you more often."

"Lily!" A man's voice shouted from the hall stairs, part in anger, part in panic.

Joe drained his glass, beckoned to Doug to do likewise, and followed Lily up the stairs. George was ranting and raving as Lily entered her room and gave a little cry of shock.

"What the hell are you up to? Running a brothel? Did he die on the job?" George was furious. Lily shook and sobbed as the full impact of the event hit her.

Joe stepped into the room, "G'day, George. What seems to be the problem?"

"Joe! What do you know about this?" the policeman blustered officiously to conceal his surprise at Joe's sudden appearance.

Ignoring his brother-in-law, Joe walked over and placed the back of his hand on the corpse. "What do I know? Don't be bloody ridiculous! He's cold as a maggot! I only got off the train forty minutes ago. More to the point, what the hell are you doing, sniffing around in Lil's bedroom, anyway?"

"I-I-well, that - " George was lost for words.

Joe glared savagely at him, "Save your excuses! Just find a pretty good explanation for my sister, because if you break her heart, I'll give you the biggest bloody hiding you've had in your life, and that uniform won't save you!"

Later, Joe and Doug called in briefly at Joe's old home.

"I don't think Jenny will have any more problems with George and Lil," he told his mother, without going into further explanation, "but if she does, be sure and let me know!"

As they drove north, Doug finally said, "You're bloody amazing! Poor old Lil, though! You really play rough!"

"She's as tough as old boots! She'll get over it," Joe told him, "but I hope George doesn't!"

12

Early 1937 saw Rosemary commence working as a junior typist for the stock and station agent at Wilga Creek. She had spent the previous two years at an Anglican girls' boarding school in Brisbane, qualifying for her Junior high school certificate in the Commercial course. Happy to have found employment in her home district, Rosie boarded with her grandparents and was usually picked up and taken home to Mt Chillingham on Saturday afternoons, then returned on Sunday afternoons again, by either of her parents in their new V8 Ford sedan. Sunday evening, she accompanied Tom and Kathleen to Evening Service in the little church, like a dutiful granddaughter. Kathleen dryly observed to Diana that Rosie's meek acquiescence to regular Church attendance probably had something to do with the weekly presence there, of a young, well-mannered geologist employed by an oil exploration company, and temporarily based at Wilga Creek.

"You could bet on that, more than on any religious fervour!" was Diana's knowing comment.

Later, in bed, Diana informed her husband, that his precious daughter was setting her cap at the young man. Diana was amused, Joe was not.

"She's too young!" was Joe's concerned comment.

"Oh, come on! At least, your mother has an eye on the situation, and he's a nice, steady chap. Not like some of the riff-raff around the town."

"He'd better not be!" Joe said.

Diana laughed, "If Rosie has set her cap at him, he'll probably need the protection, not Her Ladyship! You have always had Rosemary in one eye, and mud in the other! I love her, too, Darling, but she is a wily little minx! I'm just glad she is showing interest in a decent sort of boy."

Joe protested, "She is a good girl, and she has had a good upbringing! She might be a bit strong-willed, but you make her sound like a hard-nosed little schemer."

"She is a good girl, sweetheart," Diana told him, seriously, "but with her nature, if she got in with the wrong crowd she could easily wind up like Jersey Lil!"

Joe was shocked by Diana's uncharitable assessment of their daughter.

Meanwhile, Michael was in what was to be his final year at high school. He was boarding with Leah and Fred in Toowoomba and had firmly set his career sights in the field of communications.

A couple of years before, a young telephone mechanic had arrived with a linesman mate, at Mt Chillingham homestead to install a new telephone system. The technician was an enthusiastic, friendly fellow, with ambitions to become an engineer. He had been only too happy to answer all the questions that the inquisitive young boy had fired at him. As a consequence, Michael's interest in both telephone and wireless communication had begun. Technical publications were added to the youngster's reading interests. Soon, he was building his first simple, crystal set radio.

13

Now, while living in Toowoomba, Michael was eager to earn more pocket money to pursue his electronic interests. Consequently, he began mowing lawns and doing other odd jobs for his Aunt's and Uncle's neighbours including three young female primary school teachers who shared a house.

Two of these young ladies were outgoing, sporty girls with busy social lives. The third girl, in her mid-twenties, was a shy, retiring, slim redhead named Miss Anne Gracewell. She sometimes played tennis, but apart from that, rarely indulged in much social activity. She was quite introverted, but the more often Michael talked to her, the more he liked her. Anne Gracewell was not unattractive, but she was a mousy little thing, with her sweet, sad little smile. Fred and Leah thought she had the makings of the archetypal little old spinster lady, and Michael, though he knew little of the nature of women, would have been inclined to agree with that opinion. There was something very nice and gentle about her. "Wouldn't say boo to a goose!" Leah was inclined to describe her type.

Had her neighbours but known, Anne had not always been a mouse! When she had first graduated as a schoolteacher at age sixteen, she had been a vivacious, fun-loving lass, full of hope and bright expectations. Her parents lived in North Queensland, and she was glad of her first teaching appointment, to her northern hometown, a sugar port. Anne's social life was good, and a young male schoolteacher, a solicitor and an accountant had all competed for her affections. Then a young Second Officer from a Coastal steamer entered her life. She only saw him once every few weeks, but more and more, Alan Finch was making inroads on her affections.

Three years after Anne had commenced her teaching career, Alan had secured a position as First Officer aboard a small freighter out of Sydney on the Tasman and South Pacific run. He had asked Anne to marry him. She had accepted, resigned her teaching position, and moved to Sydney as Mrs. Alan Finch.

Her new husband arranged for her to embark as a passenger on his first long cruise, and it had been an idyllic extension of their honeymoon. Then, back ashore, she busied herself during their long separations, making a home for him at their little rented terrace house in the harbourside suburb.

At first, home duties and redecorating kept her busy, but then she found time hanging heavily during Alan's long absences. Several men, including a couple of Alan's so-called friends, tried to strike up romances with the pretty young wife, but she was very much in love with her sailor man, and gave them all short shrift indeed!

However, aware that the Devil makes work for idle hands, she managed to find employment as a teacher at an exclusive girls' school. It was just as well she had renewed her career, because, two years after her marriage, her husband, the only man with whom she had ever made love, had failed to honour his own marriage vows. Alan advised her that she had better see a doctor because he had contracted gonorrhoea and may have passed it on to her during his previous leave.

He had done exactly that, and she was further devastated to learn after medical treatment had finally eradicated her infection, that it had left her unable to become a mother.

Anne was shattered. She instituted divorce proceedings but continued teaching under her married name of Anne Finch. She was dreading the final outcome of the divorce case, however, because of the wide publicity afforded to such juicy scandals in those days, by certain newspapers. At the very least, if nothing else, current divorce listings were always published following the granting of the decrees, and being the innocent party was not likely to be much consolation, in her case.

Then, before the matter came to Court, Alan, under the influence of alcohol, fell from an island jetty at low tide, landed on a lighter moored below, and broke his neck. Instead of becoming a divorcee, Anne became a widow.

She retained her position as a mistress at the girls' school, but for the next eighteen months, she nursed her grief and wondered if she would ever really pick up the pieces of her life. Certainly, the knowledge that she would never bear children, even if she found a new, loving husband, depressed her greatly.

Gradually, Anne had forced herself to renew her interest in life outside the classroom. One of the directors on the school board, a prominent local government alderman, well-groomed, prosperous and very well mannered, had shown considerable interest in her. At a staff function, he had sought her out and invited her to dine and dance with him one evening of the coming school vacation.

She had declined, because he was a married man, and added that she hoped he had not been attempting to use his position on the school board to try and coerce her into a comprising relationship.

"Not at all," Charles Pigeon had assured her. He added that he would never have even considered anything improper; it was just that he and his wife were separated; she had a long history of marital infidelity, he "had all the goods" on her, and had only been holding off on divorce proceedings until the end of the year out of consideration for their daughter, who would be finishing her schooling that year.

Charles Pigeon was forty years old, of athletic build, and, he professed, entirely honourable intentions. He was also a very lonely man, but would make no demands on her, and would be the very soul of discretion, at least until after his divorce was over. He wanted only her friendship, and if, sometime in the future, when he was free to re-marry, things should develop into something deeper; well, they would have laid a solid groundwork for their relationship.

Anne could relate to his loneliness and his hurt over his wife's infidelities. So long as there were no improprieties or demands, and their friendship remained discreet, she could see no harm in meeting him occasionally as a friend.

As they became better acquainted, Anne had begun to see potential, possibly a real future in the relationship. He was witty, considerate, charming and undemanding. Although he was seventeen years her senior, she had felt that could be a plus factor. He had already raised his family, so her inability to conceive should not be an issue.

By the time their friendship was five months old, Anne had become very fond of Charles, to the extent that she, herself, was prepared to let their relationship develop to the next stage should he press the issue. After all, his wife had been unfaithful for years, he had collected quite an amount of evidence, and Anne knew he would feel no compunction under the circumstances, to admit to any contributing adultery in court, should Anne and Charles finally consummate their affair at this late stage.

Charles had sensed the weakening of her resolve, and, out of the blue, had suggested, one October evening, that they travel to the Blue Mountains the following Friday evening, and return on Sunday.

Anne had no hesitation in agreeing, and made a carefully disguised rendezvous with him at 4.30 p.m. on Friday. Charles was even driving a rented car so that there would be little chance of their being recognised.

As Mr. and Mrs. Brownlee, they had arrived at the small, exclusive private hotel in time for dinner at eight, and both tingled with anticipation throughout the meal.

Retiring to their room afterward, Anne had lost any qualms she might have had, two excellent double brandies having served their purpose. Slowly, savouring each moment, Charles had undressed her, caressing her eager sensuality with his kisses, then with deliberating relish, had become only the second man ever to make love to her.

Their coupling was interrupted by the metallic click of a door lock and the room light coming on. Anne and Charles had both looked instinctively to the doorway, and a flashgun had exploded with light. Two men and a woman stood near the doorway. Too late, Anne had hidden her face in startled shame, and Mrs. Pigeon had laughed with malicious delight.

"Now you know how it feels!" she had crowed to her incredulous husband, "and this should improve my defence no end!"

The gutter tabloids had had a field day, with such captions as "PIGEON CAUGHT IN LOVENEST WITH REDHEADED FINCH!" and "MR PIGEON FLIES COOP WITH MRS FINCH!"

Humiliated, the pretty redheaded Finch had taken flight back to Brisbane, applied for and resumed teaching, with an appointment to the provincial city under her maiden name of Anne Gracewell. The Brisbane scandal rag, fortunately, was unaware of her local origins and maiden name, but, her self-confidence shattered, her self-esteem never lower, Anne hid her personality in mouse-like anonymity, drab and self-effacing. Now in her second year at Toowoomba, Anne was finding the open, friendly fifteen-year-old Michael, the only male over ten years old with whom she could hold a conversation without wanting to die of shame. Sharing a house with her two younger female colleagues hadn't been much of a success, either. Not knowing her background, they thought she was quite strange! Perhaps she was!

She looked forward to transferring back to Brisbane as soon as she was able. At least, she would have her own home, the little two-bedroomed house at Red Hill, which she had inherited from her maiden Aunt last year. Anne would feel frightened living on her own again but she would have to get over that! At least, she wouldn't have to feel unable to relate to a couple of uncaring co-tenants, she comforted herself. Anne was still very much an emotional mess!

14

As the year drew to a close, events were heralding major changes in the lives of both Rosemary, and her brother, Michael.

Rosie's young man, John Roxton, the geologist, had been working further out and was only managing to visit Wilga Creek on approximately one weekend in three, but they still found ways to communicate.

On those weekends when John would be in town, Rosie flatly refused to make the trip to her home at Mt Chillingham. She had John firmly in her sights as her future spouse. John had good prospects for promotion to a more senior position elsewhere, and Rosemary wasn't prepared to let any grass grow beneath her feet waiting for his proposal since he seemed set to move further afield. He was a very decent, steady lad, and at twenty-three, was six years older than she was.

Joe and Diana by this time were taking a more philosophical view of their daughter's future plans, young though she was. "As single-minded in pursuit as her mother!" Joe teased his wife.

"Oooh! You watch it, Boyo! Anyway, you're exaggerating!" was Diana's retort, "I was nearly twenty-four when I had to bite the bullet and give you a nudge along! When I was the age she is now. I was very firmly under the discipline of a matron and several old. battle-axe nursing sisters! There is no comparison, but I suppose if we don't give our blessing, she'll go her own way anyhow. Very much her father's daughter, I'd say!"

John's family lived in a northern mining town, and it was this background that had first sparked his interest in geology, combined with a thirst for exploring new country. The Roxton family had their roots in rugged mountain range country, and their love of a good, sure-footed horse had been part of John's upbringing. Yet he was also progressive in his outlook. Technology and mechanisation, he felt, promised to be the way of the future to unlock the riches of this great continent and to lead to self-sufficiency and Australia's control of her own destiny. If only Australians would resist the temptation to sell off control of their heritage to foreigners for short-term gain, and invest their capital to develop their own industries!

As something of a nationalistic zealot. John Roxton's doubt regarding his countrymen's resolve on the last issue was the only blight on his faith in his country's future. The sweat and toil of Australians, battling distance and climatic adversity had rarely been rewarded sufficiently in the history of the nation's great achievements in the pastoral and gold mining booms of the past. Australians had all too often wound up with blisters and mortgages for their efforts, while fat foreign speculators and shrewd overseas bankers had waxed even fatter, rewarded many times over for their investment, and with no physical exertions. Politicians had continued to fawn over their Imperial masters for knighthoods and other tit-bit favours, or were outmanoeuvred as with the fledgling film industry. They'd sold this nation's interests down the drain time after time. But young men who learned the lessons of history and technology could *yet* change Australia's destiny for the better. John was idealistic, optimistic and very ambitious. He was determined to make his mark in the future.

Spending two days at the homestead co-incident with a station muster, the young geologist had been keen to put in a day with the men on the stock camp and had impressed his future father-in-law with able horsemanship. Though lacking the instinct to anticipate a beast's intentions, due to virtually no prior experience of cattle work, he was nonetheless a first-rate horseman. He demonstrated as much during several fast dashes through the timber. Though alert to the hazards of low branches and flailed by the lighter scrub, not once had he even checked the lame chestnut mare in her exhilarating stride, nor interfered with her balance. The lad possessed both skill and nerve.

"Where did you learn to ride?" asked Joe with a newfound respect for a young man whom he had previously categorised as likeable, but an academic type.

"In a lot rougher country than this," came the matter of fact reply yet with no hint of boastfulness.

Joe couldn't conceal his involuntary smile at the younger man's non-chalant answer. Despite Diana's reservations, Rosie would not be likely to walk all over this young fellow, after all.

Early in October, Joe and Diana gave their approval, and Rosemary and John were formally engaged to be married, the wedding to take place in January.

15

Meanwhile, Michael's schooldays were drawing close to an end. He was confident of a good Junior pass and had begun to write letters to various firms in Toowoomba and Brisbane seeking an apprenticeship to become a radio mechanic.

With his scholastic grounding, two years more than the requirements for his apprenticeship, two large firms in Brisbane appeared the most interested. He confidently told Miss Gracewell, his neighbour, that he was optimistic of their favourable responses. He had high hopes of becoming a radio technician. She was pleased for him and wished him well. Then, as an afterthought, she asked him if he had any relatives or family friends with whom he might board if he was to work in the capital. Mike told her, "No", but that, once he had passed the interviews, he would quickly set about finding lodgings.

Miss Gracewell, rather shyly, told him that she too, would be returning to Brisbane to teach in 1938; that her tenants were moving out and so she would be living in her little cottage at Red Hill. If Michael liked, he would be welcome to board with her in return for a small rent and for mowing the lawn. He would have his own comfortable room, and she would be grateful to have his company, as it would allay her nervousness at living alone in a near-city suburb. Mike thanked her for the offer, and the gentle young teacher wrote out her new address for him. On his return home for vacation, Mike enthusiastically informed his parents that he felt positive about his chances and that he had found somewhere to board in Brisbane.

Diana and Joe shared his joy about the first premise but had reservations about the second. "We'll see," was all his mother said.

Diana accompanied him to Brisbane the week before Christmas for his interviews, and on the way, she checked with Leah in Toowoomba as to Anne Gracewell's suitability as a possible landlady for her son.

"Oh, she is a dear little thing. Very reserved, but very nice! She and Mike were always good friends, and I'm sure she'd have offered mainly because she felt comfortable with him and that she'd be scared stiff of everything that went bump in the night if she was living alone. But she would be very conscientious about such things as making sure he ate well, behaved like a gentleman and took his Technical College studies seriously."

Diana had wondered if a young woman's social life could possibly be compatible with adequately supervising an adolescent lodger. Leah had laughed, "Wait 'till you meet her! She is the original little spinster school-marm. For the two years she lived next door, she occasionally played a game of tennis, went to the pictures or a concert, and nothing else! In fact, the other two girls who shared with her reckon she was a bit of a wet blanket!"

One of Michael's interviews went particularly well. The firm was in South Brisbane, and the manager indicated that the job was his. His application was successful! That would be confirmed in writing; indentures would be drawn up for signing after three months' probation. Mike was to start in four weeks.

Diana accompanied Michael around to the address Anne Gracewell had given and was completely reassured. Leah was right! Anne Gracewell could have been very pretty had she put her mind to it, yet she wore her hair in a tight bun and dressed in a demure, even primly old-fashioned way. Her house was tidy and tastefully, but not lavishly furnished. Anne was genuinely pleased to meet Diana and the mutual friendship and re-spect that showed between Anne and Michael were reinforced by Anne's assertion that she would appreciate the extra security of having such a steady, trustworthy young man for her boarder.

Diana thought Anne Gracewell looked to be in her early thirties, and privately wondered what had caused her to so firmly settle for spinster-hood. Leah's remark resurfaced in Diana's mind that Anne Gracewell would never have been to a wild party in her life. Diana would have concurred, unaware that Anne was barely twenty-six years old, had been married and widowed, and was front-page news on the Sydney scandal sheets.

Christmas, then New Year's Day, came and went. John and Rosemary were married and departed on a short honeymoon before moving to their new home in Roma. Michael left for Brisbane, to board with Anne and to commence his apprenticeship.

16

At Wilga Creek, Tom and Kathleen were now in semi-retirement. Tom, at 71, operated a small sawmill on a part-time basis and had done so for the past ten years, milling Ironbark and Cyprus pine to local orders. His involvement in sawmilling had started in the mid-twenties as the local tracks had improved to become gravelled roads, and as motor trucks steadily became bigger and more reliable, making his bullock team un-competitive for anything other than working in the timber stands to the North-west.

Tom had no interest in motorised transportation. Horses and cattle were his life, and there was no way he would have swapped his big, doc-ile bullocks for one of those noisy, temperamental, fuming, mechanical monstrosities that threatened his livelihood! So he'd made it his business to learn all he needed to know about the timber industry as he'd worked his team for the logging camps, or delivered to the local mill.

When the opportunity presented itself, he bought a half share in the struggling little Wilga Creek sawmill.

Tom, together with his partner, and an elderly benchman and a youth, now handled the dwindling demands of the local community's timber requirements.

The remaining seven old bullocks from the team now enjoyed their old age in retirement on the small selection. The tough, normally unsen-timental old ex-drover and bullocky had decided he'd owed his faithful old toilers something more than a butcher's block for their lifetime of hard work. Even so, the drought of 1935 was no picnic for them.

In their twilight years, Tom and Kathleen, like the old bullocks, had slowed down considerably, yet were still reasonable fit and active. But now their old house seemed very quiet since their lively young grand-daughter had married and moved away.

Ellen, whom they rarely saw these days, was forty-three years old, with five children, the contented wife of a country G.P. Joe was nearly 40, and the effervescent Diana rising 42, while Leah would be 35 and Jenny 33 this year. Leah had a good marriage with her easy-going engine driver, but Tom and Kathleen shared unspoken reservations about Jenny and George, now transferred to Central Queensland. The young sergeant had been a seemingly model husband since Joe's prank had jolted him back to earth a few years ago, yet George had a big ego that could all too easily fall prey to any crawler or manipulator prepared to feed it. In short, George was a swelled head and a fool.

It was a very different type of copper that Joe met up with onboard the Western Mail on a rare trip, in the autumn of 1938. Joe had noticed the two Queensland Police-issue broad-brimmed hats amongst the crowd in the Railway Refreshment Rooms at a major station halt along the line but had given them no more than a cursory glance. The taller of the two men was a dignified Aboriginal in an immaculate, well-starched uniform; a black tracker, justifiably proud of his considerable skills, and of the respect and community standing in which his profession was held. The shorter policeman, a nuggetty sergeant, had had his back towards Joe. There was something oddly familiar about the fellow! Joe didn't know if it was the sloppy, almost casually unregimented appearance of the sergeant's faded uniform, the red hair now showing early tinges of grey, the slight limp from a game leg, albeit common enough among horsemen as such injuries were; or a combination of all those factors. Absently, Joe's attention turned to more immediate matters, as he bought some sandwiches and a cup of tea, and thought no more of the policeman.

Later, on the train, Joe sat quietly immersed in reading a novel in the near-empty compartment. The sergeant and the black tracker strolled along the adjoining corridor, glancing automatically but unobtrusively as they passed each open doorway, with their usual professional curiosity, (or nosiness, depending on one's point of view).

"Well, I'll be blowed! Joe Merriton!" the ruddy face beamed from the doorway of the compartment.

Joe looked up at the policeman. Recognition dawned. "Bluey Thompson! After all these years! You haven't changed a lot."

"Nor you!" Bluey replied. They shook hands, warmly, and Bluey introduced Jim, the tracker. Joe motioned to the two men to sit in the vacant seats opposite him.

"What brings you fellows onto the train?" Joe asked.

"Been in to give evidence at the District Court sittings," Bluey replied, "Soon as the seasons pick up a bit, the duffers are out in force again. We've managed to get a couple of convictions this time, but considering the leniency of the courts, I sometimes wonder if it's worth the trouble! Stock-thieving seems to be the national pastime, and I don't mean merely poddy-dodging cleanskins! These two blokes we just caught are past masters at doctoring brands."

Blue continued, "Anyway, to change the subject, Joe, how are you doing? I suppose you're on your own block by now, eh?"

"No," Joe told him, "we've thought about it, but wouldn't have had enough capital to be viable. Most of the subdivided leases hardly provide an adequate living area, given development costs and seasonal variations. I'm managing Mt Chillingham, north of Wilga Creek. It's a big run for this area, nearly 200,000 acres, mostly a mix of lighter country, running back into the ranges. Good water though, but not the sort of lease the government is likely to resume and cut up. Yet I like to think I make a pretty good fist of running it for the owners. I've been there since we came home from Egypt."

"Sounds like you're pretty settled, then. I grumble a bit about the Force, but now the kids are grown up, the missus and I are pretty comfortable with it. At least, it's a secure sort of career. You got a family?" Bluey asked.

"Yes. Wife and three children. Our daughter married a few months ago, and the eldest lad works in Brisbane and the youngest is four and a half. I married that Kiwi nursing sister, Diana Smithfield," Joe told him.

"Thought you might have!" The policeman smiled his approval.

"Yep," Joe agreed, "smartest thing I ever did!"

17

John and Rosemary had settled into their new home and were adjusting well, but by mid-year, the young bride was beginning to experience bouts of morning sickness. Yet another generation was on the way, to the delight of the expectant new parents.

In Brisbane, Michael was learning that his position as a first-year apprentice entailed many more mundane duties than he had envisaged. In fact, it sometimes seemed to him that he was more of a cleaner and messenger than budding technician, but, as was evident from the complaints of other first-year lads at Technical College classes, it was very much the normal circumstances in all firms. How the new boys all looked forward to the following year, when a little more knowledge, a little more experience would make them more technically useful to their employers and earn them a little more responsibility and seniority! Then another batch of lads could worry about the frustrations of being at the bottom of the pecking order!

Fortunately, the other aspect of living in Brisbane was working out much better. Anne Gracewell was tops as a landlady! She was an excellent cook, a good friend, and had such a sweet nature it was very easy to be cheerful around her.

Anne, for her part, had also benefitted greatly from the association with her young lodger. She no longer felt lonely and isolated. Having somebody else to focus her attention upon seemed to fulfil a need in her, and Michael's ready sense of humour made her feel young again. Every Saturday night, they now travelled into the city by tram together, for a picture show, or live theatre. Anne also had taken to wearing her hair long on these occasions, and, tastefully made up, together with obvious enjoyment reflected in her eyes, looked far younger than her years.

Mike, on the other hand, was a manly, mature-looking youngster. Dressed in his dark suit, he could have passed for four years older than his tender age of sixteen going on seventeen. He was not conscious of this, but the general effect of himself and Anne out together on a Saturday evening was that they looked approximately the same age.

When they were noticed together by a couple of his Tech classmates one evening, the lads were obviously impressed. So much so, that when his awestruck colleagues commented the following week, on what a gorgeous-looking girlfriend he had, Mike did not bother to disillusion them. His ego experienced quite a lift, indeed! Funny he hadn't noticed it before, but Anne really was a good sort! He didn't tell her she'd been mistaken for his girlfriend, though. That might have embarrassed her!

Anthony David Roxton was born in November 1938 at Roma, and Diana spent two weeks at her daughter's home to assist the young couple to cope with the new demands of parenthood.

The new baby was baptised a month later at Wilga Creek, and John, Rosemary and baby Tony spent Christmas at Mt. Chillingham, before leaving for North Queensland to show the child to his other grandparents.

Michael also returned to the homestead for the Christmas vacation, and Anne travelled north to spend a couple of weeks with her parents, also. Two weeks of her summer vacation was about all she was able to endure, she found, given the oppressive heat and humidity of a northern wet season, combined with the equally oppressive hostility that sometimes emanated from her unforgiving and disillusioned mother. Her mother had been made aware of Anne's earlier escapade in Sydney by a stickybeak acquaintance, back in 1935. Indeed, Anne looked forward to returning from her parents' home to the friendliness of her own little house and Michael, back from the bush to commence the second year of his apprenticeship in 1939.

Anne had not mentioned to her parents that she had a young male boarder in Brisbane. Her mother's acid tongue would have made another issue out of that, innocent as it was! She'd eventually hear about it, Anne supposed; from another of her so-called friends, but Anne was almost past caring. She resolved that she would not make any more visits home to be denigrated and humiliated. If her parents wanted further contact with her, they could make the trip to Brisbane! And they'd jolly well have to accept the fact of Michael boarding with her if they did, she thought defensively. She was tired of being pushed around. She was twenty-seven years old. Michael was a few weeks off seventeen. If any of her nosy relatives wanted to make out there was anything improper in her having a teenage male boarder, they could go and jump in the lake if they found out! Her self-esteem, though still fragile, had improved markedly over the past year.

18

For several more months, Anne and Michael continued their platonic friendship, co-operating well as landlady and lodger at home, and socialising at tennis or the pictures, in mutually shared enjoyment of the same interests. Mike was proud to show her off to his friends, smugly omitting to tell them she was his landlady.

Anne, with her gentleness and lack of ego, frequently deferred to him for his opinions, and in some ways, seemed to look to him subconsciously when she needed masculine support or approval.

One evening in May, he arrived home from work to find her sobbing quietly to herself. She had attended the funeral of an eight-year-old pupil who had died of meningitis, and, six hours after the service, she was still deeply affected.

Mike gently inquired as to what was the cause of her grief, and she told him of the tragic end to the life of a formerly happy, considerate little girl, for whom the future had seemed so bright such a short time ago. He put his arm around her shoulders and then dried her eyes. Sweet gentle little Anne! Ten years older than himself, yet at times, she seemed so much a child herself! A wave of compassion swept over him. He drew her closer and tenderly kissed her forehead. Her response surprised him, as she lifted her face to him, clung tightly with her arms, and kissed him fully upon his lips. Then, blushing furiously, she stammered incoherently, hastily drew away, and served his dinner shortly afterward. He sensed her embarrassment, compounding the misery she already felt about the unfortunate demise of the child. He could not find the words to express his compassion. Had she looked into his eyes, she would have seen it, but she did not trust herself to look directly at him. She did not sit down at the table. She just wasn't hungry, herself, she said!

The following morning at breakfast, Anne was still very subdued and averted her eyes as she apologised, "Look, Michael, about last night… it was very foolish of me. I don't know what came over me. I'm sorry."

"Don't be," he told her, "I'm not. In fact, I quite enjoyed it."

She reddened noticeable, "Really?" she inquired.

"Really," he grinned.

She looked up and gave him a wan little smile. She was still acutely embarrassed, yet, somehow, she felt she'd get over it. "You're very kind," she said.

19

The winter of 1939 heralded little promise of cheer through southern Queensland. Once again, the summer Monsoon rains had failed to arrive. It seemed the decade would close as one of driest Joe could recall. Many areas had received less than half their normal rainfall each year since 1931-32, and for most, 1935 had been a disaster from which few had, or would ever, recover.

But Mt. Chillingham station had been fortunate. The big run, with its comparatively low stocking rates, ran back into the southwestern slopes of the Dividing Range, and was blessed with just sufficient localised storm rains to maintain passable feed and water to sustain it through the widespread drought, with the aid of judiciously timed cutting of edible trees for fodder. The size and topography allowed, indeed dictated, a minimum of three or four men employed full time, including Joe himself.

Primarily a breeding proposition, to supply store cattle for fattening, to the owners' more intensive holdings in more reliable rainfall areas on the Darling Downs and in New South Wales, Mt Chillingham, nevertheless, must have frequently appeared a liability to them. Particularly in the succession of dry years when store stock was available at near give-away prices. The big station's major advantage was as a reliable supply of store cattle in bountiful years, when even those surplus to the company's requirements found a ready market, at top prices. Yet Mt Chillingham would have been on or near the wrong side of the owners' ledger for several years now.

Such an operation was not a venture for men with limited capital, and, as Joe had remarked to Bluey Thompson on the train, some time ago, he and Diana were, in hindsight, grateful they had not become encumbered with mortgages to start on their own in this business. In many ways, Joe knew that as a relatively unfettered manager, he had the advantages of both lifestyles, of grazier and employee, with few of the risks. In return, his employers had a loyal, competent and conscientious employee, who managed the big property as carefully as though it was his own.

Again, in Europe, other clouds were gathering. Not the long-awaited clouds to darken the blue skies of sunny Queensland, but far more ominous clouds. The Clouds of War! If Britain once again became at war with Germany, then surely as night followed day, the Dominions of Canada, Australia, New Zealand and South Africa, would immediately be drawn in to assist the Mother Country.

On 29th September 1938, the British Prime Minister, Mr. Neville Chamberlain, with Hitler, Mussolini and Daladier of France, had signed the four power Munich Pact, modifying French guarantees of Czech independence, to allow for a new German frontier with Czechoslovakia.

Chamberlain had returned to London with a new joint declaration of peace between Great Britain and Nazi Germany after the German Army had marched into Czechoslovakia to take up the new frontiers on October 1st. The utterances of "peace in our time", and "peace with honour", soon gave way to British and French unease with the policy of "appeasement" as Hitler's speeches became more truculent.

On 28th February 1939, after announcing in the House of Commons British recognition of the Franco regime in Spain, Mr. Chamberlain had also repeated his belief that Hitler had no further aggressive intentions. Sixteen days later, Germany invaded what was left of Czechoslovakia.

Illusions of Nazi peacefulness were shattered. Chamberlain roundly rebuked Hitler, and soon after gave guarantees of support firstly to Poland, then to both Greece and Romania.

Britain and the Commonwealth now had few illusions left. War with Germany now seemed only a matter of "when", not "if". At Red Hill, the relationship between Anne and Michael was also changing. Not with hostility, nor with any noticeable unease. More with a sense of awareness of each other's latent sensuality, ever since the kissing incident months before.

Mike still treated her with due respect, and the warmth of their friendship remained, yet Anne was conscious of his increasing tendency to good-naturedly taunt her with light-hearted banter that left her in no doubt that he found her desirable. She didn't really find his wisecracks unwelcome. Unsettling, perhaps, but not offensive, and he never took such liberties with her in the company of a third party.

Occasionally, Anne found herself taking the initiative to give him a bit of cheek first, yet Mike usually seemed to have a ready answer to turn the tables on her. Such as the time she noticed him intently perusing an "Esquire" magazine that he'd brought home. As Anne passed behind him, she noticed the full-page photograph of a scantily dressed young model.

"Careful," Anne told him, "they say that sort of thing makes little boys go blind!"

"Nah!" he told her, "that's just some girl in a photograph. You're what I dream about!" He turned his head to give her a cheeky grin and a wicked wink.

"Michael! You're incorrigible!" she blushed hotly. He had her measure, all right, the young blighter!

September 1939 began with Germany's invasion of Poland on the first day of the month. Two days later, in compliance with their pledges to Poland, both France and Britain declared that they were now at war with Germany. Immediately, Australia's Prime Minister, Mr. R.G. Menzies, announced to the Australian people that a state of war now existed also, between Australia and Germany.

The Army Reserve, or Militia, of 78,000 men was re-activated, an Australian Air Expeditionary Force of four bomber squadrons and two fighter squadrons, and an infantry division of 20,000 volunteers, eventually to be increased by another three infantry (and one armoured) divisions, was raised as the Second Australian Imperial Force, and the Royal Australian Navy was also put at Britain's disposal.

Compulsory military training for home defence, abandoned ten years previously, was also reinstated.

Australia was once more at war, yet, even more so than in Britain, there was a feeling of unreality about the mobilisation. The period from September 1939 to April 1940 would go down in British and Australian historical records as the "Phoney War".

Although Australian Naval units were already serving with the Royal Navy, the first squadron of the Royal Australian Air Force for active service in Britain would arrive there on 26th December 1939, and the first A.I.F. units would land in Egypt early in 1940, there persisted the feeling that it would all be resolved quickly, and would be over before most of the Australian forces were there very long.

Enlistments were enthusiastic, due as much to the promise of the regular employment for many young men of the Depression and Post-Depression era, as could be attributed to any sense of Empire loyalty and craving for adventure, which had motivated their fathers, uncles or older brothers in the Great War of 1914-18. Few Australians yet realised that the new conflict would be one that would far exceed the First World War on a scale of slaughter, destruction and huge geographical expanses over which the battles would range.

Diana Merriton, though, felt considerable disquiet at the new events now unfolding. As a former military nurse, as a mother and mother-in-law, she was very uneasy.

Michael was fast approaching military age. John Roxton was already a Militia Lieutenant. Though neither showed any inclination to rush off to the European war, Diana was aware of a growing national anxiety about Japan's militaristic intentions in Asia and the Pacific.

Joe tried to allay his wife's fears. "No chance of John enlisting with the 2nd A.I.F.," he told her, "You've heard his views on British Imperialism and Europe solving its own problems this time around! He's only interested in Australia's defence. And by the time Mike is old enough, it will all be over. The Japs aren't likely to worry us. They've already got their hands full in China!

"Oh, Darling, I do hope you're right!" Diana told him.

20

War was the furthest thing from the minds of Anne and Michael, as they walked home from the tram stop. It was a fine night in early November. This particular Saturday night, instead of the usual picture show, they had gone to a dance.

Occasionally, months previously, Anne had "dragged him off" to a dance, or given him some instruction at home, "to improve his social graces," she had told him. It used to be something of a duty to Mike, to comply. Not anymore! This particular evening, with his awakened interest in Anne's sensuality, Mike had finally discovered what it was that so many people found so exciting about dancing. Particularly the waltzes, although Mike did feel slightly embarrassed about the inevitable erection he seemed to get when he danced in close contact with Anne. Fortunately, she hadn't seemed aware of it!

Actually, Anne was very conscious of the effect she had on the youth! As they walked along, arm in arm, immersed in their own private thoughts, Anne was deciding to cease worrying about the propriety or otherwise, of the mutual attraction between them, and let events take whatever course they might. No wonder she sometimes found herself in awkward situations; she ought to be locked up for her own good, she thought, but she was past fighting it.

Home again, Anne kicked off her shoes and turned to smile her thanks to Mike for escorting her to the dance. "It wasn't too much of a chore, was it?" she asked.

"No! It was great! I really enjoyed tonight," Mike told her.

"I'm glad you did," she smiled invitingly.

Michael kissed her upturned lips. She responded eagerly. Emboldened, he caressed her left breast with his right hand. She didn't resist. If anything, her kissing became more passionate. Finally, she softly asked him, "Are you sure you want to?"

He could scarcely believe his ears! Yet he did not doubt what she meant! "I'm positive!" he told her hoarsely, his throat suddenly dry with anticipation.

Silently, Anne took his left hand with her right and led him to her bedroom. They sat together on the side of the bed and resumed their kissing. Slowly, Anne reclined, positioning herself to afford him every assistance as his inexperienced fingers fumbled to undress her. She then slipped naked between the sheets as Michael quickly disrobed to join her.

Their first coupling was passionate but all too brief. It was Michael's first time, and, very quickly, his excitement and lack of experience brought him to ejaculation.

"Sorry I was so quick!" he mumbled in embarrassment. Anne's legs were entwined behind him, and her arms also helped to lock him in place on top of her.

"Never mind! Just stay there, and you'll soon be ready again," she kissed him, and whispered in his ear, "but do be a gentleman, and take your weight on your elbows!"

The tip of her tongue darted inside his mouth and ran the edge of his teeth, as, simultaneously, her lithe body wriggled in slight but sensuous movement beneath him.

Her prediction soon proved accurate, as Michael firmed again inside her. "Just take it easy. We've got all night," Anne reassured him. The second time lasted much longer. Michael's self-assurance returned.

Afterward, Anne lay snuggled contentedly in his embrace, her back to him. Michael's right arm reached around to the front of her, and his index finger lazily caressed her right nipple. He felt it stiffen with excitement, and his placid member, resting against her hip, responded likewise. "Mmmmm!" she murmured appreciatively, turning towards him.

He felt a mixture of love, pride and protectiveness towards her. Although she was ten years his senior, he sensed confidently that from now on, she would always be his woman!

Yet, as her legs again parted to his touch with eager acquiescence, he savoured a sense of smug irony. After all, there wouldn't be many seventeen-year-old lads who'd taken their landladies to bed!

Thereafter, although they were careful to conceal the change in their relationship to the outside world, within the shelter of their little home, they lived like any newly married couple. They slept together each night in Anne's big double bed, and Mike's single bedroom became a mere storeroom and study. Like any dutiful wife of a healthy, young, brand-new husband, Anne sometimes found it necessary to nag him gently, so that he did not now neglect his studies and other mundane duties.

Mike's letters home to Mt Chillingham naturally gave no inkling of his romantic involvement with Anne, yet he managed to hint sufficiently that his return home for the Christmas holiday break would leave Anne on her own through the festive season, as she would not be going north this year. Diana naturally indicated that her son's landlady would be most welcome to accompany him to the homestead for the holiday.

John, Rosemary and young Tony also spent Christmas and Boxing Day at Wilga Creek and Mt Chillingham, before leaving to visit John's parents, three days train travel away.

Rosemary had not previously met Anne and was agreeably surprised to find her brother's landlady such pleasant company. Anne also seemed to have a special gift for relating to children. Both Robert, at five years, and the toddler, Tony, loved her company.

Innocently, in the presence of the whole family on the afternoon of Boxing Day, Rosie remarked to Anne, "You've such an affinity with children! You really should be married with children of your own. I'll bet you'll make a wonderful mother!"

Mike looked decidedly embarrassed for his friend. Anne looked wistful, then turned her head away. Diana thought she saw a tear welling in the corner of the schoolteacher's eye. Anne brushed her eye lightly with the back of her wrist, and after a few moments, she regained her composure. "I've been married," she told them, "and widowed! I was very young then. But there were medical complications, and I am unable to have children."

Rosemary's face reflected her concern and sympathy. She wished she had been aware. "Oh, Anne! I'm so sorry!" she said. "Don't be. It's not your fault," Anne told her wryly.

Diana also found the young redhead excellent company during the two-week vacation. Anne had a ready sense of humour, and at times was quite bubbly. She also looked very young and pretty. Diana found it hard to reconcile this girl as the same timid little introvert she had first met two years before.

Michael spent a lot of time in the company of his father and younger brother but was also quite solicitous about saddling a couple of horses in the late afternoon of each day, to take his guest "exploring" for an hour or two. Diana was glad her son was boarding with such an agreeable companion in Brisbane.

In bed, on the evening of the day Mike and Anne had left by train to return to the city, Diana innocently expressed to Joe, how pleased she was that Michael was in such fortunate circumstances.

"Yair," her husband agreed drily, "I wouldn't be surprised if he's knocking her off."

"Joe! You're dreadful! You are joking, aren't you?" Diana was shocked. She hadn't even considered the possibility!

Joe was smiling at her startled reaction. "No, I'm not," he told her.

"Well, you don't seem very concerned!" Diana said, irritably.

"Why should I be?" her husband said affably- "If he is- at least he won't be chasing whores or tarts! And you heard her say she can't have children. No, half his luck, I reckon! Every young feller should have a steady, older woman to show him the ropes!"

Diana was somewhat intrigued by now, "Oh, yes? The voice of experience, I presume?" she asked. It was a subject about which Joe had always been tight-lipped during their twenty years of marriage.

"Matter of fact, yes -" Joe admitted.

Female curiosity was getting the better of Diana. She had momentarily forgotten about Michael and Anne. "And who was your first conquest?" she asked, "Outback barmaid? Black gin? Or Cairo whore?"

"None of those," he told her quietly, "it happened in Wellington, twenty years ago. She was a Kiwi nurse, about your size!"

"Oh, you liar, Joe Merriton! You bare-faced liar!" she laughed as she threw herself- wriggling and wrestling on top of him.

His lips found hers, then, silently, the horseplay changed to passion. Even after all these years, physical arousal still came very quickly for both of them.

21

By June of 1940, the future was looking bleak. Not only on the land in southern Queensland, where summer and autumn rainfalls had again been well below average and the clear skies of winter heralded cold frosty mornings and clear sunny days devoid of any rain, but more disastrously, the war in Europe was now a stark testimony to the effectiveness of the Nazi "Blitzkrieg", (lightning war) tactics. The Phoney War had ended on April 9th, with the virtually unopposed occupation of Denmark, and the capture of the principal ports and airfields of Norway that same day. The Royal Navy and two small allied forces enjoyed successes at Narvick in the far north of Norway, and several other locations, but were forced to evacuate their land forces over the following month or so, at considerable cost.

The low countries, Holland and Belgium were the next to fall, Holland in a few short days in early May. Fierce resistance by the Belgian Army briefly delayed the inevitable.

German Panzer divisions breached a gap in the Maginot Line between Sedan and Mézières where the French Ninth Army could not contain them. The British Expeditionary Force and the northern units of the French Army were isolated from the remaining Allied forces. The Belgians fought on until their supplies were exhausted, but by May 26th, the besieged British and French forces were withdrawn to the northern French coast at Dunkirk and the history-making evacuation commenced.

King Leopold of Belgium capitulated on May 28th. Three and a half weeks later, on June 21st, France signed an armistice under her new Petain-Weygand Government. She could do little else, as Mussolini had also declared war and was attacking from the south. Britain now stood alone, backed only by her far-flung Dominions, and the remnants of such Free

French, Polish, Czech and other forces that were able to reach her shores.

Right from the outbreak of war, however, it was anything but a Phoney War for the Royal Navies. On September 4th, 1939, the first German submarine attack of the war claimed the British liner "Athenia", with a loss of 128 lives.

Thirteen days later, the aircraft carrier H.M.S. "Courageous," became the first major British warship to be sunk, with 515 of her crew killed. This was followed on October 14th in Scapa Flow, north of Scotland, by the battleship "Royal Oak", for a further loss of 833 lives. Meanwhile, German U-boats and surface raiders extracted a terrible toll of Allied Merchant shipping, frequently, their brave but inadequately armed escorts, such as the armed merchant cruiser H.M.S. "Rawalpindi, which, armed only with 6-inch guns, and no armour plating, defended her convoy against the pocket Battleship, "Deutschland". The "Rawalpindi", ablaze from stem to stern, guns still firing and flag flying sank for a further loss of 265 gallant souls.

Then, on December 13th, 1939, the Royal Navy began to turn the tables. Off the South American coast, the cruisers H.M.S. "Exeter: H.M.N.Z.S. "Achilles" and H.M.S. "Ajax'," although vastly outgunned, damaged and put to flight the German pocket battleship "Graf Spee". The German reached the sanctuary of the neutral Uruguayan port of Monte Video, where she put ashore two British merchant seamen from nine merchant ships previously sunk by her. Faced with the alternative of internment by Uruguay for the duration of the war, or resuming the fight with the cruisers waiting offshore, her Captain scuttled her and shot himself.

On February 15th, 1940, the British destroyer "Cossack" entered the then neutral waters of Josing Fjord, Norway, to subdue and board the armed German supply ship "Altmark", thereby rescuing a further 299 captured British merchant seamen.

H.M.S. "Cossack" had defied two Norwegian gunboats to carry out the rescue, but the British Navy was no longer in any mood to compromise.

Following the German invasion of Norway in April 1940, for the loss of the Aircraft carrier "Glorious", six destroyers, three submarines and six smaller ships, the R.N. destroyed several German cruisers, destroyers, U-boats and approximately forty transports, and severely damaged two battleships. Britannia, at least, still claimed she ruled the waves.

Dutch and Polish ships had also reached British ports to serve with the R.N., but in the surrender of France, the terms of the armistice were that the French naval forces would be demobilised. Britain did not trust Hitler's assurances, nor did many French officers, who brought into Plymouth and Portsmouth two battleships, two cruisers, eight destroyers, several submarines and two hundred minesweepers and trawlers, all of which were immediately taken under British control. At Alexandria, the Flag Officer of a French fleet at anchor was less co-operative, and after several days and threats of sinking by the British, was finally persuaded to e-commission his ships.

At the French North African ports of Oran in Algeria and Dakar, French West Africa, British warships under Admiral Somerville destroyed a recalcitrant French fleet, totalling five capital ships, (among them three of the most modern battleships afloat) numerous light cruisers, destroyers, submarines and other units. The Australian cruiser, H.M.A.S. "Australia", took part in the Dakar operation of July 8th.

Eleven days later, a daring British destroyer flotilla, acting as bait for a trap, skilfully lured two of the fastest cruisers in the world, the Italians "Bartolomeo Colleoni", and "Giovanni Banda del Nere", into range of H.M.A.S. "Sydney's" guns. Excellent Australian gunnery quickly finished off "Bartolomeo Colleoni" and damaged the second cruiser, which, even though heavily damaged, still had sufficient speed to outrun her pursuers as she fled to her homeport.

Meanwhile, the Battle of Britain had started on July 10th, with heavy German air attacks on Britain and a spirited defence by an outnumbered R.A.F., including Commonwealth, Polish, Czech and other allied pilots.

News of these victories was heady stuff for young Michael, who pleaded with both his employers and his parents for release from his apprenticeship, to enlist in the Royal Australian Navy.

This was the very thing that Joe and Diana had dreaded most, yet, with an increasingly isolated and aggressive Japan making truculent noises and demands against British and American interests in China, Burma and the Pacific, it seemed to Joe only a matter of time until the lad would be conscripted into the Militia anyway. Reluctantly, they gave Michael their assent, conditional on his employers agreeing to release him. Michael's employers understood.

"We'll be sorry to let you go, but, if your mind is made up, we won't try to hold you. You'll probably be called up before your apprenticeship is over, anyway." the workshop foreman told him, "but Management wants you to know you will be welcomed back with open arms when this bloody war blows over. And that goes double for me!"

They allowed Michael a week of his accumulated annual leave to travel home to see his parents and grandparents before he enlisted. It seemed that, with one exception, everyone was supportive, albeit reluctantly so. The one exception was Anne. She was ropeable!

Michael had never seen her so upset and angry about anything previously. "You idiot! You silly young fool! Can't wait to get yourself killed! And what about me? I suppose I'll just be another one of your girls in every port until you finally get blown up, or drowned or something!" Her green eyes fairly blazed and her face became almost as red as her hair, as she launched into a quite irrational tirade.

Mike was amazed! Talk about women being unpredictable! He hadn't expected her to be pleased about his decision, but this was over the fence! He tried jocularity. "You're beautiful when you're angry," he grinned.

Normally, he could kid his way around any of her moods, and she rarely stayed angry for long, but this time she just fixed him with a grim, smouldering stare. Then she turned abruptly, ran into the bedroom and locked the door. He heard her sobbing brokenly, but his knocking at the door and concerned pleas only brought from her a response of "Go away!"

Michael slept in the second bedroom for the next two nights, and the waking hours produced a most uncommunicative attitude from her. He'd never known her to be sulky, before now. He was experiencing what some of his older colleagues had often cynically referred to as "Married man's staple diet! Hot tongue and cold shoulder," he ruefully reflected. Then it was time to take his leave and return home to Mt Chillingham. For the first time in his young life, Mike flew in an aeroplane, affording him more time at home. By the time the Qantas DC3 touched down at Roma, the closest airport to home, he was hooked! To hell with the Navy! He'd probably get seasick anyway! RAAF aircrew was his new goal.

Diana met him at the aerodrome, for the long drive home. Michael didn't mention Anne's implacable reaction. He could hardly confide anything of that nature to his parents, he thought guiltily. They'd be sure to tumble to the fact that she was a lot more than just his landlady if they had any idea of how she had carried on about it all.

Instead, he told his mother about his new decision to try for the wild blue yonder. Diana shook her head in exasperation, and let out a pained, long-suffering type of sigh, but kept the rest of her opinions to herself. In his mind's eye, Mike envisaged even more fireworks at Red Hill when he related his new goal to Anne.

The week of his vacation was also the first week of the August school holidays. Michael idly wondered if Anne would be still sitting at home sulking. Maybe she would go to Southport, or somewhere else, and play around just to spite him, he thought with alarm. Oh, to hell with her! It's time she grew up! Time they both grew up, come to that. They'd be apart for long periods when he was in the Air Force. They'd just have to get used to it! He couldn't really see their relationship ending, though.

Six-year-old Robert was very proud of his older brother. He was already visualising Michael becoming an ace fighter pilot. Joe, in his own way too, was quietly proud of his eldest son. He treated Mike with the respect due to an equal, yet soberly told the lad to have no starry-eyed illusions. War would be a tough, bitter, deadly experience. Young men usually viewed it beforehand as a coming great adventure, but soon found otherwise. With fatherly concern, Joe hoped the war in Europe would be over before Mike finished his training, and maybe common sense and statesmanship might prevail in time to prevent a war in the Pacific. "I can only pray to God that you'll never have to fire a shot in anger," he told Michael, with a fervour the young man could not yet begin to comprehend.

Diana was, if anything, even more motherly than usual. She had always had a special affinity for Michael, though she deeply loved all her children. Even if he hadn't noticed occasional tears welling in her eyes as she turned aside to hide them, the unspoken bond of feeling between them told him his mother was very apprehensive for his safety, though she tried hard to be brave. Similarly, at Wilga Creek, Tom's and Kathleen's love and pride in their grandson could not disguise the sadness they felt in farewelling Mike.

So it was, by the time the returning airliner touched down at Archerfield Airport, Brisbane, the obvious concerns of all his elders had sufficed to help Michael better understand the emotions behind Anne's angry outburst. Yet, as he walked across the tarmac to the terminal, he was pleasantly surprised to see her waiting for him. She had taken a taxi to meet him.

Demurely, she kissed him, then apologised for her behaviour of the previous week. "It was unforgivable," Anne told him, "I had no right to put you through that, because of my own insecurity and selfishness."

"It's alright," Mike told her, "by the way, I decided I'd prefer the Air Force instead." he waited for her reaction. She gave a wan little smile, and kissed him again. "You do whatever you want to, Mike. It's alright by me. I love you!"

Later that evening, after a particularly torrid lovemaking session, Anne was even more acquiescent.

"You know, I've been doing a lot of thinking, over this past week on my own," she told him. "I've been a bit of a cradle raider. You are ten years younger than me, yet I've been a selfish, demanding mistress to you! I've monopolised your life since you first moved into this house. You have never had the opportunity to socialise with girls of your own age. So, while you're away in the Air Force, I want you to feel free to go out with other women if you want to, then you can make up your mind about us."

It was quite a profound, soul-searching little speech, Mike thought. He wasn't interested in other women! She had just spent a week alone, wrestling with her conscience because convention dictated that she was too old for him! To hell with convention!

Somewhat clumsily, he tried to allay her worries, with crude levity. "Not bloody likely, you little witch!" he laughed, "You're just looking for an excuse to try yourself out with a few stray pricks while I'm away!"

"I most certainly am not!" Anne retorted indignantly, "I'm yours exclusively for as long as you want me, but I want to be sure that you have a free choice!"

"Then stop worrying! Where else would I find a sheila as sexy as you?"

"Sex isn't everything! I meant what I said. I want you to be sure!" she told him firmly.

Ten days later, Michael was accepted as a recruit, into the Royal Australian Air Force.

22

When the Ford V8 utility drew up alongside the homestead gate at Mt Chillingham late afternoon. Diana watched from the verandah as the new arrival casually allayed the suspicion of the snarling old blue heeler dog, and beamed up at her in friendly recognition.

"G'day, Mrs. Merriton. Bluey Thompson," he introduced himself, "I'll bet you don't remember me, but you've hardly changed a bit! I was in hospital in Cairo same time as Joe, from the same dust-up!"

"Oh! Of course, Sergeant! Joe told me he ran into you again on the train a couple of years back. Come on inside. Joe is working down in the yards, but he should be back up anytime now. Anyway, is this call business or social?"

"Purely social, Missus. I was passing through the district and thought this time I'd make the detour to see you both again. And please, call me Bluey."

"Alright, Bluey. On one condition! I'm Diana, not Missus, OK?" Diana told him.

"OK," Bluey grinned, "Diana."

After the evening meal the three relaxed, yarning in the cool sanctuary of the fly screened verandah, over more cups of tea. The name of a mutual acquaintance cropped up. An old, half-Afghan, half-Aboriginal drover who had worked for both Tom Merriton, and Dave Simpson, Joe's old Boss Drover.

"Old Dudley, eh? He was a really top bloke! A thorough gent, and brains to match! Should have been a droving contractor himself, but I suppose his colour would have gone against him with a lot of the station owners and managers," Joe said.

"Yair, it'd be hard to get most of them to take you seriously if you're a blackfellow," Bluey agreed.

"Is he still alive? Had a couple of sons in the game, too, didn't he?" Joe asked.

"Dudley died about five years ago. Both of his lads are in the AIF now. Joined up like a shot when war broke out,"

Thompson replied, "Which brings me to the point. Remember his daughter, Mavis?"

"Ah yes! The little bush princess, Dave Simpson used to call her," Joe remembered the happy, lively little girl. "Yair. Well, I ran into her again a few weeks ago, for about the third time in recent years. She has a fourteen-year-old son now. Nice kid, smart and direct. Reminds me a lot of old Dudley. Anyway, it appears Mavis married a decent, hardworking half-caste stockman out on the Diamantina. They only had the one child, and then, when the boy, Billy, was about nine years old, his father died. Barcoo Rot, or something. Well, ever since, Mavis has worked on stations or in pubs as a housemaid and managed to both give the boy a fair schooling and to hang on to him, which must have been a battle. She's terrified the Native Affairs bureaucrats will take him away from her, on the one hand. On the other hand, her husband's two younger, white half-brothers have recently renewed their acquaintance with Billy, and she's concerned about their influence on the boy. They're a pair of thieving, boozing no-hopers. Someday I'll manage to nail them, but in the meantime, Mavis is worried they'll drag Billy down with them, and frankly, so am I!" the policeman paused.

"Poor woman! What a quandary she must be in!" Diana exclaimed with motherly compassion.

Joe nodded silently, then asked, "What can you do, though, Blue? Shouldn't you just hand the matter over to the Aboriginal Affairs people? A minor in danger of corruption, or something?"

"Strictly speaking, I suppose I should, but I have to agree with Mavis; I don't think that would be in Billy's best interests, either. I'm prepared to bend the rules all I can for Mavis's and Billy's sake, and out of respect for Dudley, just so long as I can keep it unofficial. Look," Blue finally came to the point, "I don't suppose you would have a job for him here? I promised my wife, and Mavis, that I'd at least ask, even though it is probably straining the bonds of friendship."

"Not at all," Diana chipped in, "we are glad you can still care enough after twenty years as a policeman, aren't we, darling?" she looked at Joe, pre-empting his reply.

Joe smiled wryly, "If he is old Dudley's grandson, there will be a place here for him," he said, "We've had a chronic shortage of station hands since this war broke out!"

A couple of months later, nearly two hundred miles to the northwest, Bluey, with Jim the tracker, and a young constable, were preparing to leave by horseback from the small police station, when the Aboriginal housemaid hurried down the street from the hotel. Dawn was just breaking, but something, maybe just worried intuition, maybe telepathy, had awakened Mavis in time. One look at the loaded packhorse confirmed her misgivings.

"G'day, Sergeant Bluey! Long ride?" she feigned cheerfulness.

Thompson nodded, and then quietly reassured her, "Don't worry, Mavis. If Billy's with them, I'll do my darndest to keep him out of it!" They were out of earshot of the others.

"Thanks, Sergeant. You're a good friend," she said quietly. Hereabouts, it was sheep country, but far to the east lay the wild Carnarvon Ranges, amongst the broken gorges, ridges and forests of which lay many isolated plateaus and valleys. Generally, these afforded good, sheltered grazing for cattle, with an abundance of natural waterholes. The large grazing leases of the district relied on a seasonal contract labour force for mustering these breeding areas, particularly now that so many young men were enlisting for military service.

On unused Crown land, forestry reserves and some under-manned big runs, therefore, many remote pockets might only be visited by humans once or twice in a year, yet, since the widespread rainfall of the past few months, persistent signs of unauthorised activity indicated an outbreak of duffing. Unscrupulous cattlemen, it would appear, were busily ranging far and wide, re-stocking at the expense of their neighbours, and in Sgt Thompson's mind, Billy's uncles were two of the most likely suspects. Their small block had never boasted many breeding sufficiency of right.

Four days later, at the northern end of a big pastoral lease, Jimmy's persistence paid off. The station manager had told them the previous day, that he hadn't been near that end of the run for weeks, yet here were tracks not two days old! A small mob, with two horsemen. One of the horses was going quietly, the other, obviously hard and spirited, never off the bit. The tracker drew Bluey's attention to the irregular pattern left by the prancing, shying animal.

"Blood 'orse, or Arab, eh?" Jimmy said.

The sergeant and the constable nodded their agreement. Didn't need to be a tracker to work that out, Bluey thought. If his gut feeling was correct, there might be more concrete evidence for a conviction. Funny how a jury who might be a bit ambivalent about a few cleanskins, could react entirely differently about the theft of a valuable thoroughbred horse! "If it's an Arab, it's a ruddy big Arab" he refuted one option, praying it would be a certain chestnut thoroughbred instead.

Ten miles north, on Crown land, they first glimpsed the camp through the scattered timber. Keeping well back out of sight, a quick reconnoitre told them a lot. There was only one man at the camp, and the fresh tracks of two horses, again, one the blood horse, diverged south easterly, away from the camp, which was set at the narrow entrance to a natural pound. The steep walls of the blind gorge held about one hundred young cattle on a lush valley floor, and a spring-fed rivulet tumbled down into a chain of rocky waterholes, then meandered out of the entrance on a south westerly course. The 'man' at the camp was the boy, Billy! He was holding the mob, with a saddled horse tethered nearby, and two spare horses hobbled close at hand, while his uncles were away stealing more cattle.

Thompson left Jim to watch the camp, and with the constable, rode around in a semi-circle. They tethered the constable's horse, hobbled the packhorse and spare mount behind a jump up, and Bluey gave the constable instructions to watch for the returning thieves, then to follow them discreetly at a distance back to the camp itself.

Bluey took a coil of hemp rope back with him, ignoring the question in the Constable's expression, and rode back to join the black tracker. There were still about four hours of daylight left.

After a quick conversation with Jimmy, the Sergeant grinned. There was no need for Colin, the young constable, to be burdened with the knowledge of the plot hatched between sergeant and tracker. Quickly, they covered the distance to the camp using the natural cover. A neighed greening from one of the hobbled horses alerted Billy too late! He looked up in surprise at the two mounted lawmen, his mouth open, his eyes wide with apprehension.

"Correct me if I'm wrong," Thompson said sternly, "but those other two fellows are your uncles, right?"

"No one here but me," the boy told him.

"I'm not silly, son. Just the way my mother dresses me. We've seen the tracks, and you surely didn't put this little lot together on your own!" Thompson waved expansively towards the cattle grazing on the valley floor. "Now," he continued, "we'll assume the other two thieves are your uncles. Next question, when will they be back? This evening? Or have they left you to watch the camp while they go off on a bender for a week?"

"I don't have to tell you anything," the boy said defiantly.

"Don't be a hero. No such thing as honour among thieves!" The Sergeant seemed to be playing with the end of a rope as he spoke, "When are they coming back?"

Billy maintained a sullen silence. Thompson dismounted and hand-cuffed the boy's hands behind his back. This was the tracker's cue. "More better we 'ang 'im, I t'ink, Sarge!"

The Sergeant turned away, towards his horse. "Yes, Jim, I think you're right. Save the Government a lot of money if we get shot of him now before he gets entrenched in a life of crime!"

Thompson turned around to face Billy. The rope in his hand now formed a noose, complete with an authentic-looking hangman's knot.

Billy felt a sharp stab of cold, naked fear. The Sergeant had tied that knot so quickly and expertly! Perhaps he'd hanged men before! Billy had heard his uncles say that Thompson was a tough, ruthless bastard. Probably the hardest stock squad man in the state.

Thompson slipped the noose over the boy's head, and, holding the other end of the rope, swung lightly back into the saddle. "Start walking," he ordered, "over towards the timber!"

Billy stood riveted to the spot in fear, his throat dry, beads of perspiration breaking out on his forehead. Desperately, his eyes pleadingly to the black tracker. "You're black, too! How can you stand by and see me hang?" he asked urgently.

Jimmy threw him a look of contempt. "You not blackpfella bootlace!" he told him, exaggerating his own accent. "Proper pfella blackpfella mebbe spear 'im bullock for tucker. Not steal 'im couple 'undred! No, you not proper pfella blackpfella! Jus' white pfella piccaninny rubbish, I t'ink! More better 'ang you now! Save 'im plenty trouble, white pfella!"

Thompson had to turn away to hide a smile. Jimmy was making the most of it, and taking the opportunity to exorcise a few private demons from his own life. "That's it! Start walking," Thompson told the lad.

Billy burst into tears and slumped to the ground.

"I didn't want any part of it! They made me join them! Said they'd get me packed off to a Government reservation if I didn't," the boy sobbed brokenly.

Instantly, Thompson was beside him, lifting the noose of his neck. "Easy, son! I thought as much! Nobody's going to hurt you," the tone was compassionate, even fatherly, "Now lad, are they coming back this evening, or have they gone for a couple of days?" He removed the handcuffs.

Billy dried his eyes, "They'll be back tonight."

"Alright, son! We'll catch them red-handed, and as far as we are concerned, you were never here! Now look, get on your horse, and ride west until you pick up the stock route, then get back to your mother and keep your head down until I arrive back there. You won't be going to any reserve! I've arranged a job for you with a top man who knew your grandfather. Now, grab some tucker and take off! I'll see you next week," Bluey told him.

The boy looked at the tracker, who was smiling his approval, then back to the Sergeant, "Thanks, Sergeant Thompson. And you be careful! They've both got Winchesters and they might use them. Especially Claude!"

Thompson nodded, "Thanks, son. We'll be careful." He was grimly conscious of the fact that further to the east, in the same ranges in 1902, two other cattle thieves, the Kenniff brothers, the last of the bushrangers, had murdered Constable Doyle and Albert Dahlke, a young station manager.

The sun had just set, and an early moon rode high in the eastern sky when the returning duffers came into view with around twenty head. If you were going to take cleanskins, twenty of those wild little weaners would have been plenty in this timbered country, Bluey thought; all wanting to break and get back to their mob!

They were mostly young mickey bulls; starting to feel pretty full of themselves, but usually kept in their place by the older herd bulls. Certainly not easy cattle to keep together and drive. Whatever else these thieves were, they were good stockmen though! And that thoroughbred horse out there was still on the bit even after two hard, consecutive days of paddy dodging!

Branding irons and tools in the camp indicated to the policemen that these fellows probably intended to keep the stock in the little trap for a week or so to quieten, possibly build some yards from the abundant standing timber, then brand, earmark, and cut them before taking them home.

Cheeky, but the area was just about isolated enough for them to have managed to get away with it!

The mickeys spotted the mob already held in the enclosure and readily passed the camp to join their relatives. Police horses were hidden well out of sight, and the hunched figure, squatting in the shadows, waved cheerily to the approaching riders as they shepherded their charges through the gap, then wheeled towards the camp.

The taller of the two had already dismounted before the figure in the shadows of the fire stood up, revolver in hand, and advised him not to do anything stupid. Simultaneously, the tracker, rifle in hand stepped from the shadow of the eastern face to cover the other rider, who looked frantically to his right only to see his escape blocked by an approaching mounted constable.

"Stay well clear of your rifles, gentlemen, or be killed resisting arrest," Bluey advised.

He was mentally noting every feature of the thoroughbred and its markings. Star, snip, white sock off-fore. He'd recognised the gelding instantly, a noted bush racehorse. Didn't need enough light to read the brand to know where this one came from!

"We've nothing to hide," Claude told him, "just mustering our own strays from Crown land."

"Oh, yair? And I suppose the Colonel gave you a receipt for his horse?" was the Sergeant's sarcastic rejoinder.

Claude changed the subject, "Where's the kid?" he asked.

"No idea," Thompson lied, "we saw some kid hanging around, but he bolted when we showed up. Didn't get a good look, but he seemed awful young. And scared! The speed he was going, he's probably in Tambo or Augathella by now, maybe even Adavale. He was going west, and we knew from your tracks you'd be coming from the east, so we didn't bother about him.

"Bloody little dingo!" Claude muttered savagely.

"I don't often dispense legal advice," the policeman said, "but if I were you, I'd forget all about him. Unless you want another charge, relating to corrupting a minor into a life of crime!"

One evening the following week, Diana answered the telephone.

"Hello, Diana! Bluey here. Is your old man there?"

"Yes, he's here, Bluey. I'll call him," she said.

Thompson breathed a sigh of relief. With telephone party lines, he certainly didn't need some stickybeak putting two and two together in hindsight, and getting four! He was grateful Diana hadn't addressed him as Sergeant when what he was doing had to be in a strictly unofficial capacity.

"Hullo, Blue. What's new?" Joe asked.

Bluey suppressed an involuntary chuckle, "OK if I put your new station hand on the train for Wilga Creek tomorrow? Dudley's grandson?"

"By all means, mate! I'll ring Mum and Dad to meet the train and look after him until I come in the next day."

Thompson drove the lad in his ute for the long dusty journey to the railway and paid for Billy's fare to Wilga Creek. It would be the boy's first train trip.

"Don't worry about those bad egg uncles of yours," the policeman told him, "They won't worry you again! Be sure to keep in touch with your Mum, and heed any advice the Merritons give you. They're fine people. I'd like to hear from you, too, if you've got time. Good luck, Billy,"

They shook hands. "Thanks for everything, Sergeant. I'll make you proud of me," Billy told him.

"I know you will, son," Thompson answered.

23

It was around 4.30 pm on a Friday, in the book department of a Melbourne store, that Mike first saw her. He'd been on weekend leave since 12.00 and was just browsing, mainly. Killing time until the evening, when he'd either take in a movie or go to a dance. Little else to do, as he didn't fancy swilling beer madly at a local pub. There was little joy in the "six o'clock swill", the rush hour preceding the 6.00 pm closing time. Mike was glancing at the titles in the paperback section when he was aware of being under scrutiny himself. He looked towards her, noting firstly her expensive, well-tailored clothes. She was, obviously, not a salesgirl. Well-groomed, around five feet seven in height, with medium length, dark brown hair lightly streaked with honey blonde. It framed a very attractive oval face and her wide-set blue eyes showed an amused, somewhat challenging glint. Her left hand held up a slim woman's romance book, the upper corner near her lips highlighting, rather than hiding the impish suggestion of a smile playing at her mouth. She wore a large sapphire and diamond engagement ring, with an ornate white gold wedding ring.

As Michael turned towards her, she briefly glanced at the pilot wings insignia on his tunic, then, cool as could be, asked in an educated, well-modulated voice, "Are you on your own?"

"Yes, I am," Mike replied, bemused.

"Well?" her voice and her facial expression now carried more than a hint of teasing.

"Well, what?" he grinned good-naturedly, his curiosity rising.

"Well, silly, aren't you going to ask me if I'd like to join you for coffee or something?" she returned his smile confidently.

Mike suppressed a chuckle at her brazen impertinence. "OK," he asked, "would you like to join me for coffee or something?"

"Why, thank you, kind sir! I'd love to! There's a cosy little place just around the corner in Swanston Street," she told him, the teasing back in her tone again.

"I'm Mike Merriton," he introduced himself,

"Hullo, Mike," she flashed him a dazzling smile and adroitly managed to avoid giving him her own name by expertly launching into small talk, as they walked along together.

Michael was both amused and intrigued by her. She was warm and friendly, yet at the same time, almost imperial. He was positive that he had never met her before, yet something about her had a ring of familiarity. She could not have been more than a couple of years older than he was. "I haven't met you somewhere before, have I?" he asked.

Again, that dazzling smile, as though he was the only man in the world at that instant. "No," she told him, "you haven't!"

She was obviously well-bred and from a privileged background. He had only ever met two girls even remotely like her, and both had been the daughters of wealthy squatters.

Mike ordered coffee and asked if she'd like something to eat as well. She shook her head.

"Not just yet, thank you. Maybe later," she told him.

Skilfully, she controlled the conversation, giving away practically nothing about herself, yet drawing him out to talk more about himself than it seemed he had ever done before. She was an attentive, interested listener. By now, Mike had simply indexed her in his mind as "The Squatter's Daughter."

They had drunk several cups of coffee, and the time was approaching six p.m., when she finally suggested, "Let's have dinner. I'll pay, I insist! I know you chaps don't get paid very much. Then we'll go back to my place, alright?"

Mike nodded but protested that he would pay for the meal. She wouldn't hear of it, "No, I'll cover it, but, of course, I'll pass you the money so that you can pay the cashier to save you any embarrassment."

They finally reached a compromise, to split the bill.

During the meal, Mike silently wondered about her wedding ring, the fact that she had not mentioned a husband, and also, if she was married, the practised, nonchalant ease with which she had picked him up.

She had another surprise for him. As if she had read his mind, she put down her knife and fork. With such disarming frankness that she almost made the whole thing seem perfectly natural, The Squatter's Daughter told him, "Look, I don't make a habit of adultery. Well, not that often, anyhow, and always with a stranger, and on my terms! My husband has been overseas for two years, and, now and then, I allow myself a night with another man. But never more than one night at a time, and never the same man on two separate nights! Those are my rules, Mike, so, after tonight, you'll never have me again. Alright?"

Surprised, Mike nodded his agreement. It was funny how often she seemed to say "Alright?"

They took a cab to an address off Toorak Road, and the Squatter's Daughter led Mike into a small, very expensively furnished flat. It was not yet eight o'clock, but she didn't waste any time! Kicking off her shoes in the lounge room, she went across to a cabinet, took out a bottle of Scotch and two glasses, and poured the drinks. She handed one to Mike, who had taken the hint and was already taking off his shoes and socks. Downing her Scotch quickly, she replaced her glass on a glass-topped table, motioned for Mike to finish his drink and follow her, and disappeared through to the bedroom.

Mike finished his drink more slowly than had his hostess, placed his glass beside her's, and went into the bedroom. Already, she had hung her suit back in the wardrobe and removed her blouse and petticoat. She turned to face him, fully aware of her own visual effect. Clad only in a lace bra, panties, suspender belt and fine silk stockings, she looked magnificent!

With well-proportioned neck and shoulders, firm, ample breasts above her small waist, and curvaceous hips flowing down to meet her long shapely legs, she would not have looked out of place in a Tivoli Theatre chorus line, and she knew it! She obviously revelled in male admiration, yet the promise in her eyes declared she was not just a tease.

Michael glanced beyond her, briefly, at the framed photograph of a young Naval officer. She followed his glance, then turned and placed the photo face down on the dresser. "Oops! We don't want my husband looking on, do we?" she joked. Then, more seriously, she said, "Anyway, goodness knows what he's getting up to with the ladies of Gibraltar, Malta and Alexandria! He's a Lieutenant aboard a destroyer in the Med," she explained.

"From what I hear," Mike told her, "they are kept too busy these days to get up to much mischief."

"Do you really think so?" she looked relieved.

"Well, maybe not all that busy!" Mike was careful. She might be having a change of heart!

"No, I think not," she agreed, as she deftly removed her undergarments, then impatiently, started helping Mike to undress.

In bed, she was eager and passionate. That she also led a lonely life was evident to Michael. Between their sexual activities, she was keen to make conversation. For either of them to have stated the obvious, that she needed companionship and understanding as much as she needed the sex, would probably have embarrassed her. Yet she was plainly glad of the chance to open her thoughts to the sympathetic young airman, and to be able to articulate the rules she had made to preserve some structure in her marital compromise with loneliness.

"You know," she told Mike in all earnestness, "some of my husband's friends have asked me to sleep with them, but I never go to bed with men we know, and certainly never with any Naval men!"

Mike chuckled. "What have you got against sailors?" he asked.

"Oh, nothing at all! But you see, my husband is a career officer. He is very bright, and someday, he'll probably reach Flag rank. Well, how would it look if some of his peers, or men under his command had slept with his wife? It would be known all around the Fleet in no time!"

"If you think like that," Mike told her, "you have to look at your life-style all round. I mean, with me, for instance, I hope to make the RAAF my career after the war. Perhaps I'll finish up as an Air Commodore or an Air Vice-Marshall, and have contact with you and your husband on an inter-service level."

She was horrified! "I hadn't thought of that!" she said.

"Cheer up, sweetie," he told her, "I wouldn't be skiting about it! I doubt my own wife would see the funny side, for a start."

"Well, airmen perhaps you mightn't, but I'd better scratch all and soldiers as well, from now on. That won't leave many attractive young men around Melbourne in wartime!" She was very serious.

"There is one other solution," Michael told her.

"What's that?" she asked.

"Try fidelity," he advised.

"I say, that's a bit drastic! He mightn't be home for ages!" she protested.

In Michael's memories, henceforth she would be indexed not as The Squatter's Daughter, but as The Admiral's Lady.

He realised, with some surprise, as he strolled back to Melbourne city the following morning, that despite their shared night of energetic passion and her strict observance of her own "Rules Governing Infidelity", the main thing he did not know about her was her identity. He smiled to himself. He had to hand it to her! In spite of her mixed up emotions and values, and in spite of her loneliness and strong need for physical sex, even if it meant committing regular adultery, she kept her own rules to the letter.

She was a real lady.

Yet he felt guilty, that he had somehow taken advantage of her, that he had somehow short-changed her and the husband she obviously loved, despite her willing, wanton ways. Mike was as guilty of adultery as she was.

He also felt regret that he had been unfaithful to Anne, even though she had encouraged him to find girls nearer his own age. That was only a manifestation of her own guilt for being a "cradle raider", a "seducer of young boys", as she put it.

He knew with certainty, that although he had spent less than four weeks with her over the past fifteen months, that Anne would, herself, have been absolutely faithful to him. And she would be hurt, very much so, if she found out he had taken precisely the sort of liberty, to which she had encouraged him. Bloody women! Why were they so complicated?

24

In the early hours of the 8th December 1941, local time, a Japanese invasion force, under cover of darkness, steamed across the Gulf of Siam from occupied southern Indochina, to land and attack Kata Bharu airfield in north eastern Malaya.

Simultaneously, across the International Date Line where it was 8.00 a.m., 7th December local time, Japanese Naval aircraft from a carrier task force, abetted by three midget submarines, attacked Pearl Harbour and other military airfields and barracks on the island of Oahu, Hawaii. Within hours, further Japanese forces had virtually destroyed the American Army Air Force in the Philippines on the ground and launched attacks against Hong Kong, the Australian-mandated Nauru Island, and minor U.S. bases on Guam and Wake Island.

Japan had entered World War 2, dragging the United States of America, kicking and screaming, into the conflict as well.

Without air support, the pride of the Royal Navy, Britain's newest battleship, "Prince of Wales", with the battle-cruiser "Repulse", was sunk on 10th December by eighty-seven Japanese bombers and torpedo-carrying attack aircraft, while vainly attempting to prevent further Japanese landings in Malaya. By the 19th of December, British troops had abandoned Penang, and Japanese forces swept on down the Malay Peninsula towards Kuala Lumpur and Singapore.

American and Philippine forces evacuated in haste from Manila on Christmas Eve to withdraw into Bataan peninsula, and the island fortress of Corregidor.

On Christmas Day, the isolated British Colony of Hong Kong surrendered.

Six months earlier, a German minelayer had managed to sow mines in a huge sweep of south eastern Australian waters from Adelaide to Sydney. Together with submarine attacks, these were to sink around fifty ships, yet even this had not jolted Australia into a full realisation of her isolation, until these stunning new advances of Japanese Imperialism to our near north.

Although R.A.A.F. units in Britain and the Middle East were flying high-performance fighter aircraft, Spitfires, Hurricanes and Kittyhawks, the desperation of the European requirements had dictated that such aircraft were simply unprocurable for the defence of Australia itself. 1942 dawned, with not a single modern fighter among the R.A.A.F. strength of nearly 2300 aircraft within Australia or New Guinea.

Sole fighter protection for all of Australia and New Guinea had to be entrusted to a proportion of our 440 Wirraways. These were locally built copies of the North American NA 33 Trainer, lightly armed with .303 machine guns and having a top speed of 220 miles per hour; no match for the Japanese Mitsubishi A6M Zero, capable of over 350 m.p.h.

Our only reasonably up-to-date bomber force consisted solely of 131 Lockheed Hudson medium bombers, with a top speed slightly over that of the Wirraway, 246 m.p.h. The remainder of the R.A.A.F. inventory was made up of various trainers, transports, Army co-operation and reconnaissance types ranging from Tiger Moths to Avro Ansons, apart from 18 Catalinas and 10 DC2s!

Pilot Officer Mike Merriton returned to Brisbane in early January, posted to Maritime Reconnaissance duties. Avro Ansons and Lockheed Hudsons maintained surveillance against enemy ships, submarines and mines off the coastline. Mike's little B.S.A. Bantam motorcycle provided a link between Red Hill and the Airfield, and Anne was delighted to have her man at home with her again when duties allowed. Mike was less comfortable with the situation.

"Marry me, darling," he had asked her almost immediately he returned home.

"Oh, Mike, I can't! You're barely twenty, and I'm nearly thirty-one. Your parents and everyone else would be shocked silly, and you probably wouldn't get permission, anyway!"

"Let me worry about that! In any case, a man is a man at eighteen in the Forces. If I'm old enough to defend my country, I'm old enough to damned well marry whomever I want to! You do still love me, don't you Anne?"

"Of course I do! You know I do! Look, wait until you are twenty-one, and, if you still want me, I'll be happy to marry you, then," Anne said, "but remember, I can't give you children!"

Mike held her close. He gently kissed her forehead. "That's important to you, isn't it?" he asked softly.

She nodded, barely trusting herself to speak. "Yes," she murmured in her small, sad way.

"Then there's no problem! We'll just adopt! There'll be plenty of poor little mites looking for a loving home by the time this war is over," he told her.

She smiled up at him, "Oh, my love! I really don't deserve you."

"Nonsense!" Mike said, "And now that is settled, when are we getting married?"

Anne was still resolute. "Not for another year! As soon as you're twenty-one," she told him, "but not before! I am not going to be any more scandalous than I need be."

"Scandalous!" Mike exploded, "Hasn't it entered your pretty red head that if some interfering old biddy tumbles to the fact that we are not married, but I'm just living here and shagging the pants off you, the Education Department might just decide they don't want a scarlet woman teaching little kids?"

Anne reddened, "Do you have to put it quite so crudely?" she shot back angrily.

"Yes, dammit, I do, if it will make you change your mind! I love you too much to just want to live in sin with you! Oh, a minute ago we were all lovey-dovey, and now... why the hell are we fighting?" he asked.

She smiled ironically. "Because I'm a stubborn woman who will not change her mind, and you are frustrated! Now, why don't we change the subject and go to bed? You can do whatever it was you were just skiting about doing to me," she nibbled his ear lobe suggestively.

Mike sighed. "You've won me!" he conceded.

The Japanese continued their relentless advance. Their strategy of a simultaneous attack on all Allied bases from the Aleutians to Malaya, together with the Pearl Harbour raid, not only reduced the Allied Naval effectiveness but also assured Japan of her main concern - that no land-based Allied bombers would be within range of the Japanese homeland, as Japan already occupied eastern China.

Manila had fallen on 3rd January, although a gallant US-Filipino defence would hold Bataan Peninsula until April 9th, by which time General MacArthur would have been in Australia for three weeks. On Corregidor, their remnant would hold on for a few more weeks beyond that. Borneo and its oilfields were effectively in Japanese hands by late January, as was Rabaul, on New Britain, in Australian mandated New Guinea. Here, a handful of R.A.A.F. Wirraways and a small Army garrison bravely held off the attack for ten days, to the 22nd. With air cover destroyed and land forces outnumbered, the defenders could no longer resist. Some made their escape down the length of New Britain and across to Milne Bay in Papua, but many others were killed or captured.

The Dutch East Indies was also under attack, with further Japanese landings on Bali and resource-rich Sumatra. The entire Dutch East Indies would be in Japanese hands by the middle of March.

Then, on February 15th, the Malayan invasion ended with the unconditional surrender of the Singapore defenders. A total of 32,000 Indian, 15,000 British and 13,000 Australian troops became prisoners of war, many to die later in forced labour and brutal, malnourished, ill-treatment while building the infamous Burma Railway, along with captured Dutch soldiers.

Late February and the first few days of March saw the loss of five Allied cruisers, several destroyers and smaller vessels under the command of the Dutch Admiral Doorman in the Battle of the Java Sea, and later, in the battles of Sunda Strait. These losses included the Australian cruiser "Perth" and sloop "Yarra", and the U.S.S. "Houston", all of which were sunk after brave encounters with vastly superior Japanese forces. "Perth" and "Houston", in particular, accounted for many of the enemy in their furious night battle.

With her four crack infantry and armoured divisions, her fighter squadrons and a large part of her Navy in the North African and European operations, Australia was hard-pressed at home.

Most of the Australian troops garrisoning Port Moresby and Milne Bay in Papua New Guinea were young militiamen. These were coming under heavy, constant Japanese air attack, with no adequate air cover. They laconically referred to the long-promised Kittyhawks as "Tomorrow hawks" or "Never hawks". Even General MacArthur, Supreme Commander of all Australian, American, Dutch and British troops in the Pacific, could make little impression on his President, Franklin D. Roosevelt, who inclined towards Mr. Churchill's views that ninety percent of the U.S. land and air support should be directed towards the European theatre.

MacArthur forcefully disagreed with his President, as did the U.S. Navy, still smarting after the humiliation of Pearl Harbour. Like MacArthur, they were thirsty for Japanese blood. Wounded U.S. Naval pride was partly assuaged in mid-April, when U.S.A.A.F. B25 bombers were launched from the carrier "Hornet" in a daring raid to bomb Tokyo, then attempted to over-fly China, intending to land beyond Japanese held territory. It was a taste of their own medicine for Japanese strategists, shaking their security. But the U.S. Navy wanted real revenge. This commenced in May, at the Battle of the Coral Sea, when U.S. Carrier aircraft, together with Australian and U.S. land-based bombers thwarted a large Japanese Naval Force.

To the north of the carrier battle, the Australian cruisers "Australia" and "Hobart" with the U.S. cruiser "Chicago", under the flag of Rear-Admiral Crace in HMAS Australia, forced a large Japanese troop convoy to abandon a landing in southeast Papua.

The experience was expanded the following month off Midway Island, 1300 miles north-west of Hawaii, when U.S. air and naval forces under Rear Admiral Ray Spruance, sank four large Japanese carriers and several other vessels, for the loss of one carrier, the "Yorktown". Japanese loss of life (around 12,000) was heavy. Japan's mighty naval air supremacy had passed its zenith!

The enormous American industrial capacity would soon redress the U.S. losses, and the expanding, highly efficient U.S. submarine force would wreak havoc amongst Japanese merchant shipping on a scale far surpassing the German U-boats in the Atlantic war.

Rosemary and Tony were now living at Mt Chillingham, where Diana and Joe were delighted to have their daughter and grandson for company.

"You'll spoil him, Mum," Rosie warned her mother, "and Dad is even worse! You wouldn't have let us get away with what he gets away with, when we were little!"

"Oh, fiddle-faddle! He's only a baby, and the poor little fellow misses his dad. Your father is very proud of his grandson, as I am, but there is no chance we'll turn Tony into a spoilt brat!" Diana replied.

Rosie was pensive. "Oh, Mum! I miss John awfully! And I worry so much about him up there. It's not only the Japs; there's malaria and all sorts of things. From what I've heard, New Guinea is a terrible enough place, even without a war. At least, I'm glad Mike hasn't been posted there yet!"

"I know just how you feel, but John will be alright! He's very sensible, and from what we hear, the Japs will soon be getting a taste of their own medicine," Diana tried to reassure her daughter.

"We only get told half of it. Mum! The Coral Sea battle didn't stop them. There are still hordes of the little yellow blighters pouring into the islands." Rosie's usual cheerfulness disappeared every time she thought about it. She continued, "I believe all that stuff about the Brisbane Line, Mum! The Federal politicians must have known how serious the threat was if they wanted to move us all south of a line from Brisbane to Adelaide."

"Well, thank heavens for General MacArthur!" said Diana. "You know, your father had made up his mind that if that happened, he wouldn't leave here! He'd pack young Bob, Billy and me off, make sure Grandma and Grandpa went with us, then he'd take to the bush with a rifle and plenty of dynamite. He said we'd burn this country out before he'd let the Japs get any benefit from it! But now, we are getting reinforcements galore! There are so many Yanks coming into Australia."

Hmph! I'd settle for the 6th, 7th and 9th Divisions all returned from the Middle East. I overheard John tell another officer before he left, that from what he'd seen of them, he didn't think the average Yank could fight his way out of a wet paper bag!" Rosie said, "'All piss and wind,' he said."

Diana suppressed a grin. She could just imagine John saying that. "Well," she said, "their Navy hasn't been doing too badly lately."

25

Bluey Thompson phoned occasionally, to inquire as to how young Billy was progressing, and Joe was happy to be able to tell him how pleased he was, to have taken Billy under his wing. The boy was not only a first class ringer but also had high intelligence and a thirst for knowledge, which delighted Joe and Diana.

Like many intelligent people living in isolated locations, the Merritons had built up an extensive collection of books, both fiction and non-fiction, over the years. The diversity of subject matter covered was wide, and Billy was allowed full access to this library, which he eagerly accepted. Joe and Diana were only too willing to explain to him, anything which might be beyond his vocabulary or experience. His life in the years to come would not be an easy one, but the seeds of learning, which had been sown, would stand him in good stead.

Young Bob was much more of a problem. Although only eight years old, he had a seemingly inexhaustible penchant for mischief. He was very bright but lazy with his schoolwork, was a born practical joker and on one occasion at Wilga Creek, had almost set his grandfather's sawmill alight. In fact, the only times he seemed to be well behaved were when he was riding or working with horses, which he loved. Joe and Diana tried to mix discipline and understanding with their youngest son, yet, though he did not want for love, he was a restless little larrikin.

Kathleen, his grandmother, sometimes shook her head and advised Diana, "You'll have to keep your eye on that one. I'm afraid he is a throwback to my father!" Rosemary, who had been somewhat wilful herself, was inclined to dismiss the problem lightly, "Oh, he'll grow out of it, Mum."

Diana was not so sure. "We haven't spoiled him. He has had his fair share of hidings, but only when he has deserved them. He's also had plenty of love and attention, too. I hope and pray he will turn out alright in the end."

"Perhaps his nose is out of joint now little Tony is getting so much attention. After all, Bob is still just a little boy," Rosemary volunteered.

"No, he thinks the world of Tony. Bob has been a holy terror long before you and Tony came to stay, anyhow," was Diana's reply. She thought for a while, then added, "I'll continue to try to teach him at home by correspondence for a couple of years more, then it will have to be boarding school if he doesn't improve. I'm not sure that would sort him out, either. He would certainly be too much of a handful for your grandparents, to stay with them and go to the Wilga Creek School."

From that fateful day of 19th February 1942, when Japanese bombers first bombed the Australian mainland causing heavy civilian loss of life in the little port town of Darwin, Mike's frustrations had steadily increased. Yet home production of the Beaufort bomber, and the little Australian-designed "stop-gap" fighter, the C.A.C. Boomerang, was finally being supplemented with the arrival of the U.S.A.A.F. and a small but steady trickle of modern U.S. aircraft into the R.A.A.F. by mid-year.

The Boomerang, the prototype of which had flown just 14 weeks from the commencement of design, was a fitting example of what could be done with the right motivation.

Crates of Kittyhawk fighters, Vultee Vengeance dive-bombers and Douglas A20 Boston light attack-bombers were trickling through for the Australian Air Force, to join the Lockheed Hudsons in the north.

The long-awaited "Tomorrow hawks" finally arrived in the New Guinea area, to wreak havoc amongst the Japanese Air Force. No. 75 Squadron, defending Port Moresby operated for 44 days at an average daily strength of five serviceable Kittyhawks, yet accounted for 35 confirmed enemy aircraft destroyed, four probable and 47 damaged.

Many of the latter category would not have made it back over the rugged Owen Stanley Range to their bases.

The 75 Squadron lost 11 pilots in combat and 22 Kittyhawks destroyed or missing, and had one serviceable aircraft remaining before being relieved by Airacobras of the U.S.A.A.F. 35th Fighter group.

If there had remained any lingering doubts that Australians were up to the task ahead of them, these were dispelled in early August by the "Chockos", the young "Chocolate soldiers" of the Australian Militia Forces, who, the cynics had sneered would melt in the hot tropical heat, like chocolate!

At Milne Bay, near the south eastern tip of Papua, supported by Australian and American air units, these young Australians had participated in the first serious reverse on land to be suffered by the Imperial Japanese Army. Together with units of the 6th Division AIF, "Chockos" drove the Japanese back, with heavy losses into the narrow peninsula north of Milne Bay, destroying all the Japanese tanks and heavy equipment. John Roxton was one of these "Chockos".

Meanwhile, Mike complained bitterly about his lot. He couldn't get into action soon enough for his taste. Instead, he was flying out of Archerfield, "stooging around" off the coast of southern Queensland and northern New South Wales in Avro Ansons. For their part, both Diana and Anne were grateful. Flying was dangerous enough, they thought, and the longer the Air Force kept Mike away from the Islands Campaign, the better.

26

Along with other Australian cities and towns, Brisbane was witnessing a vast change in attitude, sense of purpose, and lifestyle.

Since the Darwin air raids commenced, followed in June by the Japanese midget submarine attack in Sydney Harbour, irritations like air raid drills and blackout curtains were being taken more seriously by the civilian population. Huge concentrations of American, Australian and Netherlands East Indies forces were encamped throughout southeast Queensland. Road and airfield construction proceeded at a rate hitherto undreamed of; primary and secondary industries were expanded enormously to supply the vast war machine. From a pre-war condition of chronic unemployment, the civilian population, directed by the Federal "Manpower" bureaucracy, worked in whatever capacity they were so dictated. The women, in particular, were magnificent. They operated lathes, heavy presses and other factory machinery, drove trucks and tractors, or laboured manually in agriculture, often hundreds of miles from their homes.

To alleviate the accommodation problems, billeting of total strangers whether civilian or military, in private homes, became widespread. There was no choice; it was by government direction. Likewise, suitable motor cars and commercial vehicles were requisitioned for official use from private owners who could not prove an essential case to retain them; (sometimes to satisfy an equally non-essential need for somebody more fortunately placed). In pre-war Australia, private motor vehicles were generally, a luxury, the preserve of a fortunate few, or of people whose very professions or remote locations had deemed them a necessity. Petrol rationing was stringently enforced in the case of those civilians able to retain the use of vehicles. Supplementing such a meagre availability of petroleum, charcoal-burning gas producers became commonplace;

mounted on extensions behind the vehicle chassis, and filling a large, ballooning, rubberised fabric "gasbag" reservoir carried either on a roof rack or on a semi-permanently attached box trailer.

Butter, meat, sugar, tea, clothing and cloth fabric were also rationed to the civilian population. Books of ration coupons became a normal part of one's personal effects. Luxuries like ladies' stockings or household appliances were either unprocurable or too exorbitantly priced for ordinary Australians.

Again, people generally responded cheerfully and unselfishly to the limitations imposed. Yet, as always, the dark side of human nature remained among a few; the inevitable smarties, the lurk merchants, the scum who will always be around to greedily take advantage of any opportunities to corrupt and profiteer, the black-marketers. These parasites existed in industry and among the predominantly decent public servants and the U.S. and Australian Military supply personnel. They were the germs who could syphon off building materials, petrol, American cigarettes, stockings, refrigerators and other luxuries from a system too large and unwieldy to maintain proper control. They were the selfish mongrels whose profiteering "enterprises" took up valuable cargo space in Liberty ships and oil tankers, while brave merchant seamen risked bombs and torpedoes to supply the war effort in the southwest Pacific.

Theoretically, penalties for black-marketing were severe. In practice, most of these criminals were never prosecuted, and ended their careers in affluence; some might even buy enough influence to become knights of the realm.

Mike Merriton called in at his former workplace to renew acquaintance with his old civilian colleagues.

"Well, will you look what the cat dragged in?" said Col, "How's the Air Force?"

"Good day, Mike! We thought you'd be a Squadron Leader at least, by now," from Ted.

"When are you coming back? Your work has been piling up!" the foreman asked mischievously.

Mike surveyed the happy faces. "Oh, I might stay in the Air Force, and become a Squadron Leader - or an Air Vice Marshall," he told them, only half-jokingly.

The foreman's face looked serious, almost grim. A fatherly man, he said, "Just make sure you come back safely, son. Poor Alby won't be back, you know!" he added softly, gloomily.

Mike was jolted by the news. Alby was two years older than himself, a serious but good-natured lad, who used to go out of his way to be helpful. Mike had considered him a good friend. Always something of a pacifist by nature, yet no coward, Alby was an only son and had three sisters, all older. His father was English and his mother was German by birth. He'd still had aunts, uncles and cousins in Germany, and, aware of his mother's sensitivities, yet wanting to do his bit, he'd elected to join the Merchant Navy.

"No, I didn't know," Mike finally said. "When? How?" he asked.

They all looked uncomfortable, sad; the jocularity of a few moments earlier now gone.

"In mid-Atlantic about a month ago. His ship was torpedoed by a U-boat and sank very quickly," Col told him.

"I'd better go and pay my respects to his parents this evening," Mike said.

"They'd appreciate that! In fact, they are probably at home today. Alby's dad is working shift work," Col told him.

It wasn't far from their home at Annerley. Alby's Mum, Dad, and one sister, Ingrid, were at home when Mike called on them. They remembered him well.

"Hullo, Mike!" Alby's Mum greeted him with a motherly hug, "Come on in!"

Her husband shook his hand, tears welling in the older man's eyes as Mike's presence rekindled memories of a cherished son.

Moist-eyed, Ingrid acknowledged him with a wan, yet friendly smile and a sisterly kiss on the cheek.

Inadequately, he felt, Mike offered his condolences. They would be a long time coming to terms with it, their only son's mortal remains somewhere in the cold depths of the Atlantic Ocean; not even the formality of a burial, just a Memorial Service.

Awkwardly, embarrassed, Mike almost wished he hadn't come. At least, not yet. It was still too soon; he felt he was an intruder on their private grief. What right had War to touch the lives of this gentle, Christian family?

They made Mike welcome, so genuinely pleased and surprised to see him. His misgivings evaporated. Mike decided he was glad he had visited.

Sitting around the table, with tea and homemade biscuits, they talked with such pride and fondness, about their boy.

"Alby was thrilled to be appointed Radio Officer to that ship," the father told Mike. "She was a modern British ten thousand tanner, refrigerated holds, and a good, up-to-date radio room. They left Hobart in February, and then after they returned to the U.K., were on their second trans-Atlantic convoy when it happened. Apparently, the U-Boats got three ships that night. The other two were tankers. A lot of poor lads were lost from that convoy."

Mike was no stranger to losing aircrew friends to this war, yet the news of Alby had upset him more than most. Alby had been such a nice, decent bloke from such a nice, decent family. The sort of people who would not have a mean or malicious bone in their bodies. And they were so proud of their only boy.

A few days later, returning from Archerfield to Red Hill, he was feeling particularly depressed. It had been a bastard of a day! Three false starts due to maintenance problems with the "old Aggie"; then a bumpy, squally patrol over the water with a sick port engine. Then a landing on one engine after the port motor gave out while the landing gear was being wound down manually. Talk about bloody Gremlins! Even the H.F. transmitter had been unserviceable for half of the flight.

The Gremlins were working overtime since well before dawn, and hadn't let up for a moment! Mike didn't normally have much use for alcohol, but Anne wouldn't be home for an hour or so yet. On the spur of the moment, he'd called in at a waterhole popular with his mates, on the chance one of them might be there. None of them were, but now he had this bloody green Yank bullshitting in his ear! Been nowhere, done nothing, but knew everything! Fresh out of the U.S. of A, and trying hard to make friends. Mike didn't particularly like beer at the best of times, but this was warm and a bit flat, to boot! And here was this Yank telling him, "Say, Buddy, if there's one thing I like about this country, it's the beer! This is great beer, man!"

"It's piss!" Mike said, disagreeably and uncharacteristically.

The young American looked hurt and affronted. He opened his mouth to debate the issue, but Mike's icy glare stopped him in his tracks. He shrugged his shoulders and turned away, to find a more congenial drinking companion than this cranky Aussie airman.

Mike turned back to his beer. It was piss, all right! But overpriced piss! He might as well finish it. To his right, a loud, flashily dressed man in his mid-to-late thirties had the ear of a quieter bloke. The loudmouth was a typical smartarse, over-dressed, over-fleshed and full of his own importance. The type who wouldn't hesitate to use any means to avoid the call-up yet seemed to think his country owed him a lucrative living. A spiv!

The quiet bloke didn't seem too impressed either. "Well, I've got to go, Harry," he said, draining his glass.

Big Harry consulted his gold watch, "Yair, me too, after I shake hands with a girl's best friend. But don't forget! Watches, Yank cigarettes, refrigerators, you name it! I've got the contacts. Anything, you need at a price, Bert!"

"Fridges, too, eh?" Bert asked flatly.

"Bloody oath! My Yank mate can get 'em in by the boatload?" Harry boasted.

Leaving, Bert shook his head in disgust, the gesture lost on Harry.

Broodingly, Mike finished his beer. He was wondering if this bloody country would be worth fighting for, by the time the Harrys of this world were through with it!

He pocketed his change and turned toward the door. Better have a squirt first. He turned back and went through the door marked "Gents".

Lost in thought, Mike heard, "Good day, my boy!" spoken in an expansive, yet patronising way. It was Harry, doing up his fly as he stepped away from the urinal.

"Ah, the frigging refrigerator salesman!" Mike addressed him balefully.

Anyone quietly with common sense would have called it a day and gone quietly with that look in Mike's eye. But not Flash Harry. "That's right, boy! Fridges, watches, cigarettes, you name it! Want some silk stockings for your girl?"

"Get rooted, you parasite! Brave men in Liberty ships get torpedoed and drowned to bring that stuff over here! And your sort of scum profiteer from it! You ought to be locked up, you bastard, yet you skite openly about it!" Mike told him.

"And why not make a profit?" Harry sneered, "They're mugs if they are bringing it in and not making a quid! And you're a mug, too, Blue Orchid! Get out of that Air Force and make some money for yourself, while it lasts."

There was nobody else present. Harry was in real trouble! A hard left hook loosened his teeth, as Mike "king hit" him. A right jab to the solar plexus doubled Harry up with a rush of air that spat one of those teeth onto the floor. He raised his forearms to shield himself, but Mike swept them aside with his left and followed through with a bone-crunching right to Harry's face. Blood gushed from the flattened nose.

"That was for Alby and his mates! But you wouldn't know about them: They only died to defend democracy for arseholes like you!" Mike addressed the blubbering heap in disgust then turned and walked out, contemplating his skinned knuckles.

What he'd done was stupid, childish; perhaps even criminal, and completely out of character. But Oh, Boy! Was it satisfying!

27

From Buna, on the northeast Papuan coast, to Port Moresby on the south coast, a line passing through a hill station village called Kokoda appeared on both Japanese and Allied maps as a road through the mighty Owen Stanley Range. An unfortunate aberration on the part of the cartographers responsible known to old Papua-New Guinea hands for what in truth, it was; this "road" was no more than a difficult, at times frightening and precipitously steep, lightly used native pathway, of great antiquity. Repeatedly, it climbed and fell, at times reaching altitudes over 7000 ft. as it passed between mountain peaks over 13000 ft. high. In very few places more than a yard wide, this Kokoda Trail clung to mossy rock faces, muddy mountainsides in the rainforest and traversed deep ravines over rushing, turbulent streams on swaying rope-vine suspension bridges. Only a handful of Australians knew this route. Neither MacArthur nor the Japanese had ever been in the area, therefore, to both Commands, it was a road or route as represented on the map.

So it was, as the crack Second AIF battalions of the 18th Brigade, Sixth Division, together with three Militia battalions including John Roxton's unit were valiantly routing the Japs far to the east at Milne Bay, a "Chocko" battalion, the 39th, from Victoria, had the unenviable distinction of becoming the first Australian Army unit to walk across the Owen Stanleys along the Kokoda Trail. Apart from the commandos of an Australian independent company living off the land and harassing the Japanese at Lae as guerrillas, 160 miles to the west, the 39th, some small, scattered Native Constabulary platoons and a volunteer Papuan Infantry company at Buna, there were no other Allied units north of the Owen Stanleys.

Some fifty miles from Kokoda, at the Anglican Mission village of Gona, and also nearer the only other coastal village in the region, Buna, some 25 miles east, Japanese landings took place on the 21ˢᵗ July 1942. This was in preparation for their planned assault on Port Moresby, via the Kokoda Trail. Because they had taken the line on the map to represent at least a primitive roadway, albeit one "almost impassable to motor transport", they disembarked some 400 packhorses at Gona, mistakenly supposing that these would be able to carry their supplies along the track to Port Moresby.

Their main base was quickly established at Sanananda, a former shipping point for rubber, midway between Gona and Buna on the 5erviceable coastal road that linked these centres. From these beachheads, a fairly easy walking track forded some minor creeks then crossed the raging Kumisi River on a wire rope suspension bridge at Wairopi, a pidgin place name that derived from the bridge. This track continued on to link up with the mountain trail at Kokoda, which also boasted a small airstrip.

Those Japanese landings had not gone completely unopposed. RAAF dive-bombers had sunk one transport, but the remainder had managed to retreat seaward beneath a fog bank and returned later to complete the landings. However, once ashore, the Japanese quickly murdered most of the Europeans soldiers of the Papuan Infantry, missionaries, plantation owners and government officials alike.

Using systematic murder, rape and brutality combined with bribery of any natives willing to cooperate, they proceeded to establish their authority over the native populace.

A large Japanese force set out towards Kokoda garrisoned shortly before by "B "Company, Aust.39th Bn., as the remainder of this Militia battalion hurried northward to reinforce their comrades. At Awala, north of the Kumisi a small detachment consisting of two "B" Coy. Platoons and Native Constabulary engaged the superior Japanese force before retreating across the wire rope bridge and cutting it down behind them. This bought them less than 24 hours of respite. They fell back to Oivi, a tin village a few miles from Kokoda, but were again surrounded by the enemy the following day.

Retreating that night by a roundabout route, to another small village on the other side of Kokoda, they dug in and were joined the next morning by the rest of "B" Company. As the Japs did not immediately occupy Kokoda, the Australians returned to its outskirts and prepared an ambush.

That night, under a ferocious bombardment from Japanese mortars, mountain gun and machine guns, "B" Coy., again was forced to retreat, this time with an elderly expatriate Australian doctor and some Papuan bearers, but the battalion's C.O., Lt. Colonel Owen was killed in the action. A few days later, joined by their new C.O., Major Cameron, and the rest of the battalion, these brave young militiamen made another surprise counterattack against Kokoda. Again, they were repelled with heavy losses.

Once more, the Chockos withdrew south, this time to another village, Isurava. The Japanese, reinforced by the crack combat troops of their much-vaunted South Seas Detachment, many of whom were even taller than most of the Australians, attacked again with mortars, mountain guns and machine guns and followed up with a wild bayonet charge. With superhuman courage and desperation, this time, though weakened by hunger, dysentery and malaria, the young Victorian militiamen forced the enemy to retreat and regroup.

Later that same afternoon, AIF troops of the 21st Brigade, 7th Division, started arriving at Isurava. Even though men of this Brigade were seasoned Middle East veterans, such was the Japanese numerical and weapons superiority that those weary, battered youngsters of the 39th could not yet be spared for a well-earned rest and return to Port Moresby.

Back and forth, across ridges and ravines, through tiny villages, the fighting seesawed. Placenames such as Isurava, Alola, Eora Creek, Myola, Efogi and Mission Ridge would be burned indelibly into history; burned as well, as memories of a living hell into the memories of those fortunate enough to survive the experience. Finally, after weeks of bloody, muddy savagery and reduced to a mere 300 combat-fit men ranged against some 5000 suicidal and well-equipped enemy, the 21st Brigade was forced back to the second ridge before Port Moresby. Here, they were reinforced by the fresh 25th Brigade. Both brigades withdrew further, to consolidate at Imita Ridge, overlooking Moresby. Then, on 28th September, the combined Australian force counter-attacked against Ioribaiwa, three miles north of Imita Ridge, only to find the position abandoned! Inexplicably, so close to their objective, the enemy was retreating! Now it was the Australians' turn to pursue, to harass and charge at the retreating Japanese back to the northern slopes of the Owen Stanleys. Even so, Jap rear-guard units defended with brave desperation to cover their main force withdrawals; to hold out as long as possible in the vain hope that Guadalcanal might be retaken, and Japanese reinforcements diverted to Papua-New Guinea.

Such determined defence exacted a heavy toll on the three battalions of the Australian 25th Brigade, their attached 3rd (Militia) Battalion and 2/1st Pioneer Battalion, as they attempted to advance in the Templeton's Crossing area. Badly depleted, over 40% killed, wounded or sick, the 25th was relieved by the 16th Brigade, 6th Division, 2nd AIF, at Eora Creek on the 20th October. Here the Jap rear-guard were well dug in, overlooking at point-blank range, the two suspension bridges and precipitous walking tracks above Eora Creek.

Nine days, 99 Australian dead and 192 wounded, was the cost of dislodging the enemy before the advance could proceed.

Finally, the Australians could again advance to Alola. The 16th Brigade and the 3rd Battalion were again joined by the 25th Brigade, who moved up and forked left along the track through Isurava and Deniki to secure Kokoda. The 3rd Battalion secured the airdropping ground at Alola, while the 16th Brigade took the right-hand track to attack Japanese positions in the Oivi/Gorari area.

A patrol of the 25th Bde found Kokoda abandoned by the Japanese: the Brigade entered the village and secured the airstrip on the 2nd November. By the morning of the 4th, Douglas C47 transports were arriving with supplies.

The 16th Brigade and 3rd Battalion again combined in heavy fighting against Japanese positions. On 7th November, 25th Brigade moved east from Kokoda in support. The campaign had lasted three and a half months. Much bitter, intense fighting still lay ahead, but the infamous Kokoda Trail had been regained and secured. Like the Milne Bay victory, it was a totally Australian Army combat role. An American contribution by way of a very large part of the joint USAAF/RAAF supply drop was greatly appreciated. Even more vital and praiseworthy had been the stoic, dedicated heroism and toil of those "Fuzzy Wuzzy Angels", those hardy, gentle, unarmed Papuan native bearers who carried stores up the track ten returned to Moresby carrying the sick and wounded so carefully, staunchly and surefootedly over such appalling terrain.

In Brisbane, meanwhile, General MacArthur, whose own U.S. Intelligence sources, (almost a contradiction in terms to Australian commanders in the field) had so badly under-estimated Japanese strength, continued to publicise all U.S. successes as "American" and all Australian achievements as "Allied Forces" victories. Privately, he continued to denigrate the Australians' abilities. Such prejudiced misconceptions were to be proven embarrassingly wrong for him a few weeks later when U.S. land forces were finally committed to action alongside Australian troops!

28

Buna, December 1942. Three young Diggers were griping about the shortcomings of Australia's great and powerful ally; it was a real "piss on the Yanks" session. American infantry units had not, on the whole, performed very well during their baptism of fire in the Buna-Sanananda areas.

"I heard they all go to ground and don't move an inch if they hear so much as a single shot ahead and if they actually come under fire, they fair shit themselves," a freckled-faced nineteen-year-old redhead said contemptuously.

"Serve the gutless smart-arses right! They've been sitting around in Australia for nearly a year, skiting to everybody about how we could all go home once they got here. They reckoned they'd go through the Japs like a packet of salts! Meanwhile, they've had the best of everything, living like Kings and eating Australia out of house and home," an older man, a twenty-two-year-old Corporal spat in disgust.

"You're telling me, Len! They don't only go to ground, a lot of them go to water as well, the emotional cry-baby bastards!" the third youngster agreed with all the wisdom of twenty years. "We kicked the Japs out of Milne Bay, we hunted them back over the ranges from Moresby; all the Yanks have been asked to do is to drive them out of a couple of coconut plantations, and they can't even handle that on their own!"

"It's got me stuffed what the bloody sheilas see in the mongrels," Len said morosely. The corporal, a married man, had recently received a poisonous letter from an anonymous, sanctimonious busybody, inferring that his wife was a little too friendly with the Yanks. As if he didn't have enough to worry about already!

"Yair, but the mob at home never hear the full story, anyway. How do you reckon the yarn about the Moresby Fishermen would go down if it was allowed to make the papers?" Bluey, the nineteen-year-old asked.

The Moresby Fishermen were an American Airacobra squadron, given their nickname due to an alleged tendency to take off and head out over the sea to avoid combat during Japanese air raids on Port Moresby earlier in the year. Supposedly, they had always returned safely intact when the Japs had left. An unjust slur, this was widely accepted as fact by many Australians.

"Fair go, you jokers!" the platoon sergeant butted in, "Some of the RAAF blokes reckon the Yank Kitty hawk pilots at Darwin did one hell of a good job, and the Yank transport pilots looking after us with supplies haven't shirked the risks, either!"

"Yair, well they must be a different breed of Yank to these bludgers we have here!" Len countered drily.

Privately, the sergeant agreed with the criticism of the American Infantry. Always better provisioned and clothed than the Australians, these Yanks also had a couple of years of training in most cases. Mainly National Guard units, the U.S. equivalent to Australian Militia, they were not a patch on our own much-maligned militia in action. Perhaps that was understandable; the U.S.A. was six thousand miles away, but only Torres Strait separated Papua-New Guinea from mainland Australia. It was only to be expected that all Australian soldiers would be more motivated, but it was beyond doubt that the entire Australian Army, from Blamey down, now had little faith in American ground forces. Weary Australian divisions, depleted by the harsh Kokoda campaign, now pressed grimly on against the Japs at Gona and Sananda. Disgusted at the lack of results from the fresh U.S. infantry at Buna, they were making their feelings plainly known. Humiliated, MacArthur had relieved the Hapless American commander, a Major General, and replaced him with his most aggressive leader, Lieutenant General Robert Eichelberger, instructing him, "Bob, I want you to take Buna or not come back alive!"

The sergeant, of course, did not know the full story, he knew only that a new, high-profile Yank General subordinate to Blamey, were given the task of turning the Yanks into an effective fighting force. Was this a new beginning, or a flash in the pan? Only time would tell, but time was a luxury they could not afford.

More than a thousand Japanese reinforcements were reported to have been recently landed to fortify their already strong, well-entrenched comrades. Aircraft and destroyers were believed to be massing in support of further landings. To the allies, it seemed imperative that the Gona-Buna area be secured in Allied hands as soon as possible to forestall renewed onslaught.

The sergeant almost felt like an American apologist as he told his lads, "Don't blame the Yanks for all of our problems. Mostly, they're good-hearted poor bastards; it's not their fault they've been force-fed bullshit from birth! Besides, you can't be crooked on them just because their mob looks after them a lot better than our miserly mob looks after us!

Had they but known, those Americans at Buna were no longer well provisioned. Their supply lines to this remote area were no more efficient than those of the Australians; if anything, they were, at the moment, even less organised. To compound the difficulties, many U.S. units, lacking discipline and accustomed to what had seemed limitless material reserves, had contributed to their own sorry plight. During the march towards their objective through difficult terrain and heavy going, considerable numbers of them had wastefully discarded what they had seen as surplus and unnecessary stores and equipment. Similarly, when they finally faced a combat situation, too many had needlessly squandered ammunition by firing countless rounds in the general direction of unseen targets. Obviously, the U.S. Army's 32nd Division could not live up to the reputation won by U.S. Marines at Guadalcanal.

Contrastingly, the experienced, disciplined Jap soldiers and marines, blooded in the China campaign, many of them also veterans of the Kokoda experience, fought with intelligent and ruthless efficiency. Now entrenched for a last-ditch stand from their cleverly positioned and camouflaged bunkers and gun pits, they exploited any element of surprise; they would hold fire until almost point blank range from their concealed fortifications. These Japanese would fight to the bitter end to protect the airstrips and beachheads behind them. Other reports had filtered through since the closing weeks of the Kokoda campaign, adding to their reputation for sub-human behaviour and disgusting barbarism. There had been several accounts from reliable Australian witnesses, of evidence that isolated; starving Japanese units had practised cannibalism of Australian prisoners and of Australian, and even their own Japanese, battle casualties. The sergeant's reflections were cut short as young Bluey changed the subject.

"This new bloke, Roxton: he's a Chocko, isn't he, Sarge?"

"Captain Roxton to you, lad!" the sergeant replied. "He transferred to the AIF from Militia and now he's our Company Commander. Just remember he was in the Milne Bay stoush, same as the rest of us, so I don't want to hear any more talk of Chockos. He's a good officer!"

29

Only a few days remained until Christmas but this was one Yuletide season that would bring only grief and mourning to hundreds of Australian and American families. Families whose sons, husbands and fathers sought to flush out the invader from his foothold on the northern shores of Papua.

From their concealed and fortressed pillboxes, the Japanese had defended the old airstrip and a series of fortified lines to the beach, approximately half a mile away through the low scrub, kunai grass and the coconut trees of the big plantation. From the start of this operation two days earlier, it was made abundantly clear why an experienced Australian Bren gun carrier troop had been cut to pieces and three American regiments were halted over the preceding weeks.

Now the task was given to a crack AIF infantry battalion supported by a hastily assembled squadron of seven Stuart light tanks and crews seconded from an AIF armoured regiment. Some of the footsloggers were battalion originals who had served in Tobruk and the North African desert. Most were veterans of that bloody but historic turnaround of the Japanese at Milne Bay, while a few had been previously unblooded reinforcements; all, over the past two days, had emblazoned a glorious new chapter in the already proud annals of their country's feats of arms. Doggedly and ruthlessly they had dealt with the enemy defences, the camouflaged coconut log or concrete and iron dugouts with earthen and grass-covered roofs treacherously hidden in the long grass and light scrub, the fallen loss placed to "belly " and immobilise the armoured vehicles and the suicidally brave Japanese snipers.

With Bren gun, rifle, grenade and bayonet, with the 37 mm cannon and Browning machine guns of the tanks, with artillery and US mortar support and with another Australian and three American battalions in reserve to mop up and secure the ground won, this spearheading AIF battalion had virtually captured the whole plantation in two and a half days. The unit's casualties ran very high; around 350 of their own, including more than a hundred killed. Yet they had achieved what others thought unbelievable.

Now, virtually at the close of the action, sporadic fire from a "woodpecker" in a well-positioned dugout was reaping further casualties. The light machine gun nest had pinned down one of Captain Roxton's most heavily depleted platoons. John motioned to a section of his Company HQ men to follow and set out in the general direction with an urgent recklessness born of tiredness.

"Drop down! Hit the ground, Sir!" the sharp-eyed young corporal shouted, simultaneously swinging his Bren upward and firing a long burst high into a coconut tree. A Jap sniper fell lifelessly, together with a section of the treetop.

"Got the bastard!" the corporal exclaimed with satisfaction. He turned to where his Officer lay on the ground. Captain John Roxton's eyes stared up at him, unseeing. There was a single bullet hole almost exactly in the centre of his forehead. The Japanese marksman, too, were deadly accurate.

To learn of John's death was merely to confirm what Rosemary had dreaded in expectation. Three days before the official notification had arrived; she had been riding some four miles from the homestead around mid-morning, heading towards the North West section of the station. Joe, Doug and Billy were cutting and splitting posts further out, to renew a fence burned out by a bushfire caused by a dry lightning strike. Fencing was a chore usually left until the cooler months. It was usually avoided during the heat of a Queensland summer unless, as in this instance, urgent reconstruction was imperative. The men were camped out for three days with a tucker-bag of tea, sugar, flour and corned beef.

Since early morning, too, Diana and Rosemary had been busy with a welter of pre-Christmas baking. They had made fruitcake plum pudding and fresh bread. The previous day, they had also made marmalade and melon Jams from the produce of the station garden. Rosemary had decided on impulse to ride out and deliver a treat to the men. The self-imposed errand was largely an excuse to get out of the house, with the surprise wrapped in tea towels inside two large saddlebags.

She had been enjoying the ride; the morning was hot but not unbearably so on this part of the property. Undulating ground, a park-like scattering of trees and a few little glens and gullies served to provide some small patches of green grass amidst the parched landscape of yet another summer with lower than average rainfall. Trees, gullies and hills provided just sufficient thermal breeze for a pleasant morning before a scorching sun would climb to its zenith almost directly overhead.

Suddenly, Rosemary was seized with fear and foreboding. Her short-sleeved arms showed goose pimples and she shivered as though cold from the indefinable fear that gripped her. Her conscious mind urged calmness, restraint. Be sensible. Look for some physical reason.

The horse had sensed no danger. The birdlife continued about its business with noisy normality and a kangaroo, two hundred yards along the shallow valley, hopped unhurriedly into the cover of the scrub. Still, that sixth sense screamed inside her head. John! Something terrible had happened to John. She was certain, in that instant, that he was dead!

Reacting instinctively, she had wheeled her mount around and spurred him towards the homestead at the gallop. Barely a dozen strides on, reason had triumphed over panic. She had reined back, turned about and resumed her original course. She told herself that she was imagining things! John was never far from her thoughts, concern for his safety and well-being had never left her, but it was irrational and selfish to dwell on her fears, she had told herself. Anyway, if John was injured or something, he was two thousand miles away and nothing she could do would change that!

Panic fought back: reason re-asserted itself; then panic, allied with her impetuous nature, began to get the upper hand once more. Subconsciously, she had urged the horse along, faster and faster. Then, over the final three miles, she was like a madwoman and her unfortunate horse was at full gallop.

The men had heard the galloping animal approaching through the timber. Joe had dropped the maul and had run in alarm towards his daughter. There had to be something terribly wrong for Rosemary to get a horse into that condition! He caught her in his arms as she swung lightly down from the saddle.

"What's happened? Your mother? Tony?" he asked in apprehension.

Doug and Billy were beside him, concern clearly showing on their faces, too. Suddenly Rosemary had felt a complete fool. She'd fought back her tear and busied herself with unfastening the straps on the saddlebags.

"No, they're all alright! Oh, Dad! I'm just a silly woman, I suppose, but I've just had the most awful premonition about John!" She had then related to them the chilling experience she had felt on the way to meet them.

To her surprise, all that she saw on their faces was compassion.

"Don't let it throw you, love. Those sorts of fears are both natural and understandable with your husband away fighting in the jungle. Come on, we'll put the billy on! You look like you could use a cup of tea," was her father's response.

She'd given them an embarrassed smile, then unwrapped her original excuses for the ride out.

"My word! That lot should beat our corned meat and damper hollows!" Doug had tried to encourage her to a less morbid state of mind.

Joe had kept his own counsel on the concerns that his daughter's fears had raised. He'd been around too long to automatically dismiss Rosie's trepidation out of hand. There had been many instances of some sort of telepathy between people hundreds of miles apart. Many of the old Aboriginals had understood it well, and he had long felt that there was something of it that existed between himself and Diana at times. Besides, such communication of minds was indisputably evident in the minds of good working dogs, particularly among sheepdogs, which could read their master's thoughts and intentions. No, he conceded to himself, it was quite probable that John had met his fate for Rosemary to have that vivid experience.

When Joe unsaddled Rosie's stressed mount, he put him with the others on the camp. Later, he'd saddled two fresh horses to ride back to the house with her, over her protestations that she really was all right and sorry for the worry she had caused. She had tried to present a brave front.

For the following three days. Rosemary was very subdued, living in the desperate hope that her worst fears were merely the result of a false, unfounded premonition. By the time official confirmation came through that John was killed in action, she was so emotionally drained and exhausted that she could not even cry.

Diana phoned John's parents. She also suppressed her own tears to explain to her grandson, as sensitively and tactfully as she could manage, why Mummy was so sad and tired, and that it would be a very, very long time before Mummy or Tony would see Daddy again.

The four-year-old boy gravely informed her that he had not seen his Daddy for a very long time already, and asked, "Doesn't Daddy love me and Mummy anymore?"

Tears flowed down her cheeks and a lump choked in her throat, but somehow Diana managed to retain sufficient composure to look her grandson squarely in the eyes and tell him, "Oh, yes, Tony. Your Daddy loves you both very much! That was why he went away to the war, to protect you and Mummy from the Japanese."

"Will we ever see him again?" the child asked.

Rosemary joined them, "Yes, my darling. One day we'll see him, up in Heaven with Jesus!" She hugged the little boy tightly to her. Diana hugged them both.

"Well, that's alright, then," Tony decided.

He went out onto the verandah. Soon after, childish impersonations of engine noise and gear changing announced the fact that he was playing with his toy truck. Diana silently reflected that it was fortunate that he was so very young and had not seen his father for such a long time. A child's limited conceptions of time and the finality or otherwise of death would allow Tony the mercy of a gradual acceptance of his father's death. Silently also, she asked God to comfort Rosemary, to allow her, too, that gradual acceptance. She was quite worried about Rosemary's uncharacteristically restrained behaviour.

Rosemary squeezed her mother's arm lightly and kissed her on the cheek. "Thanks, Mum," she said, "you handled that wonderfully."

Diana hugged her in silence, wondering as she did so, in how many other living rooms in Australia, in New Zealand, in America, in Japan and throughout the world, was the same situation being enacted that same day; probably in the thousands as a result of this monstrous war! Suddenly, she became aware of Rosemary, sobbing quietly for a few moments, and then wailing, with a full rush of tears. Tears flowed from her own eyes, too. She held her daughter close to her with a strange sense of relief.

"Let it flow, Rosie." She encouraged, "you're entitled to express your grief!"

30

Some weeks earlier, Mike had arrived home with some news which pleased him greatly but which Anne had long dreaded. I'm being posted to a Beaufighter conversion course! That should almost certainly guarantee I'll get a real crack at the Japs after all! Seems that with my twin-engined experience and all the time I've out into spruiking in the earholes of everyone with any pull, somebody has finally got the message!"

"You are already doing a useful job of coastal surveillance. I wish you'd been content with that!" Anne's reply had made plain her disapproval, but Mike was too elated to notice.

The Beaufighter, developed from the Beaufort light-medium bomber, was of considerably enhanced performance; a tough fast strike fighter, heavily armed with four 20 mm cannon, six machine guns and, at times, eight underwing ground-attack rockets. A potent new addition to the RAAF inventory, its quiet engines and low altitude exploits in the hands of aggressive Australian pilots were destined to earn it awesome dread and the nickname, "Whispering Death," from Japanese ground troops.

Anne was suddenly conscious of how little time they might have together before Michael was posted overseas. She acquiesced to his other long-cherished wish. A few weeks before his twenty-first birthday, with Joe's and Diana's somewhat hesitant blessing, they "made it legal," during a short leave period.

Newly married and with the rank of Flying Officer, Mike received his posting to the Islands a bare two months after his brother-in-law was killed in action. As Mike saw it, it was both a chance to help personally to square the account for John and others and a well-deserved graduation from the monotony of interminable but necessary patrols in old Ansons, looking for but never sighting those elusive enemy submarines. His bride, his parents and his sister, however, viewed his new role in a much more disturbing light; the light of cold, hard reality; of waiting and praying in impotent inability to influence the outcome. Theirs was the same burden of anxiety, hope and dread, which has faced the families of warriors since the dawn of history; the same crushing load, which Rosemary, in particular, had already shouldered in vain for the previous year.

Barely had Mike joined his new squadron when he received his baptism of fire in one of the most decisive and bloody victories to Allied air power during the whole course of World War 2.

Japanese High Command had already badly underestimated the courage and tenacity of the ill-equipped and under-supplied Australian ground troops in Papua and New Guinea, just as they had also underestimated the calibre of the US Marines on Guadacanal, and the ability of the United States to rebuild and expand her Naval forces in the southwest Pacific. Logistically, the Japanese octopus had finally overextended its tentacles. The nightly "Tokyo Express" of Jap destroyer flotillas ferrying provisions down "The Slot" to maintain a toehold in the Solomon has had diverted the lion's share of the Emperor's resources from the New Guinea theatre.

Attempting to redress that situation, at midnight of the 28th February 1943, eight Japanese transports sailed from Rabaul, in convoy along the north coast of New Britain. Steaming at seven knots and varying in tonnage from 950 to 7200 tons, these transports carried almost 7000 Infantry and Artillerymen of the 5lst Division plus 400 Marines, equipment and supplies. They were escorted by eight powerful, modern fleet destroyers and were headed for Lae, at the head of Huon Gulf on the New Guinea mainland.

Late on the following afternoon, 1st March, the convoy was spotted and shadowed by a USAAF B24 Liberator bomber. Commencing 10 am 2nd March, the convoy was bombed by eight, then by a further her twenty US Flying Fortresses. These attacks sank the 5500-ton troopship, "Kyokusei Maru," and damaged other transport ships. Around 850 survivors were then taken at high speed to Lae aboard two of the escorting destroyers. They were landed at Lae before midnight of that same day.

Meanwhile, surviving ships of the convoy were again attacked by eleven Flying Fortresses and harassed continually throughout the night by an Australian Catalina flying boat. This was followed by a dawn attack by two RAAF Beauforts. That morning, the two destroyers, "Asagumo" and "Yukihaze" returned from Lae and re-joined the convoy. By 9 am 3rd March this Japanese force was in Huon Gulf and only 90 miles due east of Lae, which base now provided them with a fighter umbrella of around 40 Zeroes at high altitude. On a calm, flat sea in brilliant sunshine, waves of Allied bombers commenced their attack while simultaneously RAAF Bostons of the famed 22 Squadron strafed and bombed Lae aerodrome.

Protected by a top cover of 28 USAAF P38 Lightnings to engage the Zeroes, i3 B17 Flying Fortresses bombed the convoy from 7000 feet, claiming five direct hits. Then followed ferocious low-level strafing by RAAF Beaufighters to suppress the ships' gun crews, before the next wave of 13 USAAF 825 Mitchells bombed from medium altitude. A further wave of Mitchells struck from 500 feet using a "skip bombing " technique; 500 lb (227 kg) bombs released in a dive, at masthead height, each having a five-second delay fuse which allowed the aircraft to be well clear of the target before the resultant explosions in the water against the ships' hulls. Results were devastating. The concerted bombing and strafing attacks sunk five more transports and two destroyers, one of which was the Flagship, "Shirayuki." An additional two destroyers were severely crippled, as were the two remaining transports. One of these was then abandoned. All four of the remaining destroyers also sustained damage. They temporarily retreated northward to refuel from "Hatsuyuki," another destroyer sent from Kavieng, New Ireland.

Further raids later in the day by US B17s and B25s, and by Australian Bostons despatched the last transport while the crew were transferring to one of the crippled destroyers.

One thousand five hundred rescued survivors aboard the four refuelled destroyers were transferred to one of their number and to "Hatsuyuki," which left immediately for Rabaul. The three others returned to the battle scene and worked until midnight, plucking scattered survivors from the water before themselves departing north to Kavieng. American P.T. boats mopped up and sank the last abandoned and burning transport with torpedoes.

A final Allied bomber attack on the 4th March despatched the two crippled destroyers. Over the next few days, some of the swimmers in the water survived to come ashore on the mainland or islands, only to be killed or captured. Others were killed in the water by aircraft or P.T. boats, and a fortunate 275 were rescued by two Japanese "I" Class submarines.

Of the mighty invasion force, a mere 850 men landed at Lae, three thousand had perished, all eight transports, all their equipment and supplies plus four of the escorting destroyers, were sent to the bottom of the Bismarck Sea. It was a route to rival the defeat of the Spanish Armada.

Allied air losses were minimal; three Lightnings and one B17, for 10 aircrew, were lost in combat while one B25, three aircrew and one Australian Beaufighter were lost to accidents.

At least 24 Japanese fighters were shot down, fifteen by Lightnings, eight by Flying Fortresses and one by a Beaufighter. Many other Japanese aircraft were destroyed on the ground at Lae by RAAF Bostons and Beaufighters. The Bismarck Sea Battle and its grisly aftermath of mopping up was Mike's initiation to the real air war; not glamorous, merely demanding, terrifying, messy, yet essential. Its conclusion left him feeling a curious mixture of revulsion and satisfaction, of horrific reality, yet professional achievement.

31

Six months passed. Mike had developed into a veteran; a wily-experienced attack pilot. He'd been further promoted to Flight Lieutenant. The war was going well for the Allies; its end, though still far off, now promised defeat for Japan.

His trip to Guadalcanal was an interesting diversion, a sort of taxi-driving stint, he reflected. It had had its genesis when an American submarine picked up an Australian Navy Coastwatcher from a beach on the southeast coast of New Britain and landed him in the Trobriands. It seemed that he might have learned something of a vital and urgent nature about Japanese defence dispositions on the Gazelle Peninsular, but only a full de-briefing by U.S. Naval Intelligence could evaluate the position adequately. The Navy, under Halsey's South Pacific Command, was far away in the southern Solomon Islands, time was of the essence and submarines travelled too slowly. A rendezvous with a U.S.N. Catalina was proposed and discounted, as, by the time it could be effected, the dawn light could expose the lumbering flying boat and its passenger to patrolling enemy fighters, so the submarine ran full speed on the surface through the night, arriving mid-morning.

Mike had flown the Coastwatcher from Kiriwina to Milne Bay, where a brief chat with Australian Naval Intelligence had confirmed that Halsey's men should check it out further. Next stop, Guadalcanal Island.

"Keep your finger out and your eyes peeled approaching Henderson Field, son," the RAAF Briefing Officer advised.

"Japs still pretty thick around there, eh?" Mike asked.

"Japs be buggered! Trigger happy Yank Navy and Marine Corps! They've even been known to jump our Catalinas, and bloody Yanks built them! Most of them will never have seen a Beaufighter, so stay awake in case they think you're one of Tojo's mob," came the pessimistic response.

"Thanks, Sir, you've just made my bloody day," Mike told him with laconic irony.

In the event, it had turned out to be an unchallenged arrival, following on an entertaining flight. The passenger, originally a London-born man, now in his early forties, was managing a Copra plantation in New Britain for sixteen years before the war. He had returned there in 1942 as an RANVR Lieutenant, under the very noses of the Japanese, to set up as a Coastwatcher. Just himself, a couple of loyal natives, and a transportable radio transceiver! So far, they had evaded, watched and reported on the Japs for nearly twenty months, living largely off the land and their wits! Brave, resourceful men, and obviously pretty fair sorts of radio mechanics, too, these Coastwatchers! Naturally, the fellow was close-mouthed about his area of operations and his tactics, but he was quite talkative about his pre-war experiences. Like many other Englishmen before him, he'd been seduced by the Tropics. Gone quite troppo, he freely admitted; he loved these islands and their happy, unsophisticated, dark-skinned people.

"You were an apprenticed radio mechanic, yet the Air Force made you a pilot? Wonder they didn't turn you into a Wireless Air Gunner," the Coastwatcher had changed the subject.

"Yes. Well, I'm not complaining," Mike had replied, "I love it! Even in the tough bits, like when we're lost in cloud, or have been shot up and wondering if we'll be able to walk away from the landing, at least I'm occupied with flying the brute! Kev, my usual observer, has to just sit there hoping and quietly fighting back a nervous breakdown. It takes more guts to be a backseat flyer than a pilot, in my opinion, I wouldn't change places for quids!"

There was quite an assortment of aircraft on the strip at Henderson; Dakotas, Venturas, Wildcats, RNZAF Kittyhawks, Dauntlesses and a few less common types, but it was the F4Us that Mike really noticed. The big Corsair fighters sitting high over their inverted gull wings, were the most massive single-seat, single-engined machines he had ever seen, and, by all reports, as fast as greased lightning!

His Coastwatcher friend was quickly spirited away by a couple of Yank Naval Intelligence types. It was the last Mike would see of the Englishman; the Yanks would make other arrangements for returning him home to New Britain. Probably by submarine, the same way he'd come out.

Meanwhile, a trio of young Marine pilots introduced themselves. They were as fascinated by the big twin-engined Beaufighter as Mike was by their Corsairs.

"What's her airspeed and range, man?" one asked, Mike told him, exaggerating both by around fifteen percent. Well, he reasoned, the Yanks don't hold a monopoly on bullshit!

"Is that right! Boy, she sure looks a mean mother!" the young Lieutenant was suitably impressed.

They were right-royal hosts, generous to a fault, eager to be liked. Yanks were all right, Mike decided, just so long as you didn't take their boasting too seriously. In a way, it was just a different route to the same objective--- the desire to impress, to be well regarded. Yanks, from a highly materialistic society, tried to impress by showing what great guys they were. Australians, on the other hand, were from a country much closer to its pioneering roots, and therefore more inclined to try to impress by exhibiting a hard-as-nails, laconic toughness; an attitude that they didn't give a stuff what anyone thought of them. Beneath the surface, young men of both races were remarkably similar; just little boys at heart!

Departing Henderson at dawn, the Beaufighter's fuel tanks full and a slight hangover resulting from a like condition himself the previous evening, Mike flew a north westerly heading. It wasn't the most direct route, and he'd chance meeting Japanese fighters from the Rabaul and Bougainville areas, but he deemed the risk acceptable. The long, wide northerly sweep taking him closer to Rabaul might provide some useful reconnaissance, perhaps some target of opportunity; a Jap barge or two, a light naval craft to add to his tally.

What a beautiful day! Despite the hangover, he reckoned, he wouldn't be dead for quids! He surveyed the tropical sea below, hues of sapphire blue changing to pale, translucent greens in the shallows that flanked white coral sands and dark green vegetation of small islands breaking the surface here and there, like jewelled settings. No wonder that English-born Coastwatcher loved these islands so much! Despite the heat, the malarial mosquitoes and tropical ulcers, it was easy to see how a man could be seduced by the beauty and the slow pace of life in peacetime!

Mike flew well to the southwest of known Jap fighter fields. There were likely to be heavy enemy air patrols to the east, all the way from Bougainville down to The Slot. One Beaufighter was no match for an agile Zeke, much less for a squadron of them! A Zeke could out-climb and out-manoeuvre any Allied fighter, let alone such a big, heavy twin as a Beaufighter. The lightweight Jap fighter also had excellent range, and, though lacking the outright speed of a modern Allied Pursuit aircraft, it retained a level flight speed advantage over a Beaufighter at most altitudes.

If jumped at his present altitude, Mike felt, his best bet would be to dive away, using momentum from the weight of the big kite, to reach an airspeed that would out-strip the light Jap fighter. The Jap wouldn't be able to stay with him on the way down. That was his theory, anyway! So far, he hadn't tested it personally.

Two hours on, Mike was bored. He'd scanned sky and sea continuously, almost subconsciously. His thoughts drifted back to Brisbane, to Anne, to her soft, warm kisses and her eager, passionate body. How he longed to make love to her again!

Then, in the distance, he saw them, two tiny black dots approaching from two o'clock above. If he hadn't noticed them when he had, they'd soon have been in a position to jump him from out of the sun. Jap fighter patrols often came in sections of three, but these were only two, so far as he could make out. He was bigger than they were, and they weren't looking into the sun, so it was almost a certainty they'd have seen him! He turned to port and pushed the throttles wide open, diving away.

Another black dot approached from the west, almost dead ahead. He'd been cut off; they'd obviously received a sighting report and been sent to look for him!

"Keep 'er coming, Tojo!" he muttered grimly.

The enemy fighter grew rapidly larger with closing distance. This Jap had made a fatal mistake! He'd thought he was closing on a Beaufort bomber and was lining up ahead and a little below for an easy frontal attack! Mike eased the nose down and fired a long burst from his four 20 mm cannon, commencing at 1200 yards. Two seconds later, at around 700 yards, the Jap exploded as Mike took violent evasive action, narrowly avoiding the wreckage.

Behind him now, what remained of the enemy's fuselage and one wing spiralled down to douse their flames in the Coral Sea, while the other wing followed, fluttering gently seaward like a falling autumn leaf. There was no sign of a parachute.

"Chalk up your first Zero, Mike! That should look bloody marvellous on the gun camera!" He congratulated himself elatedly. Besides the thrill of downing his first Zero, his previous tally of barges, of aircraft strafed and destroyed on the ground and other successes, paled into insignificance. Mike did not waste any sympathy on the dead Jap pilot; since his gory initiation into the Bismarck Sea Battle, he would have found it helpful to recall Japanese atrocities and to think of the enemy as sub-human, a species of bloodthirsty little monkeys.

Above and astern, the two remaining "little yellow monkeys" were gradually gaining on him. On the horizon, a large bank of low cloud was building up as the morning became hotter. He started a gentle, almost imperceptible climb. If only he could make it! He'd play hide and seek until their fuel situation forced them to abandon the chase. It was an anxious few minutes, but, he made it, and his ruse proved successful!

What a day! Mike was grateful for those earlier clouds, but now a new front was closing in from the west. He was nearly home, but the strip could be hard to find in these conditions. Oil pressure had dropped alarmingly in the starboard motor, possibly a legacy of shrapnel damage when that Zero had disintegrated in front of him! Another thing, he'd wasted a fair bit of fuel playing Chase-me-Charlie in the clouds with those Japs! Probably, he should divert to Milne Bay instead, if he could only rely on the motors. Then again, Milne Bay could also be in an equally bad situation by the time he arrived, anyway. He'd stayed at altitude in the clouds because he hadn't fancied flying at deck level for too long if one engine packed it in. Oh, what the heck! He was certain he was still over the sea; he'd go downstairs. Go below cloud base, take a look and decide then!

Banking into a gentle, wide turn, Mike commenced a steady, spiralling descent. At two thousand feet, he still hadn't found the cloud base. Suddenly, out of the mist a hundred yards ahead, loomed the menacing bulk of a mountain cliff face rushing towards him. An instant later, his mortal life was ended.

32

At Mt. Chillingham, Diana had taken the news particularly badly. Her usual calm, resilient strength, which was such a comfort to Rosie after John's death, had evaporated. Joe, too, was hurting deeply. His own grief and deep sense of loss at Michael's demise was further compounded by that helplessness he again felt at being able to offer any real comfort to Diana and the family. Diana was an emotional mess, alternating between disbelief, anger at the Japs for starting the war, and an irrational, incredible feeling of self-recrimination that somehow she, as his mother, had failed in her duty to shield Michael from the dangers of war.

Surprisingly to Joe, it was Rosemary who was reacting the most rationally and selflessly on this occasion. For Diana, and for young Bob, who bottled up his grief in a stony-faced, unfathomable silence of self-control, the acceptance of Michael's fate would be a long way off. Ever since Mike first joined the Air Force his family had lived with the distinct possibility that he might not survive the war, yet now that the worst eventuality had come to fulfilment, his death seemed so unreal; a horrible nightmare. Had his body, the physical evidence of his death, been here with them, his passing may have been a little easier to accept, but Michael's remains lay in Papuan soil.

Rosemary's first thoughts of compassion were for Anne. Over the telephone, Rosemary had established that her sister-in-law had nobody to offer real comfort and support in Brisbane. Even that girl, whom Manpower had billeted with her earlier in the year, had moved on before Michael crashed. Anne would be desolate in her loneliness! Rosemary's mind was made up in an instant.

"I'll be taking the earliest train to Brisbane, Dad! I know exactly what Anne must be going through, and I can't allow her to face it alone. At least you, Mum and Bob have one another," Rosie declared.

"Of course!" Joe agreed. "What about Tony? I'd suggest you may as well leave him here with us for the time being. It wouldn't do him any good going to Brisbane in the circumstances. Besides, if he stays here, that will give your mother something positive to help occupy her time and thoughts."

Rosemary deliberated. "I'm agreeable, provided Tony won't be unsettled by my leaving him, "she decided.

She explained to the child that she would be going to Brisbane to help Aunty Anne for a while, but if Tony would like to stay with Grandma and Grandpa and Bobby while she was away, then they would all like that very much, too. Assured that Mummy would return in a few weeks or months, the little boy had no qualms about remaining behind. Mt. Chillingham Station was his home; his grandparents and Bob were a major part of life and security to him.

During those next few weeks, life at Mt. Chillingham returned to some semblance of normality. Gradually, accepting Michael's death became less difficult. Joe and Diana found their thoughts dwelling less upon the loss and more upon the wonderful memories of his growing-up years. To Diana, responsibility for Tony's welfare and happiness was proving to be the therapy, which Joe had known she needed.

At the Red Hill cottage, too, Anne and Rosemary shared treasured memories of Michael. Their similar experience of being recently widowed as well as that bond of family between Mike's wife and sister served to strengthen the mutual liking and respect that had already existed between them for some years. Their friendship was blossoming.

Rosemary became conscious of a further need within herself. Anne had a useful occupation, teaching, but Rosie felt an increasing urge to contribute something to the National effort, herself. She telephoned the homestead to discuss the matter with her mother, and to gauge what, if any, effect such a decision might have on her young son. Diana positioned the youngster to stand on a chair so that he could talk to his mother. For a few moments, he listened then chuckled happily in the realisation that it was his mother speaking. Rosemary asked if he missed her very much.

"Just a little bit, Mummy, but I like looking after Grandma when Grandpa is out on the run," Tony said with an air of importance to his childish voice, "and Grandpa said he's going to find a pony just for me!" he announced excitedly.

"That's wonderful, my gorgeous little man! I love you and I miss you very much," Rosemary told him with a lump in her throat.

"I love you, too, Mummy," the child assured her in a carefree tone.

"I know you do! I'll be home again at Christmas time. Hand the phone back to Grandma now. Bye, bye, Darling!"

"Bye, Mummy!" Tony took the receiver from his ear and handed it to Diana.

"Well, he sounds chirpy enough, Mum!" Rosie said

An amused giggle from Diana, "Oh, he's chirpy, alright! Happy as Larry! How are you? How is Anne coping?"

"I'm doing fine, Mum, and Anne is coping well. We seem to be good medicine for each other!"

Diana was aware that Rosemary, too, needed young company and more diversions than station life to take her thoughts off John and Michael. Rosie was still getting over her own loss. A longer break in the city could be very therapeutic.

"Don't worry about Tony! He is just fine. You stay there as long as you feel you need to, dear," Diana said.

"Thanks, Mum. I miss the little blighter like mad. I'll make sure I get home for Christmas, even if only for a few days, Rosemary broke the news, "A girl I knew from school down here, is working for one of the big pastoral companies. She says that with my background and having worked for a stock and station agent. I could easily get a job with her. I'd like to, at least for a while! There is a big labour shortage in a lot of industries. Now that our boys have started to turn the Japs around there is even talk of releasing men from the forces to meet some requirements."

Diana was remembering her daughter's childhood, Rosie desperately pleading the merits of her case whenever she wished to do something that might not have the approval of her parents. So that was the main reason behind this expensive trunk-line call!

"Go to it if that's what you feel you should do," Diana gave her blessing, "but watch out for Yanks, and don't forget you have a little boy to come back to when it's all over!"

"Thanks, Mum. The Yanks have no chance, and I won't forget Tony. Bye, Mum. Give my love to Dad and Bob!"

"I will, dear. Give our love to Anne!"

It took a couple of lively exchanges with the Manpower bureaucrats, but Rosemary sorted them out to her satisfaction. One pompous clown, with a thinly veiled leer, queried why an attractive young country widow should leave her infant son with her parents and move to wartime Brisbane in search of a job. Rosemary blushed as the inference dawned on her, then immediately hit back with her customary lifelong defence, counter-attack.

"You miserable, smirking nitwit! Yes, of course, I could have stayed in the bush with my son, but my mother is taking good care of him! I came down here to be of some use, not to get out on the town! My husband was an infantry officer, killed in action. He felt a strong sense of duty to fight to protect his country, his wife and his child. He didn't sacrifice his life to let me be insulted by some impertinent, smutty-minded, glorified shiny-arsed excuse for a counter-jumper like you! I'd bet London to a brick that you're the sort of worm who has pulled every trick in the book to stay out of the Army, much less the Infantry! You look young enough, and you're obviously not crippled, so what's your excuse?"

Rosemary won that round hands down. The other incident occurred when a different twit had the gall to suggest that Rosemary must have had some pull to be favoured with an office job in a pastoral company when she hadn't worked in an office for six years. Again, she took a truculent line.

"So what? It is a pastoral concern, isn't it? I was born and raised on the land. Before I married. I worked in a stock and station agency, but I suppose you would rather put me in a boiler suit and send me to a shipyard to learn to rivet! Do you government incompetents go out of your way to be obstreperous, or is it a talent you're born with? I wish I did have some pull; I'd use it to have you sent to the Islands!" Her eyes blazed her contempt. If this little two-bob Hitler wanted a stoush she was more than ready to give him one! But the officious little fellow did not pursue the matter. This attractive young woman was not a genteel, defenceless widow of an Army Captain, a vulnerable lady to be bullied and taken down a peg; this one was a born scrapper!

33

Rosemary shared a portion of her cut lunch with the ever-present pigeons in the square. Idly, she observed a USAAF officer some twenty yards from where she sat. He stood casually relaxed, his right forearm leanings against the knee of his raised right leg, supported in turn by the rim of a large elevated ornamental goldfish pool. As though lost in some personal reverie, he was gazing absently into the water.

Tall, quite handsome in profile and around mid to late twenties in age, he wore his well-cut uniform, peaked cap and highly polished shoes almost deferentially, perhaps self-consciously. That air and the pristine newness of his tunic suggested that he was a very recently commissioned junior officer who was yet to become accustomed to the privileges of his new rank.

She looked away again, not wanting him to notice her curiosity or he might try to pick her up. It seemed most Yanks did try; apparently, they saw themselves as God's gift to women with their nice uniforms, loads of money and that soapy, un-manly way they liked to kiss and cuddle their women friends in public. Not that there was a scarcity of tarts eager to accommodate them, either! The Yanks acted as though they owned the country. Well paid in contrast to Australian troops and civilians, Yanks had a virtual monopoly of taxis, expensive liquor and other luxuries; it seemed that the city was over-run with bloody Yanks! Garrison troops, while the Australians were in the islands fighting to save the country, she reflected bitterly.

Even Joan, the girl who had steered Rosemary into her office job, had an American beau. Meanwhile, Joan's husband, a Ninth Divvy man, was in New Guinea.

Perhaps, Rosie conceded, she shouldn't judge Joan too harshly. A year

148

older than herself, Joan was married less than a year when her husband had enlisted in the A.I.F. in 1940. They had no children and the Ninth had been away for three years in the Middle East before returning home. A paltry three-week leave was followed by a brief, inadequate jungle training on the Atherton Tableland and a quick return to combat, this time in New Guinea. Three weeks of married life in almost four years! Rosie could understand Joan's infidelity even though she couldn't condone it. Yes, the burden was unfair but with their country under threat, those A.I.F. veterans had accepted their lot without rancour. After all, units of the Sixth and Seventh Divisions returned at the height of the crisis a year earlier to a mere one week of leave before being sent north. Equally, it at been unfair to all wives, families, mothers and girlfriends of the AI.F. With no close family of her own for support and comfort, Joan was apt to quip defensively that she "wasn't cut out to be a nun!"

No, Rosemary didn't condemn Joan out of hand, but neither did her understanding of the situation serve to moderate her opinion of Yanks generally. As for herself, she was sick and tired of fending off amorous Americans with their transparent ploys or "lines" and their arrogant presumptions that their fat bankrolls made them irresistible!

Her luncheon eaten, she pulled her white cotton gloves onto her hands again. She savoured the gentle breeze and the dry warmth of November sunshine. Pleasantly warm, the day lacked that humid stickiness of the summer months to come. That humidity was what she had always disliked about Brisbane's summer climate.

Although the Western Queensland sun had more bite to it, and the daytime temperatures were usually much higher than those of Brisbane, she had always found the inland climate far more pleasant. With its dryness, it lacked the oppressive steaminess of Brisbane from December through March. Fashionable dictates or not, she would not fancy wearing gloves in this city once summer began!

The pigeons had moved on in search of some other benevolent human. She leaned against the back of the park seat, stretching her arms behind her head in relaxation. Oh, no! That damned Yank was moving in her direction! For an instant, she contemplated rising and walking away to avoid him. No, she decided defiantly! Why should she?

For a junior officer, he wore an impressive number of campaign or medal ribbons! They seemed quite incongruous against the newness of his tailored uniform jacket.

"Hi! Mind if I share the bench?" he enquired amiably, controlling the nervousness he felt.

"Suit yourself. It's a free country, or so they tell me," Rosemary said frostily.

The American sat in awkward silence. He wondered if her hostility was directed at him or the world in general. Perhaps she was just having a bad day. He decided to try again. With a pleasant smile, he introduced himself.

"Lieutenant Clifford Clarke! I flew in on a B24 from Hawaii yesterday."

"My, my! A mere Lieutenant! With all that fruit salad. I thought you'd have been a Brigadier General at the very least!" Rosie observed in a brittle tone. Rubbing salt in, she asked in mock innocence. "Did you get all of those ribbons just for flying across the Pacific all by your little own self?'

He looked puzzled for a moment, then, comprehending her scepticism, he broke into a good-humoured grin. Reluctantly, she conceded to herself that he had a very nice, shy sort of smile.

"Heck, no! Anyhow, I am a flight engineer, not a pilot! I am a Regular; enlisted back in '37. When the Japs struck, I was in the Philippines, in B17s. After that came Sumatra. When we got out of there, I did a few ferry flights, then found myself based in North Queensland, flying on operations over New Guinea and the Islands. Well, I'd kept up with my studies, then after I'd gotten myself shot up for the second time, I guess somebody must have felt sorry for me, 'cause they decided to grant me a Commission." he explained modestly, almost apologetically.

Rosemary felt ashamed of herself; unsettled. This Yank was a total contrast to the archetypal image that her resentment and prejudice had shaped in her mind. Embittered by John's death and influenced by the constant sight of so many sleek, well-fed U.S. troops stationed in the safety of the Brisbane area, she was all too ready to write them off as Base Bludgers, the Australian Infantryman's term of contempt for all who wore uniform whilst pursuing a paper war in safe bases far from the dangers of combat.

"I'm sorry! It was rude and thoughtless of me to say what I said," she offered contritely.

He held his palms outward in gentle denial.

"Please! No apology is necessary! I should have respected your privacy. I guess I came on a little too strong," the Lieutenant said.

In her unease, her gloved hands felt hot and clammy, involuntarily, subconsciously, she removed her gloves and nervously toyed with her wedding ring.

The American misinterpreted the gesture and rose to his feet in embarrassment. He apologised, "I'm very sorry, Ma'am! Somehow, it never occurred to me that you might be married. I mean, you looked so young ---- aw heck, I do apologise!" He looked so earnest, so awkward in the discomfiture of knowing that the more he tried to explain, the deeper he seemed to compound the embarrassment.

Rosemary read the genuine concern in his earnest blue eyes and believed him. Here was one Yank, at least, who subscribed to the inviolability of marriage. She wanted to put him at ease.

Quickly, she reassured him, "Please, sit down! I did not intend to embarrass you. I removed my gloves and adjusted my ring because my hands were perspiring, for no other reason. It was a subconscious gesture. Actually, I am a widow, and not, perhaps, so young as you thought! I have a five-year-old son. In fact, today is his birthday. I phoned him this morning to wish him a happy birthday, and to make sure that his present had arrived. He is staying with my parents at the moment. My husband was killed at Buna almost a year ago," she babbled on. Now it was her turn to feel foolish. In case he should misinterpret her explanation, and assume that she was available because her child was living elsewhere, she added hastily, "I live with my sister-in-law."

"I sure am sorry about your husband," the Lieutenant said.

Rosemary nodded. "Goodness! Look at the time! I must get back to work!" she exclaimed.

"May I walk with you?" he asked.

"Yes, why not?" she agreed magnanimously.

As they walked, Clifford Clarke mentioned that he expected to be based in Brisbane, probably, for a few months. He wondered if he might meet her after work that evening. Coffee? Or a movie? Dinner afterward, perhaps?

She accepted, conditionally, "Alright, Clifford. Where shall I meet you? But I warn you, don't be too hopeful! I'm not yet ready for anything deeper than friendship."

"I'll settle for that," he agreed. "Please, call me Cliff. Hey, I don't even know your name!"

She laughed, "No, you don't, do you? Well, it's Rosie! Rosemary Roxton."

He savoured the name. It had a nice ring to it. "Rosemary Roxton! O.K., Rosie, I will meet you right here. What time do you finish work?"

"Five thirty," she said, "now I really must go!

She hurried inside and sat behind her desk, feeling quite surprised at herself. It must have shown.

"You look rather bemused, Rosie," Joan remarked.

"Yes, I think I am! Do you know, I've just been picked up, and by a Yank!" Rosemary replied.

Joan smiled. "He must be pretty darned good to have gotten under your guard!" she commented.

34

Before leaving work that evening, Rosemary phoned Anne to say that she would not be home until late.

"Actually, I'll be dining out, with a Yank," she added. For the first time since Michael's death, she heard Anne laugh heartily.

"Rosie! You of all people!"

"Yes, I know! I find it hard to believe, myself!" Rosemary giggled.

"Well, I think it's great because he must be very nice! Otherwise, you wouldn't be meeting him. Enjoy yourselves," Anne encouraged her.

Cliff was waiting outside. He took her for coffee, and then they filled in time at the Newsreel Theatrette. Afterward, he hailed a taxi driver and gave an address unfamiliar to Rosemary.

"I've never heard of that place," she remarked.

"I haven't been there myself," Cliff whispered, "but it comes highly recommended by a buddy of mine. I'm more familiar with Townsville, personally."

She was becoming a little alarmed. "I hope this place is on the level," she said, showing concern.

"Of course it is! Perfectly respectable, my buddy assures me!" he whispered.

"Then why all this whispering?" she asked.

"Because," he whispered, his eyes twinkling with good humour, "I don't want the driver to know that I'm a newcomer to Brisbane, or we might be taken the longest route to get there. These cab drivers sure like to soak us Americans for the very last buck!"

Rosemary laughed her relief. "Yes, I suppose they do!" she conceded.

The address turned out to be a rather swank little establishment. It appeared to be exclusively the preserve of U.S. Officers and their guests. There was no hint of rationing and austerity here! Rosemary hadn't been aware that such a place still existed in wartime Brisbane! Probably the result of some black-market deal with the U.S. Military, she thought. Whatever, it was very ritzy, and here she was, still in daywear; her office clothes!

The evening was a success, very pleasant. Quite a contrast to the shaky start of their first meeting in Anzac Square. That was something she'd prefer to forget, and for which, as she fully realised, her acrimony had been the sole cause!

A most attentive escort, Cliff was interested in everything about her. She found herself talking freely, as to an old friend, about her life, her husband, her son, and the reasons why she had elected to move, temporarily, to Brisbane to stay with Anne.

"I'm truly sorry about your brother," Cliff sympathised. "You and your sister-in-law sure have had a rough deal! Was your brother in bombers, too?"

"Fighter-bombers. Michael was a Beaufighter pilot," Rosemary's voice reflected the pride with which she would always remember him.

With his usual quiet sincerity, Cliff said, "I was privileged to see some of those guys in action. They were right down at deck level in the big Bismarck Sea scrap. Man, they were hell on wheels, if you'll pardon the expression!"

Rosemary smiled. "Thank you. I'll certainly pardon the expression since it's obviously intended to be complimentary," she said. "Michael flew in the Battle of The Bismarck Sea. Now, enough of my family! Tell me about yourself."

Again, that shy, self-effacing smile of his. "Not a lot to tell really. My family lives in Detroit, Michigan. I have three sisters, no brothers. My

Mom thinks the entire U.S. Army Air Force revolves around me, and my Dad is an autoworker. I guess he is kinda proud of me, too. We're a close family. Well, I joined the Army Air Corps straight out of high school. I guess that's about it."

"I'm sure that's not 'about it'! You're too modest! When you introduced yourself, you mentioned you were an engineer. What made you decide on an Air Force career?" Rosemary encouraged him.

He shrugged his shoulders, "Security, I guess. Like I said, Dad is an autoworker. I grew up with gasoline in my veins, but back during the Depression autoworkers had a pretty rough time. Dad was out of work for quite a while. Well, I liked fooling about with engines, and I thought airplanes had a great future, so I enlisted. The Air Corps gave me good training, and here I am."

"I see! But what about all that fruit salad you're wearing? I know I ribbed you about it today, but that was mean and spiteful of me, and I'm sorry! I really would like to hear how you earned it," Rosemary assured him.

Still, his manner was self-effacing. She had to quiz him for more than the barest details, but the more she drew him out, the more obvious it became that this young American airman had seen many of his buddies killed, and was twice wounded himself, yet appeared to have few qualms about the prospect of a further tour of combat duty. The unassuming Lieutenant Clifford Clarke was the type of man whom both John and Michael would have liked and respected.

A Quartet played swing music, and there was a small dance floor. Cliff invited her to dance with him, but she declined, "I would, but I've neither showered nor had a change of clothes since this morning. I'm sweaty, and I smell like a horse!'

"I hadn't noticed," he assured her gallantly.

"Perhaps not, but I am most certainly aware of it!" she smilingly insisted." Let's just sit, talk, and enjoy the meal and each other's company."

"Fine by me, but you sure are the most direct, uncomplicated lady I have ever met!" he laughed.

The hour was very late when they finally alighted from the taxi at Red Hill.

"You'd better hold the cab." she told him, "Anne will be asleep, so I shan't invite you in. Thank you for a lovely evening, I enjoyed it immensely!"

"Me, too! May I see you again?" he asked.

"I'd like that, she said.

"Since I only arrived yesterday, I'm not too sure of the duty roster. How about I phone you tomorrow?" he asked, taking a propelling pencil and small notebook from his top pocket. She told him both her work number and Anne's home number. He wrote them down by the reflected light from the taxi's lamps.

"Well, goodnight," he paused uncertainly, obviously desiring to kiss her. Rosemary resisted a very strong urge to comply, deciding instead to observe the propriety of first-night conventions. So much for her being a direct, uncomplicated lady, she thought wryly.

"Goodnight, Cliff, and thanks again." She squeezed his hand then adroitly turned away and slipped through the front gateway.

35

Seven days later, Rosemary and Cliff had been out together on three occasions. Despite her warning from the outset that she was not ready for anything more serious than a friendly relationship. It was clear to her that Cliff's feelings towards her were already deeper than that.

Even more disconcertingly, she had begun to feel increasing emotional involvement herself. John was her first and only serious boyfriend. She had loved him with all her heart and soul, had married and borne him a son whom they'd idolised. Now, with John dead for less than a year, although she had last seen him almost two years ago, she was keeping company with another man. She felt guilty, that she was betraying John and his memory. Nonsense! She reasoned with her conscience; after all, there was nothing improper in her friendship with Cliff. He was a congenial friend, merely a lonely soldier who was passing through and would be gone in a few months at most. Well, yes, she had allowed him to kiss her once or twice, and yes, she had found it pleasant, but she had kept it as platonic as possible.

Now she was aware that Cliff was asking her a question.

"I'm sorry, Cliff. What was that? I was miles away," she said.

"So I noticed!" he laughed, "I asked if we could maybe manage a picnic someplace on Sunday?"

"Oh, Cliff. I don't know! I mean, I came to Brisbane to keep Anne company, yet over the past week I've been out with you on two nights and last Sunday," she seized on the convenient excuse, "I feel as though I'm letting her down!"

"Why not ask her along?" Cliff countered gallantly, "I don't mind sharing myself with two beautiful women. In fact, I'd be honoured!"

Anne had thoroughly approved of the American when Rosie had introduced them the previous weekend. However, she tried to pass up the invitation for the picnic, "I couldn't, Rosie! You go, though! I'd feel a real wet blanket, cramping your style."

"Far from it!" Rosemary dismissed the protest almost pleadingly, "Look, call it moral support! I'll be much happier if you come, too! Besides, the outing will be good for you."

"Are you really and truly certain that you want me along?" Anne asked.

"Cross my heart! I need a chaperone. He's a nice bloke, but I don't want things to get too serious. The fact is, I think I like him far too much already!"

"You could do a lot worse," Anne said, "but, alright, I'll come along. I'll be glad to come."

They packed a hamper and a travelling rug. Cliff contributed some wine, sliced ham and a box of American "candy" as he called it. All were luxuries in wartime Brisbane. As usual, he was his good-humoured, gentlemanly self; Anne felt very welcome. If he were disappointed at not having had Rosemary's company exclusively to himself, he certainly hid the fact very well. Back at the house that evening, Anne invited him to "stay for tea."

"That's Australian for what you Yanks call a dinner invitation," Rosemary chipped in with an eager translation.

"Yes. I know. I was stationed at Townsville, remember! Thank you, Anne. I accept!"

The meal was simple fare, but tasty. Cliff was appreciative. "Thank you, ladies. That was great! Sure can't beat home cooking!"

"Glad you liked it, Cliff. Now, tea or cocoa? I'm sorry we don't have any coffee, but it's scarce as a hen's teeth in this country at present," Anne said.

"Is that so? Tea will be fine, thanks, Anne," He sounded genuinely surprised that coffee should be in such short supply. The next time he called for Rosie, on Tuesday evening, he brought with him the gift of a large tin of coffee.

The weeks passed quickly for Rosemary. She enjoyed Cliff's attentions, though she frequently felt that she was having far too many nights on the town for a working girl.

She and Anne had booked to travel by train to Wilga Creek for the Christmas-New Year break. The days at Mt. Chillingham passed all too quickly. She treasured her time with Tony, her parent's and Bob. To her surprise, she found herself wondering what Tony would think of Cliff. It suddenly dawned on her that she was evaluating the possibility of Cliff becoming the boy's stepfather. It had taken this journey home and her separation from Cliff for her to become aware of the depth of her feelings towards him. Before they arrived, she had extracted a promise from Anne that she would make no mention of her relationship with the American.

Not until the fourth evening of her visit did her mother ask if she planned to remain much longer in Brisbane.

"Do you feel I've been away too long, Mum? Is Tony fretting?" Rosemary was concerned.

"No. Dear. Tony is fine. I just wondered, that's all," Diana said.

"I thought I might stay until Easter," Rosie said. "I think I owe them a couple more months at work, but I do miss my little boy!"

"That seems fair enough," Diana agreed, then, intuitively she asked, "Any other attractions in the Big Smoke to keep you there?"

"Not really, Mum. Well, one, perhaps. But I don't expect that the U.S. Army Air Force will keep him there much longer. He is a very nice chap and I've grown quite fond of him. Anne says she thoroughly approves of him," she said defensively.

"Well, in that case, I'm happy for you. You have had precious little enjoyment these past few years but from what I've heard of these Yanks, I trust you're taking the necessary precautions," Diana observed with her usual directness.

Rosemary was shocked, "Mum! It's not like that at all! I'm not sleeping with him!"

"Well, that's a relief," Diana said drily.

36

The night, in early March, was warm, but not unbearably so. Joe had something on his mind. He lay on his back, eyes staring absently at the darkened ceiling above. Beside him Diana stirred, her subconscious wakening her by a realisation of his communicated tension. Sleepily, she asked, "Can't you sleep, Darling? What's the problem?"

"Nothing, Love. Go back to sleep. I guess I'm just not very tired."

"You seemed preoccupied all evening. Anyway, I'm awake now, so spit it out! What's eating at you?"

"Billy will be eighteen soon, and lately he has been going on about volunteering for the Army," Joe confided. "I'm worried he might be accepted."

"That reminds me! I was talking to Julie MacGavin in town today," Diana began, and ..."

"Just how does your hob-nobbing with the silver tails have any bearing on Billy joining the Army?" Joe interrupted with unusual testiness.

"If you'll allow me to finish," Diana told him, "her husband has been given his discharge. Anyway, you shouldn't be so uncharitable about Julie! She's really very nice. As I started to say, Major MacGavin and quite a few other fellows are being released because it is considered that they can contribute more through their civilian skills, whether they are farmers or graziers, or skilled tradesmen. "

"Well," Joe conceded, "Alan MacGavin certainly has done his fair share for the Army. He first went overseas in 1940 and I heard he was wounded on more than one occasion."

"Yes, but that's not all the news! According to Julie, he says MacArthur's strategy is to leapfrog north through the islands and hog all the glory for the Yanks. There are plenty of Japs cut off from supplies and living at subsistence level in New Guinea, Bougainville and other places, but MacArthur reckons we should leave them to their own devices then round them all up after the war is over. If our lads go in after them before the Emperor tells them to surrender, they'll fight to the death. MacArthur would be happy for Australia to just become a huge supply base in support of American troops."

"I'll bet Alan is pretty crooked on MacArthur hogging all the glory now that the Japs have been turned around," Joe said.

"Oh, he holds no brief for MacArthur, but he told Julie he agrees on one point! He thinks we should keep an eye on the Japs, but just let them tend their vegetable gardens until the war is over, wherever they have been cut off from supplies and reinforcements. He says that to send in our troops to root them out will only be a sheer waste of Australian lives," Diana said, "He is more annoyed with Blamey and the Australian Government for continuing the Islands Offensive and unnecessarily sacrificing more of our soldiers."

Joe thought about all that Diana had said.

"At that rate," he concluded, "Billy should be in an exempted category, too, if he tries to volunteer, but I wouldn't count on it!"

"But why? Surely they wouldn't take him!" Diana exclaimed.

"Because he's an Aboriginal!" Joe said bitterly, "The Government may not consider his occupation at all. You know what the bloody public service attitude is like! They'd have taken him from his mother and raised him in a mission if they'd had their way. They don't concern themselves with bothering to count Aboriginals in the Census, but they'll accept them as cannon fodder readily enough. One of his mother's brothers was killed at Tobruk and another is still fighting in the Islands, remember?"

"Yes. I know, Darling, but you shouldn't get yourself so worked up about it all," Diana squeezed his hand sympathetically.

"Darn it, Love. I can't help getting worked up! I care about that kid almost as much as if he was one of my own'"

162

"You couldn't wait to join the First A.I.F. when you were that age yourself," Diana gently reminded him.

"Yes, that's true," Joe agreed, "but we've lost John and Michael to this war already!"

37

Rosemary was in no doubt that she had fallen head over heels in love with Cliff, and he with her.

Neither had yet given spoken affirmation to the fact; for her part because she already feared losing him to battle casualty on his return to combat, just as she had lost John.

Cliff was mindful of her apparent reluctance to accept a deeper commitment. He was mindful, also, as she had often reminded him, of the strict "friendship only" ground rules which she had laid down conditional to the beginning of their relationship. He longed to declare his love for her but feared that to do so might force the issue to a point where she would panic and break off the budding romance. She had turned out to be a very complex girl, after all; on the one hand, blunt and outspoken, yet on the other, so intensely guarded and protective of her deepest emotions!

That often flippant, sometimes angry refusal of Australians to admit to the intensity of their own emotions was, Cliff had observed, almost a national characteristic. Perhaps it had something to do with the inherent reserve of British ancestors, but whatever, Cliff was convinced, that the sometimes laconic, sometimes aggressive Aussie was a darned sight more of an enigma than the stiff-upper-lip Englishman!

Yes, Rosemary was certainly passionate enough when they kissed and cuddled in private. Sometimes, the petting got very heavy but never would she allow it to go all the way. At times, she would terminate it quite angrily, saying as she was saying now, "I don't know why all the responsibility for saying 'No' has to rest with the woman! Why can't you exercise some self-control, too, damn you? After all, I'm the one who could end up with a tummy full of arms and legs if I let you have your way!"

Her eyes blazed with the anger of an outraged virginal goddess. Cliff thought she looked beautiful, even magnificent in her fury. He knew that he could delay his move no longer: the news he'd received that morning dictated that. This might not be quite the appropriate moment, but he had to say it.

"Damn it. Rosie! Listen to me! I love you and I want to marry you!"

The colour drained from her face in shocked surprise, yet she did not look displeased. Eventually, she laughed a little unsteadily.

"I'm sorry, Cliff, but was that a proposal or a proposition that I just heard?" she tried to regain her composure.

"It was a proposal, darn it!" he told her heatedly. He felt embarrassed, hurt and angered, thinking that she was refusing to take him seriously. Worse still, the fear of rejection gnawed at the pit of his stomach!

What he saw next in her eyes quickly banished all apprehension.

"I didn't mean to laugh, Darling. Yes! Of course, I will marry you. Just as soon as this war is over," Rosemary promised. She kissed him tenderly as she nestled back into his embrace.

"I was kinda hoping it might be a little sooner, like for instance, next week," Cliff ventured. It was time he told her the news. "I've been posted again, leaving for Stateside next week. Sure hoped I could rush it through; you know, pull a few strings and get us married before I leave? Uncle Sam has a brand new bomber becoming operational. It's top-secret, but I heard rumours of it before I last left the States. Bigger, faster, flies higher than any other bomber ever built! Well, the first of them are due to fly combat missions any day now, with a lot more in production. I have been assigned for training in Kansas to join one of the new Very Heavy Bomber Groups. After that, we probably will be flying out of southwest China or the North Pacific islands, depending on how quickly the Navy and Marines can take them off the Japs. Hopefully, we will then be bombing the Japanese homeland to shorten the war. I don't know how long it will be until I get back here to you. but I'd sure like for us to be married before I fly out next week."

"Oh, Cliff, my poor darling! I'll wait for you no matter how long it takes, you can be sure of that! And I'll follow you anywhere once the war is over! You've been very patient and understanding with me, and I love you for it. But please, Darling, let's wait until the war is ended. Already, I have one fatherless child to raise as a legacy of war. I don't think I could cope with yet another one if anything should happen to you on active service, nor could I accept being widowed twice in such a short time! Those are the reasons I've been such a straight-laced bitch with you right from the start. Don't you know I've ached to have you inside me time after time? Do you think I'm made of stone? Please, Darling, be patient! We must both be patient! Let's wait until the war is over before we marry. It will be just as hard for me as for you, I promise. Do you understand, or do you think I'm being a silly, irrational woman? I can't help the way I feel," she pleaded.

"I do understand," Cliff chivalrously consoled her. "I don't think you're being silly or irrational. Naturally. I admit to disappointment, but I do see your point of view."

"Thank you, Darling. Your gallantry is exceeded only by your good looks!" Rosemary once more concealed her relief with flippancy. Playfully, she nibbled the lobe of his ear.

"You sure as hell make it hard for a guy!" Cliff sighed.

38

Cliff returned to the U.S.A. A couple of weeks later at Easter, Rosemary kept her promise to Tony by returning home to Mt Chillingham. Giving up her office job didn't bother her, but she was concerned about leaving Anne on her own.

"Don't be such a worry-wart, Rosie. I'll manage quite all right on my own now. It's been almost eight months since Michael died. I'll never forget him, but I'm quite resigned to the fact that he has gone. It was kind and generous of you to offer your comfort for so long, but you have your own life and little Tony to consider. I appreciate your love and friendship and I always will, but I really will be all right on my own now. I'm no frail little flower that everyone seems to imagine I am, you know" Anne chided her mildly.

It was true; Anne had come to terms with her grief. She had even resumed some of her social activities, including tennis and voluntary Red Cross work.

Yes, Anne would cope well.

"I know you're not," Rosie smiled, "but do remember that you'll always be welcome out home, so don't sit around on your own feeling lost and lonely over the August or Christmas school holidays. Mum and I would always love to see you!"

Diana, Tony and Bob met Rosemary at Wilga Creek railway station. Diana was quick to notice the new engagement ring that her daughter was sporting.

"Well, that's a surprise! You didn't mention becoming engaged! You only said that your Yank had gone back to America. I presume that he is the one. Your fiancé?" Diana sounded less than enthusiastic.

"Of course he is, Mum! I asked Anne not to mention it, either, because I wanted to surprise you myself," Rosemary said.

"You've certainly done that, my girl!" Diana told her, tight-lipped. "I suppose you've given some thought to your son in the matter?"

"Yes, I have, Mum! I have had Tony's future in my mind ever since I began to think seriously about Cliff. He's a wonderful man; I love him very much! He is kind, considerate and he likes children. I'm positive that he'll be a good stepfather to Tony. If I wasn't sure, I wouldn't have said 'yes' when he proposed!" Rosemary countered huffily.

"No, I don't imagine you would have." Diana's tone was more conciliatory. "It's a pity you couldn't have brought him out here to meet us, especially Tony, all the same!"

"Oh, Mum! There wasn't time! There is a war on, you know," Rosemary said defensively.

Diana relented. She gave her daughter a motherly peck on the cheek. "Yes, I know. I'm sorry. Love! Let's not argue."

Rosemary gave her son another hug. She wiped a tear from below her eye.

"Why are you crying, Mummy? Are you sad?" the little boy asked.

"No, Darling. I'm not sad. I'm just so happy to be back with you again!"

Tony looked bewildered. Crying for happiness was beyond his childish comprehension. Bob merely looked disgusted. Rosemary drew comfort from the secure environment of Mt. Chillingham. She sorely missed Cliff, but with her son and her family together around her, in the familiarity of her childhood home, she felt at ease just as she'd drawn solace from returning home after John had gone north with his battalion. Goodness! That seemed a lifetime ago, she reflected, when she had made her previous retreat to the scents of the bush and a kerosene refrigerator and carbide lanterns.

Anne visited in August and stayed for five days. She was bright and cheerful, but to a confirmed townie like Anne, a visit of longer duration would have resulted in sheer boredom with the quietness of the bush.

The year drew to a close with savage fighting as Australian and Dutch troops continued their costly offensive against the beleaguered Japanese in the islands of our near north. Much further north, Royal Australian Navy warships were components of the U.S. Fleet during the Marine and Army landings closer to Japan.

B29 Superfortresses from newly constructed airfields on the recently captured Marianas Islands of Guam. Saipan and Tinian were bombing the Japanese mainland cities. Cliff was flying regular missions over Tokyo and other targets.

While the war in Europe drew swiftly to its inevitable conclusion, early 1945 saw Japanese fanaticism increasing in intense desperation. Germany fell, but the Japanese fought on to the death. U.S. troops met fanatical opposition before capturing Iwo Jima and Okinawa, while Australian and Dutch troops with Australian Naval and Air support landed at Balikpapan and Tarakan to bloodily wrest the rich Borneo oilfields from the enemy. Nearer to Okinawa the suicide pilots of the Kamikaze, the legendary Japanese Divine Wind flew their aircraft loaded with high explosives directly into Allied warships, sink1ng or crippling many. The cruiser, HMAS Australia survived no less than five hits to her hull or superstructure by Kamikaze planes.

American Mustang and Hellcat fighters reigned supreme over their rapidly diminishing Japanese opposition, whilst B29 night and day incendiary bombing raids continued an unprecedented obliteration of Japanese cities. Even so, it was estimated that any invasion of Japan would cost two million allied and countless Japanese lives unless the Japanese Government was made to surrender beforehand. Therefore, at 09.15 hours on the 6th August 1945. Colonel Paul W. Tibbets' B29, Enola Gay, dropped an atomic bomb from a height of 31,600 feet above Hiroshima. A stunned Japanese Government was tardy in surrendering, so three days later, another B29 piloted by Major Charles W. Sweeney dropped a second nuclear bomb over the city of Nagasaki. Still, the Japanese delayed another five days before finally surrendering on the 14th of August, at which time more than eight hundred B29s were airborne on conventional bombing missions over Japan. Captain Clifford Clarke was in one of these aircraft when the surrender was announced. So, it was that the most destructive chapter in human history was finally concluded.

39

By the commencement of 1946, a general demobilisation of the Armed Forces was well advanced in Australia, as it was in Britain and the U.S.A. The economy was facing massive re-adjustment, jobs were in short supply, materials were scarce and so was housing. Many utilitarian uses were found for war surplus items such as military Jeeps, Quonset huts, Blitz wagons and other things, which had never been designed with any civilian usage in mind.

Thousands of expensive warplanes were dumped at sea or in old quarries or were in storage awaiting sale to be recycled for scrap metal at prices that were ridiculously low fractions of their manufactured costs. Transport-type aeroplanes were more marketable for conversion to the civil register, as were some light and medium bombers. Such was the accommodation shortage that a few enterprising and imaginative souls among the more desperate home seekers were known to purchase the hulls and fuselages of flying boats and large bombers for a pittance. They then converted these to living quarters, caravan style, for their temporary use.

With the shortage of and demand for building materials, there was no doubt it would become a boom time for suppliers, even in remote rural communities.

At 79 years of age, Tom Merriton knew it was time to retire and make way for a younger, more enthusiastic businessman. Gratefully, he accepted a fair, even generous offer for his half-share in the old sawmill, and sold out to a son of his partner. Once the long drought broke, the young fellow would be well rewarded for his foresight.

Tom Merriton had earned his retirement after a lifetime of uncomplaining toil, but like so many other active, hard-working men before him, he did not have long to enjoy his earthly reward.

Four months later, he suffered a mild stroke. Two months after that, he died peacefully in his sleep.

While most Australian and American servicemen welcomed being de-mobbed with heartfelt joy, there were others, particularly amongst war-time emergency Naval and Air Force Officers and N.C.O's who sought permanent careers in the peacetime defence forces. Mostly, they were to be disappointed, but for Cliff Clarke, a regular airman since 1937, the choice did not arise.

Based in Okinawa as a member of the U.S. Occupation Forces, Cap-tain Clarke's biggest problem lay in arranging his return to Australia to marry his sweetheart. Eventually, in August 1946, with one month of accumulated leave, he hitch-hiked his way by USAAF C54 and RAAF C47 Transport planes, to Amberley RAAF Base, Ipswich, near Brisbane.

Rosemary had travelled to Brisbane to meet him and to arrange wed-ding details. It was almost two and a half years since she had seen him last. Although their correspondence was intense, Rosie was nervous be-fore their reunion. What if he had changed? What if she had changed? Could it be possible that the anticipation, the long wait, might end in anti-climax, in disappointment for them both?

The moment she saw him, she knew any fears were groundless. Hun-grily, she clung to him, kissing with such wanton abandon that he was momentarily taken aback before responding in kind. When eventually, they paused to catch their breath, Rosemary spoke.

"Now, Cliff, I have some good news and some bad news! First, the bad news! The wedding is not until Saturday, another five days!" she teased him.

"Five days!" he yelled, "Five days? Baby, you mean that after that, you'd make me wait another five days?"

"Shhh! Keep your voice down!" she pleaded, "I said the wedding is not for another five days! The good news is that I've booked a room for Captain and Mrs. Clarke. The honeymoon can start this afternoon!" she smiled temptingly.

"Yippee!" Cliff threw his cap in the air. He lifted her off her feet and spun around, holding her high. "You living, breathing doll, Rosie!"

The Brisbane City Hall clock struck seven. Rosie smiled to herself in the darkened hotel room, lit only by reflected light filtering up from the street below through the window to bounce softly off the ceiling. She sprawled shamelessly on her back; legs slightly parted, hands clasped behind her head as she stretched her body in contentment. Beside her, face downward, one arm flung haphazardly across her torso, Cliff slumbered in exhaustion.

Poor darling, she thought, two days of continuous aeroplane travel followed by four hours of her sexual demands. No wonder he was sleeping; he must have thought her insatiable! With idle detachment, she wondered if her four and a half years of celibacy had been too much. Perhaps she was now in danger of becoming a nymphomaniac. She giggled. Well, if she was, she would only be Cliff's personal nymphomaniac and nobody else's, of that she was sure.

Her tummy growled a protest: all that activity had given her quite an appetite! Should she wake Cliff so that they could go to dinner, or should she let him sleep? She'd let him sleep a while longer, she decided.

Afterward, they could find a late-night cafe. The evening air was turning rather cool. Not surprisingly, they were both naked as jaybirds. She managed to pull the covers up over them without waking Cliff. Tomorrow, they'd keep the appointment with the U.S. Consul, then perhaps, they'd pay Anne a visit.

Anne had remarried a few months earlier, in May. By all accounts, she was blissfully happy in her new role of housewife and stepmother. She had met Ken, her husband, through his sister, a teaching colleague.

That was in the previous October. Ken, at that time an Army Major awaiting demobilisation, was a widower, keen to return to his legal practice and his two children; a boy of ten and a girl of eight. For most of the war, since mid-1942 when his wife was killed in a road accident, his mother had been the children's guardian. If Anne's friend had intentionally assumed the role of Cupid, she had chosen well. In his late thirties, the lawyer was a considerate, caring family man whilst Anne would be suited eminently to the roles of wife and mother, the latter of which had so tragically eluded her in her previous marriages. Ken's son and daughter had accepted Anne readily, which was not surprising given Anne's nature and her affinity with children.

Many people. Rosemary included had sometimes wondered how the soft-natured Anne could have been an effective schoolteacher; she gave little hint of possessing the necessary stiffness of character to cope, yet cope she always did, and very ably too, by all accounts! Anne's hidden determination was masked by a pleasant exterior and adept psychological skills. She persuaded and encouraged children to give their best and mostly they co-operated willingly. The few recalcitrants were quickly pulled into line with iron-hard authority.

Anne's motto could well have been Theodore Roosevelt's classic advice to talk softly but carry a big stick!" Popular and respected, a real professional, she was one of a breed who was all too scarce in her day. Now retired, she would make an excellent stepmother.

Rosemary prayed that Cliff would pass muster with Tony as readily as Anne had with her stepchildren. She felt confident that he would. Her parents would be driving to Brisbane with

Tony and Bob on Thursday morning for Exhibition Week, the time of the big annual Brisbane Royal National agricultural Show. They would attend her wedding on the Saturday in the same little suburban church where Anne and Ken had married. Anne would be Matron of Honour and Ken was co-opted to be Best Man. Thursday would be the first time that any of Rosemary's immediate' family met Cliff. Her father would have a pink fit if he saw her now, she giggled mischievously; but then, fathers were prone to think of their daughters as paragons of virtue.

Cliff stirred. Sleepily, he observed, "I must have dozed off, Honey! Sorry about that."

Laughingly, she told him, "You've been asleep for over an hour! I'll bet you never dreamed your little Aussie tease could be so insatiable!"

"No," he confessed, "but I sure have lived in hope all of these years! I don't think I could ever get too much of you!"

He took her in his arms again. Playfully, she wriggled beneath him, pretending she wanted to get out of his grasp. It excited him more.

"Let's have dinner first," she feigned a protest, "got to keep your strength up!"

"Later, Rosie. Later!" he insisted.

It was after eight-thirty before they finally ventured downstairs to seek out a cafe or a restaurant.

40

Mount Chillingham Station, like most of Queensland, was in its third year of drought. Tantalisingly, clouds would gather then blow away without any fulfilment of their promise. Dust storms were frequent but rainstorms remained little more than a memory. Were it not for Nature's blessings of a couple of good permanent waterholes in the range foothills and an abundance of Wilga, Selah and Bottle trees, the big run would have been long since destocked and the remaining workforce of Joe, Doug and Billy paid off.

However, as things were, a small nucleus of breeders had to be kept alive. When finally the drought did break, such cows would be in heavy demand and their replacement values would skyrocket, so the pastoral company who owned the property had taken another financial gamble. They had decided that the crippling burden of retaining good men for maintenance and for cutting branches for fodder was preferable to destocking and closing up the place completely. To restock, rehire reliable men and rebuild and replace valuable buildings and improvements left without caretakers, could well prove even more expensive in the longer run.

It was a prudent decision, yet one that only large, well-structured pastoral interests could afford. Joe and Diana were keenly aware and appreciative of the situation. Had they been on their own selection and carrying a mortgage, they probably would have gone under in the current circumstances. Such is often the lot of the battler.

Paradoxically, it was the fact that both Doug and Billy were also retained that now allowed the Merritons the luxury of a ten-day vacation at Brisbane for the Show, and to attend their daughter's wedding. It was to be the first time in more than three years that Joe had spent more than a day and a night away from the station. Doug and Billy had continued to enjoy more normal annual and recreational leave. They were capable and willing to carry on alone with station duties for the period. Both were totally trustworthy. Joe looked forward to the brief holiday.

The family stayed at a hotel in St. Paul's Terrace within easy walking distance of the Showground. Brisbane was abuzz with festive activities. Although still a time of drought and relative austerity, the rural economy held the promise of future expansion.

Queenslanders from near and far flocked again to the State capital for Exhibition Week, or as the more facetious of Brisbaneites were apt to label it, "Bush Week." For country folk and their city cousins alike, the big Show or "Ekka" and its spinoff functions, Balls, Dinners, Annual General Meetings, etcetera, had long provided the highlights of the peacetime social calendar.

Rosemary brought Cliff to meet her family for the first time on the afternoon of their arrival in Brisbane. Later, to allow Joe and Diana an evening out together, the younger couple treated Tony and Bob to an early evening picture show followed by dinner at eight, then a leisurely stroll around the city centre, window shopping. The two station-reared lads considered everything new, interesting and exciting. The tram ride, the Disney feature film and supporting cartoons, the posh Dining Room at the hotel where Rosemary and Cliff were staying, and the Neon lights and shop-front displays of the department stores were all objects of adventure and pleasure to the unsophisticated youngsters.

Cliff shared their enjoyment unreservedly. His own enthusiastic laughter at the antics of the cartoon characters on the screen were as natural and as unforced as that of Tony and Robert. Furthermore, a genuine rapport between her fiancé, her son and her brother was established. Rosemary's prayers were answered.

Two tired but happy youngsters went to sleep that night, looking forward to a big day at the "Ekka" on the morrow. Rosemary and Cliff chatted a while with her parents before leaving for their hotel.

The following day's activities at the Showground provided more excitement for the boys. Bob was five years old on his only prior visit to the

Brisbane R.N.A. Exhibition. For Tony, this was his first such experience.

Joe and Diana relaxed over afternoon tea and sandwiches at a C.W.A. run refreshment kiosk and hall on the grounds. Rosie and Cliff had taken the lads across to Sideshow Alley. Ferris wheel, Chair-o-plane, Bumper car rides and the mysteries within the Sideshow tents were dubious attractions that the older Merritons were happy to forego.

"I'm glad she found herself such a nice bloke. He's so good-natured, with a real zest for life!" Diana said, "Those kids think he's the bee's knees! Rosemary always told us he'd make a good stepfather for Tony."

"Yes," Joe conceded, "but I wish they didn't have to move to America. We'll miss Rosie and Tony!"

"I don't imagine that will be for a while yet," Diana said, "Not while he's stationed on Okinawa!

It's a shame he and Rosemary will have to remain apart until he gets another transfer. They've waited long enough already."

"I've got a feeling that they're doing their best to make up for it," Joe remarked wryly. He didn't approve of his daughter shacking up in a hotel room with Cliff before they were married.

Diana knew what he meant.

"Joe, don't be such an old stick-in-the-mud, for goodness sake! They're good as married already!"

The Saturday wedding was a small, unsophisticated one; a simple church ceremony followed by a cosy reception at a riverside catering venue afterward. The entire guest list was comprised of Anne, Ken, his two children, Joe, Diana and the boys; ten in all including the bride and groom.

Distance and short notice dictated by his USAAF commitments had meant that none of his family or service buddies were able to attend. Therefore, he was privately thankful that only Rosemary's closest friend and immediate family were present. Though friendly, articulate and seemingly outgoing, Cliff was, as Rosemary knew well, essentially a shy, reserved man.

With none of his own family or friends in support, she had known that the alternative prospect of scrutiny by her entire family and friends at a larger wedding breakfast at Wilga Creek would have been an ordeal he'd have found more frightening than a fighter attack at 35,000 feet.

As it was, this small reception among the friends and relatives who'd had the opportunity to get to know him over the past couple of days, made for a much happier, more relaxed occasion all around.

On Sunday, the newlyweds left by train for a one-week honeymoon at Coolangatta. Whilst making the wedding arrangements two weeks earlier, Rosie was very fortunate at such short notice for a school vacation period, to book accommodation against a cancellation in a guesthouse on Marine Parade.

The Merritons and Tony remained on holiday in Brisbane. For the adults, it was a time to catch up on shopping, socialising, new rural technology and long-postponed business appointments; for the juveniles, it was a time to enjoy further delights of show sample bags, amusement stalls, hair raising carnival rides, more fairy floss and hot dog stands, as well as movie matinees.

Tanned and relaxed, Cliff and Rosie returned to Brisbane the next Saturday. All six travelled home to Mt. Chillingham in the big car.

A city boy born and bred, Cliff enjoyed the novelty of the Australian bush, station life and the unhurried, even sleepy, atmosphere of Wilga Creek township. To his uninitiated eyes, the drought-stricken landscape resembled the American Old West come to life again. Ten days later, he had to leave his new bride and stepson, to fly out of Amberley Air Force Base on the first leg of his journey back to Okinawa. Early in the New Year, there would be another posting, Stateside to a proper married life, a normal family life at long last!

41

Rosemary had chosen to remain in Australia until she and Tony would be able to join him at some base on U.S. soil. As with those Australian war brides who had sailed to America earlier in the liner. "Mariposa", U.S. bureaucracy again had demanded as part of their Immigration procedure, a series of answers to demeaning, insulting questions such as, "Are you a prostitute, or have you ever been engaged in prostitution?"

"Certainly not, but if I was, I'm damned sure I wouldn't tell you, anyway! I suppose the next thing you'll want to know is whether or not I'm still a bloody virgin!" Rosemary had roundly berated the hapless Consulate staffer.

"Only doing my job, lady! I don't formulate the questions," the poor fellow had answered in a tone of resignation that implied that this was far from the first time he had heard that answer from a spirited Aussie girl.

"I should hope not! Many more questions of that ilk, and I'll tell you what you can do with your bloody country!" Rosemary was riled. That legendary Australian chip on the shoulder was alive and well.

The man sighed in exasperation. He put his pen down on the desk and patiently explained. "Ma'am, I daresay your own Australian Immigration Department procedures would require answers to a similar range of questions which might offend. It is the lawful expectation of every Sovereign State that it has the right to veto any application that might not measure up on grounds of moral character, criminal record or National security. In your case, as the wife of a serving United States Officer, these Questions have even more relevance. Please do not take them so personally. It is not our intention to maliciously exclude you from the U.S.A. I am sure you have nothing to be concerned about. Now, can we get on with it?"

Cliff's new appointment as of January 1947, was to Hickham Air Force Base, Oahu, Hawaiian Islands. Rosemary and Tony flew from Sydney to join him at their new home. Hickham Field was a major base by U.S. standards. Compared with Australian Air Force traffic, the number of aircraft movements was very large. Oahu and its capital, Honolulu, primarily owed their prosperity to being the locations of several Army, Navy and Marine Corps barracks, installations and airfields, which in turn existed largely to support the giant Naval facility of Pearl Harbour.

An island of great natural beauty, the compact 608 square miles of Oahu boasted high volcanic peaks, fertile plateaus and coastal plains, lush tropical vegetation, crops and market gardens, surfing beaches and majestic headlands. The populace was a mixture of polyglot origins; native Polynesians, white Americans, Chinese and Japanese who again coexisted in remarkable harmony and tolerance, although local Japanese, who had considered themselves loyal Americans, understandably had experienced a rough deal between the time of the Pearl Harbour raid and the end of the war.

Island architecture varied from simple rustic shacks or seamy Honolulu hotels and whorehouses, through comfortable middle-class residences to imposing mansions and hotels.

Climatically, Oahu was near perfect, a gentle oscillation between pleasantly cool to pleasantly warm, with no extremes. Structurally, the Clarkes' rented weatherboard home was comparable to a contemporary Brisbane house with a front verandah. Here the comparison ended. Few Australlan houses could boast such a range of modern electrical appliances, from a huge refrigerator and freezer to a dishwashing machine.

Tony found the change from correspondence school supervised by his mother and grandmother, to a regular classroom situation, to be a little difficult, even traumatic at first. However, his classmates were friendly. Most were impressed by his background, which they saw as a kind of Australian Frontier cum Wild West environment.

Rosemary found her new lifestyle very acceptable. There was a new freedom of mobility with her own Chevrolet convertible, abundant social life and new friendships with several other young Officers' wives who were American girls around her own age.

"Happy, Darling?" Cliff was asking her. They were together on Oahu for four months. Tony was adjusting well to his new life. She felt so much at home now that even the crazy Yank rule of driving on the wrong side of the road, in cars with the steering wheel on the left instead of the right, now seemed only vaguely disconcerting. Her husband had arrived home from his desk job at Hickham to find her staring pensively through a side windowpane at Tony, playing 'Cops and Robbers' with the kids next door. Cliff had interpreted her pre-occupied gaze and the lack of her usual welcome as either homesickness or potential trouble.

"Oh, hello Darling! I didn't hear you come in," She kissed him long and lovingly, then continued, "I'm not just happy, I'm delirious! I'm pregnant! Just found out this afternoon!"

42

The drought had broken and new growth was flourishing. All of the work and expense of cutting branches and of hand-feeding was worthwhile. The breeding herd had survived reasonably intact.

Billy had stayed on, out of a feeling of loyalty to see the Merritons and Mount Chillingham through the hard times. Now, with plenty of green pick and full waterholes, it was time for him to move on. He would miss the place; it was home to him, and Joe Merriton his friend and mentor since he was fourteen.

Seven years, almost! More than just a job, it was a learning experience, an incentive to better himself from people who cared; from Sergeant Thompson in the beginning, from Joe and Mrs. Merriton, from Doug. Bill was twenty-one now, a man, and a competent ringer who could look any man squarely in the eye on equal terms. With the skills he'd learned on Mount Chillingham, he could hold his own on any cattle camp; Joe had told him encouragingly when Bill had given his notice.

But Bill was looking to a future far from station life or droving routes. Joe wrote him an excellent reference and asked him to keep in touch. Bill promised that he would. Now, he'd be trying his luck in Brisbane.

"Bill, if things don't go quite how you've planned, don't hesitate to let me know. We'll work something out," was Joe's paternal advice.

"Thanks, Joe, but I'll make a go of it in the Big Smoke. I'll never take up the grog," he vowed, "and I mean to make a home for my mother in her old age."

Joe nodded. Billy had always kept in touch with Mavis. He was a son of whom any mother could be proud. Bill said goodbye to Doug and Diana.

"I'll stop by and say goodbye to young Bob before I leave Wilga Creek," he assured Diana. Bob was completing his primary schooling in town, staying with his Aunt and Grandmother during the week. Jenny knew how to keep the young larrikin in line, and he got along well with her son, Tom.

Joe drove Billy down to the road to wait as arranged for the mail contractor on his way back to Wilga Creek. Tactfully, he attempted to warn the lad that attitudes he might encounter in the outside world would not always be encouraging. Joe had given the matter much thought.

"Bill." he said, "people around here know you and they respect you. They know you're a good ringer and a top bloke. But you'll often encounter others who will see you as different. Some of them are that way because they're bigots and some are that way because they are frightened of anyone or anything that is outside of their own limited experience. You'll find some who'll be hostile to you just because you're black or who'll be disdainful simply because you haven't learned their particular skills. You're a stockman and a good one, but what you know about the bush, fencing and cattle won't have a lot of relevance to most city jobs and there'll be a lot of competition for unskilled work. On the other hand, there will be people who will give you a fair go, so don't let the negative ones wear you down. With the reference I wrote, you should have a good chance at the stockyards or the abattoirs to get started. Maybe someone at the Hostel may have a suggestion.

Another thing, until you get to know your way around the city, don't be too open about how much money you have in your wallet or your account. There are always some people around who will try to take advantage. You've had to work too hard for your savings to lose them! Brisbane is a big place for any bushman to get to know. It's a hell of a lot bigger than Wilga Creek or Roma and there are a lot of sharp operators who think we bushies come straight off the Christmas tree. Oh, and make sure you don't get paid less than award wages!

"Well, Bill. Good luck, son. Keep in touch," Joe finished, feeling somehow inadequate. He extended his hand.

Bill shook it, appreciating the older man's concern. It was an unusually long speech for Joe.

"Thanks, Joe. I will watch out for thieves and con men. But you don't have to warn a blackfellow about bigots! I've run across them for as long as I can remember, even in Wilga Creek!" the young Aboriginal smiled knowingly but uncomplainingly.

There was a depth of spirituality that was something special, in Billy; a spirituality latent in all human souls, yet usually suppressed or corrupted by the pressures and trivial concerns of everyday life. It was a spirituality unrecognised by the world at large; yet to those few who were capable of such recognition, a serene, gentle strength of spirit. It could be seen in a good number of Aboriginals who were corrupted neither by wine, grog or rejection, nor in sensitised by their desperation in striving for acceptance amidst the fickle values and mores of contemporary Western civilisation.

Of course, this depth of spirituality or soul was not an exclusive pre-serve of a few uncorrupted

Aboriginals. White people, too, sometimes possessed it. Invariably though, these were people unspoilt by a surfeit of material success. Tolstoy had observed it frequently amongst the Russian peasantry; Joe had seen it clearly in his own parents, Tom and Kathleen, as well as in Billy.

Life would never be easy for the lad, yet it would bring its own re-wards. God, and a guardian angel, would watch over Billy! Joe drove back to the homestead with a tear in his eye and a lump in his throat.

43

Hilton Brocksbank was wrestling with some hard decisions. The family's grazing and meatworks empire would have to be dismembered to accommodate his English cousins. The long Queensland drought had ended, only to be replaced on many holdings by the ravages of plague locusts. Kangaroo and rabbit numbers were again building up. Industrial unrest once more disrupted the abattoirs; the final straw, so far as his relatives were concerned. The Poms had declared they'd had enough and Hilton didn't blame them, though he didn't agree with their reasoning. To them, in the circumstances, a huge increase in their Argentine equity and complete divestment of their Australian interests appeared on paper, to be a wise financial move.

Hilton conceded their right to that viewpoint even though he held it to be a foolish one. The young General, Juan Domingo Peron had led a Coup d'état in 1943. For nearly three years, he had then remained the real power behind the Argentine Presidency before being popularly elected President himself, in February 1946. Peron was a Nationalist and a populist; he had no love of foreign Capitalists. If Hilton's cousins thought that the Peronists were a passing aberration or that Peron would see the wisdom in modifying his Nationalism, they could prove to be sadly mistaken. Besides, rumours were rife since the war's end that Argentina had become a refuge for fleeing Nazis and Italian Fascists. No, despite the rich grazing and farming lands, despite the relative proximity to British, U.S. and European markets, political risks far outweighed any short-term advantages from the bounteous Latin American jewel of Argentina, in Hilton's estimation. Conversely, Australia's disadvantage of old, tired soils, long drought periods and great distances from her markets were more than compensated for by a sound, stable system of Government! This was a huge advantage that should have been clear to those English relatives in the aftermath of World War 2.

Hilton was Australian-born and bred. His grandfather had come out from England and built a pastoral dynasty, yet only one son, Hilton's father, had not returned to Britain. Now that the family's various partnerships and companies were to be dissolved, Hilton determined to preserve a viable nucleus of the Queensland operation. He was formulating a plan to salvage for himself a new, smaller private pastoral company which would retain four key properties plus the half interest which he already held in a small meatworks operation. In a structure designed to hedge his bets against fluctuating rural fortunes, Hilton's plans included Mount Chillingham, which would continue as his, restructured group's mainstay, supplying young store cattle. The lease had twenty-three years to run. Due to the nature of its soils and topography, it would most likely see out that period without being compulsorily resumed for subdivision (from Pastoral Lease to smaller Grazing Selections under Queensland's unwieldy and complicated system of Land tenure). Despite its proximity of only thirty miles from Homestead to Railhead, Mount Chillingham was not the type of country that would be viable for closer settlement soon.

For its current use, it was an admirable proposition. Rent was relatively low as befitted the unimproved value, and being a lease, land tax did not apply. While rents were of little importance in profitable years, (being tax-deductible from income) land tax was a burden to be avoided except in such higher rainfall areas where Freeholding of land was essential for the security of tenure. Capital improvements on Mount Chillingham were currently valued at 21,550 Pounds, consisting of dog netting, other fencing, yards, and water provision to paddocks. etc., and value of Station homestead and outbuildings. Relative to the value of the livestock it could carry, this property must be regarded as a very cost-effective asset! Joe and Diana Merriton were another prized asset. They ran the place as conscientiously, as honestly and intelligently as if it was their own.

Good employees, loyal men who put their hearts and souls into their work, were worth their weight in gold! They were the backbone of any successful pastoral enterprise. More than just employees, they were friends; to be respected, to be listened to, to be amply rewarded, and to be subjected to no more outside direction than was essential.

His shrewd old grandfather had built his fortune on that creed. With Hilton, as with his father before him, this philosophy was so ingrained, so proven as to have become a virtual article of faith governing management strategy.

'Curly' Harris, the bald-headed Manager of "Cordoba Downs" was another employee held in similar esteem. Like Joe Merriton, Curly was with the old Company for almost three decades. Curly had started as a jackaroo on a Brocksbank sheep run in New South Wales; had worked on several of their properties before becoming Manager of Cordoba Downs in 1938. A top man who had forgotten more about sheep and wool than some Managers had ever known!

Cordoba Downs, in the low rainfall, semi-arid far southwest, eighty miles from the railhead, had eighteen more years to run on its current lease with a near certainty of lease renewal over its entire area.

Converted to Pastoral Development Lease terms in 1936, its 305,000 acres carried around 50,000 sheep and up to 2,000 bullocks in good years. Mainly Mitchell grass country, the improvements reflected the higher costs of netting, fencing, buildings and more intensive bore and watering provisions for successful sheep husbandry. An improved value of 170,000 Pounds attested to this. It had long been the showpiece of the old family Company's Australian operation. Typically, even the name was indicative of that partnership's Anglo-Argentine preoccupation! Hilton saw this property in a similar light to Mount Chillingham, as a lynchpin to his future viability. These two stations would be the only ones of the company's seven big leases that he would retain.

As subsequent booming wool prices in the 1950s were later to prove, through the shifting minefield of amendments to rights, obligations and conditions of tenure that applied under the Lands Acts of both Queensland and New South Wales. Hilton's judgement was sound. Equitable disposal of the other five big leases held by the Anglo-Australian partnership would become a running battle of wits with Lands Department officials. Mindful of their governments' wishes to implement decentralisation and closer settlement, these administrators were not always sympathetic towards a large landholder's expectations of fair compensation on investments and improvements made, once the time was due to surrender or transfer leases.

Hilton decided to restrict his purchases of smaller properties to freehold only. Although these also could be resumed at the whim of the Crown for specific purposes, at least both land and improvements were then subject to a fair market valuation. Thus, for smaller blocks in the closely settled areas. Freehold always had a firm real estate value. On the debit side, land taxes were payable, but one could not expect to have one's cake and eat it, too!

Perpetual leases were almost as safe as freehold tenure. They had no land tax obligations and rents were charged at 1.5% of unimproved value, per annum. However, perpetual lease conditions were normally only applied to smallholdings, under 2560 acres in area; on average, 460 acres.

Pastoral leases held little security against Crown resumption rights, whilst grazing selections, though completely secure throughout the currency of the lease, were normally subject to the condition of personal residence by the owner.

Such were Hilton's headaches in trying to establish a new pastoral enterprise in Queensland while winding up the old partnership.

His own base of operations would be the freehold fattening and grain block of 5000 acres that he owned on the north western edge of the Darling Downs. In addition, he was negotiating to purchase a 3700-acre run suiting both sheep and cattle, in the Southern Border highlands. Additionally, he sought to buy a further five hundred acres close to his coastal abattoir. Such an area would be useful in the short term and would return substantial capital gain against subdivision potential in the long term.

Together, with his other diversified investments in rural and retail fields, he felt confident that he was accruing a sound, manageable pastoral conglomerate, totally Queensland-based as he had divested himself of all interstate and overseas interests. His payout to the English cousins would be more than offset by their purchase of his equity in the Argentine operation. Yes, on paper, it was working out! Hilton and Celia, his wife, looked forward to the forthcoming trip to London to formalise the deal.

"Well, Hilton will be here tomorrow. I can't help wondering what's in the wind! It's only six weeks since his last visit. Remember, he seemed to be fishing to find out whether we had ever thought of buying our own place? Then, there was all that talk of rationalizing and restructuring. I didn't follow much of what he was saying, except that he wanted to dice his South American interests and that the Pommy side of his family wanted to pull out of Australia. He talked a lot but I don't think he told us much! Oh, well, I daresay we'll find out tomorrow," Joe said.

"Yes," Diana mused, "but he did say we'd be looked after! Joe, you don't suppose he intends to offer us the chance of first refusal to buy this place?"

"Surely not! He's a trained accountant, he must realise we'd have no hope of carrying a mortgage on a place this size, even if we could find a bank manager silly enough to lend us the money. We'd have to win a ballot for a Brigalow block to have any chance of getting out on our own!"

"If you've any illusions of getting me onto a Brigalow block at fifty-two years of age, you'll have a fight on your hands, Joe Merriton!" Diana declared.

Joe laughed, "I wouldn't dare suggest such a thing, mv sweet! We have had a great run here though, and you have invested all those bonuses we've been paid over the years. Perhaps Hilton does think we can afford to buy the run!"

Diana had managed their finances well, banking or investing their savings to accrue quite a handy nest egg. Those bonuses were an incentive that was appreciated. The Brocksbanks were consistently considerate of their managers and stockmen, in the belief that by rewarding men initially chosen for honesty, integrity, loyalty and effort, such men would scarcely abuse that trust by stealing; something quite common amongst managers and head stockmen on runs where owners were less appreciative of effort.

"Hilton would not know our financial position, Joe. For all he knows, we might have blown the lot! No, I doubt he will offer us an option on Mount Chillingham. My guess is that he'll offer a promotion or a shift to another station" Diana said.

44

Hilton spread the draft of his intended prospectus upon the dining room table and outlined his proposition to them. Joe and Diana were lost for words, "Well, Joe, Mrs. Merriton; what do you think of it? Hilton asked eagerly.

His strong young face was boyish with enthusiasm. At thirty, he was four years older than Michael would have been, had he survived. Like Mike, Hilton was fair-haired with a direct gaze from guileless blue eyes wide-set in an open countenance. Like Mike, he too had seen wartime active service in aircrew. Hilton had flown Catalinas with both RAF and RAAF squadrons. He'd served in both the Indian and Pacific Ocean theatres. From Trincomalee to Rabaul, from Bowen to the China coast, there was little of the vast tropical sea-lanes and enemy-held island territory that he hadn't flown over at 100 knots in the big, lumbering machines. He had rescued downed airmen, bombed enemy supply dumps and shipping, searched for submarines and laid mines far inside Japanese-held waters. The big black Cats had enormous range and though well-armed, had only one-third the airspeed of those deadly swarms of Zeroes. Such duties had demanded a special sort of calm and steadfast courage from the crews of the slow yet rugged reliable flying boats.

The offer Hilton had just extended to the Merritons was typical of his big heart. In addition to their retaining managership of Mount Chillingham, Hilton had proposed that Joe should accept a Directorship of the new company, together with a gratuity of 10,000 shares to himself and Diana. He'd also offered them the opportunity to purchase a further and similar share allocation at issue should they so desire.

"I'm flabbergasted, Hilton. I don't know what to say! Me, a Director?" Joe said incredulously.

"Thank you, Mr. Brocksbank, it is extremely generous of you" Diana responded graciously.

"Not at all. Mrs. Merriton! It is merely sound business sense. I will be offering a similar proposal to Mr. Harris. Look, I have a sound under-standing of the meat processing and finance aspects as well as an overall affinity with the whole box and dice, but I must rely on the input of good, practical men who are thoroughly familiar with all of the animal husbandry and property management aspects and pitfalls. For those, I could not go past Joe for cattle or Curly Harris for sheep and wool. An-other point, a selfish one; I view it as an incentive which might enable me to be sure of retaining two valuable, trustworthy Managers and in your case, an excellent station bookkeeper into the bargain!" Hilton was fully cognisant of Diana's meticulous control of the ledgers and typically modest in playing down his generosity.

"That's very kind of you to say so," Diana acknowledged. "When would you need to know how many further shares we'd like to take up?"

"Let's say two weeks? That should give you time to discuss it with your accountant or share advisor. You are under no obligation to take up any unless you want to! Either way, your decision won't affect the gratu-itous issue or my invitation to Joe to become a Director, Mrs. Merriton."

"Thanks, Hilton, I accept the Directorship, since you're so confident I'll be of some use in the position," Joe said appreciatively.

Joe and Hilton were on first-name terms ever since Hilton had come into the business. Diana normally wasn't one to stand on ceremony, but although she and Hilton shared a mutual liking and respect for each oth-er, she had always addressed him more formally. The reason lay in Hil-ton's upbringing. No snob despite his education at one of the country's most prestigious private schools, Hilton's nature was that of an Officer and a Gentleman. There was no way that he could bring himself to ad-dress this warm, gracious woman, old enough to be his mother, and his Manager's wife to boot, by her Christian name! To Hilton, it would have seemed neither respectful nor respectable.

Diana instinctively recognised this and responded in kind, always ad-dressing him as "Mr. Brocksbank. Such scrupulous propriety was something that Joe found faintly amusing, though he would have readily conceded that should Hilton ever address her by her Christian name, Diana would be equally comfortable with addressing him as "Hilton."

The following day, after Hilton had left for Cordoba Downs, Joe and Diana deliberated upon what additional shareholding they might consider purchasing. With an asset backing roughly commensurate to an issued capital of two million five shilling shares, the worth of the company would be half a million pounds.

Hilton, Celia and their family would retain the controlling interest. The share market was one mystery that Joe had never sought to probe. Diana, however, had invested most of their savings in bonds or shares over the years and had done so in a way that had maximised capital gain whilst minimising taxation obligations.

"I don't mind paying tax on healthy dividends when our capital investment is appreciating," she had explained to him in the past. "But I do object to being taxed on the pittances from low bank interest rates! After tax, savings accounts scarcely keep pace with inflation. That's why we should only keep a prudent operating reserve in our savings and cheque accounts"

Investing was second nature to Diana: a hobbyhorse on which her father had instructed her well during her school years. If Joe were to serve as a company director, it would behoove him to start paying attention to such things. There was no doubt that his wife would prove an excellent tutor.

"Look, Joe." she was saying now, "what say we divest ourselves of these, these and these?" She had spread out three sets of shares certificates on the table. She continued. They are all currently riding high on the market and together with this bond maturing next month, we will realise enough to take up the other ten thousand shares Hilton offered us. We'll not only hold twenty thousand shares with a sound asset base, but we'll also be showing our faith in our employer".

But, that sounds like putting all of our eggs in one basket! We'll be putting 2,500 pounds of our life savings into one venture! Surely that must leave us little over?" Joe was cautious.

"Heavens, no!" she smiled smugly, "We still have 300 pounds in Bonds, around 350 pounds in solid Industrials and another 500 in Oil and Mining explorations, which are a darned sight riskier. Oh, yes. We've over 300 in our bank accounts as well! Our total portfolio stands at around 4,000 pounds at present values; plus, of course, Hilton's extra grant worth 2.500!"

Joe considered for a few moments. "That's eight or ten year's wages! I didn't just marry a good sort, I married a blooming genius!" He reached across and squeezed her hand, "We're rich!"

Diana laughed, "well, maybe not all that rich but certainly, comfortable! Not having had to service a mortgage has helped us, but sometimes there are easier ways of making money than working hard for it, provided one doesn't come unstuck! I'll admit to being more than just a pretty face." she added immodestly.

The prospectus to float the new company was issued a month later. Hilton had described both Joe and Curly in such glowing terms in the Directors' biographical notes, that the two unsophisticated bushmen hardly recognised themselves.

45

Cliff now had both a stepson and a natural son. Cliff Junior was three months old, a source of great pride to Cliff, Rosemary and Tony. More than ever, Cliff had an urge to retire from Air Force life and commence to build that small engineering workshop in Michigan that had long been a dream in the back of his mind. Surely there must be handsome opportunities for new suppliers to the booming automotive industry!

When he'd taken Rosie and Tony to the mainland to meet his family last furlough, he'd explored the possibility. With his deferred retirement pay and the possibility of some appropriate training course under the G.I. Bill of Rights, he perceived a real chance to become an industrial manufacturer, albeit on a small scale. Rosie was fully supportive of the idea. There would be long, hard hours and financial risks, but they shared confidence in each other and in the viability of the venture. At least, they could be together as a family and no longer separated again by Air Force postings. Yes, it was a future to look forward to, but his immediate concern had more to do with West Berlin. He was enroute to Germany with Air Transport Command for Operation Vittles, whilst Rosie and the boys were returning to Australia until the crisis was resolved.

Just how far the Soviets would take this chilling intransigence was anybody's guess. He sure as hell hoped it wouldn't lead to World War Three, but right now, in June of 1948, they had reneged on their agreements to allow rail and road travel through the Russian Zone from West Germany to West Berlin. Their intention was to choke off the city from provisions.

All that now remained open to the Western Powers, the U.S.A., Britain and France, were the three respective air corridors, each twenty miles wide and each rigidly enforced by Soviet fighter aircraft.

Through these corridors the two million inhabitants of West Berlin would have to receive their entire supplies of foodstuffs and essential supplies from the West, a city under a virtual siege. Douglas C47 and C54 transport aircraft would need to fly a 'round the clock' schedule into Tempelhoff Airfield to keep the city alive.

So began the historic operation which was to become known world-wide as the Berlin Airlift. There would be little. prospect of Cliff returning to civilian life while the emergency lasted and USAF Air Transport maintenance requirements were to be so sorely tested. It was not surprising that in this time of uncertainty, Rosemary had elected to return with her sons to Wilga Creek rather than to join his family in Detroit for however long the separation might last.

Despite the huge strain upon military air logistics by the Berlin crisis, the previously decided amalgamation from June 1st. of the USAF Air Transport Command with the US Naval Air Transport Service to form a giant new Defense Department airline, proved to be a wise move.

The newly formed Military Air Transport Service was to have benefits for Rosemary as well. Though now in Europe, Cliff had been able to exert some influence through colleagues at Hickham. Rosemary and children remained on Oahu until August, then, household effects placed in safe USAF storage, they flew into Sydney in some spare seats aboard a MATS C54 flight to Australia via Palmyra and Canton Islands, American Samoa and Auckland. It was a long, tiring, roundabout journey, but being at no charge, was very welcome. A further seven hours in the air by two TAA DC3 flights from Sydney via Brisbane, and the young family arrived at Roma aerodrome three days after leaving Hawaii.

"Hello, Mum! Hi, Dad! Hi, Bob! It sure is great to be home! Isn't it, Tony?" Rosemary announced. She looked tired but elated. She had put on weight, but otherwise appeared tanned, fit and glowing with health.

"Sure is, Mom! Hi, Bob! Hi, Grandpa, Grandma! How do you like my baby brother?" Tony asked as he hugged Diana.

"He's beautiful!" was Diana's verdict as soon as she got a good look at him. "My, you two have certainly acquired Yankee accents!" she smilingly chided.

"Goodness me! Is it that noticeable? One tries not to, but it must be infectious!" Rosemary exclaimed.

"Never mind, a few months back home will soon knock the edges off that. We'll turn you both back into Aussies again," Joe laughed. "I'll grab your ports, then we'll get a feed in town before we head home, eh?"

Rosemary smiled reminiscently. She certainly was back home in Queensland! Her father's usage of the uniquely Queensland term, "ports" for suitcases or luggage was a normal, everyday part of the local vocabulary, yet was greeted with amusement, even with derision by Melbournites and Sydneysiders, and with absolute bewilderment by nationals of some other English-speaking lands.

"What's the joke, Love?" Joe asked her.

"Nothing, Dad, really! I was just remembering a cabbie's face in Honolulu when I referred to them as ports. He didn't have a clue what I was talking about! They usually call them 'cases or bags. Gee. it's great to be back!" she replied.

The word was apparently derived as an abbreviated form of the French "Portmanteau," from "Porter," to carry, and "Manteau," a coat; literally, almost the equivalent of "suitcase," but then, what dinki-di red blooded Queenslander would be caught dead using some sissy French word, or even the Anglicised equivalent, "suitcase." when the short, succinct "port" sufficed?

At any rate, to the average Banana Bender the origin of the word was long lost in antiquity!

46

Rosemary decided to rent a small house, which had become vacant, at Wilga Creek. Bob declined the offer to stay with her; as it was less than four months until the end of his final school year, he elected to remain with his grandmother, aunt and cousins. Rosemary could enjoy a private life with her two children yet be within easy access of her extended family and also spend frequent weekends at Mount Chillingham.

Tony, whose previous Queensland schooling was at home through the Queensland Primary Correspondence, now attended Wilga Creek State School for the first time.

For simplicity and convenience, he was known as Tony Clarke by his schoolmates, sharing the same surname as his mother and half-brother. He hadn't been consulted in the matter, and though Rosie and the Headmaster had acted with the best of intentions, it was a liberty taken which the boy deeply but secretly resented. He was proud of the name Roxton, proud of a father killed in action, yet when he tried to explain that to his young schoolmates, they didn't understand; it went beyond their own youthful experiences.

The December-January school vacation was spent at the station with his grandparents. How he wished that they were his parents instead of Rosemary and Cliff! Mount Chillingham was his real home, he felt; not Hawaii, not Wilga Creek! Bob was more like a big brother than an uncle, but even Bob was moving on!

Bob had finished primary school with a State Scholarship Examination Pass at age fourteen and declared in no uncertain terms that his formal education was complete.

"I'm not going to be a boarder with a lot of smart-arsed bastards at some flash private college! If you try to make me, I'll shoot through and get a job droving," he defiantly informed his parents.

Diana and Joe quickly realised that no amount of threatening or cajoling would alter the situation. Bob would carry out his threat to run away; he wasn't the sort of kid to meekly remain at boarding school if his mind was set against it. The time for compromise had arrived!

Following a couple of phone calls to Hilton and Curly Harris, it was arranged that Bob would be "apprenticed" to Curly as a jackaroo on Cordoba Downs.

"You could probably use him yourself, couldn't you, Joe?" Hilton had asked.

"Yes, I probably could, except that I might be tempted to murder the little buggar! I'm too close to him to remain fair and impartial," Joe admitted. He added, "Besides, he's been born and raised here; it may do him the world of good to broaden his experience!"

Hilton had concurred. Curly was quite amenable, "Sure thing, Joe! He's not a bad kid and at least, he's already a competent horseman, unlike some of the young blokes who've started here in recent years. Send him out in January!"

It was a relief to have found such a niche for Bob. Curly was a good, sound manager; also, he hadn't been soured by fourteen years of Bob's silly antics. In this instance, Curly surely would be a more suitable boss and teacher than would Joe.

Joe was only too aware that his patience had worn a bit thin so far as Bob was concerned, and he, therefore, was inclined to over-react when Bob made any mistake. Another factor was that Bob regarded working on Cordoba Downs as an adventure. Born and raised in Maranoa country with Mt. Chillingham his sole yardstick of station life, the lad saw the prospect of working on a semi-arid Channel Country run as an exciting challenge. The irony of this compromise was that it was similar to the start of Joe's own pastoral career some thirty-seven years earlier, though at least, Cordoba ran cattle as well as sheep.

Deep within Joe's soul, he nursed a hope that one day when Bob had knocked around and matured, he might eventually return to take over the reins and succeed his father as manager at Mt. Chillingham. Whatever the outcome, Joe yearned for that closer father and son relationship which thus far had continued to elude them.

47

On May 12th, 1949, the Soviets lifted their blockade of West Berlin. Cliff immediately applied to return to the U.S.A. and to resign his commission. In July, Rosemary, Tony and Cliff Junior, now a sixteen-month-old toddler, flew out of Australia; Tony most reluctantly.

"Why can't I stay here with Grandpa and Grandma?" he wanted to know.

"Because I'm your mother, Cliff is your stepfather and your place is with us! You didn't want to go to Hawaii either, but you have to admit that you liked it once we arrived there, didn't you?" Rosemary argued with the weariness of one who had made the same point a dozen times before.

"Yair, but, I don't want to go to Detroit. I'm not American, I'm Australian! I'd rather stay here!"

"Well, listen. You're coming and that's final! I love you and Cliff loves you just as much as he loves your baby brother. He wants us all to be together, a real family, and I want that too! Why else do you suppose he's given up a good career in the Air Force? It wasn't an easy decision for him, you know! Besides, you've always got along well with Cliff; you like him and so you should! He spoils you rotten trying to keep you amused, so why all this fuss?" Rosemary was in no mood for an argument. Tony's tantrums had taken the edge off the excitement that had thrilled her upon receiving the news of Cliff's return from Germany; she was dejected by her elder son's unsettled feelings and general negativity.

"Come on, Mate! Keep your chin up, look on the bright side! You'll make new friends in Detroit. Don't upset your Mum! It won't be forever; we'll all get together again someday! I'll even save a job for you when you finish school if you still want to be a ringer or a Jackaroo." Joe promised, hugging his grandson.

"I think I might become a Flying Doctor pilot instead," Tony refused to concede completely.

"That's the spirit, lad! You will have to study hard at school, but you can do it! Meanwhile, you can think about it and imagine you're the pilot on the plane going back to America. You're a lucky bloke! Wish I was going, too. I've never been in an aeroplane!" Joe attempted to inject some enthusiasm into the youngster.

"Haven't you, really, Grandpa?" Tony asked.

"No, Mate, I haven't!" Joe said. "So, off you go and look after your Mum and little brother for me, eh? Goodbye, son!"

A final round of hugs and kisses left Diana and Rosie moist-eyed. It was time for the little family to board the aircraft.

As the airliner taxied out for take-off, Diana watched reflectively. She squeezed her husband's hand. "Poor Rosie! The little blighter was determined to give her a hard time right to the end! Oh, Joe, I'll miss them!"

"Yes. Love, I will too! Well, with Bob out west and Rosie and the kids off to America, the old place is going to seem terribly quiet. Just you and I now, old girl, for the first time in, what; twenty-eight years or more?"

48

To a world still recovering from the ravages of World War Two and warily learning to live with the frightening possibility of future Nuclear warfare, the Cold War era was epitomised by deep distrust and international brinkmanship between those former Allies, Communism and Western Capitalism.

Though smouldering tensions and ideological hatred had stopped short of open warfare during the Berlin Crisis, some Asian nations were less fortunate. Nationalism, already rampant in Malaya, Singapore, Indo-China and the former Netherlands East Indies, was further fuelled by Japan's earlier demonstration, which proved that European colonial powers were far from invincible.

Indonesia won her independence through a long and bitter struggle, India and Pakistan won theirs by negotiation with a Britain driven to accept reality by her war debts and a new conception of the rights of Man irrespective of skin colour. Yet these three were among the few Asian countries in which Marxist idealism was not a significant driving force. For others, local Nationalists, Communists and die-hard Imperialists ensured that the final results would be the outcomes of three-cornered contests. In both Malaya and Indo-China, wartime resistance to the Japanese had been primarily the preserve of Communist Revolutionary insurgents; therefore, it followed that once again these would be at the forefront of the new struggle against European Colonialism.

Again, in China, no sooner had the Japanese capitulated than full-scale civil war broke out between Communist and Nationalist regimes. The resultant 1949 Communist victory saw the Nationalists retreat to regroup and consolidate in the offshore islands of Formosa, Quemoy and Amoy.

Further north, unhappy Korea, for 35 years a Japanese puppet appendage, was under occupation by the Soviets in the north and the Americans in the South since 1945. As a result, two separate Korean governments claimed a legitimate right to represent their nation. Friction boiled over on 25th June 1950, as North Korea invaded the South. Though already committed to aiding Britain against Communist insurgency in Malaya, Australia did not shirk the United Nations' call for military support in Korea. The Korean War was only seven days old when RAAF Mustang fighters of No.77 Squadron became the first non-American unit of the U.N. Forces to see action, being re-deployed from service with the British Commonwealth Occupation Forces Fighter Wing at Iwakuni, Japan. Later, the Third Infantry Battalion, Royal Australian Regiment, as well as RAN ships and aircraft were added to Australia's contribution.

To a nation seemingly inexhaustible in her enthusiasm to throw herself into other peoples' wars, the onset of the Korean conflict brought Australia only one benefit; a worldwide surge in demand for wool as participant nations sought to kit out their Armies to fight in the dreadful cold of Korean winters.

As was the case with other pastoralists, this wool boom brought new prosperity to the Brocksbank Pastoral Company. Hilton's decision to retain the big Cordoba Downs property in his portfolio had paid off handsomely!

Across the Pacific, for Cliff and Rosemary, their fledgling engineering workshop was also boosted by the dreadful requirements of the Korean War contracts. At first, they were apprehensive that Cliff would be recalled to active Duty from the Air Force Reserve, but with his factory fully set up and his knowledge of defence specifications, the powers that be had decreed he could better serve his country as a subcontractor manufacturing Military hardware.

The career path of Bob, too, had altered. As a jackaroo, with comfortable living quarters and dining with the Manager's family instead of with the station hands, he'd been spoiled in the culinary department.

The Harrises had lived well on the Channel Country run; the meals were equal to the good cooking of Bob's mother back home.

However, Bob had moved on after his third year at Cordoba Downs. Curly was a good boss, if a little fussy and strict about the standards required of a future manager, but before Bob reached the age of eighteen, he'd developed itchy feet. He then spent six months working for a drover around the Gulf Country. The tucker was barely edible, the drover was mean; tight-fisted, bad-tempered, abusive and frequently violent. Bob quit, and following a drunken bender in Mount Isa to celebrate, had gone looking for another job. This took him to a run-down Territory cattle run, isolated and in the process of renewed development and restocking. He'd spent more than a year there by late 1953, mustering, fencing and yard building. At nineteen and a half, he was fit and well-muscled from hard work. He'd enjoyed the stock work, particularly the challenge of catching and throwing big, wild cattle and training his horses. But there was little mental stimulus. It seemed that the very isolation of the place served as a magnet for deadbeats, criminals, wife-deserters, gin-jockeys and other no-hopers, so Bob had kept his own counsel mostly.

Ted, the overseer, probably was a good man in his time but a lifetime of hard work, war service and injuries had dulled his spirit. He was tough enough to exercise control over his motley crew when necessary but appeared to show little real interest in his job. Essentially, a time server.

Again, the tucker was nothing to write home about. In fact, the camp had seen four cooks come and go since Bob had first arrived; not that one could blame Ted for that, Bob conceded. The location was scarcely one to attract a competent chef.

Of those who'd held the position, one was lazy, unreliable, dirty and halfway mad; two more were closet alcoholics as well as grubs while the fourth was incompetent and so carelessly unhygienic that he'd earned the nickname "Silversleeves" from his nauseous habit of wiping his perpetually dripping nose on his shirt sleeves. All four had received their share of abuse from Bob, resulting in punch-ups on occasions. Bob, however, was well able to defend himself in a fistfight, and at least, he felt, it served to break the monotony.

Eventually. "Silversleeves" had proven too much, even for Ted's apathy. The overseer had sacked him instead of waiting for the grub to quit. For once, the time-honoured joke of "Right Oh! Who called the cook a bastard?" and the standard rejoinder of "Who called the bastard a cook?" was a little too close to the truth.

Ted took over the cooking for the following three weeks, while he awaited a replacement. It was a task the overseer loathed, but at least he was clean and reasonably adept at turning out good, if plain, fare. When the new replacement cook arrived, Bob's quick wit, coupled with his instant dislike of the fellow, turned out to be his nemesis in an off-hand way. The young ringer was tired and irritable when he came in off the run that evening. He noticed the new car, a Vanguard, and wondered what visitor had arrived.

Ted and the new arrival approached. The newcomer was of fat, soft and effeminate appearance. The fellow even walked with a limp wristed, mincing gait.

"Ah, Bob, this is Ralph, our new camp cook," Ted introduced him. It was an unfortunate choice of phrase.

"Well, Ted. I reckon you've got to be at least half right," Bob quipped drily.

"What do you mean?" Ted was unusually slow to comprehend.

"Well, I can see the bastard is camp, but can he cook?" Bob jested rudely.

Ralph's moon face reddened. "I didn't come all this way to be abused and insulted! I'm a trained chef with excellent references, and I demand an apology!" he complained in a girlish, high-pitched tone.

"Well, what do you know? Not only a poofter but a Prima Donna into the bargain!" Bob observed unrepentantly.

"Excuse us for a moment, Ralph!" Ted said. Angrily, he drew Bob aside a dozen or so paces.

"Now, young Bob, I don't give a stuff whether this bloke is a fairy or not, so long as he doesn't pester me; but I've had a gut-full of running this place and being the bait-layer as well! At least this fella seems neat, tidy and capable. A decent cook is a lot harder to find than another ringer! You can either humour him with an apology or you can finish up!"

"Suits me, Ted," Bob said equably, seizing the opportunity. "In that case, I'll snatch my time!"

He'd been thinking already of going back and finding work around Wilga Creek, maybe a job with his father at Mount Chillingham before the wet season commenced and isolated the roads for weeks at a time.

There was a good chance he'd have been laid off for the three months of the "Wet," anyhow! Ted's ultimatum had merely decided the issue for him.

49

The pastel blue Holden F.J. ute slewed sideways on the dusty road in a hair-raising handbrake turn. Gravel scattered like machine-gun fire as the vehicle halted. Two very surprised stock horses shied and spun, then, nervous but under control, snorted their alarm as they faced the now stationary ute.

The rider of the grey gelding swore, and then asked tersely, "You bloody piss-wit Perry! Were you trying to start a roadside rodeo, or what?"

"G'day, Tom! Just thought I'd check and see if you jokers were wide awake," the Holden driver offered cheekily.

"Yair, well now you know, what else is on that hare brain of yours?" Bob Merriton inquired nonchalantly, without malice. Beneath him, his bay Arab mare danced her protest at such shenanigans, her nostrils dilated wide, her eyes huge and round as saucers. "Easy, girl," Bob comforted her, gently stroking her neck.

Perry Maddison was a mate of the two cousins since boyhood, though that was something that pleased neither Bob's parents nor Tom's mother, Jenny. A likeable rogue, Perry had the reputation of being a little too free and easy with a branding iron. He had never been convicted of the offence, but for a ringer who didn't appear to spend much time in gainful employment, he seemed remarkably affluent. Witness the new F.J. utility! In some ways, Bob was a kindred spirit, much to the chagrin of Joe and Diana.

Thus far, Bob had never actually engaged in cattle duffing, but as his father frequently cautioned, "if you fly with crows, you're bound to be shot at!"

Tom, on the other hand, was more ethical, though equally as high-spirited and full of bravado as his older cousin. Also, true to that occasionally misguided Australian tradition, Tom was no dobber, no matter what!

Perry, therefore secure in this knowledge, was prepared to risk Tom's disapproval as he informed Bob, "Granville's got around three hundred head of young Baldy steers in a nice quiet back paddock. By a handy coincidence, a mate of mine has a brand and earmark that'll be dead easy to fix up! Now, Granville has only just put them there, and I hear he's off to Sydney again for the Royal Easter Sow and a bit of the high life. I reckon we could lift those steers next week, and Granville won't know they've gone for another fortnight! With Granville away, you can bet your nuts that Fred will bludge. He probably won't bother checking that paddock again until just before Granville's due back! Want to be in on the action?"

"I dunno, Perry. Granville's not a bad bloke for a silvertail," Bob said.

"Oh, come on, mate! He's rolling in dough! He'll never miss them. Are you turning into a social worker in your old age? How about Saturday arvo? Any passing traffic will have gone into town for the evening before we get them near the road. We'll have 'em delivered, cash in hand, by ten Sunday morning and you blokes can be on your way! Bill and I will doctor the brands at his place. He's got a good set of yards. There'll be thirty quid in it for each of you; not bad for a night's work, eh?" Perry was like a used car salesman trying to close a deal. "Not bloody likely!" Tom declined.

"Suit yourself," Perry said, "how about you, Bob?"

"Ah, what the hell --- yair, I'll be in," Bob decided.

"Good, mate! Knew you would! And, Tom, if you change your mind, the offer is still open! Be a lot quicker and easier with the four of us. See yer about two o'clock Saturday by the old hut, Bob," Perry said as he re-started the motor of the ute.

"Right, mate. See yer," Bob told him casually.

Perry put the Holden into gear and departed in another cloud of dust and gravel.

The cousins rode off, Tom in troubled silence, wrestling with his conscience; Bob mentally spending an extra thirty pounds.

Eventually, Tom broke the silence, "You buggars must be mad! Three hundred head! You're bound to attract attention, especially next to the road."

"We'd have to be pretty stiff to be seen," Bob said, "much less recognised! After we've crossed the road, the route only parallels it for a couple of miles. It'll be dark by then; any traffic going to town for the night probably will have passed before then. Anyway, if we keep them on the far side we can stay a few hundred yards from the road everywhere but where we actually cross it and there is enough timber on that far side to hide 'em amongst if we see any headlights in the distance. There is so much feed about they'll just put their head down and graze as soon as we stop pushing them. There's so much grass they'd hardly be able to stir up a dust cloud in hot daylight."

"They're white-faced cattle, for Pete's sake! On a clear night, they'll be visible from the road!" Tom protested.

"Not once they're steadied up amongst the shadows from the timber. It's movement that catches the eye! Anyway, there are never more than three or four cars in twenty-four hours on that road. We'll be safe as the Bank of England!" Bob insisted.

Tom regarded his cousin suspiciously, "Are you sure you haven't already done a bit of poddy-dodging? It seems to me that you've got it all worked out!"

"I haven't yet, but I have considered it, just for the heck of it. Perry has given me a few pointers on how he's got away with it. Seems it's mainly just a case of planning, common sense and keeping your eyes open."

"It's stealing! Your Mum and Dad would have a pink fit if they even suspected you thought that way. I may be younger than you, but I wish you'd grow up and act your age! You're just a half-smart kid at heart!" Tom remonstrated.

Bob laughed good-naturedly, no offence taken.

"You take life too seriously, Tom! Where's your sense of adventure?"

Ahead, the track forked and they parted company. Tom to return to his job on a neighbouring station, whilst Bob had a further ten-mile ride to Mt. Chillingham. He'd been back in the district for over two years and was once more becoming restless.

"Well, see you 'round, worry-guts!" Bob said cheerfully.

"Grow up, you silly buggar!" Tom replied.

Despite different temperaments and outlooks, they had remained firm friends since childhood. Tom, steady and reliable as the grandfather after whom he was named had long since ceased trying to change Bob's wayward ways.

50

Six days later, Bob rode up to the old derelict hut near the reserve, ten miles north of Bradford, a small settlement situated on the railway eighteen miles west of Wilga Creek.

Tom was thoughtful as he watched Bob approach on his favourite mount, Bint, that flashy little blood bay Arab mare. She was a pretty little thing; alert, proud; tail carried high like a battle ensign. She was hard as nails, too; untiring. But she stood out like dog's balls! If anyone saw them today, well, there wasn't another like her within two hundred miles, Tom thought.

Not that there were too many dark greys quite like his own mount, either, but at least there were some! Tom was edgy, guilt-ridden already. He was almost envious of his cousin's easy nonchalance as he thought about it. Just look at the silly bastard! You'd think he was on a picnic!

Bob's face broke into a broad smile," Hullo, Tom! I thought you weren't going to be in it?"

"Yair! Well, somebody has to look after you, you great galah! Perry only looks after himself! Couldn't you have ridden a less showy horse, something a bit less eye-catching? Just in case we're noticed?"

"Ah, stop fretting! Those steers won't be missed for weeks! Nobody is going to suspect every bloke to pass through on a horse in that time, mate! Any sign of Perry yet?" Bob asked.

"Not yet," Tom told him.

Half an hour later, Perry and Bill arrived.

Tom's unease increased. He knew Bill only by sight: a shifty little bush-rat with a selection in the hills to the northwest!

"Well, let's get on with it," Perry decreed.

The paddock was about three miles to the east and lightly timbered. It was around fifteen hundred acres in area. They cut the wires, rode through and soon got a clean muster of the quiet well-handled steers in the paddock.

A quick repair of the fence to avoid attracting any suspicion unnecessarily early and by nine o'clock bright starlight found them on the stock route a mile to the north of the derelict hut. Perry led the mob on his brown gelding, at a calm, steady rate. Bob and Bill covered the wings, keeping them far as practicable from the parallel road, while Tom brought up the rear.

They were travelling well, being pushed along at a nice balance between browsing on the move and enough pace to be clear of the area quickly enough to suit. Still about fifteen more miles to go. Not too excessive for an overnight drove in this pleasant coolness, but one dare not push them too fast at night or they might rush, quiet though they were.

By nine-thirty, the duffers were breathing a little easier. Just a few hundred yards further and they would diverge along a little-used lane to the left. This would lead eventually to the southern boundary of Bill's run.

A pair of headlights approached in the distance, coming fast from the north, but still quite a long way off. Quickly, efficiently, the riders bunched the mob behind the shadows of a stand of box trees, but the grove wasn't very thick and the slight bend in the road ahead served to deflect those headlight beams momentarily onto the white-faced steers.

"Bloody Hell! What's this bloke doing on the road at this hour, anyway?" Perry wondered aloud.

He motioned to the others to move further back, into the shadows as the car slowed down then warily crept towards them across the stock route from the road, two hundred yards away. He cracked his whip lightly, like the sound of a bough snapping, and the mob started moving forward again. The headlights swung further to the right, following the cattle away from the trees, then doused completely to avoid spooking the animals. The driver paralleled the path of the stock, half talking, half crooning to them in a soothing tone as he caught up to them. Tired and quiet-natured through regular recent handling, the beasts settled down again.

Talking softly, encouragingly, the driver left his car and walked closer to the stock, moving in as close as he judged they would allow him in the dark. Still talking to them, he momentarily flashed a torch over a steer, then switched it off before the mob could react to this intrusion. Now, it appeared he was returning to his car.

Nervously, a woman's voice called from the vehicle, clear as crystal on the still night air. "What do you think, John?"

"I think they're probably Granville's, and I don't think they got here by themselves. We'll call in there and we'll let that copper in Bradford know, too!"

Bob recognised the voice. It belonged to the stock and station agent from Wilga Creek! The fellow returned to his vehicle, switched on his headlights and drove back to the road in almost indecent haste.

"That's stuffed it! Let's get the hell out of here! Forget the bloody mob!" Perry was close to panic.

"Hang on! Why not start them back towards home first? At least that might help cover a few of our tracks in case that copper is really on the ball. Only takes a couple of minutes to turn 'em round and it can't do any harm, anyway," Bob suggested calmly.

"Good idea," Perry concurred, collecting his scattered wits, "Then we'll disappear PDQ ourselves! Sorry, fellas: all that work for nothing!"

Tom's first reaction was to feel a huge wave of relief. Their troubles might not be over yet, but at least the duffing attempt hadn't come off. He wasn't ever a thief and now, he knew, there was no way he'd ever become one if he was lucky enough to get out of this mess! It mightn't hurt to leave the district for a while, either, he thought. Might even join the Navy for a few years and see a bit more of life than just horses and cattle. He was toying with that idea for some time, anyhow.

51

Lady Luck changed her ever-fickle mind; now she favoured the failed cattle duffers.

When the stock and station agent called in at Bradford, the sole policeman, a Senior Constable, was out of town, investigating a road accident. Tired and overworked, he, with Fred, Granville's man and a local honorary stock inspector, returned the steers to Granville's property apart from eight head to be held as evidence in the Bradford Police paddock. He'd phoned his District Police Inspector to request the assistance of a black tracker but was too hard-pressed to take any plaster casts of the duffer's horses' hoof prints. They could do that later in the afternoon after the tracker arrived. Snatching a few hours of sleep was more of a priority. Those casts were never made; a sudden thunderstorm swept in from the North West after lunch, obliterating the tracks.

Perry Maddison was seen in Bradford Saturday morning; a likely suspect, but where was the proof? As Perry himself said in an injured tone when the matter was broached, "It's a free country, isn't it? Sure, I was in town Saturday. What's wrong with that?"

Somebody else had seen an unidentified rider on a grey horse near the old hut early Saturday afternoon. Then again, Simpsons had seen Bob Merriton on their way home from town around 1 pm. Bob was riding that flashy bay mare of his, about twenty miles north of town. The policeman knew he was, figuratively, clutching at straws. Bob was an old mate of Perry's, but then, so were most of the young fellows in the district. Besides, all of these sightings were singly, none together, even though they could well have been headed for some rendezvous.

Entirely circumstantial! Bob was a bit wild, but there was nothing mean or nasty in his make-up. The Merritons were a well-respected family; Joe was straight as a die, with an outspoken contempt for cattle duffers. Not the type to let his kids grow up with any illusions about clever, noble bushrangers, etcetera.

However, the policeman would have to check out what Bob was doing in the area. He'd need to be tactful in his enquiries at Mt. Chillingham. He couldn't appear to be accusing young Bob outright.

Nonetheless, he presented himself at the station homestead on a Wednesday afternoon. He put it to Bob that he'd been seen on the stock route on the Saturday, a fact which Bob readily confirmed, "Yes, that's right! I took a long ride and did a lot of thinking about my future. I've been getting a bit restless lately. Then I came home to keep an eye on the place Saturday night while Mum and Dad went into Wilga Creek for the evening."

"You spent Saturday night at home?" the policeman asked, "Can anyone corroborate that?"

"Only my cousin Tom! He dropped over for a while. Far as I know, Doug was in town; nobody else on the place."

"Notice anyone else along the stock route when you were out, Bob?"

"No, Jim, and only one car went down the road as I remember, Simpson's Chevy, I think," Bob recollected evenly.

"That checks out with what I know. Thanks, Bob. It was just a long shot that you might have seen something," the officer was satisfied. Bob and Tom had prearranged the alibi, but Bob hoped Jim wouldn't quiz Tom. Tom had always been hopeless as a liar, never could fib!

After the policeman had left, a concerned Joe asked his son, "You did return home Saturday night as you said, I hope, Bob?"

"Of course I did! A bit after sunset, Dad. I'd run across Tom along the road and he came back with me, stayed for tea and went home about tennish, I guess."

"Good!" Joe said, obviously relieved, "I'd hate to think you'd been up to some lame-brained caper then roped in poor Tom to lie about an alibi for you, son."

"I'm not as silly or as irresponsible as you seem to think, Dad," Bob lied with a touch of indignation, as he looked his father in the eye with practised ease.

"I'm glad, son, and I apologise," Joe said with sincerity.

52

Another week passed. Bob had given some more thought to his future directions, and had decided that in the short term, at least, it lay elsewhere; certainly, until the duffing investigation died a natural death, hopefully. Perhaps, like Tom, he could join the Navy for a while. However, he was keeping that option close to his chest. Instead, he informed his parents that he might try to find work in the Rockhampton area for a change. Midweek, he rolled a change of clothes and a few personal papers inside a two feet width tight roll of his swag wrap, strapped it to his saddle pommel; then dressed in his leather jacket, cesarine shirt, best moleskin trousers, newest hat and kangaroo skin Cuban heeled boots, he left Mt. Chillingham. He rode into Bradford first; later, arranged, he would go on to Wilga Creek, leave the mare at the old selection and catch the next day's train to Brisbane.

Police enquiries at Bradford, meanwhile, had reached a stalemate. Stock squad officers were "pursuing a certain line of investigation," or that was the public relations story. Factually, the case stood little chance of being solved, though the eight steers held as material evidence still resided at Her Majesty's pleasure, dining on Her Majesty's grass, in the Bradford police paddock. Another daring prank formulating in his mind was the real reason for Bob's detour via Bradford to Wilga Creek; to remove the evidence and return it to its rightful home! Riding into town from the northeast along the stock route, he noted a paddock gate, some two hundred yards behind the police station and residence. It wasn't padlocked! The stock route crossed the Warrego Highway near where the gravel ended and the short, town stretch of bitumen commenced.

Just across the highway, a couple of K wagons were unloading some sleek Hereford breeding cows into the railway siding stockyards. It was almost 4 pm! If they were to be held overnight before delivery, this could provide a bonus to his madcap scheme, Bob laughed inwardly with further inspiration.

He reined right rode the remaining quarter mile into Bradford, dismounted and gave her a nosebag of chaff and grain behind the pub. He'd come back and give her a drink from the trough in half an hour or so. Casually, he sauntered into the bar of the Commercial Hotel. It was a time of spreading unrest in the shearing industry; a massive industrial strike loomed on the horizon. Five or six shearers in the bar were starting on a bender and were loudly denouncing all scab labour.

Good! Thought Bob. They should keep the copper. Jim, busy at this end of town tonight! He settled in at the other end of the bar, catching up on town gossip from the barman and a couple of locals, but careful not to give away too much himself. He remembered to go out and water Bint, then a little after 5 pm, one of the Railway's lads dropped in for a couple of beers.

"G'day, Les. Got a couple of K wagons in, eh?" Bob inquired off-handedly.

"Yes, Bob. Sandy MacAlister bought some stud cows at Toowoomba. They've been fed, watered and settled down for the night; he'll pick 'em up in the morning. By jingo, they're nice types! Just as well that Perry's gone up to the Dawson, he might not have been able to resist them!" Les joked. Bob laughed and steered the conversation onto a different tack. Three-quarters of an hour later, the constable turned up on his rounds.

"Hullo, Bob! What brings you to town mid-week?" The question was sociably spoken, with no hint of suspicion or nosiness. Jim liked young. Bob and still felt some embarrassment at having had to query his movements the previous week. Bob had always seemed open and frank, and he was a top horseman. He certainly loved that flashy little bay; rode her everywhere but looked after her well. He'd see to his mount's comfort before his own, any time! Not like some of the young blokes who were interested in nothing but hooning around in bomb cars!

"G'day, Jim! I'm having a bit of a bludge; gave Dad my notice and quit. I've been a bit restless lately. Must be catching, eh? Don and Phil have gone farther out, my cousin Tom is joining the Navy and just a few minutes ago I heard Perry has gone north contract mustering."

"Yes. Told half the town I was persecuting him before he went," Jim's eyebrows narrowed in a frown. "Oh, well, he's some other poor copper's worry now, thank heaven."

Bob smiled. "This district should be a lot quieter without him," he conceded.

"Yair," Jim reflected." Anyway, where were you thinking of heading?"

"Dunno, really," Bob lied, "probably Rocky or Bowen. I might even shout myself a week or two at South Molle Island and break a few female hearts first."

The policeman grinned at Bob's cocksure remark. The lad was certainly capable of doing just that with his cheeky nonchalance that had served to charm many a local lass.

"But right now, "Bob continued, "I'll grab a bite in the dining room and head off for Wilga Creek before it gets very late. All the best, Jim! I won't see you again before I go north." He extended his hand, looking the Constable squarely in the eye.

Jim shook the proffered hand warmly, "You too. Bob. Good luck, wherever you end up."

At the end of the bitumen, Bob dismounted and took four home-made green hide over boots from his saddlebag and fitted and tied one to each of Bint's hooves. He remounted and reined her left, down the stock route in the darkness, swung open the gate of the Police paddock and rode through. He took very little time to locate the steers' camp and quietly walk them out onto the stock route. Three miles on, he opened Granville's front gate beside the grid, took them through, then cheekily, through a holding paddock beside the yards. Finally, he turned them loose in the adjoining well-timbered paddock, which now held the remainder of those steers returned earlier. He'd been very observant during his ride to Bradford that afternoon! Back on the road, he slipped the boots from the mare and returned them to the saddlebag. No point in wearing them out yet; they still had a little more work to do. When he arrived back at the highway, he re-fitted the boots on the mare and rode the short distance to the railway yards, almost opposite the police station. His heart nearly stopped as the police ute started up, headlights came on, and it raced out onto the road.

Bob breathed again when the ute swung right, its taillights growing smaller with distance as they traced its path to a rapid halt outside the hotel.

He mentally blessed those shearers, at the same time hoping Jim didn't get himself hurt. Not too bright, but a good bloke for a copper! Bob almost felt sorry for the embarrassment that Jim would suffer in a day or so!

He released eight of the stud cows from their pen in the railway yards, took them smartly but quietly along the stock route, and then through the gate into the paddock behind the police station. He rode back to the highway, took the boots off the mare for the last time, and rode eastward to Wilga Creek. Along the way, he threw the green hide slippers under a low, leafy roadside thicket.

He arrived at his grandmother's place around 10-30 pm, to a darkened house and the originally suspicious, then welcoming growl of a chained blue heeler, then a light came on. His grandmother, Aunt Jenny and Tom all appeared on the verandah in their dressing gowns. While Bob unsaddled and saw to the mare, Jenny lit the kerosene primus stove and put the kettle on.

Over a cup of tea, Bob announced his intention to join Tom on the Westlander the next day. He asked politely if he could leave Bint at Wilga Creek until his father could arrange to return her to Mt. Chillingham.

"I'll be happy to look after her," his Aunt promised, "she'll be good company for Tom's grey!"

53

Around 10 am the following morning, as Bob was pulling the shoes off his mare at Wilga Creek, Sandy MacAlister and his two sons arrived at Bradford rail siding to collect their stud cows.

MacAlister was a sheep and cattle breeder with a first-class property about ten miles south of the railway line. He counted his cows: only twenty-two head, not thirty as expected! Not by nature a patient man, he angrily stormed up to the Station Master's office and exploded, "Where are the other eight cows? You've lost half a K wagon load!"

"Eh?" the startled railwayman protested. "There were thirty when we unloaded them yesterday evening!"

"Well, there ain't thirty now! Bloody public servants! I'll bet they're mixed in with whatever came off the other five trucks you unloaded!" the grazier shouted belligerently.

"Uh, those! No, they came in empty. We're loading out a hundred head of Simpson's for Warwick this afternoon," the Station Master explained.

"Well, you'd better come over to the yard and show me where the missing eight are hiding!" MacAlister said sarcastically.

Nearly an hour of verbal abuse, argument and recrimination passed before one of the MacAlister boys drew his excitable father's attention to cow tracks accompanied by what appeared to be muffled hoof prints, leading out and onto the roadway.

The grazier sent the other lad to fetch the policeman, while the rest of them followed the trampled grass and occasional hoof print along the stock route, past the police paddock, Jim soon joined them, very worried. More stolen cattle! Stud cows this time and right out from under his nose! Well, just across the road from the police station, anyway! He looked across the paddock; at least, Granville's young bullocks were camped securely in the shade of the box trees. Jim and the MacAlisters followed those tracks along the route until they were almost at Granville's property; then the tracks were covered up by Simpson's mob enroute to the rail. No, Simpson and his lads hadn't passed any stock on the track that morning.

Hungrily, almost accusingly, MacAlister's eyes swept over Simpson's mob, looking for any cows of obvious quality.

Simpson noticed; his temper flared, "Do you think I stole your bloody cows, you toffee-nosed piss-wit?" he snarled at MacAlister.

"Hold your horses! Nobody's accusing you!" Jim intervened.

Surly, unsatisfied, MacAlister returned with Jim to the Police station and formally lodged a statement describing the stolen cattle and their brands. Something else bothered his subconscious but he couldn't put his finger on it! He and his sons left to take the rest of their cows home. Jim telephoned his inspector to report this latest theft, then belatedly put a chain and padlock on the paddock gate. If the duffers were bold enough to steal from the rail siding across the road, he was lucky they'd left Granville's steers in the police paddock. Not that a chain and padlock were much of a deterrent anyway; it was enough to cut the wires! He'd better get some hay from the agent and move those steers into the little police stockyard if he got enough time later in the day, but he didn't; not that afternoon, nor any other!

Aboard the Westlander that evening, Bob told his cousin of his doings the previous night.

At first, Tom was incredulous, then he realised that Bob wasn't kidding. "You're a bloody nut case! What are you? You ought to be locked up for your own good!" He responded.

"Nah! I had a bit of a yarn to Jim, the cop at Bradford, yesterday. There's no way in the world that he suspects us. Anyhow, what have they got to go on?" Bob asked.

"Probably your fingerprints all over the paddock gate," Tom said morbidly.

"Fair go! I'm not bloody stupid! I wore gloves," Bob protested.

"I'm amazed," Tom remarked sarcastically.

Bob ignored the sarcasm. "Poor old Jim must have looked pretty stupid when he found he had those cows of MacAlister's impounded instead," he said.

"Maybe I wouldn't get too cocky yet, mate," Tom was pessimistic.

"Yair, you could be right! I've been thinking, I might join the Navy myself. I've got my birth certificate and references in my swag wrap. Still, it might be an idea to join up over the border, eh? In Sydney? If anyone cross-checked, there wouldn't be enough to bring us back from interstate. It'll all die down in a couple of months, anyway."

"If you join the Navy, you realise it will be for at least six years?" Tom said. "You can't just change your mind the next week, you know!"

The more they discussed it, the more sensible it appeared to be to enlist in Sydney. The train rolled on through the night.

MacAlister hadn't slept a wink all night. There was something that just didn't add up! What was it? Tired and worried, it escaped him. Around 5 am, he was almost asleep when suddenly, the connection registered in his brain. He got out of bed, now wide-awake, dressed, and then drove to Bradford. The sun was rising when he arrived, pounding impatiently on the door of the police residence.

None too happy, Jim answered the door testily, "What's the matter now?"

"Those cattle of Granville's in your paddock! Weren't they supposed to be steers?" MacAlister asked the sleepy policeman.

"Yes, they're steers," Jim said crossly.

"Well, I think you'll find they've grown teats!" the grazier crowed triumphantly.

"What!" Jim roared incredulously.

The train pulled into Roma Street Station, Brisbane. Bob and Tom walked across the Grey Street bridge in the early morning light, booked on the Sydney Express and left their baggage in the South Brisbane Interstate Cloakroom for the next few hours. Then they found a cafe and had a good hot breakfast; bacon, eggs, toast and strong black tea.

Eight days later, after sampling the delights of Sydney, the two bushmen boarded yet another train and were headed southwest to Melbourne and Flinders Naval Depot, Cribb Point, Victoria.

54

Three and a half years later, at sea with a Carrier Air Group of the Royal Australian Navy, Radio Electrical Mechanic 1st Class (Air) Robert Lawrence Merriton reflected on the odd choices he had made since impetuously joining the Navy along with Tom.

His cousin, too, had become a Fleet Air Arm rating, but as an aircraft engines fitter. Bob had frequently regretted not having chosen engines or airframes as his specialisation; he'd found radio and radar theory dull, abstract and boring. He supposed he'd only chosen it because his elder brother, Mike, had started his career in radio and to Bob, with the limited technical interest of a cattleman, it had seemed like a good idea at the time. At least, he was at sea on draft to a squadron. Bob liked aeroplanes; he enjoyed working on them, somehow identifying with their sleek, clean metallic beauty in a similar though less animated admiration that he might have for a well-bred horse, dog or bull. On the other hand, he'd found the various radio workshops exceedingly dull and lacking inspiration. In that respect, he was the complete anti-thesis of a dedicated radio technician and was very thankful that his draft to the ship was with a squadron, rather than to Air Radio Workshops.

Tom was at sea the previous year with HMAS Melbourne's Air Group and had visited Hawaii and Fiji in addition to the annual South East Asian ports of call. By all accounts, it was a good trip. Tom was ashore once again, at the Nowra Naval Air Station, HMAS Albatross.

Bob was content with this draft, though; New Zealand before Christmas, then the Air Group would disembark off Jervis Bay, go on leave from Albatross, working up there afterward before re-embarkation early in the New Year. Then would come the yearly commitment to the Far East Strategic Reserve area, highlighted so the "buzz" had it, by leave in both Manila and Yokohama.

The New Zealand goodwill visit was very entertaining; the ship had even sailed into Milford Sound for a morning. This magnificent spectacle was a new experience for Bob. A few days later came leave in Wellington, sufficient to both visit his mother's family and still have time to romance a pretty girl he met at a dance. Later, Auckland too was equally enjoyable. Even some of the New Zealand beers weren't bad provided they were served cold enough! Not, of course, that he would admit that fact to a Kiwi!

However, flight deck duties during night flying exercises, particularly when both fighters and anti-submarine aircraft were launched in the same programme from the crowded deck, would long remain his most vivid impression of his introduction to Carrier operations.

Aircraft maintenance personnel, such as he was, were required to attend each launch, to deal with any last-minute equipment malfunctions. With land-based flying, that was always straightforward but in the crowded confines of a small flight deck with Sea Venoms firing up along the starboard side abaft the "Island" superstructure, and the Gannets with their big contra-rotating airscrews down the port side; the only lighting being aircraft navigation and downward deflecting spotlights on a darkened flight deck above an even blacker sea forty feet below, it was bedlam!

For deck crew, it was hairy enough until one got used to it; Bob surmised that it must really have the aircrew adrenalin pumping for their first few times and probably never completely abated irrespective of experience! To follow up with having to land on again an hour or so later onto a pitching, darkened deck with no assistance other than the coloured lights of the Mirror landing device, must have all the excitement of a night rush through the mulga!

Meanwhile, ashore at Nowra, Tom had no regrets concerning his chosen career, and was rapidly gaining a high degree of proficiency in his chosen trade. As well as a good wage, three nights and three weekends of leave out of every four, he had a very nice fiancée in the nearby town. It beat the daylights out of station life as far as he was concerned!

For a brief year or two, Bob also had nurtured career ambitions. Having finished school at fourteen, he'd availed himself of the Naval Education Branch facilities whilst still an O.D., or Second Class rating, at Flinders Naval Depot on his specialist qualifying course. In fact, he'd shown considerably more interest in those voluntary studies than he had in his radio theory course. He'd quickly achieved his Higher Education Test Certificate and had applied for aircrew training on three occasions. On the initial application, his then Divisional Officer, having noted Bob's singular lack of enthusiasm for his radio theory studies, had declined to recommend him.

A later D.O. had advised him to "pull your socks up and try again in the future" not long after Bob had narrowly avoided landing in trouble with a stupid, drunken escapade.

The final effort, with Bob's D.O. once again the officer who had rejected his first application, again met with a similar fate as a result of yet another of Bob's escapades which had backfired; the Lieutenant did not think Bob had the stability to be entrusted with Commissioned Rank. However, three weeks later, that same officer had sought to make partial amends by recommending R.E.M.1 (A) R.L. Merriton for a Leading Ratings' course, the first step towards Non-Commissioned Rank. With his usual intransigence, Bob again burned his bridges with a blunt, insubordinate dismissal of that proposal, in terminology that would have convinced the Electrical Officer beyond any lingering doubt that Bob Merriton was not cut out to become an Officer and a Gentleman!

55

Early February, the Air Group re-embarked and commenced flying exercises around the southern coast of Australia. There were port visits to Melbourne, Adelaide and Hobart before the ship headed north to her annual commitments of participation in joint exercises with other navies of the SEATO Pact countries. Merely a light fleet carrier of the British "Majestic" or more properly, "Modified Colossus" class; laid down in 1943, launched in 1945 and finally completed, modified and modernised in 1955, her original design specification had been for escort duties in the North Atlantic and Arctic oceans, operating smaller, piston-engined aircraft for convoy protection.

Her limitations in size, speed, range and her inadequate ventilation meant that she was not suited to the task of operating jet fighters in a tropical environment despite her new, state-of-the-art features; mirror landing aid, semi-angled flight deck and steam catapult (albeit a small 103 ft. one, the largest physically possible given her restricted size.)

Her fighter complement of De Haviland FAW 53 aircraft was the sole type in Australia's inventory, Naval or RAAF, which possessed true night, or all-weather capability. Of obsolescent engine and airframe design, their adequate service ceiling and excellent AI 17 on-board air interception radar nevertheless rendered them highly potent in their designated roles, provided they could be launched. Therein lay the "rub." The critical proviso, especially in often mirror flat stillness of equatorial seas was that operating from such a ship, these fighters required a minimum of 32 knots of wind down the flight deck to allow the short catapult to launch them at flyable airspeed. Even at the ship's maximum speed of 24 knots, this meant that unless she could find and steam into a minimum eight-knot breeze, the fighters could not launch.

Thus, they would be unable to provide air cover for either the fleet or the slower Gannet anti-submarine aircraft, which could still operate in these same calm, windless conditions.

A further cause of frustration to Air Group was that unlike the big American carriers with their side-mounted lifts and more open hangar design permitting a freer air circulation through their hangar decks, the British light fleet carriers had fully enclosed hangars beneath a steel flight deck, and had their two lifts positioned fore and aft along the centre line. Hence, maintaining aircraft in humid temperatures around 140 degrees Fahrenheit was a normal work environment in tropical waters. The poorly ventilated mess decks fared little better. Sailors were particularly scornful of those journalists who were prone to visit the ship in temperate climes then write with almost expected inaccuracy in their Sydney and Melbourne newspapers that the flagship was fully air-conditioned throughout!

With that morning's sorties being all that the Venoms had been able to fly for the past three days due to still-air conditions, and with night flying once more scheduled for the coming evening, Bob recalled his introduction to these aircraft at Nowra two years earlier.

"And this," the Line Radio Chief Petty Officer had announced to four newly qualified radio mechanics on draft from Flinders Naval Depot, "is a Sea Venom Mark FAW 53."

"What does the FAW stand for, Chief?" Trev had asked innocently unaware of the designation; Fighter, All-Weather.

"F---All Wind, son!" the Chief had responded with a wry smile. All since had come to learn just how appropriate the sobriquet could be!

Now, in the late afternoon, Bob sat in the right-hand seat of a Venom, closing down the radar after a satisfactory test run. As he switched off, a young air electrical mechanic looked into the cockpit.

"You finished now, Bob?"

"Yair, Jim. She's right as rain now!"

"Good! I'll do my N.F.C. now." Jim said.

Bob swung down from the cockpit and Jim was stepping from atop the ladder into the left hand, or pilot's seat, to commence his Night Flying Conditional inspection when the shrill whistle of the Bosun's call came over the ship's Tannoy system. They listened to the announcement that followed, "D'you hear there? Night flying for tonight has been cancelled!"

"Beauty!" remarked Jim, "with a bit of luck, we might score a beer issue tonight in that case!"

His words were scarcely out when the Bosun's Call cut the air once more, followed by, "Belay the last pipe! Night Flying will commence at 19.00 hours."

"I wish they'd make up their bloody minds!" Bob said. The metropolitan forecasters must have gleaned some new data, though personally, Bob was inclined to doubt that sufficient breeze would eventuate.

Disgustedly, Jim whistled in shrill imitation of the pipe. "Do you hear there? There will be no moon tonight! There will be two moons tomorrow night'" An instant later, he mimicked the Bosun's Call a second time and then announced. "Belay the last pipe! Up moon! Duty crane driver, close up!"

Bob laughed at the cynical burst of humour.

"Well, the bastards seem to think they're God!" Jim commented drily.

56

Novelty begets fascination in meeting a very different culture for the first time. Even so, the journey through beautiful Lombok Strait then westward along the northern coasts of Bali and Java and north west across the Java Sea to the arrival of Singapore, the morning degaussing exercise offshore, and passage along the narrow Johore Strait to the huge British Naval Base on the island's north shore scarcely prepared Bob's senses for the exotic sights, sounds and aromas of the tiny former colony.

Founded by Sir Thomas Stamford Raffles in 1819 on an island merely 25 miles long and 14 miles wide, it was less than three-quarters the size of Mount Chillingham station yet the diversity within was stunning! Between the naval base and airfields along its north shore and the bustling city on the south coast, the road wound through villages, rubber plantations and rice paddy fields to a city of the 1960 era, which yet bore all the hallmarks of an outpost of the British Raj.

There were exotic bazaars, street stalls, fine Victorian colonial-era stone government offices, well-tended parks, a crowded canal or creek where families still lived aboard sampans; there were crammed and decaying two-storied terrace houses facing a waterfront roadway. All of these co-existed within easy walking distance of the new, modern British NAAFI Club and the majestic old Raffles Hotel. So different to the sprawling, gradually delineated sections of any large Australian city, Singapore with its tri-shaws, Asian music and spicy odours from Oriental cooking, was a fitting introduction to the legendary mysterious East!

Late one evening, as the big "Happy World" fairground wound down its activities for the night, Bob, Jim and another mate, Jake, lingered over their Tiger beers in conversation with three bar hostesses at one of the many little open-air bars in the grounds.

Jim was twenty; Jake was in his late twenties, recently married. Both were steady, decent, thoughtful blokes. All three of the women were around forty years of age yet youthful-looking, with smooth skin and unlined faces. Bar hostesses worked on a commission basis from the bar proprietor, paid to chat up customers and encourage them to buy as many rounds of drinks for both themselves and the bar girls as was feasible. Of course, in the interests of sobriety, the bar girls' drinks usually consisted of cold tea or coloured water in a wine or spirit glass, at spirits' prices. It was a normal practice of which most customers were aware, but as a higher proportion of what they spent, therefore, resulted in higher net bar profits, the bar hostesses also reaped a better commission.

These three ladies also made clear the fact that they would be prepared to supplement those incomes later with other services, should the sailors so desire.

Neither Jim nor Jake had the inclination to sample these other services, yet all three ratings had continued to buy more rounds and enjoy a conversation which was taking on a depth of fellowship and human interest that Bob, of his own accord, would not have sought, yet found quite touching.

Bob and Jake were surprised at the depth of wisdom their young friend displayed, as Jim, ever interested and concerned with the cares of the average battler, drew out these intelligent Chinese women to talk freely of their own hopes, lives and families to a lad half their average age; eagerly, as though to a sympathetic father.

All three women had suffered starvation, hardships and beatings during the Japanese occupation, all had seen the white colonial masters return as liberators and now, in the transition, with Malaya, to independence, each hoped for a better life and an education for her children. Each seemed to welcome the opportunity to bare her soul. The conversation entered a surprisingly theological bent, as one spoke feelingly of her deeply held faith and trust in God. Although whether or not she was referring to our same Christian God was not completely clear to Bob, her unswerving belief in an Almighty Being was abundantly evident!

Quite possibly, none of these women had ever previously confided so completely in any other person of European race: quite probably, no previous white person had ever shown them such fellowship and genuine human consideration as Jim had. Bob felt unaccustomedly humble.

57

At sea once more, this time with units of other SEATO Powers, for operations in the South China Sea and off North Borneo, they were reminded that navy life was not meant to be a pleasure cruise. Then came five days of leave in Manila, the chance for sightseeing by day and womanising or boozing up on the good San Miguel beer or the rough Manila Rum by night. After working tropical routine in harbor, 06.00 to noon, the city's 01.00 curfew then in force presented few worries as few had either the sobriety or staying power to be inclined to party-on beyond that.

Bob took an instant liking to the friendly Filipino people. It was a hard life for most of them in a country where official corruption was a way of life for centuries; where forty-six years as a U.S. Dependency from 1900 until 1946 had left the predominantly Roman Catholic population with an abundance of college degrees, high ideals, a high rate of literacy, but sadly, an even higher unemployment rate and a virtually non-existent Welfare system; where fierce and bloody resistance to the wartime Japanese occupation had left the legacy of a surfeit of handguns and other offensive hardware.

Tourists, American bases and a constant stream of port visits by foreign warships provided a large percentage of the national income. Though Filipinos were generally, gentle, optimistic people, Manila was still a city where Marxist Huk terrorists sometimes made incursions into the outer suburbs. The carrying of personal small arms, therefore, far exceeded even the liberality of United States practice, and virtually every Manila bar, club or dance hall displayed a prominent notice directing patrons to "please deposit all guns, knives, knuckle-dusters and other lethal weapons at the Cloak Room. Same will be returned to you on departure."

Bob had received a letter at sea between Jesselton and Manila. It was from Julie, a Sydney stenographer of whom he had become fonder than he cared to admit. Long unsure of her own feelings towards Bob, Julie had liked him a lot but had wondered if he was a little too wild, unreliable and prone to getting drunk. Now she had written to break off their association, informing him that she had become engaged to someone else.

As a result, Bob had hit Manila with a mission; live it up, to hell with Julie! He'd enjoy himself! Over the five nights of liberty that visit, Bob found himself on duty watch for only one of them, and that was on the shore patrol roster. Normally, he disliked shore patrol duty, but this one proved to be different. It was a multi-national patrol, under the charge of a Royal Navy Chief Petty Officer, with a mix of RN, USN, RNZN and RAN ratings. The truck dropped them off in twos and threes at various little bars in their designated sector. Bob, along with an American, was delegated to keep an eye on a friendly little bar with a Spanish name. An easy-going Australian Petty Officer and a Kiwi Leading Seaman were allocated for general supervision over several such small establishments in the area.

All four of them entered the bar room, looked it over and made their introductions to the proprietor/barman, who welcomed their presence. The two senior ratings left after advising Bob, Paul the American, and the barman that they would be a hundred yards or so up the road should anything get out of hand.

The bar wasn't very busy, probably twenty-five to thirty patrons and half a dozen hostesses trying to solicit business.

"Looks like a quiet night, eh?" Bob remarked.

"Might get busy later" the Filipino barman said hopefully, then asked, "What would you like to drink?"

"Whisky, on the rocks, thanks! What are you having, Paul?"

The American was a little shocked and very conscientious, "No alcohol for me, Buddy! Hell, we're on dooty!" he said.

"Suit yourself," Bob told him, "but I'm having a whisky. That doesn't mean that I'm planning to get drunk."

Paul decided he would have something non-alcoholic. After all, it was a hot night. Bob offered to pay, but the barman brushed it aside. "It's on the house! Glad to have you guys here, in case of trouble!"

Paul cautiously sipped on something that looked like a soda squash. "You know," he confided, "I would have asked for a glass of water, but they say you can't always trust the water in these foreign places."

"Yair. That is my excuse for not drinking water anywhere! It's only meant for washing in," Bob quipped facetiously.

The conversation soon drifted from suspect water to other foreign ports. Paul turned out to be an interesting fellow. He planned to join his brother in Europe when he left the Navy. Paul's brother, who was some years his senior, was currently in Italy, driving sports-racing cars professionally. Paul nursed an ambition to do likewise. He appeared to have some knowledge of the major European circuits, having previously visited Italy, France and Germany and was particularly enthusiastic about Italian women.

"That surprises me," Bob admitted, "the few I've met have been mostly sulky, overweight and usually heavily chaperoned!"

"Hell, no!" Paul protested, "Around the race car circuits and the resorts, there are hundreds of them in the Lollobrigida category. Man, some of those babes are living dolls!"

The barman generously kept the drinks coming. Bob decided he'd better make a conscious effort to slow down and stay sober. The premises had received a few more customers, some of his mates among them, but all were well behaved so far.

One of the hostesses, taller than the others, had attracted Bob's attention several times. In her white, low-cut dress suggestively slit Cheong Sam style all the way to the top of her thigh; she was doing a brisk trade, taking customers for "short time" romps in a back room. She caught Bob looking at her, and smiled sensually at him. He returned her smile. She came over to where he sat on a barstool.

"I think I like you," she said, impudently perching herself on his lap. She took his hand and immediately placed it beneath the slitted dress.

She wore no panties" Bloody Hell! She didn't waste time in coming to the point! And she was a real good looker!

"Want to come with me?" she asked huskily.

Bob's throat went dry. "Love to," he said, "but I can't, I'm on duty!"

"That hasn't stopped you from drinking." She teased, "why should it spoil our fun?"

"Because I can sit here having a quiet drink and still keep an eye out for trouble. I can't do that if I'm in the cot with you'"

He heard his American colleague breathe an audible sigh of relief. The bar girl pouted prettily in mock indignation, slid off his lap and flounced away with exaggerated hip movements.

It was much later in the evening, about an hour before the bar was due to close, that the only incident, a minor one, took place. Two young English seamen began punching each other across their table. Bob and Paul moved swiftly to restrain them. The other two RN ratings at the table appeared singularly unconcerned by the fracas. It transpired that the combatants were from two different ships, but otherwise looked almost identical in appearance.

"They're brothers," one of the other matelots explained to Bob, "and every time they get together ashore, they finish up in an argument!"

"Right! Well, you can't settle your family quarrels here. Now, behave or piss off!" Bob told the brothers bluntly.

"Ah, I'm sick of the idiot!" the more belligerent one said. "I'm leaving, anyhow!" He walked out onto the street. The other brother followed, attempting a reconciliation.

"Sympathetically, Bob restrained him, not wanting the brawl to resume in the street. The first lad stormed angrily away.

"Forget it, mate! It's past the talking stage. No point in belting each other! It won't seem so important in the morning," Bob consoled the second lad.

"You know," the young RN rating observed, "You're a very decent chap for an Australian! I've only ever met another three Australians, and each one beat me *up!* Everybody seems to want to beat me up, even my own brother," he continued morosely, "but you're a very decent chap! Are you quite sure you really are an Australian? Not English originally, perhaps?"

No wonder this bloke copped a few hidings! He certainly wasn't born to be a diplomat, even though he was obviously a little drunk but trying hard to be friendly.

"No, I'm an Australian from way back," Bob assured him patiently.

The two other RNers joined them. "Come on, Peter. We're going back to the ship. Thanks, Aussie!" one said.

"You go on ahead; I'm talking to my friend," Peter announced, assuming an amusingly inebriated attempt at dignified independence.

"I reckon you ought to leave with your mates, otherwise I just might be tempted to live up to your expectations of an Australian. Good night, mate!" Bob said good-humouredly.

Peter blinked owlishly, pondered the advice, then started to protest but his friends led him away, still insisting that he couldn't understand why people always wanted to fight him.

In the mess deck next morning, Jake asked, "How was shore patrol in Manila?"

Bob thought for a moment, then replied, "I guess it was pretty much like an ordinary run ashore, Jake, except they wouldn't let me pay for my grog!"

58

Back to sea and more exercising with the USN and RN. Off watch in the late afternoon. Bob viewed flying operations from a high vantage point; the small platform deck atop the island and abaft the funnel. On a parallel course some two to three miles off the p beam, a big American carrier was launching aircraft simultaneously with the Australian ship. Bob was aware that she had two forward catapults against the single one of the Australian carrier. Interested in her performance, Bob timed her launching intervals. There was a light chop on the water but no swell, therefore planes could be launched as fast as deck crews could handle them and the Yankee was getting them away at a rate of one every forty seconds, averaged over five launches. Quickly, he switched his attention to his own ship, whose deck was clearing rapidly with four only remaining to launch. The Australian catapult crew was launching at a constant interval of only thirty-four seconds. It was a matter of pride, yet not surprising. Probably most of the USN deck crew were draftees, conscripted to man their huge navy, given rapid but narrower, more specialised training to be utilised quickly, then were considered "veterans" after two years' service and looking forward to resuming their civilian occupations soon. It was likely that the American catapult crews may have averaged less than eighteen months service, whereas most of the RAN aircraft handlers had anywhere from four to twelve years of experience, much of it at sea.

Royal Navy crews, on the other hand, would be in a much better position to really test the Aussies. Even so, it always brought the Australians a degree of smug comfort to measurably out-perform the Yanks!

Even more so than Singapore had, Hong Kong, Pearl of the Orient, lived up to and beyond Bob's expectations. Uniquely and vibrantly, it epitomised the stereotyped Hollywood concept of old, traditional China, yet was saturated with a modern mixture of westernised metropolitan characteristics that was so integrated into and absorbed by the Oriental lifestyle as to display no hint of incongruity.

The beautiful island of Victoria, dominated by a central peak; the harbour; the numerous small islands which dotted the approaching sea lanes; all contributed a harmonious, timeless, natural beauty to the colony, against which neither the hillside shacks nor the bustling commercial centres flanking the shores of Victoria Island and the Kowloon Peninsula on the mainland opposite, detracted to anywhere like the extent which might have been expected from a metropolis of three and a half million people.

It was plain, from the tens of thousands of Sampan dwellers and wide proliferation of traditionally primitive but seaworthy junks to the scores of modern Merchantmen and Naval vessels, that this was one of the world's foremost Maritime cities. Her trade and the sea were synonymous; her arteries, her lifeblood. Apart from the British Army and RAF garrison and a small percentage of British and European business, airport, Police and diplomatic personnel and their families, the lucrative retailing and hospitality industries relied to a large extent upon visiting Mercantile and Naval ships and crews for their profits.

Prices of most Japanese manufactured goods in this duty-free port average around one quarter to one-third of the then-current retail prices in Australia. European items were only marginally more expensive. Made-to-measure suits and shoes of excellent quality were similarly competitive in price as were the wares of the liquor and other entertainment industries.

Hong Kong had yet to become an international tourist Mecca. Americans in particular, were very thin on the ground, possibly dissuaded by their government's requirement that a Certificate of Origin, to verify that such goods were not products of the communist Peoples' Republic of China, accompany all U.S. purchases of Hong Kong merchandise. Without such verification, doubtful items would not be allowed into the United States of America. Since Hong Kong served as China's main commercial link to the western world, there was little of Oriental origin that could be shown convincingly, not to have originated either wholly or partly in Red China.

The American presence in the Colony, therefore, was limited mainly to a small Diplomatic and Press enclave and to the crew of whichever USN destroyer was rostered as "Station Ship" on secondment from the Seventh Fleet to wait in readiness in the harbour to evacuate all American citizens should the dreaded Chinese Communists invade from across the border with Kowloon and the New Territories.

British policy to deal with any such eventuality was one of stoicism and sacrifice. At best, the British garrisons could hope to delay such an advance by no more than three days, time to evacuate British civilians and some business assets. However, reality dictated that there would be no logic to any such communist attack, as this would cut off China's principal commercial link with the West. Obviously, much depended on British diplomacy and cool-headedness.

For a first-time visitor, Hong Kong was a sightseer's delight, shopper's paradise and a feast of nightlife and entertainment, all rolled into one compact package. As in Singapore, the simple purchase of a watch, camera or transistor radio became an exercise in bargain foreign to the easy-going Australian character. Usually, it began with firstly deciding what may be a reasonable local price, asking the price of the vendor in a sort of simple Pidgin English then making an offer absurdly lower than that which the intending buyer assumed to be a fair price.

An average storefront might have approximated the size of a double garage fronting the footpath and crammed with cartons of radios, cameras and other appliances. A trader eager for business might have accosted a likely potential customer passing by, by waving an item before him and inviting its purchase. Persistent and needing to close a sale, the vendor was rarely easy to ignore. Should the possible customer indicate an interest in some item among the merchandise, there could follow a friendly debate in which both parties might trade light-hearted insults, each stressing his own reasonableness contrasted with the other party's supposed greed. A typical Cantonese-speaking trader, while not fluent in any other language, could well be capable of driving a hard bargain in English, French, Portuguese or one of a variety of other tongues; a quite remarkable, street-wise versatility.

In English, the usual form of address was "John" or "Joe" if the client was clearly American. A trader seemed always to appreciate matching wits with a good haggler: but should a client accede too readily and pay something like the asking price, the vendor usually completed the transaction sullenly; whether this was due to feeling cheated of stimulating exchange of repartee, or merely self-annoyance at not having asked a higher initial price was not clear. On the other hand, to beat the trader down in price to accept the lowest profit margin would be met invariably with good humour and the invitation, "You come back again, John!"

Bob, seeking to buy a particular make of high quality eight transistor Japanese portable radio receiver for his parents, found one in a little Kowloon warehouse.

"How much you speak this one, John?" Bob inquired, knowing full well that the item in question would cost at least 36 pounds from a Sydney retailer. Therefore, he estimated that the Hong Kong price should be around ten or eleven Pounds equivalent, say HK$140, give or take a few dollars.

"Very cheap! I give you special price. Only 180 dollar!" the Chinese responded.

"Cheap, my foot! You're a robber, John! I give you 90!" Bob told him.

"I not robber, John!" the vendor pretended indignation, "You robber! Australia boy all same, all Ned Kelly. You know how much you pay in Australia?"

"Yair, I know! Australian Customs are the real Ned Kelly with their Import Duties, but we're not in Australia now, and this is duty-free. I'll give you $95," Bob foxed.

"You very hard man, John! I give you very special price, only $17 dollar, if you promise you not tell!" the shopkeeper tried another tack.

"Come off it, John! I didn't come off the Christmas Tree! I'll give you 100," Bob countered.

The vendor shook his head, "I not sell for 100, I lose money! But I give you very, very special price. 160, okay?"

"Tell you what, I'll make it 110!" Bob felt mean spirited and tight-fisted, continuing the expected charade.

"My last price, 150 dollar!" the merchant bluffed.

Bob merely shook his head and, feigning loss of interest, turned as though to leave.

"Okay, Okay! How much you speak, last word?"

"$130," Bob said flatly.

They finally agreed at $140, equivalent to around ten pounds ten shillings in Australian currency. The retailer insisted he was making no profit on the deal, but his good-humoured smile said otherwise.

"You come back, now; you bring friends, John!" the Chinese said.

Bob nodded. He too, was smiling. Both were happy with their deal.

59

All in all, there were many memorable aspects of shore leave in the Colony. Bob, with a busload of shipmates, participated in a tour of the New Territories, the small, rural slice of the Colony adjoining the Kowloon peninsula. Here were quiet roads and examples of traditional, rustic Chinese architecture. From one vantage point alongside a British Police outpost, the tourists looked across paddy fields and No Man's Land to the Red Chinese border post, a mere few hundred yards distant across a narrow causeway. Beyond lay the mysterious, feared and misunderstood China of the Cold War period; sinister, brooding and dangerous, in Western eyes, ever since the Korean conflict. Far away, a city lay sprawling over a plain flanked by more mountains, yet the interlying countryside of this, the world's most populous land, seemed almost as empty and rural as inland Australia.

Because of deliberate jamming of English language radio transmissions by the Communist Chinese, the English-speaking community relied on newspapers, landline-based communications for their news in the Colony, therefore, English language, and music was virtually unheard of on the normal radio broadcast frequencies.

Bob, in company with three shipmates, was walking on the footpath in Nathan Road, Kowloon, when a trader trying to drum up business and brandishing a transistor radio, waylaid them outside his premises.

None of the four friends was interested, all having already made any such investments previously. Three waved him politely aside, but Jim pretended some interest in the six transistor portable.

"Alright, let's hear it play, John," he said.

The merchant enthusiastically switched on the receiver. Loud Oriental music blared forth.

"Good sound, okay?" he asked.

Jim nodded in agreement. "Let's try another one, John," he suggested.

The Chinese happily turned the dial. More Oriental music blared forth. "Okay?"

Jim nodded sagely. "Okay. Let's try again."

This time, a male voice spoke in Cantonese or Mandarin. The sailors couldn't tell the difference.

With a poker face, Jim requested to hear yet another station, while his mates watched attentively. Jim's dry sense of humour was obviously at work.

Dutifully, the shopkeeper, in growing exasperation, exhausted the dial's range of frequencies.

"You like? Very nice?" he asked.

"Oh yes, it's a very nice radio," Jim conceded, "but it's no use to me!"

"Why for, John? I give you very cheap! Special price," the trader said, "only 150 dollar!"

"That sounds very fair," Jim said agreeably, "but it's no use to me at any price!"

"But, you like! You say fair price! Why you not buy?" the Chinese was puzzled.

"Because," Jim managed to retain a straight face as he earnestly explained, "it doesn't speak English! You've been right through the dial, and it only speaks Chinese' I don't understand Chinese, only English."

The shopkeeper raised both arms and rolled his eyes in a gesture of total exasperation, and then with a pleading manner, he looked in turn at the others. Two were doubled up with laughter at the trader's clear dismay. Bob managed to restrain himself long enough to look sympathetically at the fellow, to shrug his shoulders and shake his head to indicate that it would be a waste of time to try to convince Jim otherwise.

The following day, a sudden typhoon warning was issued. Ships flew the Blue Peter from their yardarms and made haste to recall men from shore leave as they prepared to put to sea. It is naval practice to ride out such huge storms at sea in preference to being caught in harbour and risk being sunk or washed aground in confined and crowded waters. Even so, the carrier put to sea with little more than half of her usual complement. Men caught ashore found shelter in the China Fleet Club or in less reputable hostelries.

Many miles offshore that night, in mountainous seas, Bob reported to his duty watch post as Flight Deck Sentry a little before his allotted time of 23:59. He came from below through the sheltered gallery deck beneath the island superstructure and found the rating he was to relieve very pleased to see him. They looked out through the hatchway into the wild, wet blackness of the flight deck.

"All secure? Nothing working loose?" Bob asked.

"I don't know! I last checked it with the Duty P.O. a couple of hours ago, but I wasn't going out again on my own," came the frank admission.

Bob nodded understandingly. From the ship's bridge above, it would be difficult to keep constant track of a man moving amongst the aircraft lashed to the deck in this torrential rain, howling gale and wild seas. A man swept overboard would be lost for sure!

"Let's check it together before you turn in," Bob suggested.

They adjusted their foul weather gear, fastened the hoods tightly about their faces to keep the rain out and ventured onto the deck with their flashlights. Most of the aircraft, all that would fit, were stabled below in the security of the hangar, but seven or so were lashed down to rings in the flight deck. Canopies and air intakes were covered or sealed up with protective blanking plugs. A temporary, or jury-rigged, rope hand-line at waist height wended its way around the aircraft; a sentry's sole protection against being swept overboard. Bob and his colleague checked the lashings securing the planes; only two needed minor adjustment. They were stoutly secured and no significant movement had taken place. Should one aircraft work adrift and bump against its fellows, all could well be lost or damaged as a result of the violent pitching and yawing of the ship on such a night. Even the safety of the ship herself could well be compromised.

Satisfied, they returned to the sanctuary of the island. The other rating retired below and Bob stood by the hatchway alone, peering out into the dark.

An hour later, the wind had dropped somewhat. Bob physically checked the deck again. Around 02.00, the Air Department Duty Petty Officer paid a brief visit. He and Bob checked the deck once more. The worst of the storm had passed but the sea was still very rough. Finally, the rain ended.

The first glimmer of dawn a little before the completion of Bob's watch at 04.00 provided a stirring spectacle. Standing in the centre of the flight deck looking aft, Bob noted three smaller warships keeping station on the flagship in an almost perfect line astern amidst these huge seas.

The first, a little Royal Navy "C" class destroyer, disappeared momentarily from view in the trough between two crests. Astern of her, a larger Australian "Daring" class rode high on a swell whilst still further astern, an Australian fast anti-submarine frigate held her station.

Suddenly, the RN destroyer reappeared, crashing through a wall of water, with spray flying high into the air and the sea cascading from her deck coamings. She shuddered visually from the effort, like a small dog shaking the water from itself before plunging back into the surf.

Now the Australian destroyer disappeared from view, into the trough, while the frigate in the rear rode high on yet another crest. Lost in admiration of the spectacle, Bob reflected that all that was missing was a Navy band on deck to play "Hearts of Oak!"

60

After the storm, they returned to Hong Kong to embark crewmen who were unable to join the ship in time for the sudden departure precipitated by the typhoon. Further mail from home also awaited them, amongst which was a letter addressed to Bob, with a Sydney postmark. It was from Jan, a girl he had met in Adelaide. When first he'd made her acquaintance, she had confided a yearning to move to Australia's oldest and largest city but was hesitant to do so because of stories she'd heard about the crime rate and the highly-priced rental accommodation.

Bob had lightly dismissed her timidity, telling her that there was a seedy side to every big city or port, but that most Sydney residents led normal suburban-type lives, and managed to avoid the unsavoury areas of town; provided she could arrange a good, well-paid job before she made the move, wages were also generally better in Sydney. Accommodation and cost of living, therefore, should be no great problem for her as the city had an excellent range of public transport systems. He'd thought no more about the possibility of her acting on her impulse until he received this letter.

She had "taken the plunge" as she put it, and had transferred to a Sydney position with the company for which she had worked in Adelaide. Her letter told of the loneliness she now felt in the harbour city, and of how eagerly she awaited his return. Bob felt very surprised. To his recollection, little had occurred between them in Adelaide beyond a pleasant evening of dancing, supper in a coffee lounge, and some mild petting and kissing after he'd escorted her to her home. He hoped that he hadn't inadvertently given her hope and encouragement to make a move, which she now regretted. Bloody women! A man never could tell what was going through their minds!

Yokohama, in the early morning sunlight! A mild, foggy haze was clearing, lifting above a huge calm harbour, which extended for some twenty miles further north, into Tokyo Bay. So this, finally, was Japan! Homeland of an enemy who was hated, detested, resisted and finally defeated not quite fifteen years previously, yet now generally conceded by mariners of every race to be the finest destination in the Orient for shore leave!

Busily, the small, modern, powerful Japanese tugs pushed the carrier into her allotted berth alongside Yamashita Pier. Through the blue haze, the great U.S. naval base at Yokosuka, far to the south, lay silhouetted against the skyline.

Later, ashore in Yokohama, it became evident that very few buildings were more than two stories high and that there were many bare and vacant building sites, particularly in the Port area, obviously a legacy of the wartime American bombing. Yet there was much recent post-war construction, too, a lot of which was currently in progress.

Another major difference between this seaport and Singapore, Manila, or Hong Kong was that very few taxi drivers or other locals either spoke or understood English. After almost fifteen years of Allied Occupation, the Japanese remained an insular and independent people, absorbing from the West only that which they chose and rejecting that which they did not need.

It was true that in shops along the Isezaki, the main thoroughfare of downtown Yokohama, there were usually some shop assistants who were conversant in the English tongue. In the popular bars and nightclubs, too, the same applied, but to find any other address, the easiest solution was to first obtain a relevant business card or brochure from an information centre, then to show the required destination to the taxi driver. However, the Isezaki, a street more than a mile in length, was closed to vehicular traffic from around 7 am until 10-30 pm each day and became a great pedestrian shopping mall, proudly illuminated at its main entrance by a spectacularly multi-coloured neon archway.

With three shipmates, Bob arrived in Downtown Yokohama that first afternoon of leave. He and Johnno sought out a well-patronised bar, while the other two set off to explore the Isezaki. The dimly lit bar was noisy, already frequented by other Aussie sailors.

After buying drinks from the barman, Bob and Johnno sat at a table in a low cubicle along the opposite wall. A bar hostess soon joined them. Bob bought her something that looked like whisky but was probably cold tea.

She wore a figure-hugging, silk brocade, ivory coloured dress that had elements of both Chinese cheongsam and modern Western style. It showed her superbly rounded curves and shapely legs to advantage. Her English was very good, though she was obviously Japanese; yet there was something else unusual about her appearance. Above her high cheekbones, her round, doll-like eyes seemed enormous and in vivid contrast to her delicate Oriental features. Certainly, she was one of the most beautiful women Bob had ever seen and she was already looking at Johnno with unmistakeable infatuation. Her name, she said, was Machiko. She rested a hand on Johnno's thigh and caused him to choke nervously on his drink.

"My, what big eyes you have, Grandma!" he quipped to hide his embarrassment.

"Yes," she acknowledged, "I want to look like Western girl, not Japanese girl, so I have operation."

"How does that work?" Bob asked, fascinated.

"They cut wider at corners; make eyelids open more so more of eyes show," Machiko explained matter of factly, "Many Japanese girls have such operation! You like?"

"Yes, but it seems a lot of trouble for you to go through," Bob said.

"Oh, no trouble! You like, too?" she prompted Johnno hopefully.

Johnno was slightly built, boyishly youthful-looking, with fair, curly hair and light blue eyes. Perhaps it was this attraction of opposites that caused this girl to want his approval so strongly.

"Yes, but I'm married! Now, Bob isn't married!" Johnno showed her the wedding band on his left hand, "Why don't you put some work into him instead?"

It was a sentiment that Bob endorsed wholeheartedly. The bar girl shook her head. Plainly, the suggestion held little appeal. "No, you much nicer! Besides, I not want to marry you! Why you worry?" she asked.

Johnno told her that he believed in being faithful to his wife. Machiko told him that his wife was very lucky.

"Someday, maybe I marry Australian or American man!" she added, "I not like Japanese man very much! Too bossy, not very nice, I think!"

Poor little buggar! She had such a fad for all things Western, even to having her eyes changed so that Caucasian men would find her more attractive. Fat chance she'd have of becoming the wife of any caring man, white or Japanese, from her present status as a bar hostess! Even if she could find some gullible Yank or Aussie prepared to marry her, it was unlikely that immigration in either country would care to know her once they had checked out her background! And what self-respecting Japanese would take on a barroom whore with Westernised eyes?

No, once her good looks faded, the best she could hope for might be a tenuous life with some seedy old pimp, or perhaps as Mama-san or Madame of some sleazy brothel! Yet here and now, in the full flush of youth and beauty, she was as full of hope and dreams as any aspiring young starlet with great Hollywood ambitions, Bob reflected sadly.

Johnno had ordered another round and Machiko had temporarily departed to speed the delivery along.

"Bloody Hell, Bob," Johnno told him, "If she puts her hand on the inside of my thigh again, I'll be gone for certain! I wish you'd race her off and remove the temptation!"

"You might have noticed; I've been doing my damnedest, but it's you she's wrapped in, old son!" Bob drily observed.

"If my missus could see her, there's no way in the world she'd believe I'd pass that up!" Johnno told him. "Let's finish the round and piss off before my prick takes charge of me!"

Machiko returned. Johnno pleaded tiredness.

"I had a rough duty watch last night. I think I'll go back to the ship and get some rest," he said. Instantly, Machiko produced a keyring with two keys and offered, "You go have a sleep at my apartment. It's not far; here, I give you address. You rest, then I be along in about three hours when I finish here!"

This girl didn't give up easily!

"No, I wouldn't feel right, but thanks all the same," Johnno evaded.

Machiko misinterpreted. "I not want your money! I like you!"

"I like you too. But I told you, I'm married! Look, why don't you and Bob stay here until you finish your shift, then you can take him back to your place instead?"

Her disappointment was plain to see. Bob drained his glass. "Hang on, mate. I'll leave, too!"

They left the premises, Johnno's precious virtue still intact.

"Boy, she sure had her heart set on you! I wouldn't imagine she gets too many knock-backs," Bob said.

"Yair, well it's got me tossed, too! She didn't have a very professional attitude, did she? For a bar girl, she's an incurable romantic!" Johnno said.

"I've never met one like her," Bob admitted, "I reckon the poor little buggar is so keen to latch on to an Aussie or a Yank for her ticket out of Japan, that she's letting it affect her judgement!"

Beyond the neon archway, they spent the rest of the evening exploring the shopping bargains.

61

Taking the opportunity offered, Bob was one of those who had put his name down for participation in an organised bus tour the following day. The ship's public relations and welfare people were always most diligent in providing for such excursions. For any interested ratings of the non-duty watches, such occasions were beneficial in promoting understanding of, and friendship with a wider cross-section of a host country's population; also, no doubt, it served the purpose of keeping a few young sailors out of potential mischief.

The large, immaculately prepared Japanese tour bus manoeuvred through a five-point turn on the wharf. Unusually modern by Australian standards of the era, the big Hino featured a rear-mounted engine. Busily, the coach driver alternated between first and reverse gears as he easily spun the powered steering wheel, while the young, smartly uniformed bus hostess, the tour guide, walked alongside the rear of the bus and blew continuously on a shrill whistle each time the vehicle was reversing. Whenever she ceased to blow and the noise stopped, so did the bus; the sudden silence was her signal to the driver that he could not safely reverse any further. Again, he would spin the steering to the opposite lock and go forward, before once more, twirling the wheel back and re-selecting reverse gear, to the accompaniment of resumed whistle blowing. One further silence, then the bus again swung left and went forward to stop, the tight manoeuvre finally completed.

"One would think," Bob observed, "that it would have been much quieter and simpler to have scrubbed all that noise and just given one loud blast for each signal to stop!"

"Yes, but I've noticed already that the Japs seem to do a few things the other way round to how we'd do them." Jake reflected.

"Yair. Might be a bit of French influence somewhere, eh?" Bob surmised wryly.

Cultural differences aside, the outing proved to be both stimulating and educational, with commentary in near-perfect English by the attractive Japanese guide. The first stop, at Kamakura, was to view the 'Great Buddha', an enormous bronze statue of the seated Buddha, rising some fifty or sixty feet above its base. A tremendous achievement, cast in one single piece in 1297 A.D., the idol was originally housed within a temple, but that was demolished by a tsunami or a tidal wave surge, around 1314. Being too heavy to be moved by the water, the Buddha stayed in position, sitting in the open air for more than six and a half centuries.

Back aboard the bus, they were transported into the mountain regions, past small farms, through an area of thermal resorts, hot springs and geysers, then upwards through forested hillsides and mountain hamlets to the beautiful medieval village and National Park of Hakone. Located on the shore of the magnificent Lake Hakone, so large that it accommodated big, modern multi-decked ferryboats, and with the majestic snow-capped cone of Fujiyama towerin8 above and behind the smaller mountains, which flanked the far shore, the overall scenic views were truly breathtaking. Some ninety percent of Japan's land area was forested mountain terrain, but here, as earlier in the thermal region, Bob was reminded of a geological similarity to New Zealand's North Island.

That evening, amidst the Yokohama nightlife, Bob and Jake over-imbibed on the sake. They were not excessively drunk in the usual sense; their mental faculties appeared little impaired and their later recollections were total. Instead, it was the motor and balance functions that were interestingly sabotaged by the warm, dry-tasting rice wine. To attempt to walk was to reel about in an exaggeratedly burlesque manner.

"I think it must have toppled our gyros!" Was Jake's bemused but appropriate comment.

Duty watch the following day precluded Bob's sightseeing until the weekend, then he decided to see something of Tokyo before they sailed. He went alone, his mates either on duty or having already made the trip. At Yokohama railway station promotional posters proclaimed the pro jected new standard gauge super-fast trains under construction. The Shinkansen railway would link the 517 kilometres between Tokyo and Osaka, via only two intermediate stops at Nagoya and the ancient Capital, Kyoto, by the Hitari (lightning) services. These streamlined bullet trains would be transporting passengers in regular services before the Tokyo Olympic Games commenced in 1964.

Bob boarded a less glamorous electric interurban train of the customary Japanese 3ft 6in· gauge for his twenty-mile trip to Tokyo. He was the only Occidental in a carriage of Japanese, mainly men, who were seated on benches down either side and who were universally immersed in reading their newspapers. Bob took one of the few vacant seats. Two stations further on, he glanced upward and saw a young, very pregnant woman "strap hanging" in the aisle. He stood and gestured to offer her the seat. She looked acutely embarrassed yet grateful as she accepted the courtesy. She looked pale and drawn, not at all well. Standing in the aisle, he became suddenly aware that several of the male passengers were watching him with what could only be described as silent animosity, over the tops of their newspapers. Apparently, he'd committed some grave social gaffe.

Bloody hell! No wonder Machiko, the beautiful round-eyed bar girl, had hoped to marry an Australian or an American, he decided. These blokes certainly had an unchivalrous attitude! Yet the paradox he'd already noted during this visit was the obvious love and conscientious caring so apparent within their family groups.

62

Between Yokohama and Djakarta, the carrier ran a course to take her between two typhoons. One had caused considerable damage to Hong Kong, demolishing refugee shacks and swamping or overturning thousands of sampans, which were home to many others. Many lives were lost. Another equally devastating storm had caused flooding, homelessness and loss of life in the Philippines, and now both typhoons had returned, on nearly converging courses, to the China Sea and were regenerating in intensity.

The flattop steamed for twenty hours at her maximum capability, having regard to sea conditions, to avoid being caught by either storm.

Bob contemplated the angry sky and the turbulent grey sea from the weather deck opening of the Paravane storage space on three deck. A mile away, a small, converted tuna boat headed north flying a Japanese ensign. A seaman Petty Officer coming off watch descended the ladder from two deck. Bob remarked, "Here we are running flat out to get away from it, and that little blighter is heading blissfully into it!"

"Yair," the seaman aired his knowledge, "she is a Jap weather boat. She is going right into the thick of it to take readings!"

Bob shook his head in amazement. "Those blokes must be gluttons for punishment!"

"You're telling me!" the seaman P.O. agreed.

The following day found them once again in brilliant sunlight and calm tropical seas. Tomorrow, Indonesia!

Lining the flight deck to enter Tanjong Priok, the former Dutch colonial harbour serving the capital Djakarta, some twenty miles away, the sea was smooth and still. It was a sultry overcast morning.

Several Indonesian Navy vessels were anchored nearby; mostly modern-looking sloops or light frigates, but two of the three long, low, Soviet-built destroyers lay in the foreground.

These recent Indonesian acquisitions of the latest Baltic Sea type, with a shallow draft, (around nine feet), were well suited to the requirements of the archipelago nation with its thousands of islands and atolls. Lean, hungry-looking, of very modern design, their profiles took on a somewhat sinister appearance in the light of Cold War tensions.

The wharf, too, was dotted with Russian-built trucks and jeeps, and with Indonesian Marines carrying sub-machine guns. Two days previously, a rebellious Indonesian Air Force Lieutenant, flying an old B25 Mitchell, had bombed the Presidential Palace, President Soekarno had escaped injury, but this attempt had placed the country under Martial Law.

Tension seemed to hang in the air like a form of static electricity; while leave was granted, it was not an ideal liberty port at this particular point in time.

Money changing facilities were available on board at the official rate of 80 Rupiah to the Australian Pound, and the crew was warned that possession of any non-Indonesian currency ashore was punishable by a three or four-year term of imprisonment. This was because the unofficial black market exchange rate was 800 Rupiah to the Australian Pound – ten times the official rate - and because rebel groups in the inflation-ridden country required foreign currency to finance their gunrunning and smuggling operations.

Needless to say, the Navy had organised as many supervised leave activities as possible, with the full cooperation of the Australian and British Embassies, whose staff and families were excellent guides and hosts.

The bus trip to the capital along the road parallel to the canal was conspicuous for its contrast. On the one side, spacious Dutch Colonial-built houses fronted the road, whilst across the canal; the grinding poverty of the squatter's shacks was evident. The polluted waters of the canal had to serve the cooking, washing, drinking and sewerage needs of the poor simultaneously, yet those people strove hard to maintain both personal hygiene and dignity. A gentle, cultured race was being manipulated and pawned by national and international, political and financial exploitation and vested interests. In hindsight, it would seem that further revolution and distraction were inevitable in a society where corruption and patronage had prevailed for three centuries.

Later, divided into groups of four or five, each hosted by personnel from the British and Australian diplomatic communities, the Navy men were treated to sightseeing, a lavish function at the British Cricket Club, and most congenial dinners in diplomatic residencies. A very pleasant, informative and unusual shore leave! Bob was glad he had availed himself of the opportunity.

63

Dusk of the following evening found the ship homeward bound, through Sunda Strait, past the smoking volcano that was "baby" Krakatoa, to the spot where "Perth" and "Houston" had fought their last battle eighteen years earlier. A brief ceremony, a wreath dropped overboard to commemorate the fallen of the two cruisers, and of the gallant little sloop "Yarra" which was sunk defending her little convoy against overwhelming odds a couple of days after the Cruiser battle, in these same waters.

Brief stopovers in Fremantle and Port Melbourne, then the air group disembarked at Jervis Bay before the ship carried on to Garden Island Naval Dockyard, Sydney.

Bob arranged to meet Jan the following Friday evening in Sydney, a 105-mile drive north of the Naval Air Station. He had left his little Austin car in his cousin, Tom's, care at Nowra. It was good to have his own wheels again, but he was recovering from a bout of influenza and did not particularly relish his reunion with Jan under those circumstances.

Tired, with a headache and with little enthusiasm, he met her as arranged, in the lounge of the Australia Hotel. She was her usual bright, bubbly self, all excited and talkative; whereas Bob was feeling out of sorts and uncharacteristically moody.

Jan was very attractive: auburn, curly hair, hazel eyes and a figure like a pocket Venus. Combined with natural, almost naive, unsophisticated charm, she had attracted his interest when he'd first met her in Adelaide. Now, he let her make all the running, conversationally. Bob was not attuned to her happy frame of mind; he contributed little comment beyond the sufficient "Hmm," "Yes," or "Do you think so?" necessary to save his lack of attention from appearing to be total rudeness.

Idly, he glanced towards a nearby table where two attractive, well-dressed secretarial-type girls were sharing some giggly, whispered confidence. He looked back towards Jan, pretending interest in her conversation, but she had misinterpreted his glance at those other girls.

There was evidence in her tone of voice as she addressed her next remark, that she felt alarmed; that she was losing her attractiveness to him. She nervously feigned an amused chuckle, and said, "I'll bet you're thinking if you weren't stuck with little old me, you'd probably be able to get set with one of those real good lookers!"

Bob felt a flush of irritation with her. It wouldn't have mattered at the moment if a Hollywood starlet had walked up to him with her panties in her hand and tears in her eyes; he wouldn't have been interested, he felt so jaded and tired! Jan was a lot nicer sort than either of those other girls; so, damn it, why did she put herself down? He didn't bother to communicate a denial, though. He did not explain to her as to why he was not the brightest companion for her that evening. Instead, he merely grunted a reply, "You'll do! Finish your drink and we'll find a restaurant. What do you fancy for dinner?"

Eagerly, Jan drained her glass. "I'm ready! How about a Chinese Cafe?"

"OK, Chinese it is!" Bob agreed. He had become heartily sick of Oriental cooking after six months of shore leaves in the Asian area, but he'd already made himself disagreeable enough for one night.

Strolling arm in arm with Jan along Pitt Street, then along George Street, Bob began to feel a little more sociable in the cool crispness of the July evening. They found a nice, unpretentious little Chinese Cafe down towards the Haymarket. Jan enjoyed the meal and his more convivial attitude. Bob even found the dinner more palatable than he had anticipated.

They talked some more, as they dawdled through the three courses and the green tea. Bob was finding her more desirable, her conversation more interesting as his headache cleared.

It was nine o'clock. A bit late for a movie, perhaps. He glanced at his wristwatch. Yes, same time as the wall clock. Jan seemed to read his thoughts.

"What shall we do now?" she asked.

"I'm open to suggestions," Bob told her, "but I'd just as soon we booked into a hotel room for the night."

Nothing like being blunt about it! She could only say "no" if she wanted to keep her honour intact. She didn't!

"I'll go along with that," Jan agreed.

They found a little private hotel, nothing flash, but clean and comfortable. The desk clerk discreetly ignored the fact that they had no baggage. An obvious shack-up joint! Bob would keep this place in mind! Nothing worse than taking a girl to a more-upmarket establishment, then finding some disapproving old biddy in reception glaring at the girl as though she was a harlot.

As they kissed and fondled each other on the bed, and Bob commenced to undress her, Jan fixed him with that direct, honest gaze of hers.

"Look," she said, "I'm sorry I knocked you back in Adelaide, but it didn't seem right on the first night."

Bloody hell! She had a lot going for her, so why did she always seem to be either apologising to him or putting herself down?

"That's alright," Bob told her, "it's a woman's privilege! Contrary to what you seem to believe, I don't claim to be a Don Juan, anyhow!"

She was exciting, willing; also grateful that he was considerate enough to come prepared with a packet of condoms. If there was one thing Jan didn't need, it was an unwanted pregnancy, yet she would have taken the risk for him. She was not a promiscuous girl, but neither did she attempt to hide the depth of her sexual attraction to him.

Bob's tiredness was forgotten. Neither one of them was concerned with sleep that night. Around five a.m., they dressed and Bob drove her home to her boarding house, arranged to collect her that evening to go to a drive-in movie, and returned to "Johnnies", Royal Naval House, to snatch a little sleep.

At the drive-in, their mutual lust took precedence over patience, and they "did it" twice on the rear seat of the little car. Sunday, they went for a picnic to Coal and Candle Creek, interspersed with more lovemaking.

The following week, Bob went home to Wilga Creek for three weeks' leave and the weekend after his return, he met her again.

64

Once again, Jan was transparently eager to see him. She looked radiantly happy and more desirable than ever. He took her dining and dancing, and she was all over him like a rash in her eagerness to please. He felt a twinge of uneasiness. Poor little buggar was acting like a woman in love! Bob liked her, but he wasn't ready for a more committed relationship. "What have you been doing with yourself these past five weeks?" he asked her conversationally.

"Not a lot," Jan said, "just going to work, coming home again, writing the odd letter to Mum and the family."

Bob's discomfort increased. "Haven't you had an evening or two on the town, or gone to a movie?"

"No," she shook her head, "I wasn't inclined until you came back."

"Jan," he told her seriously, "don't get too serious. I like you, you're a lot of fun, but I've never made you any promises, and I don't intend to; I don't want to hurt you!"

She averted her gaze momentarily. A look of disappointment fleetingly crossed her features.

"I know that. I'm not asking for anything heavy! I don't want to clip your wings, so let's just live for the moment. When we make love, I enjoy it too, remember!" she said brightly.

They spent Friday night at the same little George Street hotel where he'd first made love to her. He dropped her back at her boarding house on Saturday morning, then returned to "Johnnies" for a shower and a change of clothes. In the afternoon, he called for her again. They went for a harbour cruise on one of the big ferries, and enjoyed a steak dinner later at a little Circular Quay restaurant, followed by a movie in the city.

Bob had not intended to sleep with her again that night. He knew he had already taken too much advantage of her feelings for him, but as the night wore on and desire increased, he put the hard word on her once more. As usual, she readily acquiesced. This time, the little private hotel in George Street was already booked out, as were any other halfway reputable establishments. They found a vacant double room in a dump that was little more than a flophouse for deadbeats.

The old chap at the desk, a decent sort of fellow, took Bob aside and whispered, "Son, you don't want to take a nice little girl like that into a hole like this! There will be drunks coughing and yelling half the night, and the cops sometimes arrive with flashlights and turn the place over looking for some no-hoper who's got himself in strife."

Bob told Jan what the man had said, but she would not be put off. "We can't get anywhere else and anyway, I feel safe as a house when I'm with you!" she told him trustingly.

"We'll take the room," Bob told the clerk. The old saying was true, in Bob's case, that a standing prick knew no conscience.

It was a dump, all right! The walls seemed almost paper-thin, but at least, the cops didn't arrive. Jan didn't seem too bothered. She'd have slept on a granite rock in the open, just to be with him. Poor little, willing, self-made door mat! Bob felt disgusted with himself. After an hour or so, he slapped her bare bottom, "Come on, honey! Get dressed, I'm taking you home. I'm sorry I brought you to this dump!"

"I don't mind! So long as you're here, too, it's not all that bad," she said as they dressed.

"Rubbish! The only good thing about this place is that so far, we haven't been bitten by bed bugs!" Bob told her.

The Air Group re-embarked in the "Offal barge", as the Carrier was less than affectionately known. Travelling from "Albatross", R.A.N.A.S. Nowra, to Jervis Bay, in a Navy Bedford bus, Jim remarked to Bob, "That little girl you were with in Sydney; wasn't she the one you met in Adelaide?"

"Yes, that's Jan," Bob admitted.

"Must be serious, if she followed you across from there," Jim commented, "She looked as doughy as a Pusser's bun!"

"Oh, well, you know what sheilas are like! Always taking seriously what is only poked at them in fun!" Bob dismissed the subject lightly.

"You're a hard-hearted bastard," Jim told him drily.

"Oh, I don't know! Barnacle Bill once told me I was too soft-hearted with my women!"

"He'd be a great example!" Jim disapproved bitterly, "Bill has had that girlfriend of his on a string for three or four years! Treats her like shit, drops her for any other sheila that takes his fancy, and picks her up again when he feels like it! You know, she's had two abortions to him already, but Bill reckons that's her problem! Just because she's a nurse, he thinks she should be able to take care of herself! He's got no sense of responsibility at all!"

Injustice always got Jim steamed up. The youngest of five children, raised in a close-knit family by a widowed mother, Jim was a gentleman graduate of the school of hard knocks. Probably one of the most decent, caring human beings Bob had ever met, but no wowser.

"You missed your calling, Jim! You should have been a missionary!" Bob lightly chided his friend.

"No, I wouldn't say that. If one of my sisters ever got caught up with a bloke like Bill, I'd probably shoot the bastard," Jim said levelly.

65

They visited Brisbane during the R.N.A. Exhibition week, together with an R.N. submarine, and units of the R.N.Z.N.

Show Week traditionally attracted visits to the northern capital from Navy ships. The following week saw combined anti-submarine exercises off the coast, before they "dropped the pick", in Hervey Bay to prepare the ship for the yearly Admiral's Inspection.

Bob's major recollection of that period was of spending hours of time and elbow grease on a brand new radome, fitted after a nose wheel hydraulic malfunction to the particular Venom for which he was primarily responsible. To achieve the shiny black finish on the fibreglass radomes was a surprisingly unsophisticated and non-technical exercise; i.e., endless polishing of the dull resin-coated surface with black boot polish, after preparation with raven oil. It seemed absurdly out of character with the jet age and electronic technology but was effective.

In a little over a year since he'd joined the Air Group, they had lost a Gannet ditched at sea, with no casualties, had six equally fortune-favoured Sea Venom landing incidents and a helicopter making a forced landing on Fraser Island; repaired and recovered without injury.

This short six-week embarkation for Brisbane and Hervey Bay ended at Jervis Bay after a further Sydney visit. This time, Bob deliberately avoided getting in touch with Jan. He was feeling guilty over the way he had used her but knew only too well that if he saw her again, he'd probably take advantage of her feelings for him once more.

No, he decided, it was better to allow her time to cool her passion. It wasn't fair to lead her on. If she didn't see him for a while before he told her the news that he was the only radio mechanic in the Air Group that year who would remain with his squadron for a further year's sea duty next year, it should lessen the probability of either of them making an unwise personal commitment.

For all of his experience with women, he was still surprisingly naive. The fact that he chose to ignore further contact with her for the time being, must have been more hurtful and humiliating for her than if he had made a clean break but Bob didn't see it that way at the time.

It was November before he finally wrote to her, informing her that he would be with the Carrier Air Group for a further year and, tactfully, he failed to mention that the Air Group would not re-embark until the end of January. He told her, more bluntly, not to wait for him, but wished her well for the future. That done, Bob commenced to put her out of his mind with a sense of relief. He had never been in love with her, although he had found her very agreeable and very sexy. Yet, though he had never made any promise of commitment to Jan, he knew a sense of disgust with himself for his casual acceptance of her favours. Bob was aware of her unspoken hopes that he might come to care for her much more deeply; he also knew that to prolong the relationship would mean that he would continue to exploit her willingness to let him use her. For the first time in his many affairs with women, he had become aware of a fact of his own nature that he despised. Previously, "love 'em and leave 'em", was par for the course.

Perhaps, he mused, he cared for her more than he was prepared to admit. Whatever, there would be no future in it, he had decided!

66

Kathleen died peacefully in her sleep that year at the age of eighty-eight. In her ill, she had left the little Wilga Creek selection to her four children equally. No doubt, the old lady had fondly imagined the well-maintained old weatherboard bungalow, the old iron-bark and galvanised iron sheds and stables, and the three hundred and twenty acres of marginal grazing land, to be worth much more than was the case.

In fact, the generous valuation of a reputable rural valuer was a market price of three thousand nine hundred pounds; equivalent, perhaps, to that of a modest three-bedroomed brick veneer in an established Brisbane suburb.

Split four ways, after allowing for duties and legal fees, this would amount to less than nine hundred pounds each. Such an amount would be of little consequence to Ellen and her husband, now living in semi-retirement on the coast, with diverse business interests. For Leah and her husband, a senior officer of the Queensland Railways mechanical engineering branch, it would be a handy windfall sufficient to pay off the balance of their home mortgage and leaving a little extra for luxuries.

For Jenny, however, it was little reward. Approaching 56 years of age, she had raised three children as a single parent and had, cheerfully, been both devoted companion and nurse to her aged mother. Nine hundred pounds would do little to secure a roof over her head, as she was too old, and her employment skills too limited, for a mortgage to be a viable option for her. Not that Jenny would complain. Cheerful acceptance of whatever life offered or retracted had long been her forte.

"Not to worry, something will turn up!" could well express in one sentence, Jenny's basic philosophy to life's unremitting struggle. That and her unwavering faith in the Almighty. Joe, seated in the hammock-like comfort afforded by the sweeping canvas of a squatter's chair, reflected on these matters in the cool of the evening. A waning moon bathed the darkened verandah with its soft light, a faint breeze rustled the leaves of the shade trees. The strident call of a night bird floated up from the timbered gully, temporarily shattering the tranquillity of the Mount Chillingham evening.

Diana switched off the kitchen light. Joe was unusually subdued for a couple of days, now. He hadn't told her what was troubling him when she had asked, he simply smiled reassuringly and said, "It's nothing, love, just a bit of daydreaming."

But there was something! He wasn't merely exercising his mind with station problems or logistics; it had nothing whatever to do with the big cattle run. She knew what was bothering him, why he was sitting alone out there on the darkened verandah, the light purposely turned off, though there were few insects abroad this evening.

Quietly, she joined him. She lifted his left arm from the extended armrest-cum-leg rest of the squatter's chair and replaced it with her own long, still shapely right leg as she sat beside and above him on the broad wooden side plank. Diana let his arm fall back to rest along her thigh and knee. She rested her right arm on top of the seat back and ran her fingers lightly through his hair.

Softly, she said, "Don't bottle it up, Darling! You're worried about Jenny." It was a statement, not a question.

"Yes," Joe admitted.

She leaned over and kissed him, "Well, Boyo, after forty years of marriage, don't you think you might've confided in your wife? After all, she might even be able to come up with a solution."

Her tone was light-hearted, but beneath the banter, she was very serious.

"Yes, I'm sorry, Sweetheart. I didn't see it as your problem, too," he said.

"Well, I like that! After all this time, am I just some blow-in from across the Tasman?" she asked in mock reproof. "Anyhow, as I said, there might be an easy answer, if you'd care to discuss it!"

Joe glanced up at her and laughed. Her irrepressibility had always been infectious. It was one of the many precious things he loved about her. Playfully, he squeezed her thigh, gently, so as not to bruise. "Alright, you've got the floor," he said.

"Steady, Boyo! Get your mind off the funny business. Anyhow, I presume you would like Jenny to have security, and you would also like the Wilga Creek property to stay in the family?" Diana asked.

"You've summed it up in a nutshell," Joe told her.

"Well, why don't we sell some shares and buy out all three of your sisters, with the proviso that Jenny can stay on at Wilga Creek, rent-free, for life? She and I have always been close friends, and even if we retired to live there ourselves, I'm sure we would all continue to get along famously together," she said.

"But those shares are part of your security, as well as mine," Joe told her, "and if we sold out now, I don't know if I'd be justified as staying on as Manager here!"

Diana shook her head. "I wasn't talking about our private company shareholding, Darling. I meant our stock market shares, oil and mining!"

Joe was astounded! He had never taken much interest in those types of shares, regarding them more as a hobby for Diana.

"Are they worth that much?" he asked incredulously. "Oh, yes! In fact, if we sold just half of our oil shares, and half of our mining shares, right now, we would realise over three thousand pounds! We could afford to buy out your three sisters and pay legal costs and transfer fees," Diana informed him. "Both of those companies are running hot at the moment, particularly the oil exploration! I'd just as soon take some profit now to invest in real estate and lessen the risk with the share market."

He jumped to his feet and hugged her. "What a clever girl I married!" he said.

"Yes, didn't you?" Diana allowed herself a moment of unaccustomed smugness, and then returned his embrace.

"I'll phone the broker in the morning," she added, "Merriton! You're particularly fresh for an old fellow!"

67

It was late May of 1961. Bob had scarcely given any thought to Jan. He hadn't seen her for ten months, hadn't written to her for almost as long. The ship's programme was sufficiently varied from the previous year to be interesting, to say the least.

Their last Australian port was Fremantle, always known for its great beer and friendly women. Then with other Australian units and a New Zealand cruiser, they had become part of a huge British Commonwealth Naval exercise with carriers, cruisers, destroyers, frigates and submarines from Britain, India and Pakistan.

Forty-four ships in all. Afterward, the combined fleet had anchored in the magnificent natural harbour of Trincomalee on the North east coast of Ceylon. The lush green jungle-clad hills met the blue waters of the port with little sign of man's interference except at the northern end, where a village and a small naval installation were the sole remaining in-dications of a major World War 2 base. Back then, Trincomalee had been the largest and by far the most significant naval and seaplane base in the Indian Ocean; even now, the huge fleet had no difficulty in anchoring at intervals of half a mile offshore and with a minimum of half a mile distance between ships. Heaps of room for all forty-four ships to "swing on the pick" in perfect safety, yet the huge harbour still gave an appear-ance of being comparatively empty. There was little commercial interest in the town, except for the Colombo jewellers who had travelled across the island to sell their fine selections of sapphires, rubies and diamonds at prices that seemed ridiculously cheap by Australian or British values.

The town itself appeared to take little interest in their naval visitors. Apart from beer sales at the Ceylon Navy canteen, the visitors generally showed a mutual lack of interest in the town, yet a walk along its streets, and to the beaches on the ocean side, revealed much to interest the pho-tographically minded.

Their next port of call was Bombay on the north-west Indian coast, a beautiful but overcrowded city, where so many poor, patient, homeless people managed to retain a remarkable sense of dignity; where ox-carts and horse-drawn gharries shared the streets with locally built taxis that were versions of an obsolete English small sedan, all busily going about their journeys while the undernourished homeless slept or rested under whatever shade they could find on the adjacent, hard Macadamised foot-paths.

Total prohibition was in force, but that, of course, appeared a to-tal irrelevancy in a country where the average annual per capita income amounted to less than twenty-five Australian Pounds. It was a humbling experience, which left Bob with a new appreciation of his good fortune in being born both white and Australian.

A two-day stopover in Karachi was abbreviated to one day due to high winds, so he didn't get ashore there. Singapore and Manila were much the same as the year before, but the big surprise was the U.S. Navy base at Subic Bay, where the Cubi Point Naval Air Station on the periphery, home of the 1st Marine Air Wing, seemed to house a huge number of modern aircraft, including several squadrons of the new F8U Crusader fighters. Their Mach 2 performance would make the Sea Venom appear obsolete, and this was only the Marine Corps!

The Naval port installations were also on a huge and impressive scale, yet through the gates, the supporting Philippine village of Alongappo looked pathetically like a boom shanty town, its main street almost exclu-sively the domain of bars and bowling alleys.

At sea, the yearly SEATO exercise was cut short; the big American carrier which was participating was diverted to the Gulf of Tonkin due to a rapidly deteriorating situation in Laos, while the Australian carrier's crew were notified that they would remain on standby to proceed to the Gulf also; meanwhile, mail outward would be subject to censorship, as she continued south-west to Singapore.

The following night, an unidentified submarine, obviously a Soviet, was detected on sonar, shadowing from beneath the surface. Blackout conditions were rapidly reinstated as the carrier increased speed and adopted a zigzag course, while the five escorting destroyers, British, Australian and American, wove a tight, high-speed defensive pattern around her in the dark. The submarine effortlessly continued to shadow her prey. It was one of those tense Cold War situations that routinely tested the nerve whenever international tensions and suspicions increased. As one young fitter anxiously exclaimed in the mess dock, "Hell, if World War Three starts tonight, the first we'll know of it will be a homing torpedo in the guts!"

But the crisis passed, and a week later, was almost forgotten in the anticipation of shore leave in Hong Kong. As they had done during the Singapore visit, the Squadron disembarked to fly out of an R.A.F. station while the ship was in Hong Kong. In this case, the airfield was Kai Tak, which was also the Colony's International Airport.

The Sea Venoms, together with the R.A.F. Venom Fighter Bombers, flew daily sorties over the Colony and the New Territories for the next five days. Ground testing the VHF radio after replacing a unit, Bob wondered how the R.A.F. pilots, the civilian aircrews, and the Air Traffic Controllers managed to retain their sanity! Loud, continuous jamming of the frequencies with Chinese music originating in Communist China deliberately frustrated radio communications.

There were many advantages for the Australian ratings, which made for a pleasant stay at Kai Tak, though. They were working Tropical routine, from 0600 to noon daily, after which they were free to enjoy leave in the Colony until next morning; the menu at the R.A.F. cafeteria Mess Hall was always excellent, both in variety and quality; the Pommy airmen were a friendly co-operative bunch, and, best of all, civilian clothes could be worn on leave from the base.

That first afternoon, Bob, with four others from the squadron, wore civilian clothes into a Kowloon Bar. They were quickly joined by the Chinese bar hostesses, one of whom immediately said, "What are you guys at Kai Tak for?"

Bloody hell, Bob thought. What a bush telegraph! How the hell did she know they had come from Kai Tak?

"What makes you think we came from Kai Tak?" Bob asked.

"You guys all Australian Navy?" the girl said.

How the heck did she know that? Bob had never been near this particular bar the previous year, and the other four were having their first leave in the colony. She certainly could not have recognised any of them!

"No," Bob lied "we're all civilians. Navy blokes wear uniforms, don't they?"

"Horse shit!" the girl said, "You Australians, and you from Kai Tak!"

"Oh, all right, if you must know, we're Qantas pilots, and we're here on a course!" he told her. The other Aussies were enjoying the exchange but managed to keep straight-faced as Bob fibbed. Bob wondered, himself, why he bothered! Perhaps, it was in some way connected to his annoyance with the jamming of the frequency that morning, but he felt this bar girl was after information, more so than merely exchanging pleasantries.

How else could she have known they were from Kai Tak, and not tourists or merchant seamen?

"He not Qantas pilot!" she cried triumphantly, pointing at Frank.

Frank was dark, wiry, and looked younger than his twenty-four years.

"No," Bob admitted, appearing to give ground, "but he's not as young as he looks! He's an aircraft Captain. This is Captain Frank Sanson of Air India."

Frank glowered as though he would like to throttle Bob. He was Australian and proud of it, but he went along with the deception as did the other three, perhaps also wondering suspiciously, how the girl knew they were from Kai Tak.

But they didn't fool the bar girl, although she gave up on trying to pump them for any further information now that they all appeared to be guarded as to why they were stationed at Kai Tak.

It's a bit bloody silly, Bob thought, we wouldn't know one worthwhile military secret among the lot of us! Yet there again, was the cautious distrust, part and parcel of the Cold War era; the expectation that even the most innocent small talk from foreigners about naval matters, somehow masked a covert espionage intent.

68

During the stay at Kai Tak, Bob and a couple of other dedicated sightseers managed, courtesy of the Royal Air Force, to fly in a V.I.P. Hastings transport during an extended test flight over the Colony and adjacent islands. It was a beautiful sunny day and provided some great views of the Pearl of the Orient. They were in the air for around an hour and a half, including several "touch and go" landings on the runway from the overwater approach between the islands to the strip jutting into the sea on the causeway.

He wished he had bought that new 8-millimetre movie camera before the flight, and decided to do so on his next trip into Kowloon.

It was a new semi-automatic, three-turret lens job, a type he had seen in Sydney. Bob was aware that this would be his last visit to Hong Kong, as he intended to leave the Navy next year.

There were plenty of home movie cameras on sale in the various little shops around Kowloon, but this particular brand and model didn't seem to be stocked by any of them, so he went to a larger, specialised store where Les had bought his identical model.

This was a more westernised type of specialist camera shop, much like those in Sydney or Brisbane. For once, price tags and glass showcases were in evidence. The prices were reasonable, but it was evident that there would be none of the usual bartering and haggling in this shop, with its higher overheads. The price tag in the showcase was for the amount Les had said he'd paid for his camera.

One shop assistant was busy with a customer as Bob looked around. Another assistant appeared behind the counter as a new customer arrived in the shop. Bob could not help staring at her as she walked towards the shop assistant. She was obviously prosperous Chinese, beautifully groomed, not a hair out of place. Her expensive-looking, western-style, purple coloured dress hugged her curvaceous body, and her quality, high-heeled shoes accentuated her slim ankles and shapely calves. Probably in her early twenties and strikingly beautiful. She was a real heart-stopper!

The shop assistant obviously thought so, too! He was already babbling away at the rate of twenty to the dozen in Cantonese or Mandarin, or whatever, before she had reached the counter. Somewhat embarrassed, the girl explained in a broad American accent, "I'm sorry, but I don't understand a word of it! I was born and raised in San Francisco!"

The first shop assistant meanwhile had attended to his previous customer, and now approached Bob.

Bob bought his camera, but by the time he had made his purchase, the Chinese-American girl had left the shop.

Outside, there was no sign of her, either. "Must be slipping in my old age," Bob told himself, "to let that get away without at least trying to chat her up!"

When the Squadron maintenance crews returned to the ship before sailing, there was an unexpected letter awaiting Bob. Postmarked in a western New South Wales town some two months previously, and at the surface mail rate, it was following the ship around for some time. The writing looked vaguely familiar, but he didn't know anyone in Broken Hill.

He opened and read it. It was from Jan and written from a hotel room. She had a new job, travelling, as a sales representative, she said. As she was alone in town, knowing nobody, she was filling in the evening with a bottle of vodka, and thought she might as well drop him a line.

Typical of Jan, she pretended to sound cheerful, but, reading between the lines, she was clearly quite drunk and very depressed. She was doing quite a lot of travelling and staying at country hotels. She hadn't given an address, apart from the name of the hotel at Broken Hill, but that was two months ago!

If she had set out to make him feel guilty, she had achieved her purpose. He dismissed the uncharitable thought, out of hand. Of course, she hadn't! Emotional blackmail was not a weapon in her armoury. She was too guileless, too open for that! No, it would have been loneliness and the vodka that had motivated her to write. Bob hoped she wasn't going to become an alcoholic. Part of him wanted to write to try to comfort her, and most of all, to gently persuade her that the bottle was no crutch; yet to write at all, would only prolong her hopes of a relationship that he could not, in all honesty, hold out to her. In any case, she had left the boarding house, and the Broken Hill address was only a temporary stop, two months earlier. Damn! Why the hell didn't the girl go home to her family in Adelaide? Women were strange cattle, all right! This one, in particular, made him very aware of his lack of chivalry, although she wouldn't have seen it that way herself.

69

Rabaul, where the smell of sulphur hung in the air, where volcanic cones came right to the water's edge. A beautiful tropical anchorage, a pleasant town living tenuously in the ominous presence of dormant, smouldering volcanoes.

Reminders, too, of the Second World War. Japanese army helmets turned upside down as hanging plant pots, and an old Betty bomber fuselage at the local club. A street named after the doomed little Wirraways, whose young Australian pilots had put up such a gallant, hopelessly outnumbered and unequal struggle to defend the little Pacific outpost town in early 1942.

The town, the market, the harbour were all highly photogenic, and Bob's new movie camera was sufficiently novel for him to soon exhaust his film supply. He went into a large, airy general store that seemed to sell everything, judging by the signs outside. It was a pleasant place, airy and well-lit by natural light. A long counter ran the width of the shop, and two Chinese women were serving a local family and a young stoker from the ship. Bob located the area where the photographic film was showcased.

A young Chinese man approached behind the counter. Bob prepared to ask along the lines of "How much you speak eight millimetre Kodak colour reel, John?"

Fortunately, the Chinese man spoke first, in a broad Australian accent, "Yes, mate, can I help you?"

Of course! This was Australia's territory! Those Chinese features had momentarily lulled his perceptions after months in the Orient, where English was merely a second or third language. Lucky this bloke spoke first or I'd have made a proper dill of myself, Bob thought!

"Yair, I'm looking for a reel of eight mil Kodachrome movie film, mate," Bob said.

He bought the film. The fellow was a very pleasant, gregarious type, and the shop not very busy. They yarned for about five minutes. The Australian-expatriate Chinese man was educated in Sydney, at high school and university, and had his professional office in Rabaul. He helped his family in the store at weekends. Like the American girl in Hong Kong a week earlier, the only thing oriental about him was his ancestry.

On returning to the Sydney-Jervis Bay area, the Air Group disembarked for Nowra in mid-June, re-joining the carrier mid-July. The highlight of those next few months was another visit to the New Zealand ports of Auckland and Wellington. It was to be Bob's final seagoing service.

Unlike Tom, who had elected to make the Navy his career, Bob would be leaving after his initial six-year enlistment, the following April. He'd had enough of the sea, of brass and bullshit. Nostalgia for leather, horse sweat and even the pungent, rank smell of gidgee called him back to the dusty, dry heat of the inland.

Bob was drafted off the Carrier Air Group in December, to the R.A.N. Air Station, "Albatross", at Nowra. His deployment there was to Ground Radio workshops, a move that did not please him at first. He had always preferred working on aircraft and had hoped for a line or maintenance unit posting. However, his Ground Radio assignment was to the H.F. Transmitter Room attached to the Communications Branch. He soon decided it was an agreeable enough way to spend his final few months of naval service. In fact, it was a downright bludge!

The transmitter room was pleasantly cooled and ventilated to a controlled temperature; not for the benefit of the ratings, but for the benefit of the big transmitters, as overheat could cause frequency drift, component failure and other problems. The radio operators were a pleasant, friendly bunch; Bob and the leading hand, an old friend, were left pretty much to themselves insofar as electrical branch supervision was concerned. Their duties were routine maintenance and tuning or retuning of the powerful transmitters as required.

Perhaps this final posting was part of the Navy's psychological effort to persuade him to re-enlist. Certainly, the Senior Service was anxious to stem the drain of its highly and expensively trained technical workforce. Bob was approached on several occasions by his Divisional Officer, Section Chief or Senior Electrical Officer to consider reenlistment.

Bob had firmly decided against it, to the point of even refusing flatly to sign on for the inactive listing in the RAN Fleet Reserve, the day before his final draft ashore, "Engagement Expired". The officer was dumbfounded for a few moments. Then he had patiently reasoned, "You might as well, Bob! It's only for five years, and it's money for jam! You would only be called on in the event of a total wartime mobilisation, but if you don't sign, it could prejudice your receiving the full amount of your O.F.R.B. payment. If a war breaks out, you'll be called up anyway."

"I don't care about the extra money! What I don't have, I won't miss, and it would be taking money under false pretences because there is no way I'll be back in this outfit! I'll be happy to serve my country in wartime if that occurs," Bob told him with a typically insubordinate grin, "but if that happens, you'll have to race me to the Air Force Recruiting Office! I've had a gutful of the Navy! Nelson might be dead, but it's high time this mob gave him a decent burial and forgot about outmoded R.N. traditions!"

"I'm sorry you feel that way, R.E.M. Merriton, but it's your decision," was all the flabbergasted Officer could muster by way of reply.

The following day Bob completed his draft out. A young Ship's Office Writer handed him a foolscap-sized folder, which was instantly taken back by a worried Chief Writer, who gently admonished the youngster, "You can't hand a man his 264, son! That's a libellous document! A man could sue the Navy for thousands if he got his hands on that!"

"Yair," Bob said laconically, "particularly since it has been repeatedly denied in both Press and Parliament that Form 264 even exists!"

The Chief looked more embarrassed, still. Silently he handed Bob the correct, official Form AS459, Certificate of Service, duly endorsed

'Discharged Shore. Engagement Expired' and 'Recommended for Royal Australian Fleet Reserve (not a volunteer)'.

Bob also had a Certificate of Competency in his trade and an attachment noting that REM (A) Merriton was 'a competent and capable rating, who has shown neither the desire nor inclination for advancement, although he has both the intelligence and ability to do so'.

"That's odd!" he'd mused aloud, "I wonder whatever made me apply for aircrew, if that's the case!"

He said his goodbyes to old mates, and responded to the chorus of "You'll be back!" with a heartfelt, "Not until Hell freezes over!"

Bob headed north with a kitbag, a few personal items, and a sense of freedom. Those and a Defence Force Retirement Benefits Fund cheque still to come were all that he had to show for six years of his life. As it turned out, the D.F.R.B. payment was for the full amount due, despite his refusal to sign for the Fleet Reserve.

He was also to find, to his surprise, that like most former permanent navy men, the psychological adjustment to civilian life was not the simple transition they had expected. Unlike men demobilised en masse following the two World Wars, Bob found he had an entirely different outlook on life to that of his civilian counterparts. Supposedly easy-going, casual and thoughtless, Bob's six years of orderly, disciplined living and working in an exacting environment had changed him more than he knew. Old mates he had known since boyhood now seemed slack, undisciplined, in both their personal and work habits, as well as racially and religiously intolerant and bigoted, obsessed with petty trivialities; shallow-minded. It took Bob twelve months or more before he was to lose this sense of impatience and annoyance with his old friends and his situation. A year later, he had a few beers with an old Navy mate, Billy Mac recently discharged from the Service.

Bill had articulated the problem accurately and succinctly, "You know, Bob, it's a strange thing, you can't wait to get out of Pussers; you think you hate the Navy! Then, as soon as you have to live and work in Civvy Street again, you start feeling all civilians are as wet as piss! Didn't it strike you that way?"

"You're telling me! It's taken me a year now before I can handle it again," Bob said, "suddenly, I knew exactly why so many blokes re-joined after only giving it a few months on the outside, blokes who were so definite that they wouldn't be back!"

70

Diana had enjoyed her day's outing, long and exhausting though it was. Joe was too busy to accompany her. All week, he was mustering, drafting, branding and marking. It was a time when she would have preferred to remain on the station, both in case of an accident, and to ensure that the men were supplied with plenty of good tucker, but she'd had an appointment in Roma with a visiting consultant. To miss that would have meant either a further three-month wait or a trip to Toowoomba.

Joe had told her, "You go, and make a day of it," so she had.

She'd collected Jenny on the way, and they had managed to combine business, shopping, and visiting a couple of old friends. Diana had dropped Jenny at Wilga Creek shortly after dark.

Jenny had invited her to stay overnight and return to Mt Chillingham in daylight the following morning, but Diana had declined the offer, "Thanks, Jen, but I'd better get back!

Joe will have had a hard day, and I like to pamper him a bit. We're not as young as we used to be!"

The headlights of the FC Holden station wagon pierced the darkness of the night as Diana sped along the recently graded gravel road. When it was in such good condition, she usually made the Wilga Creek-Mt Chillingham trip in around forty minutes - much too fast by Joe's reckoning. It was one of their few bones of contention. He had once exploded with, "You're a bloody maniac, woman! You leave no margin for error! If there is a 'roo on the road, you always hit it! Someday you will come over a jump-up to find cattle all over the track and you'll never have room to stop in time!"

But she loved fast driving. Sure, she had collected her share of kangaroos, but hadn't everybody? Sometimes, they came straight out of the timber so quickly; one couldn't have avoided them even at twenty miles per hour! Even at that speed, they could be dangerous, though. Diana considered herself a good driver. Even Joe had grudgingly conceded that, but it hadn't stopped him from worrying.

"A 'roo, at speed, might not only damage the car! It could cause a loss of control; it could even crash through the windscreen and join you in the front seat. That has happened before, causing write-offs at least, injury or death to the occupants at worst!" Joe had warned, "Besides which, you're supposed to be a Grandma, not a rally driver!"

Already, this evening, she had almost collected one young kangaroo, standing dazzled by her headlights. Quickly, she had flicked the floor-mounted dipswitch with her left foot, gently braking with her right. The roo had just enough time to recover from the glaring light and hop aside before the Holden slowed to the spot where he had been.

Her thoughts turned to her children, and her grandchildren, Bob was out of the Navy for about a year. There could have been work for him at Mt Chillingham, but he was working on a station in the Charleville area, his third job since leaving the Navy. She had only seen him three times in the past year. He had seemed restless at first, though by his third visit, two months ago, happened to be more settled. She wished he would find a nice girl and put down some roots, but to Bob, distant pastures had always been greener. A pity; he had enough ability and potential to succeed Joe as Manager.

Rosie had visited with her two younger children, almost two years previously, for a few weeks during the U.S. summer school vacation. Cliff Junior and Mary-Beth were attractive, polite adolescents but very pale-skinned. City kids from a northern latitude where the sunlight was not as strong as in Queensland. Even Rosemary had looked very light-complexioned now, although all were obviously in good health. The grandchildren were enthusiastic to meet Joe and Diana, and interested, at first, to ride horses and see the property where their mother had grown up, but by the third week, the novelty had worn thin and they had reached the threshold of boredom. They were nice kids, but the visit was more exciting to their mother than it was to them. Rosemary had brought some photographs of Tony, now a Navy pilot, and his wife - rather a pretty girl, although Rosie described her as "a spoilt brat". It appeared the marriage had its stormy moments. Diana had advised her daughter, "Make sure you don't interfere, Rosie! They have to work it out for themselves."

"I know that Mum, but Laura has been brought up as a politician's daughter. She can be very manipulative!"

"Well, I'm sure Tony will be able to deal with that. After all, he must be pretty cool and clear-headed if the Navy trusts him to fly jet aeroplanes," Diana had reassured her.

Privately, Diana shared her daughter's worry. For the early part of his life, Tony was more like a son than a grandson, to her and Joe. Reading between the lines of Rosie's latest letter, it appeared that Tony still had problems, but that he was happy to be back at sea, doing what he liked most and "living on his own adrenalin", as Rosie put it.

The road swung away to the left, not suddenly; it was rather a gentle curve, but the car was cruising at around 65 miles per hour; much faster than Diana had realised. Her preoccupation with family matters had allowed the speed to build up unnoticed. She applied a little more downward deflection with her left hand on the steering wheel, but the tyres had reached their limit of adhesion on the smooth gravel and dirt surface.

Instinctively, as the rear broke away, Diana changed lock and steered into the direction of the slide, at the same time easing off the accelerator. Another few yards and she would have corrected the drift, but the road was too narrow. The right-hand side of the road fell away sharply down a low embankment. Front and rear offside wheels left the road simultaneously as the car hurtled airborne, almost sideways into the darkness of the roadside scrub.

71

Joe was tense. Diana was very late! Had she decided to camp at Jenny's for the night, surely she would have phoned! It was almost eight o'clock. His anxiety had sharply increased around seven-thirty, a sense of fore-boding. He was being silly, he told himself! Every time she had had to come home at night, he had worried unnecessarily. She was a much better car handler than most men, himself included. Her reflexes were sharp and she never panicked. In fact, when it was her turn at the wheel on a long journey, he had always felt confident enough to nod off to sleep. That was something he rarely did when travelling with anyone else!

The Wilga Creek exchange was manual and non-continuous. He'd ring Jenny now, before eight. The postmistress understandably ended to get a bit shirty with unnecessary after-hours calls.

He made the call and was connected promptly. Jenny answered bright-ly.

"Hello, Sis! Is Stirling Moss still there? Joe asked.

Jenny understood his jest. Diana was a lead-foot, alright! "No," she said, concerned, "I thought she would have been home by now! She left just an hour ago because when I came into the house and turned the wireless on, I was just in time for the seven o'clock news. Now, don't worry, Joe! She has probably just had a puncture or something."

"Yes, you're probably right, Jen. I'll head off down the track to look out for her," Joe said, trying to sound casual. He hung up the phone, and quickly grabbed a flashlight and the keys to the Land Rover.

God, please let her be safe and sound, he prayed as he sprinted to the four-wheel-drive ute.

Seconds later, he was accelerating down the track towards the boundary gate, his mind filled with foreboding. Two miles on, he opened the gate, drove through, and disciplined himself to close it behind him, fighting back the dreadful sense of urgency tugging at him. He swung the Land Rover south, towards Wilga Creek, eyes peeled, his mind racing.

They should have been retired by now. He was sixty-five, but being a Director and shareholder of the private company, there was no compunction to retire until he was ready. Both Joe and Diana had hoped that Bob would come back and be trained to take on the managership.

Bob had known the run so well, and he was smart enough to learn quickly. He had developed a sense of responsibility, too, from his naval service. Oh, he was still restless and footloose after his discharge, but he seemed to be settling down. The last time Joe and Diana had seen Bob, they had asked him about coming back to take over.

"What about Doug?" he had asked.

"Doug has made it clear for years, that he is a ringer first and last! He won't take on the responsibility of being a boss himself, at the age of sixty-one, but he reckons he'd be happy to work under you as manager. You know, he has been in this place for thirty years! He could have left, he could have had moves upward in the company, but he has always said he is happier with the devil he knows and left it at that."

Bob had thought for a minute or two, and then said, "Thanks, Dad, but no! I'd feel awkward about filling your shoes here. Half the mob in this district still thinks I'm a bit of a bushranger. They'd all reckon you gave me the job and I'd be robbing you blind! You know what they're like."

"I know you wouldn't be robbing us blind," Joe said, "and, OK, supposing you are getting a leg up because you're my son, so what? This industry is built on nepotism!"

Bob had still declined.

"Well," Joe had said, "I'm not retiring just yet, so if you change your mind in the meantime, the offer is still open!"

He and Diana planned to give it another year, hoping Bob would re-consider. If not, they would have to accept the fact.

When they did retire, they planned to have a good, long holiday. New Zealand; a cruise; a visit to Rosie in America. He would even tolerate a few Operas and Art Galleries if that gave Diana pleasure.

Eight miles from the homestead, he saw dim headlights ahead, appearing then temporarily disappearing as he approached and clumps of trees sometimes blocked the view. As he drove nearer, it appeared that the car was off the road, but angled slightly towards it. She must have run off the road but at least the lights were still on! Probably bogged in the sandy topsoil.

He slowed and then turned off the road towards the Holden parked beneath a big old box tree. Funny she wasn't waiting for him beside the car!

The headlamps of the Land Rover now illuminated the Holden in a flood of light. Joe's heart almost stopped! The body of the station wagon was badly distorted, wrapped around the big tree trunk, intruding above the buckled roofline over the driver's door. He raced to the Holden, flung open the already sprung front passenger side door; Diana was slumped, half turned towards him, like a broken rag doll, those beautiful, dark eyes wide open in the stare of death; a massive, crushed wound to the right side of her head. Her right arm was flung above the broken steering wheel, the right side of her torso pressed against it, her back supported by the door that was pressed around the outline of the tree trunk. It was only then that Joe noticed the horn was still blaring, albeit faintly, from her weight against the horn bar.

Tenderly, Joe lifted her, extricated her from behind the wheel, and cradled her in his arms as he sat, numb with shock, in the front passenger seat.

The headlights and the ignition light were still on, though the engine had stopped. Shattered fragments of glass from the two offside doors littered the interior, their slivers cutting him, though he wasn't aware of it. Oddly, the windscreen and other glass was still intact, and the car had not caught fire. Gently, he closed her eyes, and they stayed closed as he carried her back to the Land Rover utility. He propped her up, somehow, in the left-hand seat of the cabin, against the door, and drove, scarcely seeing the road for tears, towards Wilga Creek. Once, she slumped awkwardly forward. He stopped the ute, repositioned her body against him, and after the vehicle was again in fourth gear, he held her against him, in the crook of his left arm. To lay her out in the tray of the utility never entered his mind. She was his wife, his beloved Diana! Even in death, she belonged beside him in the cabin of the Land Rover.

When they reached the township, he drove across the railway line, along the main street and up to the little hospital. He didn't know where else to take her, and once there, he was loathed to leave her.

The Sister at the hospital was very sympathetic. She asked if Joe had any relatives in town, with whom he could stay. He told her about Jenny, and that Jenny did not know yet, as he had brought his wife directly from the accident to the hospital. She phoned the policeman, who broke the news to Jenny and brought her to her brother's side.

The Senior Constable, with whom Joe was only vaguely acquainted, took a few basic details and suggested Joe spend the night in Jenny's care. "I'll go and have a look at it, Joe, and I'll arrange to bring the vehicle back to the Police Station. I won't worry you for a statement now; that can wait 'till the morning. Anything else I can do?"

Joe asked him to let Doug Gray know, at Mt Chillingham. "They'll be wondering where I've got to in the morning, otherwise."

"I'll take care of it," the policeman promised.

Joe was a shattered man. At the funeral, two days later, Bob thought his father had aged another ten years. Jenny, and Doug Gray, though very affected themselves, were a source of strength. Ellen, Leah and their husbands came west to pay their respects, but Diana's siblings were, like Rosemary, defeated by distance and could only send their condolences. Funerals, after all, are an indulgence for the living, not the dead.

But it is the suddenness, completely unexpected, which always shocks so much with a road accident death. Though vibrant and outgoing, Diana, at least, had led a full life of love with her man. She had not been cut down in her prime, as had John or Michael, or those millions of other young lives so tragically sacrificed in the human futility of war; yet those awful losses had seemed, somehow, more to be expected, though just as fully missed by their loved ones. It was a cockeyed world, Bob thought! He felt more like the parent than the son, as he comforted his father, "Cheer up, Dad! Mum would have no complaints; she had you, and for her, that was always enough."

72

By the mid-Sixties, in line with overseas trends, Australian society had changed considerably and not for the better, in Doug Gray's opinion. It was the eve of a big Rodeo in one of the larger Western Queensland towns. The old stockman entered the dining room at the best Hotel in town. Most of the guests had already dined and left the room, but Bob Merriton was seated alone at a table next to that of four rowdy and enthusiastically forward young city women, seemingly oblivious to their good-natured banter, which was aimed at making his acquaintance. He'd been pretty much a loner since he'd left the Navy, Doug reflected. It was almost as though Bob carried a chip on his shoulder at times. More conservative though; no longer that easily-led young fool who, rumour had it, had nearly been caught cattle-duffing. Doug reckoned Bob must be around thirty or thirty-one by now; certainly not before time if he'd grown up at last.

Bob saw him and gave a welcoming grin, "Hello, Doug! Nice to see a friendly face!"

A waitress hovering nearby handed a Menu to Doug as he joined Bob at the table. Doug waived the Menu aside and ordered his usual Hotel fare, "Just a rump steak, medium rare, with two eggs, chips, onions and peas, and black tea to wash it down, thanks."

Bob asked if she could organise a couple of beers for them while Doug's meal was being prepared. She nodded and left.

"I'd have thought you already had four very friendly faces at the next table," Doug continued the interrupted conversation.

Bob grunted his disapproval. "I'm not that bloody desperate! I wouldn't even chat them up for practice."

Doug was surprised at the disgust evident in the younger man's tone. Bob usually chased anything in a skirt, and all of these girls looked attractive, elegant and keen to get to know him. The older man shrugged and changed the subject.

"Riding this weekend?"

Bob nodded. "Yair, three events. I'm entered for saddle bronc, bull riding and bulldogging."

Doug shook his head in mock concern, "Must be some good sorts of nurses at the local hospital if you're so keen to get yourself busted up!"

"What do you mean? I'm indestructible!" Bob assured him with a confident grin.

A barmaid arrived with two beers on a tray. Bob paid, "Thanks, Kate. See you a bit later, eh?"

The barmaid departed, smiling rather smugly. The two men yarned about old times as they drank their beer. Finally, Doug's steak and eggs arrived. At the next table, champagne flowed and the laughter became more raucous and unladylike.

"Bunch of spoilt brats, the type whose parents have bent over backward to give them a good education and careers, shelter them and protect them from the big bad world," Bob observed, "then the minute they get to the University or the workforce and hear their first really rough four-letter word, they develop a compulsion to work it to death. If they manage to shock some poor bastard, they feel quite sophisticated and liberated. Well, they don't do much for me, I'm afraid!"

"Well, that's a turn-up! I never knew you to be a Puritan," Doug remarked. His hearing was no longer as sharp as it was in his youth, and he'd taken little notice of what the girls were saying, anyhow.

"No, I'm no Puritan," Bob said seriously, "but it's one thing for blokes to talk like that in a Navy mess deck or on a cattle camp, but it's quite another thing for women to carry on like that in public."

"You old stick-in-the-mud! And I thought that long-haired blonde would have been right up your street," Doug laughed.

"No way! I've met her sort before; come out West for the weekend and screw a Rodeo rider so that she can go home and brag about the experience to all her toffee-nosed girlfriends. It's a bit like slumming to them; they wouldn't give a bloke the time of day in Brisbane! Well, I'm damned if I'll give the sluts the satisfaction! Anyway, I've been putting a bit of work into that barmaid, Kate. Could even become serious. Well, see you around, Doug!" Bob excused himself.

After Bob had left, only Doug and the girls remained in the dining room. Now Doug couldn't help but overhear the conversation. He quickly concluded that Bob's assessment was accurate. Doug was rather shocked. His somewhat limited categorisation of women was restricted in the main to unpretentious country types, a diversity of plain-spoken barmaids, an occasional whore and a few real ladies, into which category he would count Diana Merriton and one or two others. At this point, all, even the whores and that immoral publican, Lily Lonnigan, seemed perfect paragons of ladylike propriety by comparison with these spoilt young would-be sophisticates from the city. Beautifully groomed and elegantly tailored, all four looked far too fashionable for a country pub, yet their conversation would have been better suited to a Sydney waterfront dive.

"Alison, would you like a reefer?" the longhaired blonde asked.

Alison's thoughts were miles away, "Sorry, what did you say?"

"Would you like some Mary?" The blonde asked.

"What's Mary?" Alison queried innocently.

"Mary bloody Warner, you silly moll! Do I have to shout it from the rooftops?" the blonde was becoming exasperated.

"Margaret, we can't smoke marijuana here!" Alison sounded alarmed.

"And why fucking not? I'll bet none of these bloody yokels ever heard of it!" Margaret said defiantly.

"Look, you're going to become a solicitor. Why risk arrest before you're even qualified? You could ruin your career," Alison argued.

"Speaking of which, I might as well have been done for soliciting, for all the notice that fucking cowboy took of me," Margaret observed drily, changing the subject. She addressed Doug, "Hey Old Timer, is your mate coming back?"

Doug bristled at being called, "Old Timer." The stupid girl must have watched too many Yank movies.

"No," He said curtly.

"Is he a poofter or something?" The one called Gwen queried arrogantly.

"No, he isn't!" Doug was becoming annoyed.

Margaret had lit a cigarette. She exhaled bluish smoke, then re-joined the conversation in a tone that clearly indicated that she was neither used to being disregarded by men nor liking the experience. "In that case, why doesn't he like girls?"

"Oh, he likes girls alright, but he definitely prefers ladies," the old ringer told her with perverse delight. This distinction did not impress her.

"Choosy, is he? Well, he's not exactly Robert Redford himself!" she countered in a brittle mood.

"That's true," Doug agreed, "Harry Redford might be nearer the mark!"

Harry Redford was a magnificent stockman and the greatest, most daring cattle duffer of all time. Brought to trial in this very town in 1872, Harry was acquitted by a jury of bushmen who had plainly admired the nerve and the superb overlanding skills of this master cattle thief. Redford's life was finally ended many years later, by a drowning accident; swept from his horse in a flooded creek on his Northern Territory station, "Corelia Downs." Almost every bush kid in the west had heard of Harry Redford, but Doug's passing remark was lost on these young city-educated women.

"Well, whoever he might think he is, he's still an arsehole," Margaret announced flatly.

"I have two arseholes. One of them is my fiancé," the fourth girl said morosely.

"Then why are you engaged to the bastard?" Gwen asked unsympathetically.

"Because he's filthy rich and I'm mercenary," came the brooding, self-recriminatory reply.

"But, Hilary, That's no reason!" Alison was shocked.

"Of course it is! Anyway, she can always find herself a boyfriend on the side," Margaret argued.

"Did you hear about Christine's appendicitis operation?" Gwen changed the subject.

"Christine who?" was Alison's typically naïve response.

Gwen glared at her, "Oh, you know, you nincompoop! That Christine was always in the news a couple of years ago. Anyhow, she said 'don't sew it up, Doc. I like a bit of cock on the side!'"

Amidst the uproar of laughter from the other three, Alison stole a glance at the leathery old chap at the next table. He'd finished his meal and was drinking his tea. Disgust showed plainly on his face. There was something oddly familiar about him; perhaps she'd met him years before. She summed him up. He reminded her of her father, a cattleman of the old school from the boots up. Ashamed, she fervently hoped he didn't know her dad.

"I'd love a root! I'm horny as Hell!" Gwen announced to nobody in particular.

"You're not Robinson Crusoe there!" Margaret said. Then, with vicious enjoyment, she observed the distaste of the old stockman as he drained his cup and prepared to leave. Loudly, she baited him. "Old Timer, are we upsetting you? Surely, you must have done some rude and dastardly deed in your time! Tell us all about it!"

Doug rose to leave, and then inspiration hit him. Coolly, he looked her in the eye and lied.

"Why, yes! I fucked a pig once, but up until now I've never been in fit company to mention it."

73

Across the Tasman, Helen Zietarski tried hard to find an excuse that would satisfy her friend, Angela.

"Oh, come on Helen! Don't be such a wet blanket" Angela pleaded, "I practically had to crawl to wangle our invitations for tomorrow evening! Look, we may wind up meeting a couple of really terrific blokes! Where's your sense of adventure?"

"Angela, I've never had much time for Yanks, and I'm certainly not interested in picking up sailors! You go on your own, or ask someone else," Helen said.

"Oh, for goodness sake! What are friends for? I was so looking forward to it. We don't have to pick them up; it's simply a cocktail party to welcome them to Auckland. Besides, they're not just sailors, they're Officers!" Angela persisted.

"Well, alright, just this once! But don't make any plans involving me for afterwards," Helen cautioned.

Moonlight bathed the northern approaches of Hauraki Gulf as the American aircraft carrier steamed majestically towards Auckland. She would anchor for a few hours, then, on a dawn tide, would make a spectacular entrance into harbour in the early morning light, along with her escorting destroyer and the two immaculate RNZN frigates, which had joined them two days previously for brief exercises.

Lieutenant Senior Grade Tony Roxton leaned his lanky frame against a sleeping A4E light attack bomber on the silent flight deck. Absently, his thoughts skipped fleetingly over the scenery and the coming visit to friendly, picturesque Auckland. His thoughts dwelt on his future and his past. He was aware that his wife, Laura, was already part of the former. They had no future together; he had accepted that, without rancour. Their marriage was a mistake from the very start, based on little else but physical attraction. Now that Laura had asked for a divorce on his return to the States, he'd agreed with a sense of relief. When he had first met her, he'd been a fresh-faced young Ensign. It had seemed to be almost a case of love at first sight to Tony, newly assigned to his first sea-going squadron aboard a Sixth Fleet carrier, and to Laura. The Congressman's daughter had a secretarial position in nearby Washington, DC, when they first met at a party in Norfolk, Virginia. Impulsively as always, Laura had taken leave from her job soon after, to travel to Europe to follow the Fleet around the ports of the Mediterranean. Oh, yes, he'd enjoyed her attention at the time! Several other Officers had wives who were following the ship and making a sort of European second honeymoon out of the tour. It was a fairly common practice, and undoubtedly saved a few marriages that might otherwise have foundered because of those long absences that are part and parcel of service in any Navy. Yet Tony and Laura were not even married at that time; then her parents had come over to the south of France on one of those fact-finding junkets so beloved of politicians worldwide. It had seemed like a good idea at the time, so the young couple had taken the opportunity to be married by a US Navy Chaplain in Toulon. Eventually, Laura went back to Washington, and they wrote to each other almost every night.

Later, as a Lieutenant Junior Grade, Tony had found himself posted to some trumped-up-excuse-for-a-job at the Pentagon. He was very angry about it at the time; his wife had cajoled her father into using his influence to bring the young couple together in the Capital.

Nobody had thought of consulting Tony in the matter. Hell, he was a Navy pilot, damn it, not some office boy/taxi driver for Pentagon Brass!

From then on, they had fought like Kilkenny cats. The lack of real job purpose, the endless round of parties, Laura's social-climbing friends; Tony had found it all worse than boring, it was downright depressing! Her father's well-intentioned advice hadn't helped either. "Just go with the flow, son! Sure, some of them are hard to stomach and sure, the Pentagon may be full of red tape, hot and bullshit, but the right connections now will be the fastest way up the ladder later on. Stay cool, meet the right people now and make the right impression; it'll pay dividends in the future. You could make full Commander around thirty-two!"

Tony had shaken his head and answered, "I just don't operate that way, Sir. In any case, I can't escape the conclusion that the lunatics have taken over the asylum."

"Hell, boy! Lunatics have been running the whole show for decades, not merely the Pentagon! It's just part of the system; the way things are in the lust for power. If you can't beat 'em, join 'em!"

Tony hadn't answered that one, rather than state the thought that came immediately to mind; 'yes, and end up like you in a three-way tussle with conscience, bourbon and hypertension! Not on your life!'

His father-in-law was a decent man, a liberal-minded politician who had newly gained some influence within a new Democrat Administration at the time. Had he expressed his private viewpoints publicly a few years earlier, in the era of McCarthyism, he wouldn't have escaped the attention of the Un-American Activities Committee. Even at the time, he was advising Tony to play it cool, in the Camelot of Kennedy, he wisely held his tongue in cheek on many occasions.

Finally, Tony had replied more tactfully, "I do appreciate your trying to help, Sir, but I'll continue directing whatever influence I may accrue to direct myself right back to carrier flying. It's what I enjoy, what I'm trained for, and what I do best."

All told, he'd spent a year in Washington by the time he eventually escaped back to the real Navy. A whole year of his life wasted! Perhaps his attitude was too uncompromising, too pig-headed since Laura had set her heart on trying to make their marriage work the only way she had known, whilst he had continued to show such open contempt for the type of lifestyle which she saw as natural, normal and secure. It must have seemed to her that he was rejecting her in favour of his need to fly jets. Perhaps he was; in that case, their marriage was no deeper than a sexual need.

Tony returned to flying at Alameda Naval Air Station; a brief sojourn followed by attachment to a new carrier squadron; Seventh Fleet this time around.

Laura had come out to Hawaii to join him for a brief leave, then again, after the Air Group had disembarked off San Diego, they'd set up house together on the West Coast for a while. They had both tried, but that initial closeness was never to return to their marriage. He'd sometimes wondered if she had taken to playing around during their long absences, like many another lonely Navy wife. Later, he had heard that she was having affairs since shortly after he'd left Washington DC.

But here and now, off Auckland, he was halfway through his third tour of sea duty with a Carrier Air Group. This would be his last, he'd decided. He would leave the Navy at the end of this year, tidy up his loose ends; give Laura her divorce and return to live in Australia.

His mother had a good marriage, to a fine man. His half-brother and half-sister were ten and twelve years his junior, respectively; as American as hot dogs and baseball. Though he loved them all dearly, Tony felt he shared very little common ground with them anymore. Increasingly, his yearnings were for the land and culture of his birthplace. Perhaps, he might even fulfil that early boyhood ambition to become a Royal Flying Doctor Service pilot. He smiled reminiscently.

Whatever, there would be plenty of scope for a career aviator in a place like Queensland. Oddly, he'd rarely felt he'd belonged in America. Maybe now he would feel that way in Australia also, after all of these years, but he knew he'd sure as hell give it a darned good try!

Tony wondered if his growing discontent with the U.S.A. had started with the realisation of the way things were done in Washington. To be fair, they were probably done no differently in Canberra! He did know that he had frequently felt frustrated and embarrassed that the U.S. so often and so readily alienated herself by self-righteously forcing her will on weaker, acquiescent Governments, thereby fuelling a smouldering resentment among the populace of those Nations. So often, Americans were left feeling genuinely hurt, by what they perceived as rebuffs, ingratitude or contempt of their friendly overtures. The fact that what was good for the U.S.A. might not necessarily be good for others, and the fact that America's often heavy-handed treatment of others was usually so transparently apparent in U.S. self-interest, seemed never to occur to most Americans. Indeed, were it not for his own time spent in the Capital, and his father-in-law's cynicism, Tony would never have noticed, either.

As he saw it, too often those lackeys who were supported by the U.S. were seen by others as incompetents, or self-serving opportunists, or worse, outright dictators whose very actions invited counter-revolution.

Tony recalled Laura's father once commenting, "What a bunch of ego-trippers, born losers or arrogant fascists we squander our taxpayers' money on! A whole host of goose-stepping roosters in banana republics, pious Chiang Kai-shek, Batista's thugs to name a few. Not a real Democrat in the whole motley crew! Then we organise the Bay of Pigs debacle! And we have the gall to wonder why others don't like us and even our friends think we're fools! Back in '56, we had Castro's goodwill, but we screwed up and pushed him into the Soviet camp. We almost brought World War 3 to our very doorstep! And now, we're getting suckered-in to Indo-China, taking over France's inglorious disasters! We are our own worst enemy, I tell you!"

In the latter case, the U.S. was actively encouraged by Australia and New Zealand, both of which were subscribers to the 'Domino Theory' of encroaching Communism creeping down from South East Asia. AN-ZAC fears were further fuelled by Indonesian President Soekarno's long flirtation with the Soviets, and his confrontation with Malaysia, Britain and Australia over Malaysian Borneo, though the latter was seen as a ploy to divert Indonesians' attention from their sorry economic mess, and promote national unity within.

The Australian Army had been providing Military Advisory Officers to South Vietnam for the past couple of years, following the example of the U.S. Also, with events worsening, Australia was now following America in despatching combat troops to the escalating conflict. This had incensed his grandfather. According to his mother's last letter, Joe Merriton saw his government as "Grovelling, prostituting itself, about to sacrifice young Australians to ingratiate itself as a compliant American Ally at any cost. If the right-wing, anti-communist Indonesian Army ever topple Soekarno, let's hope they don't have any designs on this country, or Australia and New Zealand will find the ANZUS Treaty isn't worth the paper it's written on!"

For an old bushie with only an elementary education, the old guy sure had a keen interest in world affairs. Tony's mother was a little shocked; she was worried that her father was becoming anti-American radical. Privately, Tony was inclined to endorse his grandfather's point of view. It might not be in American interests to oppose any future Indonesian ambitions once that country was safely out of the pro-communist camp. Wryly, he reminded himself that as a serving United States Naval Officer, he'd better keep such observations to himself!

Or perhaps his current cynicism, his discontent with the American way of life, was simply the result of his marriage break-up combined with the fact that he had spent most of his first ten years of life on a Queensland cattle run. He'd never found himself able to develop any liking for those cold north winds or the industrial drabness of Detroit; even less for the lechery and treachery he'd seen in the social and political rat race of Washington, DC.

The U.S. Navy, though, was a different kettle of fish. It was a good outfit and it had given him some good buddies. Yes, he would miss the Navy, but now that he had resolved his future directions in his mind, Tony looked forward a little impatiently; to the end of this chapter of his life; to a fresh beginning next year in Queensland.

74

As usual, Angela hadn't let any grass grow under her feet, Helen noted. The moment they'd arrived, her friend had attached herself to a tall, fair-haired Lieutenant with mischievous eyes and a witty turn of phrase. Helen had circulated, making polite but somewhat stilted conversation with several people. She felt awkward, ill at ease, and wished she hadn't let Angela pressure her into coming. Though Helen had no intention of being too available, an easy pick-up, she had no wish to be a damper on the party, either. Angela and her new friend suddenly reappeared at Helen's side.

"C'mon, Honey," the Officer said, "let me introduce you to my buddy Tony. You will like him. He's a real swell guy and he's not pushy!"

Helen felt embarrassed as she read Angela's ingenuously eager expression. She had obviously put him up to making the offer! It was well-intentioned, but Helen felt patronised; they were treating her like a shy child who couldn't make friends on her own! Brusquely, perversely, she declined the offer.

"Thanks, but I'd prefer to circulate for a while, and make up my own mind!" She wished she could have taken back those words the instant she'd uttered them. "I'm sorry," she said," I don't mean to appear ungracious, but I'd rather you two left me to my own devices. I'll be alright, really I will!"

She helped herself to another drink and a savoury from the waiters moving through the gathering. At least, she thought with relief, everybody else seemed immersed in conversation. That excused her from having to make any immediate attempts to be sociable. She stood alone but trying to look inconspicuous, at the fringe of a laughing, rowdy group. Around five paces away, in a more serious group, a tallish dark-haired young officer and a short, stocky middle-aged Commander were earnestly discussing something with the host and hostess, an elderly couple of somewhat Military bearing.

The young Officer, a Lieutenant, looked a very attractive man in a reserved, serious way. She studied his features for some time. Now that, she decided, was one Yank she WOULD like to meet! She found herself wondering why such a ruggedly good-looking young flyer seemed more interested in talking with his elders than in pursuing the local female talent. Suddenly, as if aware of her gaze, he turned his head to look directly into her eyes. She quickly looked away, turning towards the nearer group and pretended to join the general laughter at some quip she hadn't heard.

Tony had noticed the slender ash-blonde earlier in the evening. She'd been with Al and that vivacious chick with the tight auburn curls and wide, fun-loving eyes. You could always count on Al to find himself one like that! He attracted them like a light bulb attracts moths. Good old 'Girl in every port Al.' He always managed, somehow instinctively, to keep them content with a wild, brief fling and no promise of any lasting attachment. Yes, Al could leave them laughing, with nary an instance of a broken heart. He sure could pick 'em!

The little blonde had looked out of place, almost aloof. She had politely but charmingly given a few of the guys the brush-off, Tony had noticed. Perhaps she considered that she graced the party sufficiently with her regal presence, he had mused. Or perhaps, like himself, she had recently ended a love affair and wasn't yet ready to risk hurt again. Then, a few moments ago, he'd turned suddenly to find her studying him intently. She had averted her eyes, blushed noticeably and turned towards the nearest group, pretending to be part of it. So much for the "aloof and sophisticated" theory!

The Commander and the Host had verbally sunk most of the Imperial Japanese Navy between them, and a lull in the conversation allowed them both to catch their breath. Tony glanced to his left again; she was still there, and again, she was looking directly at him. He flashed her a smile, and this time, she did not turn away. Instead, she grinned self-consciously then nervously drained her glass. Quickly, Tony excused himself from the conversation and approached her.

"Hi! I'm Tony Roxton. May I get you another drink?" he asked

"Yes, please! I'm Helen Zietarski, and I'd like a Dry Vermouth," the blonde answered in a pleasant but unusual accent.

Tony soon returned with the drinks. As a conversation opener, he asked, "tell me, that's not a New Zealand accent, is it?"

"No," she smiled, "It's English West Country!"

"Aha! A Pom! I thought so!" he said, his eyes twinkling with good humour.

He really had broken the ice! "What do you mean, Pom?" She chided him, "That's what Aussies and Kiwis call us. You Yanks are supposed to call us Limeys!" She laughed.

"That's because I'm really an Australian, from just outside a little town called Wilga Creek, in Queensland. You can't get much more Australian than that!" he told her.

"You're pulling my leg." she responded in quaint imitation of a nasal Australian accent, "So why don't you talk like that?"

Tony laughed. He was sure he would enjoy this Auckland stopover. Angela and Al, with Helen and Tony, spent much of the following day, a Saturday, seeing the sights of Auckland. Later, the two flyers showed their new lady-friends over the big aircraft carrier.

The only other ship that Helen had ever been aboard was the passenger liner in which she had travelled to New Zealand. She was quite unprepared for the utilitarian starkness of living conditions aboard a warship, even for Officers. Tony and Al shared a cabin, which was virtually a tiny cell where upper and lower bunks shared a miserable few cubic metres of space with lockers, writing desktops and a myriad of pipes, shielded cables and ventilation ducts. On the flight deck and in the hangars, huge helicopters and twin-engined aircraft reposed, together with the comparatively tiny A4E Douglas Skyhawk which Tony and Al flew.

When Tony showed her his usual aircraft, 'Lt. A.D. Roxton' proudly stencilled in black beneath the cockpit canopy, Helen passed comment on the tall, frail-looking undercarriage legs supporting the little plane. She ventured the opinion that the undercarriage, indeed the whole aeroplane, looked far too slender and fragile to be flung into the air and later, landed back aboard ship in heavy seas sometimes hundreds, even thousands of miles from land.

"These babies are the toughest, most manoeuvrable jet airplanes ever built," Tony told her confidently, "and they're as safe as a Bank!"

His professional pride in his aircraft and in his ability to fly her was obvious. Helen discovered a new sense of respect and admiration for the men who lived, worked and flew in shipboard Naval Aviation.

Later, they dined together in a city restaurant. Angela and Al had left their company, hired a rental car and driven off to find themselves a quiet country motel somewhere. Tony escorted Helen to her flat. They talked, well into the night. He'd been a perfect gentleman and had made no attempt to seduce her. He'd told her the previous night that he was married, and that he and his wife had agreed to divorce upon his return to the U.S.A. From another man, it might well have led to a "my wife doesn't understand me" type of plea, but not from Tony! He seemed content with just her company and friendship, though it was obvious to both that a strong and mutual attraction already existed between them.

Helen's admiration for him increased even further. She was certain that she had never before met a man so honourable in intent, so completely devoid of any bitterness towards his estranged wife, yet so cheerfully looking forward to moving on to a new stage in his life. She fervently hoped he wouldn't lose contact with her after he sailed.

Tony talked about his early years at Mount Chillingham Station and his grandfather, still alive, at Wilga Creek. Helen told him about her parents in England; about her Polish father, in particular. She explained how, after her father's Regiment, along with the rest of the incredibly brave but obsolete Polish Cavalry was decimated in the Blitzkrieg of 1939, the young Farrier-Sergeant was fortunate enough to escape death or captivity. Eventually, in 1940, he had managed to reach England and was re-mustered for training in an Armoured Regiment. It was there and then that he had first met her mother. Shortly after their marriage and Helen's conception, her father was posted to North Africa. He'd served with the Polish Army there, also in Italy and in France as the Allied tide had rolled back the hated Nazis.

After the war, with Poland now under Soviet domination, her parents had settled in her mother's hometown in Dorsetshire, where Helen, her younger brothers and sister had grown up. Her father had worked for a local blacksmithing and engineering firm at first, repairing and rebuilding trucks, tractors and farm machinery. By hard work and sheer ability, he had prospered and now owned a garage with a motor vehicle and tractor dealership. Helen was very proud of her father, and of her mother, who had staunchly supported him through thick and thin.

"Maybe I'll meet them someday," Tony said.

"I certainly hope so!" Helen told him. Her heart skipped with joy; she was starting to figure somewhere in his future plans! She had only met him a little over twenty-four hours previously, but already she knew that she had fallen in love with him.

Sunday was another idyllic day. Helen and Tony picnicked in a park near the foreshore. Later, they spent a few hours at Auckland Zoo. It wasn't sophisticated entertainment; just the simple kind of pleasure they enjoyed in each other's company.

Back at her flat that evening, Helen cooked dinner. Tony helped with the washing-up, and then they relaxed with soft music and white wine. It felt so cosy, so natural. Helen thought. They had the place to themselves; Angela and Al either were still at whatever motel they'd spent the previous night, or were 'living it up' elsewhere.

"I've got duty tomorrow night, so I won't be able to see you again before Tuesday. May I pick you up outside your workplace Tuesday evening? We could go to dinner maybe, followed by a movie or something?"

The ship would sail Wednesday morning. They would have only what remained of this evening, and Tuesday night, before they would be parted for goodness knows how long.

"I'd like that," Helen kissed him, "and I'd like it even better if you'd stay with me tonight." Her grey-blue eyes appraised him with a mixture of sensuality and sincerity as she added, "I don't make that kind of offer to any old Tom, Dick or Harry, you know!"

"I realise that," Tony blurted out, taken aback by her directness.

"I know you realise that," she said simply, "if I didn't, I wouldn't have offered."

He held this gentle, direct English girl in his arms and kissed her tenderly. She responded with a degree of passion more intense than any she'd ever felt with any other man.

For each of them, Monday, Monday night and most of Tuesday passed with that moony, adolescent-like combination of anticipation and daydreaming normally presumed to be the sole preserve of lovelorn teenagers.

Tony went about his shipboard duties. Never one to wear his heart on his sleeve, he'd made no mention of his true feelings for Helen to anybody else. Even so, Al noticed the change in him. "Man," Al summed him up, "you really have done your balls over that Helen, haven't you?"

Tuesday evening finally arrived, and with it, for Tony and Helen, further ecstasy.

Wednesday morning, Al and Tony returned to a carrier under sailing orders. Angela and Helen phoned in to their office to say they would be an hour or so late in arriving, then waited on the wharf in company with numerous other Auckland girls, to farewell the big ship.

As the grey flattop got underway, Angela, enthusiastically waving and blowing kisses, smilingly turned to her friend. 'Miss Cool' was sobbing unashamedly, tears fairly streaming down her cheeks. For that matter, so were a few other girls, but it was Helen's uncharacteristic display of emotion that surprised Angela. Only five days before she practically had to twist Helen's arm to persuade her to attend the cocktail party! Not much time for Yanks and not interested in sailors! Not much!

Angela put a comforting arm around Helen's shoulders. "Cheer up, Love!" she said light-heartedly but tactlessly, "There'll be plenty more fish in the sea!"

"Not for me!" Helen blubbered adamantly, "I'm going to wait for that one!"

75

Eight weeks later, Helen was writing her twelfth letter to Tony. He, too, wrote at least once per week to her, but with limitations of mail deliveries that are part and parcel of navy life, some weeks she would receive no word from him. At other times two, or even three letters had arrived simultaneously.

She worried about him; the war in Vietnam had hotted up beyond the 'advisory' stage. A U.S. Marine Brigade was committed at Da Nang since March, to protect American bases, but now a continuous aerial bombardment of North Vietnam had begun. More U.S. troops were committed, an American and South Vietnamese ground offensive was in progress, and an Australian infantry battalion was on its way, with a New Zealand field battery also promised.

Tony's letters were very vague, "routine operations", doing what he was trained for, etc. In her heart, she knew his ship was operating off the North Vietnam coast, and the "routine operations" he'd mentioned were, in fact, air strikes against North Vietnam.

Helen had deliberated long and hard, whether or not to tell him the news. She didn't want to worry him, he had enough on his plate! And he was still legally married to someone else! But, she'd decided that he would want to know; she felt he would not be displeased, and that he loved her as she loved him. So she had started this letter cheerfully, optimistically; "My dearest, darling Tony, I have some wonderful news for you. All though I guess you will, at first, feel as surprised and shocked as I did, I am confident you will be as pleased and proud as I am.

If not, my darling, then I will understand and you need feel no obligation. I have just learned that I am going to have your baby, our baby!"

She continued the letter, in that vein of happy optimism with which she'd started, and, in closing, she stressed again that he'd been honest with her about his marital status from the start, and that if he was unable to accept responsibility or commitment, she would understand. She would not hold him to anything, but she would give their child all the love and care possible.

Before mailing, Helen re-read the letter. She wondered if it sounded a little too dramatic, even too noble. No, she decided, it would have to suffice! Whatever, he mustn't feel pressured or obligated. After all, he'd hardly seduced her! She'd offered herself to him quite unreservedly. Anyway, that was academic! She was sure he loved her as much as she loved him.

One week later, at the southern end of the Gulf of Tonkin, Tony was in a reflective mood. He had not yet received Helen's letter to inform him he would become a father. His thoughts were related, rather, to the bombing and strafing of North Vietnamese positions. It was a calculated risk he supposed. True, the Red Chinese were not likely to intervene directly on behalf of North Vietnam. Besides a traditional antagonism between China and Vietnam, there was, apparently, a strong Russian-Chinese rivalry for influence in the Communist Parties of Indo China, in which Vietnam was leaning towards the Soviet camp. Would China stand aside indefinitely, while the hated capitalists continued to pound North Vietnam? And did the South Vietnamese Government really have the support of the population outside of the capital, Saigon? Or was it merely a case of America propping up a convenient, corrupt puppet? Some marine and army officers had already indicated their strong mistrust of the whole rural population; it was hard to tell the friendly waving peasant from a guerrilla contemplating instant hostility. Certainly, the Viet Cong appeared to have enormous support to be able to operate as widely as they did! Anyhow, even if the U.S.A. and her allies eventually achieved what the French, who knew the country and its people far better, had failed to do against General Giap and his peasant Army, would there be anything left of the country to rebuild? Or would there remain a bitter, divided country in ruins, with lasting, savage North-South, and anti-American hatred which festered, never healed, as was the case in Korea? And how many innocent, suffering civilians had he, Tony, bombed and strafed over the last six weeks since the carrier was diverted to the conflict after leaving the South Pacific?

Another prospect he did not relish, should the war continue to escalate, was the possibility that he might no longer have the option of leaving the Service. Although he had increasingly identified in his own mind as Australian over recent times, there was no doubt that he was still an American citizen and an Officer of the United States Navy. Upon discharge, he would automatically go on the Naval Reserve list, and that Reserve could well be activated to provide for the Navy's rapid growth in manpower requirements.

His thoughts returned to Auckland and Helen. How he longed to hold her in his arms again! The mail plane had landed a few moments ago, just before he had made his way to the briefing room. No doubt, there would be a letter or two awaiting from his little English blonde when he returned from this sortie.

A couple of the younger pilots wisecracked, and then laughed at their own wit to hide their nervousness. Most of the assembled aircrew were, like Tony, quietly immersed in private thoughts.

The Commander, Air Group, or 'Cag' as was the more usual title in Navy parlance, entered the room and brought their minds back to the reason they were there. This was the same officer Tony was talking with at the cocktail party when Helen had first seen him. A valuable, professional officer, first blooded in action in 1944 flying a Hellcat against the Japanese in the 'Great Marianas Turkey Shoot', and later, F9F Panthers in the Korean War, Cag was now approaching his forty-second birthday. A motivated, dedicated communist-hater and a brilliant and forceful leader, Cag had virtually reached the end of his flying career and, had this war not broken out, might well have had to consider an early retirement due to lack of promotional opportunities. Now, it was highly likely that he would soon be promoted, first to Captain, and possibly, later, to command a whole Task Force as a Rear Admiral.

Despite his gruff exterior, Cag was a fatherly type of man. His own son was on the threshold of a career as a Naval aviator. Cag's pilots had always found him approachable, and Tony knew he felt deeply the deaths of the three aircrew that the Air Group had already sustained since their involvement in this war. Tony liked Cag, even envied him a little! Cag had no doubts, only an unequivocal belief in the justness of America's cause and of her obligations to defend the Free World, no matter what!

Tony jotted down times, coordinates, course headings and positions, as Cag handed over to the Marine Intelligence Officer for a more detailed summary of the target. It was a large column of North Vietnamese Regulars and supplies headed for the Laotian border and the Ho Chi Minh Trail. They must be stopped before reaching the sanctuary of Laos, to infiltrate down the eastern side of that country and re-emerge deep in the highlands of central South Vietnam.

Tony was to lead the second division of four. Al was his wingman. They would be attacking with air to ground rockets and then adopting a ground-fire suppression role before another squadron commenced a bombing run. F4 and F8 fighters would fly top cover to counter the expected Mig threat. Air Force and navy would be providing aircraft, and the large concentration of enemy troops could be expected to provide a stiff defence, possibly including Russian built surface to air missiles.

Timing and coordination were of the essence. Tony launched at 0938, the big catapult slinging him into the air with an acceleration of zero to 130 knots in around two seconds of stunning G-force. The Pratt and Whitney J52-P-6 took over the task as its 8500 pounds of thrust continued to lift the little warplane higher and faster into its natural element. By 0941, eight Skyhawks of Tony's squadron were streaking northward, crossing the coast some six minutes later, northeast of a large Vietnamese town, at 7000 feet. It was a ruse to lull the enemy into the impression they were headed for Hanoi. Quickly, they dropped down to deck level and then swung in a wide arc to a new heading of 235 degrees.

The Annam Range bordering Laos, was on their starboard beam after they turned to the southeast and climbed another six hundred feet. There, in the open country directly ahead and right where it was calculated to be, was the column. A line of light trucks carrying troops and supplies, some towing field guns. All were camouflaged beneath canopies of freshly cut branches. They moved along a bare dirt route through a patched savannah plain that was itself a mixture of grassland, bare earth and lightly timbered woodland. From a high altitude, the convoy would have appeared as a line of trees flanking a narrow country road.

Almost on the dot of 10.00, the squadron leader's flight of four caught the soldiers by surprise, raking them with air to ground rockets from behind, before breaking away to the left. Some of the ground fire followed some swung back in a deadly curtain of hail to the North, expecting a further wave of attack from the original direction. Thus, Tony's division, now approaching from the west to the right of the Vietnamese, again caught them by surprise a few seconds later as his planes turned tightly to run the length of the column from southwest to north. The first flight returned from the southeast to rake the disorientated troops with cannon fire and to nail a few trucks desperately attempting to disperse off the roadway into the adjoining open forest country.

More A4s swept in, this time with bombs for a single pass, and then vacated the area. The North Vietnamese regulars were effectively halted in a sea of carnage, yet more was to come. High above, USAF F105 bombers now rained further death upon the hapless soldiers, the target marked by rising plumes of smoke. It seemed a case of overkill; surely there could be no survivors from that dreadful, burning plain of scorching Napalm, that devilish, searing concoction of jellied petroleum, which burnt human flesh and destroyed buildings, vehicles and the environment with heat that must be second only to a nuclear blast.

The Navy A4E aircraft were heading back to their mother ship, leaving the continuing prelude to Armageddon far behind; comforted by the fortunate absence of surface to air missiles. It would seem the enemy's pressing needs further north, defending the Haiphong and Hanoi areas against the "Rolling Thunder" bombing offensive, had meant no "Sams" were yet deployed in this southerly sector to defend the convoys bound for Laos and the Ho Chi Minh trail.

The tension of the battle had gone; they were still deep inside enemy territory, still reasonable alert, yet possibly lulled a little by the aftermath of action. Out of the sun, from high above the Red section, two Mig 17 fighters dived. They were closing on the Blue section at a rate of one mile every three seconds. Two that had evaded the F8's and F4's of the top cover! Al saw them first, called the warning "Vandal Blue, Bogies! Above! Eleven o'clock!" Simultaneously he eased back on the stick, with some left rudder and left aileron as he broke formation. Now above and behind Tony, he rose to meet the approaching Migs with almost zero deflection as he fired. It was a fast, instinctive reaction, but too late. The first machine had already gone, narrowly avoiding a collision as it passed below him and astern of Tony. He saw a small grey puff float away from the fin of the second Mig as the last round from now-depleted cannons tore a hole that looked impressive but was little more than nuisance damage.

As suddenly as they had appeared, the Migs had gone, streaking west. From 'go to whoa', the whole action had lasted perhaps four seconds. Al's warning was too late to enable the others to take anything but belated evasive action. Only Tony flew unswervingly on his original heading. The C.O. called for a damage report from the Blue leader. No answer. "Blue two?"

"Negative!" came Al's reply. Blue three and four were also unscathed. Tony remained silent. He was also losing altitude, though very gradually. The Squadron Commander called his attention to that, too, but still no reply. Al resumed station alongside to starboard of Tony. Obviously nothing wrong with the engine; it was maintaining normal airspeed, although trim had obviously altered slightly. The airplane looked complete, at first. Cockpit canopy was intact; then Al saw it, the refuelling probe line buckled awkwardly. Close to that, on the lower right side of the cabin, were two holes where cannon shell shrapnel had egressed; one directly forward of the external 'Rescue' release, another slightly abaft and below the first. It was this, which had twisted and buckled the refuelling boom. Tony slumped lifelessly, his head forward over a chest restrained by the tight ejector seat harness.

Morbid curiosity overcame sickening apprehension. Al expertly slipped beneath his friend's aircraft routinely checking for visible damage on its underside, then re-emerged to the port of Tony. He had to look hard to see it, a surprisingly small, neat hole at the edge of the matt black antiglare surface below the windscreen frame! One lousy hit on the whole damn airplane, but just in the right spot at the right angle to have blown Tony's guts to smithereens! If he wasn't already dead, Al prayed he wasn't conscious, either. Yet, Tony must have taken his hand off the column to clutch at his stomach, and his legs had probably retracted up and back in pain, off the rudder bar. Otherwise, how could the airplane have maintained its heading?

"Pull her up, Tony! Take it easy, buddy! Don't go to sleep on me! We're nearly home!" he heard himself say. It was ridiculous, of course! Hoping against hope! Even if Tony was alive, even if Al could will him to hang together until they were well out to sea; even if Tony would have the strength to eject where the rescue chopper could reach him, it would be doubtful if he would survive the shock. Alternatively, not even Tony could land on a deck with his guts blown away! He was probably dead already, anyway.

Tony must have caught that 23-millimetre shell right at the beginning of the Mig leader's opening burst, a fraction of a second before Al's aggressiveness had caused him to switch his attention away. To have had that accuracy at such a range! The Commie was good, all right, and he'd had the drop on them! If he'd carried missiles and used them beforehand against the fighter over, Al was grateful. The Mig 17 was an obsolete airplane, yet Al would not have appreciated those guys looking up his tailpipe with missiles!

The Gulf of Tonkin was visible about ten miles away, beyond a low range of hills, perhaps 300 to 500 ft. high, a few miles inland from the sea.

"Come on, Tony! Lift her nose, buddy!" Al pleaded, refusing to accept that his friend was already dead. Following beside the track of Tony's Skyhawk, Al was already four miles south of the true course, at an altitude of 600 feet.

To the Squadron Commander, now back above, astern and to the north, it was obvious that Tony could not make it and was not even conscious. If Al wasn't careful, the squadron would lose two pilots on this mission. The dead pilot's plane was sinking too fast to make the seas, but Al was sticking to him like glue, judgement seriously clouded by the emotion of their close friendship.

Gently, but firmly, Vandal leader consoled, then ordered Roxton's wingman, "There's nothing more you can do, Al. Get back topside, Lieutenant! Now!"

The command was heeded none too soon. Al cleared a ridge by no more than one hundred feet; his Skyhawk rocking from the percussion of Tony's plane exploding into the hillside below. Al climbed in a slow, rebellious spiral to fly a final salute over his friend's funeral pyre, before re-joining the formation. No further comment was necessary. All six of the other flyers shared this loss of a friend, fully cognisant that the burning wreckage below could just as easily have contained any one of them! Four minutes later, they were over the carrier, joining circuit to land on.

76

Helen's last two letters to Tony were returned to her unopened, accompanied by a short, sympathetic letter from Al, informing her of Tony's death. Al had assured her that it was a mercifully swift end and that Tony would have been either dead or unconscious before the plane hit the ground. Al was thoughtful enough to send it all by way of a covering letter to Angela, so that Angela was there to break the bad news and to offer what comfort she could.

Nevertheless, Helen's overwhelming grief was not helped by the now obvious feeling that Tony had died without knowing that they would have a child in less than seven months. She was more determined than ever to cherish and protect this baby!

Nine or ten days later, Helen had put aside her tearful grief long enough to write to Al, thanking him for letting her know through Angela, and asking if Al could put her in touch with Tony's mother. Helen intended to write to Tony's mother, offering her sympathy and the information that she, Helen, had quickly grown to care deeply for Tony in the short time she had known him. It would be dependent on what type of response, if any, that came from Tony's mum whether or not Helen would inform her about the baby.

Fate again intervened. As before, her letter to Al never reached him. His squadron commander had the sad duty to write with the information that Al's aircraft, too, was shot down! It was of some comfort that Al was seen to have successfully ejected, although deep inside of North Vietnam. The probability was that he was taken prisoner of war.

Helen could do little more than to pray for Al, and, in turn, attempt to console her friend. Angela was far more deeply affected by Al's apparent fate than Helen had expected she would be.

What a terrible toll this war must be taking! Helen wondered how many of those young flyers who were at the cocktail party, would make it home to America. The publicised losses, on both sides, began to take on a more personal aspect in this horrendously impersonal struggle, so glibly portrayed by the nightly news bulletins!

It was several months later that Helen wrote, addressed to the "Personnel Department, U.S. Navy, C/- The Pentagon, Washington, D.C, U.S.A." She hoped that her request might reach the right quarters, although she felt strangely humiliated and even undeserving, in writing for information as to the mother of a dead Naval Officer, to whom she was pregnant. She was also naive in wording it.

A young Officer into whose hands the request fell did not relish the circumstances either.

"Damn it!" he swore. His wife was a close friend of Laura Roxton. Although he had not known Tony, he was aware the Roxton marriage had been in difficulties before Tony was killed. He did know that Laura had taken it particularly hard, blaming herself to a large degree of guilt, for her husband's death.

How the hell would she cope if she heard back through Tony's family, that some tramp in New Zealand was now claiming Tony had gotten her pregnant! He could almost visualise the broad! Some good time party girl; the kid could be anybody's, no doubt! The best thing he could do with this request was to lose it, preferably into a shredder! If she had the persistence to follow it up, he'd worry about that at some later time!

Helen did not follow up with another request. She decided that as she had not heard back from the personnel people, it must be either that the Navy had a policy of ignoring such unsubstantiated requests, or that it was passed on to Tony's mother who had chosen to disregard it. At least, Helen had Tony's memory, a couple of photographs, and, soon, his baby! That was all she needed. She had some savings and would get by until the baby could be left in day care and she could resume work. It would be a struggle, but Helen had no regrets. Her parents had asked her to return to England; Helen had declined. Perhaps, in the future, she would consider it, but to return to the small town where she had grown up?

No thanks! Pregnant and single? She would be better off in Auckland, with a few good friends like Angela. They could accept her and her baby without passing judgement!

The baby was a girl, with dark hair and brown eyes. Helen could see a strong resemblance to Tony. She'd thought of naming her daughter Toni, or Antonia, but decided, instead to christen her Stefanie Zietarski, in honour of her own father, Stefan. Helen's parents were both support-ive and concerned, and her mother had written to say her father had felt bewilderment, even rejection, that Helen had not returned to the family nest to have her baby. Naming the baby Stefanie might go some way to re-assuring him, Helen hoped.

77

The summer of 1968 in the southwest of England found Helen wondering why she had waited so long to return home. Persistently, since Tony's death, her parents had pleaded for her to come back. Obstinately, she had always declined until now. Her father had provided return airfare and told her that whether or not she decided to stay in England when she arrived, or to return to New Zealand, would be her choice, but at very least, to have the courtesy to bring his grand-daughter home to meet the family, so she had finally relented. Her family had made it clear that should she decide to bring up her child at home in England, nothing would make them happier.

That was so evident! Despite his deep Polish-Catholic convictions, Stefan would never for one moment intimate that his daughter had in any way disgraced her family. Nor had her mother, Janet, but then, her mother was always extremely understanding and tolerant.

They were a close, loving family; Steve and Paul, Helen's brothers, and Grace, her young sister, all doted on their pretty two-and-a-half-year-old niece.

Steve was a tradesman mechanic now well on the way to becoming his father's right-hand man in the family motor dealership. Paul was also learning a relevant trade as an apprenticed panel beater whilst Grace was still in her final year of high school.

Helen was home for almost a week. Her pleasure at renewing old acquaintances and friendships in the small town was a welcome source of surprise to her. Perhaps her mother's assessment was accurate after all when she had said, "Oh, you're far too sensitive and over-protective of

Stefanie! There are a lot of single mothers around nowadays."

Janet, like Stefan and the siblings, was very keen for Helen and Stefanie to remain in England. Stefan had offered his daughter part-time work in the office with flexible hours to tie in with the demands of motherhood should she so desire to remain in England yet retain her independence. Janet, too, was eager to assist with raising her granddaughter. Helen found such promises of family support most encouraging, very tempting. Life at home could be much easier in many ways, than in Auckland, yet she knew that there would be times in the goldfish bowl existence of this village when she would crave the anonymity of the large New Zealand city. Auckland people were also friendly, yet less intrusive.

Oh, her mother was right! She had become too sensitive and over-protective. Helen was coming around to the idea of resettling in England.

Another week passed by. Helen frequently visited Aunt Peggy, her mother's sister. Peggy had always been her favourite aunt, a gentle, sunny-natured woman in whom Helen had sometimes confided her problems when she was a little girl. How odd it seemed that Aunt Peggy and easy-going Uncle Bill should have been the parents of the malevolent Mandy! Two years Helen's senior, her cousin was an overbearing bully as a child and spiteful as an adolescent and young woman.

Mandy was of that ilk who crawl to and curry favour with those who they regard as equals or superiors, yet go out of their way to be spiteful and humiliating to those whom they regard as fair game. In Mandy's eyes, Helen had always fallen into that latter category, possibly because of Helen's own prettiness, lack of cattiness and air of soft vulnerability, and no doubt partly because of jealous resentment of Helen's friendship with Peggy. Whatever the reason, Mandy's constant needling in the company of their peers had always hurt; such inferences that Helen was somehow inferior, "not really British" with a name like Zietarski, or of being "not very bright" whenever Helen had not been quite conversant with subjects of interest to the older girls. Such slurs soon taught the gentle little blonde to avoid her cousin and cronies so far as was possible. Those insults were all the more hurtful because the younger girl had never consciously done anything to offend Mandy and Co.

Indeed, Mandy was a subconscious influence in Helen's eagerness to flee her home environment and to seek greener pastures at an early age. In turn, this had fanned the flames of a desire to travel; that which had eventually led her, less vulnerable and more worldly-wise, to the Land of the Long White Cloud some five years past. Helen had not encountered Mandy for some six or seven years now, for which she was grateful. Mandy was married and living some twenty miles distant. Sitting in Aunt Peggy's parlour during a short afternoon visit. Helen noted again that patient love and affinity which Peggy had always seemed to show to all children. Her aunt was listening intently to the prattling toddler on her lap. Peggy whispered some shared confidence in Stefanie's ear. The child giggled spontaneously, then hugged and kissed the elderly woman.

At that moment, the doorbell rang. Peg stood up, carrying the youngster and went to answer it.

"That will be Mandy! She usually drops by on Tuesday afternoons," she explained.

Helen involuntarily stiffened, that old fear and loathing clawed at her stomach. She forced herself to relax; it had been years, Mandy had probably changed for the better, with any luck! At any rate, Helen told herself, she had learned to handle herself in most situations now. She heard Mandy's voice at the doorway.

"Hello! Who's this, then?" Her cousin sounded bright and cheerful.

"This is Stefanie!" Peggy announced fondly, by way of introduction.

"Stefanie? Oh, yes! Helen's little Yankee bastard," Mandy recalled flatly.

"Shhh! Helen's in the parlour, and you be nice to her!" Peggy admonished in a hushed tone of suppressed fury.

At that moment, Helen arrived consciously at the decision she had known already in her heart. There was no place for her here in her home village. Determinedly, she fought back the tears threatening to well in her eyes. Her aunt and baby re-entered the room, followed by her cousin.

"Hello, Helen! Back home for good, then?" Mandy asked, feigning friendliness.

"No, Mandy. We'll be going home to Auckland in a couple of weeks." Helen forced herself to be polite.

"What on earth is there for you in the Antipodes?" Mandy wondered aloud.

Coolly and casually, Helen looked her cousin over, and then replied, "Oh, you'd be surprised! It's a much nicer environment to bring up Helen's little Yankee bastard!"

Poor Aunt Peggy looked as if she could have died! Helen wished she had been less forthright for her aunt's sake. Mandy, the imperious bitch, looked taken aback for no more than an instant, then changed the subject to the weather. It was all of little importance to her, anyway.

78

The early 'Seventies. Joe was ageing but still very active; he had not retired. Since relinquishing managership of Mt. Chillingham soon after Diana's death, he'd attempted to keep himself busy and his mind occupied by dealing in cattle and occasionally, sheep. He had bought a six hundred and forty-acre paddock adjoining the old Wilga Creek family selection. It had come onto the market cheaply enough, being far too small to be a viable run in itself. However, in combination with the three twenty of the old Merriton block in front, the resultant nine hundred and sixty acres made up a good little dealer's block, situated just across the road from the railhead.

The old man spent quite a lot of time on the stock routes now, buying, selling or delivering stock. He'd never become another Kidman or a Tyson; in fact, he eked out a fairly austere living but his wants were few and he was reasonably contented.

Jenny sometimes returned to stay for weeks or even months with her brother. She had developed a wanderlust in recent years. Armed with her pensioner rail concession, she divided her time between Wilga Creek, her two married daughters, one at Toowoomba, one at Caloundra, and her son Tom and his family in New South Wales. Unlike Bob, Tom had made a career in the Navy and had reached the rank of Chief Petty Officer. He'd married a nice girl with whom Jenny shared a good rapport. Jenny liked to feel useful and helped out willingly with home chores and babysitting whenever she visited her children and their spouses. She was always careful never to overstay her welcome and returned often to the sanctuary of Wilga Creek.

It was a way of life that she had come to cherish and she felt fortunate indeed, to be able to avail herself of it. Gregarious, well-meaning but never intrusive, Jenny had always had a great zest for life. Joe had often wished that fate had treated his youngest sister more sympathetically in her marriage and in her struggles as a lone parent, but there was no denying that she now loved that very independence which she had developed.

As for Bob, he was now head stockman on a big northern run and Bob's wife, Kate, was cook on the same property. Kate was one of those friendly, uncomplaining bush women who was born to a life of hard work and simply accepted that. She was intelligent but lacked formal education; domestic, barmaid, waitress and cook, she was almost as restless as Bob until they'd met in the mid-'Sixties. They had just sort of clicked, apparently, and Bob had become quite responsible, even conservative, as the relationship had matured. No longer was he the brash, impulsive rebel who had given his parents such cause for concern in his youth.

It seemed unlikely, though, that the Merriton name would be perpetuated as Bob and Kate were both nearing forty and had no children. Joe saw them once each year; they always dropped in and stayed for a few days during their annual holiday break. The older man would have liked to have been able to spend more time with Bob and Kate; there was a closeness now between Joe and his son, which earlier had eluded them.

Cattle prices were buoyant and Joe dealt well but wisely. City speculators had started to pour money into buying and stocking country properties. There was a good dealers' market if one could read it. Joe knew, however, that such a boom could not last. Always, there were cycles of boom and bust in the pastoral industry, normally linked to good seasons or severe drought.

Occasionally, though, an artificial boom would materialise as a result of greedy speculation, and this was one of those latter examples. No longer heeding the lessons of supply and demand, many people, it seemed. from clerks to industrialists, from labourers to lawyers, were using borrowed capital to pay unrealistic sums for hobby farms and run-down stations alike, then overstocking to blazes in their ignorance and optimism.

Their ranks were swelled by genuine producers switching from sheep to cattle ever since the collapse of the wool market. Foreign wool buying cartels had reduced that market to unprofitability by exploiting the lower costs of synthetic substitutes.

Eventually, of course, history would record that the woolgrowers were reprieved by the actions of courageous, far-sighted and often maligned industry leaders who persuaded the Federal Government that the industry was, indeed, worth saving. An Australian Wool Corporation was formed with government underwriting to provide a minimum floor price by which the new authority could purchase and store much of the flip, hereby providing competition to the foreign cartels. It was fortunate for Australia that she grew the lion's share of fine and medium wool fleece production. Together with the minimum floor pricing and a growing acceptance by world consumers that substitutes were inferior and could provide few of the qualities of natural fibre, the 1973 world energy crisis provided a further key by massively inflating costs of the competing synthetics. It was a close-run thing, the salvation of Australia's wool industry, yet those very men who had shown the leadership, the initiative and the courage to see it through, had to endure abuse and name-calling from many of their fellows; "Socialists", "Interfering with the freedoms of the individual", "The beginnings of collectivization" and other such ideologically motivated taunts.

Australia would be in no such position to call the tune a few years later when the beef industry would plummet. Speculation and over-borrowing, followed by drought and exacerbated by massive subsidisation of EEC farmers with resultant "dumping" of beef on world markets, would decimate Australia's cattle herds.

Joe, of course, was no agricultural economist though common sense and long experience urged him to be cautious. During the Sixties, big wheat prices had provided a similar impetus for world overproduction and overcapitalisation. Unsuitable land was pressed into rain production, trees pulled, topsoil lost and marginal rainfall country cultivated. How well he recalled the words of one disillusioned DPI man, "They'd try to grow wheat on Ayer's Rock if they got the chance!"

Joe knew that it would be the same for the beef industry and that many fingers would be burned once this boom finally ended. In the meantime, like snake oil salesmen, various entrepreneurs and self-appointed fountains of knowledge were promoting more than a dozen new or exotic breeds, all claimed to be the magic solution to all fertility, calving, drought survival, climatic, weight gain and feed conversion problems. Everyone and his brother had become instant "experts", and the smart money was there to make a few quick quid promoting, breeding and selling these new breeds, (if only first crosses) to the gullible. The con merchants would move on to fresh ventures in a year or three when the silly prices returned to more realistic levels. As time would prove, very few of these newer breeds would have much impact in the long term. With his old-fashioned integrity and conservatism, Joe was content to dealing steers and bullocks mostly Hereford or Shorthorn.

The 'Eighties. It was not until the early 1980's that Joe Merriton finally began to slow down. He still kept a small mob of his own cattle on the nine hundred and sixty acres at Wilga Creek "to keep my hand in." as he told his friends and family. The truth of it was that two decades after Diana's death, he was still a very lonely man.

Pottering around, riding the boundaries daily or keeping the yards and gates in good repair, mustering regularly, whether to rest a paddock or to draft out a few for sale; these were things which kept him occupied and very fit for his advanced age. Jenny spent little time at Wilga Creek, now. For most of the year, she lived in her new "granny flat" adjoining Tom's residence on the New South Wales south coast. Tom, now retired from naval service had, with his wife Jill, invested their savings and a quite substantial retirement benefit in bricks and mortar. They enjoyed a congenial lifestyle as proprietors of a modern medium-sized motel in a pleasant tourist and fishing haven beside the Princes Highway.

Joe spent a few weeks there in 1984, with Jenny. It was a relaxing holiday, a little too much so, he felt. Tom and Jill made him very welcome, took the trouble to show him the district and introduced him to many of the locals. Joe enjoyed the holiday but soon found himself impatient to return to Wilga Creek.

"Do you ever miss the bush, Tom?" he once asked his nephew.

"Never, Uncle! Mind you, I don't like the Big Smoke any better, either. This little town has everything that Jill and I need. It's home to us now. I've been away from the dust and the horse sweat for nearly thirty years now, remember!" Tom replied with a smile of understanding.

"Yes, I can see that you have a good life here. You're a part of this place now, just as I'll always be a part of Wilga Creek and the cattle country, Tom!" Joe conceded.

79

Stefanie Zietarski and two girlfriends had decided to holiday in the big brash country to the west of the Tasman Sea. Although she and Helen had shared a second brief trip to England before Stefanie commenced her nursing career, they had never made that relatively short hop across "The Ditch" expressly to see Australia.

The young nurse had long felt an urge to explore the vast old land; ever since she had become old enough to realise that Australia was the birthplace and spiritual home of the young American Naval Officer in the photograph. This photograph, the name and rank, Anthony David Roxton. Lieutenant, USN, together with a precious but pitifully minute store of trivia, represented all that either she or her mother knew of Stefanie's father.

She'd grown up determined to find out all she could about him and her own origins. She therefore took the opportunity early in her vacation to register her qualifications as a dual certificate Sister with the Queensland Nurses' Registration Board. Surf, sun and Expo 88 accounted for most of the holiday visit, but the three friends managed to spend two days exploring some of the hinterland with their Ford Laser hire car.

Stefanie resolved to see Queensland in much greater depth as soon as she received confirmation of her Queensland nursing registration. She was particularly hopeful for a position if one should arise in a western Queensland hospital, a prospect which neither of her friends found in the least appealing.

"Oh, Stef! Why move out to the dust and the flies? Why not look for a job here, on the Coast?" she was asked.

Stefanie smiled enigmatically and drawled a gruff reply, a send-up of a John Wayne impersonation. "Waal, a gal's gotta do what a gal's gotta do!"

Neither Stefanie nor her mother had known for certain, the name of Tony's hometown in Queensland. Helen had remembered it as a pretty, girlish-sounding name.

"Wilma's Creek, I think it was!" had always been Helen's recollection, yet there was no name even remotely like that; neither in Stefanie's school atlas nor in any other map of Queensland that they had seen in Auckland. Yet here, in the "Hospital Medical" section of the Employment Classifieds of the Brisbane broadsheet newspaper of the Wednesday before the girls were due to fly home to Auckland, this just had to be the very place! It must have been fate, Stefanie decided!

The advertisement for a double certificate Sister required a State Registered Nurse for Wilga Creek Hospital. Written applications were invited, requiring details of full name, date of birth, previous experience and two recent professional references. Single accommodation was available and a telephone number was quoted for further particulars if desired.

A geographical location was stated in the advertisement and Stefanie realised with a thrill that this Wilga Creek, not Wilma's Creek, was the very same place that had long occupied her thoughts. Those maps which she had scrutinised in New Zealand hadn't mentioned a Wilga Creek, either. Still, that wasn't surprising. After all, from the advertisement, this was a very small hospital, in the number of beds and average daily occupancy rate.

Stefanie dialled the number given and the tired female voice at the other end inadvertently expressed surprise at such a quick response to the advertisement. Stefanie eagerly explained that she had already applied for State Registration, which she was expecting to come through within a week or two, and that she had resigned from her previous position before commencing her vacation. She advised that she would mail her application forthwith and planned to return to Queensland immediately after she received her State Registration.

"When you have that, come out here and we can look each other over," the tired voice drawled. "If your application stands up, from what you've told me you should have no trouble."

"You don't think the position might have been filled by then?" Stefanie asked anxiously.

There was the slightest hint of humour in the tone of reply, "I doubt it, Dear, but give me a bell before you come if you like. In the rare event that we do get someone straight away, I'll let you know at your Auckland address!" the tired voice promised.

Stefanie thanked the woman and hung up the receiver, wondering just what she might be letting herself in for; it seemed obvious that State Registered Nurses weren't exactly falling over one another for the chance to work at Wilga Creek!

80

Helen's face betrayed her concern when her daughter arrived home with the news that she'd applied for a nursing vacancy at Wilga Creek.

"Don't count on being too welcome if and when you do locate your father's family," Helen cautioned gently, "They may very well regard you as an unexpected embarrassment after all these years. Then again, there may be no family left by now, except in America. His grandfather surely must be dead by now!"

"I realise that, Mum. I'll keep a low profile anyhow, but I do so want to live and work in the sort of environment that shaped him. I know virtually nothing else about him but at least I should have a better understanding of my roots once I get to know the district and its people. It's very important to me; I need to know, Mum!"

Silently, Helen nodded her understanding of why Stefanie had applied for a vacancy in that distant outback town. Far from a girlish impulse, this was an opportunity for which her daughter had always yearned. The fledgling must leave the nest to search out her own territory. Indeed, she was much younger than Stefanie's present age when she had left England for the far side of the globe.

Mother and daughter had always been very close and still were. They had done almost everything together, cheerfully accepting life's ups and downs, up until Stefanie began her professional training. Helen was so solicitous of Stefanie's welfare and upbringing that she had resolutely denied herself any male friendships capable of developing beyond the strictly platonic until Stefanie turned seventeen. So determined had she been that nobody else should discipline her daughter or jeopardise the girl's sense of security that Helen had allowed herself no thought of romance. Not that she had looked upon her attitude as a burden; as some noble, self-sacrificing duty. Helen's conception was that it was the only right and proper course open to herself. She smiled in recollection of how, at the age of fifteen, Stefanie had broached the subject herself.

"You know, Mum," the youngster had told her seriously, "you are still a young, very attractive woman. You had better start looking around for a nice boyfriend or you'll be very lonely when I fly the coop."

The wisdom of youth! Yet Helen considered herself very fortunate; when Stefanie did become a student nurse and developed other interests, Helen, at last, became aware of the interest of a fine, caring man whom she had known for many years.

Trevor had been divorced since the mid-seventies. He had quietly bided his time, knowing and understanding Helen's concern because he'd been frustrated and denied in his relationship with his own children. They were in his ex-wife's custody and he was allowed access all too rarely, apart from such school holidays as he was able to arrange with his employer for his own annual leave periods to coincide.

After Stefanie had begun her training, Helen and Trevor had commenced keeping company. Love had blossomed, they had married in late 1986 and had made a secure, loving marriage. Stefanie need have no fears that her mother would suffer from her absence abroad.

Wilga Creek was accessible by both air-conditioned train and bus services, but Stefanie had felt that she would need a greater degree of personal mobility in such a distant area. She had invested $2500, most of her savings, in a fifteen-year-old Toyota Corolla, had joined the RACQ, and then driven westward from Brisbane, hoping that she would not have to call on the services of that august motoring organisation. Thankfully, the long journey had not found the small, old car to be wanting.

It had performed very well all the way along the hot bitumen road. With all windows wound down for ventilation, it was a pleasant enough drive. Though still only late spring, Stefanie found herself a little surprised at the intensity of the dry inland heat and the proliferation of insects. She saw a harsh beauty in this seemingly endless landscape, a plain land of black and red soils with sunburnt grasses, grey-green trees, broken very occasionally by a sign-posted creek; usually no more than a dry depression or a narrow puddle over which the highway traversed on a modest bridge. Driving through this particular stretch of country, she became aware of an uncanny feeling; an almost spiritual empathy with new, yet oddly familiar surroundings. It was the feeling that her very soul somehow belonged in this particular stretch of country; something she had never before experienced, not on the rolling downs and broad grain fields further east, nor even in the lush green beauty of New Zealand's North Island where she was born and raised.

In her student days, Stefanie was introduced to an Australian Aboriginal activist in Auckland. The Aboriginal had attempted to explain a case for Land rights, something about being at one with the land in a way that bore no relationship to the white man's conception of material ownership. Apparently, the concept espoused by that Aboriginal was something to which very few white Australians could relate, or even care about.

At the time, Stefanie herself had not understood, either. In fact, she felt that this so-called spirituality thing was merely some form of Aboriginal confidence trick to advance their Land Rights argument. After all, she had felt, land was just that; land, with grass, trees, rocks and things. One owned it or leased it, and used it to grow things, or to live on and to build homes upon. Surely, one piece of land was similar in that respect to the next, be it much better or much worse. Now, driving through this particular stretch of country, visually new to her yet projecting this feeling that she was somehow part of this hard, parched land of misshapen trees and dry watercourses and that it, too, was a part of her, she finally comprehended something of what that Aboriginal activist was trying to impart. She found herself wondering whether she, through her father, might have had some Aboriginal ancestry.

81

That tired voice at the other end of the line a couple of weeks previously had belonged to Joan Kirkyard, Matron of Wilga Creek General and Maternity Hospital. A tall, gaunt woman whose laughter lines and compassionate nature belied the absolute authority that was hers within this small domain, the Matron summarised her hospital's role and position as "catering to the requirements of a small population spread over a very large area. There are only half a dozen or so hospitals scattered along more than 500 kilometres of the railway west of the Darling Downs, with fewer still at the northern and southern extremities of the region. This particular little establishment serves an area of some forty thousand square kilometres, including three settlements even smaller than Wilga Creek, and about three hundred grazing properties."

Stefanie was surprised that such a small facility could cope. Joan Kirkyard enjoyed the younger woman's amazement. She laughingly replied, "There isn't a very large populace, and we do breed them tough out here! Roma is by far the largest town on the western line, with around six and a half thousand people. Second would be Charleville with less than four thousand, and anywhere else is little more than a flyspeck on the map. We are a far cry from Brisbane or Auckland, but we need to be up to the tasks required. There isn't a lot of backup out here! Think you can cope?"

Stefanie said she could, and would welcome the challenge.

"That's the spirit, Dear! I'm sure you'll be able to handle it. Your references are excellent but don't be afraid to holler for help if you need it. When can you start?" the Matron asked.

"As soon as you need me. Today, if necessary! I've brought all of my baggage with me," Stefanie said.

Joan Kirkyard was delighted. "That's terrific! I shan't expect you to start today, but I'll introduce you around and help you settle into your quarters now. I'll roster you to start in the morning."

Registered and enrolled nurses alike all welcomed Stefanie with that relaxed air of competent professionals, at the same time, no doubt, shrewdly making their assessments of her likely competence and the likelihood as to whether or not she would remain long in Wilga Creek.

In the late afternoon of that first day, Stefanie strolled the five hundred metres or so from the hospital, past a few old wooden houses with mostly cracked or blistered paintwork from the hot, dry climate, to the business centre. Not that the commercial heart of the little town was of any great extent. One side of the main street fronted the railway station and three high-set railway residences. Opposite were the Railway Hotel, a stock and station agency. a cafe, a post office/Commonwealth Bank Agency, two small cottages, a garage and service station, an intersecting side street leading to the local state primary school, two churches and a few private residences. Beyond the intersection, the main street continued; a level crossing and a wooden hall on the railway side, opposite the Commercial Hotel- Motel adjacent to a pharmacy that also served as a building society agency and C.E.S. Agency. Next to that was the doctor's residence and surgery, then another private residence, and finally, the police station and residence. Here the bitumen ended and a gravel road led on for a short distance before curving away to the right to follow the general direction of the creek through the trees. A few short residential streets behind the business centre completed the town environs.

To any traveller on the Warrego Highway along the far side of the railway line, a humble homestead fronting the highway, a small railway station and goods shed, the railway houses and hall, a roadside hoarding advertising the existence of the modern air-conditioned Commercial Hotel-Motel, and the top of the town's water tower were the only visible indicators to this thriving little community.

Stefanie found the architecture fascinating. Apart from the concrete water tower and the modern Hotel-Motel, not one other structure in the town would have seemed out of place at the beginning of the twentieth century. All were of wooden construction, mostly low-set with high roofs and wide verandahs or awnings. The Railway Hotel was the only building of more than one storey and to Stefanie's eyes would not have looked out of place on the set of a Western movie.

The stock and station agent, who traded in a wide range of rural merchandise and real estate as well as livestock, operated from a barn-like structure with a plate glass frontage, enclosed yard and loading dock attached. The cafe cum milk bar was a plain but neat, clean-looking establishment of 1940s internal decor and framed picture-posters on the walls. Typical of many inland Australian restaurants and snack bars, the friendly proprietors appeared to be of Greek or similar Mediterranean extraction. Stefanie bought a cold soft drink at the front counter and had a cheerful conversation with them.

Refreshed, she continued her exploratory walk along Wilga Creek's main street. The recently painted post office was of otherwise un-prepossessing appearance, as were the two slightly dilapidated cottages nestling behind their picket fences and neglected, dried-out front gardens.

A sprawling general store with imposingly large plate glass windows, all but one of which were blanked out with greyish-white frosting and heavy signwriting, hinted plainly that it had seen better days as well. Two people, a middle-aged woman and a gangling youth stepped from the doorway as Stefanie strolled by. The woman smiled a pleasant "Hello" to the stranger in town, while the young man stared with a look of undisguised interest and approval. Stefanie smiled shyly in passing. The natives certainly seemed friendly enough!

On the corner, the garage and service station was another surprisingly large building for such a small town business. Had the young nurse but known its history she would have been less surprised, for it had started life as the town's livery stables and buggy hire premises.

Across the intersection, the sprawling, modern, brick single storey Commercial Hotel-Motel occupied what had originally been two sites; the former Stagecoach depot and the old Royal Mail Hotel, both of which had burnt down long ago. A smaller, re-named Commercial Hotel had replaced the Royal Mail for some years until the advent of the bitumen highway across the line had emboldened the licensee to borrow finance and to update the premises. As Stefanie walked past, she noted several cars parked in the carports fronting the units, whilst a tourist bus waited by the Lounge Bar and Restaurant entrance. Obviously, this modern facility enjoyed a good reputation.

Across the street, beside the railway line the weathered Memorial Hall, built in the 1920s, with its two outside toilets, would have been equally at home in any of a thousand small towns throughout Australia and New Zealand.

Beyond the Hotel-Motel, a narrow fronted weatherboard building housed a crammed chemist's shop with a couple of small 'Agents' signs in the window. The next building was of well-maintained appearance with a small, tidy garden, a green, cared-for lawn with ornamental shrubs and a pinkish coloured concrete path leading to the front doorway and enclosed porch. A lamp was mounted above one of the brick gateposts, which also carried the brass nameplate of the medico who was both general practitioner to the town and medical superintendent to the hospital. In fact, he was currently the only doctor within a hundred kilometres or more. Matron had spoken of him as a gifted surgeon. She had also said that very few young medical graduates would be prepared to tolerate the demands, the lack of social life and the comparatively low financial rewards associated with serving in places like Wilga Creek. A dedicated man!

Another large house, this one a bungalow with what appeared to be fully fly-screened verandahs on three sides, stood next door. The last building in the street was a combined police station and residence, with a small but substantial weatherboard building in the backyard. In assuming that this must be the local "lockup", Stefanie was correct, although aside from an occasional drunken ringer or two being "yarded" just long enough to sober up, the gaol was rarely used nowadays.

She turned and retraced her steps. So this was Wilga Creek, the town that Lieutenant Tony Roxton, USN, had continued to regard as his true hometown! Apart from the newish brick Hotel-Motel, Stefanie did not doubt that Wilga Creek was essentially unchanged since her father had last seen it more than thirty years before.

She glanced at her watch. Ten minutes to five! She hurried back to the little post office to buy some postage stamps. There was much to tell her mother in the letter she would write this night. The elderly postmistress was friendly, talkative and in no hurry to close the doors.

"Just passing through, Dear? I'll bet you're finding it a lot different to New Zealand, eh?" she enquired as Stefanie paid for the stamps.

"No, and yes," Stefanie replied, "I'll be nursing at the hospital and I hope to be around for a while, and yes, it is different to home; but I'm enjoying that difference."

"Good for you, Love! You're only young once, and they say travel broadens one's outlook! I suppose that a pretty girl like you will find herself married and tied down with a family soon enough. Best to see a bit of the world while you have the chance!" the Postmistress said.

"Probably," Stefanie conceded agreeably, having no desire to debate the issue. She introduced herself. They talked generally for a few minutes, then casually, but concealing her intense interest, for she sensed that the woman might be inclined to gossip, Stefanie asked, "Do you know of any people named Roxton who still live in the district?"

"No, Stefanie, not around Wilga Creek! We've been here since 1950. Funny, the name rings a bell, vaguely. I'll just ask my husband. He's busy with the paperwork for month's end." She raised her voice and called, "Bert, does the name Roxton ring a bell with you?"

Busy, long-suffering Bert did his best, "Isn't he that R.S.L. bloke who's always making the headlines, Love?"

"No, Bert, that's Ruxton. We want Roxton!"

"Search me!" Bert said.

The postmistress shook her head and smiled apologetically, "Afraid not, Stefanie."

"It doesn't matter. The family I'm thinking of moved to America before I was born. I just thought they might have still had some relatives here," Stefanie hid her disappointment.

The woman shook her head, "No, Love. Joe Merriton's daughter is the only one I know who married a yank, but their name is Clarke."

82

Over the following weeks, Stefanie settled into a quiet but pleasant life-style. She enjoyed a close friendship with two other single nurses, Pam and Susan, and joined the Wilga Creek Social Tennis Club. Most Saturday nights, if not on duty, she attended a dance or a cabaret evening at Wilga Creek, Bradford, or, on one occasion, Roma; a long car drive for her and Pam to seek entertainment that particular evening.

Other weekend activities, which she found interesting and novel, were a picnic race meeting and a polocrosse match. Along with their friend, Wendy, the town's sole unmarried female schoolteacher, the nurses were a focus of attention for the district's eligible young bachelors. One, in particular, was a jackaroo named Terry, who was very good-looking but supposedly saw himself as irresistible to any red-blooded young woman. Forewarned by Susan and Wendy, Stefanie ably parried this local charm-er.

He introduced himself to her, then immediately followed up with a self-assured spiel that Stefanie found blatantly condescending, "I've been looking forward to meeting you, Steffy. I heard that you were the prettiest flower in the garden and I must say, I'm not disappointed!"

So this conceited, transparent clown was reputedly, the smoothest line-shooter the district could muster! Stefanie returned his smile, lower-ing her eyelids demurely in mock modesty as her brain searched for an appropriate reply.

"I've heard about you, too!" she countered, "The honey bee who flits from flower to flower! Well, I'm sorry, but I'm not yet ready to be polli-nated!"

Only momentarily off guard, Terry bounced back with a further condescending attempt at good humour. "O.K., so I spread myself around a bit! That's my contribution to P.R.! I always do my best to make new talent feel right at home on the local scene."

Stefanie felt uncharacteristically catty. "Very public-spirited of you, I'm sure," she observed with a hint of sarcasm.

Disconsolation showed plainly on Terry's countenance. No sophisticate, his friendly smile, good looks and breezy self-assurance had usually sufficed despite his corny lines, but it was obvious that he'd met his match this time. Perhaps he had deserved to be taken down a peg, but Stefanie felt almost sorry for him. She extended the olive branch.

"Cheer up!" she said, "It wasn't such a bad try! I'm just not ready to be swept off my feet. Friends?"

"Friends!" he conceded with a rueful little grin. Stefanie thought she liked him better, already!

The hospital had first opened in 1950, so there was little point in searching its records for Tony Roxton's birth details. Stefanie asked the Matron what likely maternal arrangements might have been the general rule before that.

"Possibly home-birth with a Doctor or a mid-wife attending, but more usually an extended visit to a larger centre which had a hospital; particularly if the mother had friends or relatives there with whom she could stay until the baby was due," Joan Kirkyard said.

Stefanie felt annoyed with herself for not having searched the records of the Registrar of Births in Brisbane before driving to Wilga Creek. Naively, she had presumed that the name of Roxton would be well known in the little town, but thus far, she had found nobody who recalled it. She now realised that many of the townspeople, such as railway or hospital staff, the policeman, the Doctor and their families were comparatively recent arrivals, and that many of the older, adult residents of thirty or forty years before had died or had moved east to retire in larger, more climatically congenial centres such as Toowoomba or the Coast. Nobody else whom Stefanie had asked had remembered, either, so she had ceased to ask. Instead, she decided to do what she should have done at first; to write to the Registrar of Births, Deaths and Marriages in Brisbane, for a full copy of her father's Birth Certificate. That should give his mother's maiden name and other relevant information but she wasn't certain as to the date or the place of his birth. All that she could assume was that Anthony David Roxton was born somewhere near Wilga Creek in 1938 or 1939 from what little her mother had known of his age and background. Stefanie nominated 1938 as the likely year of his birth and southwest Queensland as his birthplace, enclosed a cheque for $14.50 in payment of the fee, and then mailed her request.

83

Now well into his ninety-first year, Joe had turned ninety some seven months previously. On that occasion, he was quite surprised at the amount of fuss that his family had made of his birthday, and had jokingly declared, "I'm not sure I'd care to reach one hundred! I don't think I could survive the celebration"

Rosemary and her family had phoned from the U.S.A. Bob and Kate had taken a couple of days off work to drive south from the big northern run where Bob was overseer; Billy and his wife, Joan, had also driven more than five hundred kilometres; the old Wilga Creek home hadn't accommodated so many people in nearly three decades! As well, a constant stream of visitors from all around the district had attended the 'open house and birthday bash' organised as a special surprise by an enthusiastic, animated Jenny, herself no spring chicken at eighty-three years of age.

Yet, amidst the special feeling of warmth and humility engendered by so many people so genuinely expressing their friendship and appreciation of his help and concern over the years, Joe could not escape a tinge of sadness. So many of his family and so many old friends had long since predeceased him, especially his beloved Diana, Mike and Tony. Ellen, Leah and their spouses, as well as Doug Gray, Bluey Thompson and a host of other old mates from the cattle tracks or the Light Horse had had a pretty good run in terms of years, but many more, like John, Mike and Tony; like young Davo, killed in a night rush of bullocks on the Diamantina, or like so many of those young mates in Sinai and Palestine whose lives were cut tragically short of their true potential, had deserved better. And Diana! Still so vibrantly young and active at sixty-seven, so loyal, so loving and uncomplaining, had been snatched from him only months before their planned retirement would have been achieved. Often since, he'd felt he should have taken more holidays and travelled with her, perhaps even to have retired earlier and moved to a more populated, sophisticated area where she could have indulged her cultured nature after forty years of living in the bush. How he loved her still. How he missed her! But now, like the others, she slept, awaiting the promised Resurrection. No, Joe Merriton felt no desire to live to be a hundred; not without Diana!

Not given to introspection or self-pity, he wasn't consciously aware that all that still drove him was the human need to keep his mind occupied, his hands busy and his heart from breaking. He was a born battler, a compulsive worker, yet with empty motivation since his wife's death.

Joe had yarded a few young male weaner cattle from the back paddock, without the knowledge of the Geriatric Gypsy, his frivolous nickname for his sister. Jenny had recently arrived back at Wilga Creek after eight weeks with her eldest daughter on the Sunshine Coast. Jenny had decided to "make the place habitable before Rosemary arrives," and to generally fuss about after her brother, for a couple of weeks. After that, she intended spending Christmas and the summer season with Tom and his family on the New South Wales south coast. Jenny was exceptionally active for her age, Joe reflected. It didn't cross his mind that he, too, was quite spry for an old bloke, but what he did realise was that Jenny would have raised plenty of objections if she'd been aware of his intention to cut and brand these young mickeys. It was true that they were pretty advanced; in fact, too well grown. He should have marked and branded them a couple of months earlier, so he had better get on with it.

Rosie and her husband, Cliff, that son-in-law of more than forty years, whom Joe still barely knew, would be visiting for a few weeks of the Christmas-New Year season. Months earlier, when she had phoned to ask her father, Joe had suggested, "Why not come a little earlier still and take in the Expo in Brisbane? You'll really feel the Queensland heat if you arrive in December!"

Laughingly, Rosie had replied, "I wouldn't be able to contend with the crowds at an Expo, Dad! I guess I'm still my father's daughter in that respect. Anyhow, if there is one thing worse than a Queensland summer, it would have to be a North American winter! No, Dad, December-January is fine for us if it's O.K. with you?"

"Anytime is O.K. by me, Love!" Joe had agreed warmly, "I haven't seen you in more than twenty years!"

That was another good reason to do these cattle now. Couldn't have the kids thinking he was getting too old to manage on his own!

He was alone in the yards, having purposely waited until Jenny had gone to a C.W.A. function, before yarding these mickeys. Had she known, she'd have first said her piece, then insisted on helping him when she realised he was determined to go ahead with it, and he didn't want a frail old lady in the same pen as these boisterous young cattle.

He swung the gate behind them, driving them up towards the little forcing pen. The lead beast baulked near the apex of the triangle feeding the crush, and turned back, turning two others with him. Joe had almost shut the gate as the rearmost animal jumped aside, bouncing its hip back hard against the gate. Joe had waved his hat and shouted, urging them back as he struggled to slam home the sliding gate bolt but slipped and lost his footing. He fell heavily, the gate swinging freely above him as a startled mickey dashed for the relative freedom of the bigger yard beyond the gate. Others followed in a stumbling, nervous rush that caused the gate to crack wide open, with no dog to block them, for Joe had left the tough blue heeler on the chain. The dog was considered too forceful and enthusiastic to be other than a hindrance in the yards.

Rolling quickly and instinctively to the sanctuary beyond a bottom rail, he was too late! Caught underfoot, he heard one rib give an audible 'crack', felt pain in his chest, numbness in his left lower arm and a blow to the back of his head. With failing strength, he rolled himself under the yard rail. Away down in the house yard his chained dog barked in frenzied excitement as Joe faded into unconsciousness.

How long he lay there he did not know, but he came to, eventually. Part crawling, part staggering, he made his way through the back gate and onto the low stairs of the side verandah of the house. He rested for a few minutes, trying to regain his breath as he nursed his gashed arm. Jenny, returning from town, found him there.

84

Although Joe was conscious when first admitted to hospital with two ribs cracked and one broken, which fortunately had not pierced the lung, Doc Rogensen and the matron had anaesthetised him for some minor corrective surgery. Also, the hoof wound in his left forearm had required seventeen "stitches", but the blow to the head luckily had not been as serious. After the surgery, the rest of the evening had passed in a blurred haze beyond which he had little recollection other than of a saline drip tube in his good arm, a craving thirst for water to satisfy a parched throat from which, in laryngitis-like frustration, he seemed unable to make them understand he was so thirsty. Finally, someone gave him a tiny sip of water that was barely enough to wet his mouth. "Sorry," the woman apologised. "But we mustn't overdo it."

Instead, they were more concerned with getting him to exercise his lungs to clear the anaesthetic from them. Later, they gave him a short period back on the oxygen mask, but still, he really craved a decent drink of water. Eventually, they left him alone in the semi-darkened ward and exhaustion claimed him. He slept soundly.

He awoke in the early morning light as the little hospital stirred into life. A blue-uniformed nurse, Pat Deskins, young Jerry's wife, gave him a cheery greeting as she stuck a thermometer underneath his tongue, as she had just done to the other three patients in the tiny male ward.

"Good morning, Mr. Merriton! Sleep well, I trust? Like a cup of tea? Milk? Sugar?" she was a buxom, good-natured woman in her early forties. Dispassionately, Joe wondered why she had first placed the thermometer in his mouth before asking such a rapid succession of questions. Obviously, they were meant to be assumptions more than questions. He smiled as he removed the thermometer and replied, "yes to the first two, Pat, but black, no sugar!" and replaced the thermometer under his tongue.

She momentarily disappeared from view but soon returned to check pulse rates against her little lapel watch, and to record these and the temperatures on the patients' charts at the foot of each bed. As she read and replaced each thermometer in its receptacle, she would sound an approving "Mmm!" without elaborating further. All part of her little charade to keep the ward atmosphere as bright and cheerful as possible. Joe suspected. Another nurse appeared carrying a stainless steel receptacle and asked Joe whether he wished to urinate or anything.

"With what? I've been dry as a bone ever since I arrived," Joe wryly informed her, "I'd love that cup of tea, though!"

She nodded her understanding and left the vessel atop the bedside locker, with the assurance that the tea would be served very soon, as indeed it was.

Afterward, Pat and the other nurse folded back the bed covers, and then Pat sponged and dried Joe's face and body. She then cranked up the bed, re-arranged his pillows to prop him into more of a sitting position and extracted from the bedside locker his shaving gear. Jenny must have fetched that for him the previous night he surmised. Pat wheeled a mobile stainless steel bench into place for him, placed a dish of hot water on it and unfolded a built-in mirror.

He had finished shaving before the duty Sister made her first appearance into the little ward. She conscientiously perused each patient's charts; a pretty, fresh-faced young slip of a girl whose manner indicated that she took her work seriously nevertheless. Finally satisfied, she then exclaimed, "Right! Now, what are we all having for breakfast?" and detailed a couple of options.

Cheekily, the young fellow in the bed next to Joe's, replied, "I'd settle for Pam and eggs!"

She tolerated the quip with a good-humoured smile, "Sorry, Alan, but I'm just not on the menu, neither with nor without eggs! Nor is a kiss and a cuddle," she forestalled his anticipated reply and continued, "Now, let's have some decorum around here! What's it to be?"

They listed their preferences; she noted them and left the ward. Joe introduced himself to the other patients. Bert, he already knew. The Postmaster suffered from severely high blood pressure and was admitted for a few days of tests and observation. "More of a rest, really," he told Joe.

Ted, whom Joe did not know, was a veteran of the infamous Burma Railway. The ex-P.O.W. and his wife were visiting a married daughter in Wilga Creek when he was taken ill. In chronic poor health since the war, Ted was to recuperate in the little hospital until well enough to travel back to Brisbane and the specialised care of Greenslopes Repatriation General Hospital.

Alan, the cheeky young ringer who had asked the young Sister for "Pam and eggs," had suffered a fractured right leg and a torn cartilage of the left knee. He was eager to recount in detail how those injuries were sustained, being something of an extrovert.

"Accident?" he grinned," It was no bloody accident from the horse's point of view! It was dead-set deliberate! She was a big blood mare, but a real rank cranky bastard, and hard as nails. We'd already put in a good morning's work but she was still full of fight. The first chance I gave her, she grabbed the bit and bolted. I had no chance; she could pull a coal train on the bit. Well, I'd heard the old blokes tell that the only way to pull up her type was to spur her like crazy and pretty soon she'd quit runnin' and start buckin', and it seemed like a logical idea."

Joe concurred, "I've been known to use that psychology myself, once or twice."

"Yair, well," Alan continued, "I put the hooks into her and it worked in no time! She had her head well down, all the rein she needed to make a fist of it, and I made the fatal blue of trying to pull her head up instead of riding out the first few and taking it from there. She pulled me forward, right over the pads and skyed me well and truly! I landed skew-whiff, with one leg on a big tree-root and the other wrenched back under me as well, so here I am!"

Sometime after breakfast, the doctor and the matron arrived on their rounds. Joe assured them that he felt fine and was ready to go home.

"I think we ought to keep you here for a couple more days. You've had some nasty injuries and a fair sort of bump on the head, to boot. Nothing too terrible, but I'd be happier to have you where we can keep an eye on you for a little longer," Doc Rogensen insisted.

After "Rounds" Pam and Pat got the patients onto their feet; Alan with the aid of crutches. The movement helped his circulation, but Joe was surprised at how weak he felt. This was only the third time in his long life that he was hospitalised, and it didn't sit easily with him. As they sat in the modest armchairs at the end of the ward enjoying morning tea while the nurses re-made the beds, he and Bert conceded that there was nothing wrong with the service.

"I reckon I could get used to it," Bert said.

"I hope for your sake that you won't have to; it wears pretty thin after a while!" Ted advised, as one who'd had more than his fair share of hospitalization over the previous forty-three years.

"I'm only here for the scenery," Alan quipped, "speaking of which, I hope Stefanie's on again tonight!"

"Don't you ever get your mind off sheilas? There is more to life than women, booze and horses, you know!" Bert chastised.

"Yair? Like what?" Alan asked incredulously.

A second Sister, whose shift overlapped with Pam's, was a middle-aged married woman. Efficient and pleasant enough, her manner, nevertheless, brooked few liberties. Alan meekly addressed her as "Sister" or as "Sister Abrams."

Joe chuckled, "I see that one has got you bluffed!"

However, there was a young enrolled nurse, Robyn, whom Alan pestered flirtatiously once Sister Abrams was out of earshot, until Robyn turned on him in exasperation, "I wish you'd dry up! I have some news for you. You're not God's gift to women! I've got other patients to attend to and you're getting to be a pain in the neck!"

Jenny arrived for the afternoon visiting hour and brought with her

Joe's bifocal reading glasses, some figs and some oranges. She looked flustered and upset, so Joe assured her that there was no cause for alarm.

"I'll be home in a couple of days," he said, "by the way, are those young weaners still yarded?"

"No, they're not! I let them out into the small paddock, and you leave them there when you get out of here!" she scolded, "Bob and Kate will be coming through next week. I'm sure Bob will be glad to see to them for you!"

"Yes, and I'll be happy to let him," Joe conceded, relieved that his sister was still enough of a bushie to have remembered the welfare of the cattle amid the drama of the previous twenty-four hours.

"Well, that's one weight off my mind," Jenny said, continuing to fuss about with sisterly concern.

"Now, don't work yourself up into a state, Sis dear. I'm O.K. and I'll rest a lot more settled if I know that you're all right. It's lovely to see you, but don't try to come again in the dark tonight. Stay home and have a good night's sleep and I'll see you tomorrow afternoon, alright?"

Jenny agreed that she would. They talked for a while, then after she left Joe nodded off to sleep.

85

He awoke around six p.m. The wards were a hive of activity preparatory to serving the evening meal, and evidently, there was another change of shift. He picked up the spectacles which Jenny had brought to the hospital for him and was about to put them on, intending a quick perusal of the newspaper which Jenny had also brought when he was startled by what appeared to be an apparition; a youthful Diana, much as his earliest recollections of her, yet with modern uniform and hairstyle.

"Good evening, everybody!" she announced brightly.

"Good evening, Sister." from the beds opposite.

From the adjacent bed, Alan quipped, "You're looking particularly gorgeous tonight, Steffy!"

Joe continued to look on in amazement. "Flattery will get you nowhere, Alan," the apparition smiled self-confidently as she approached Joe. "You're looking a lot fitter than you were last night, Mr. Merriton. I hear you're making remarkable progress!" She adjusted his pillows and assisted him into a more upright position.

Joe could manage only a surprised stare.

Assuming it to be merely a lack of recognition, she continued with, "Don't remember much of last night, eh?"

"No, I don't. Things were pretty much out of focus," he admitted.

"I'm not surprised. You'd had a very tough time of it."

Her nametag read "Sr. Zietarski" yet even that beautifully modulated voice could have been Diana's!

An hour later, with dinner cleared away and the patients freshened up, teeth brushed and toiletries attended to, another visiting hour was underway. Ted's wife, daughter and son-in-law sat talking with Ted in the chairs at the far end of the ward. Bert and his Postmistress wife exchanged news from Bert's bed opposite. Occasionally a nurse would look in on them all, unobtrusively. Few duties could be carried out until visiting hours were over. Neither Joe nor Alan had visitors. They were quietly discussing cattle breeds when Sister Zietarski made another brief appearance. Alan, as ever, was quick off the mark.

"Be nice to me, Kiwi," he coaxed, "after all, I'm an old Rugby player!"

"Ohhh, that's too bad; I'm not!" Stefanie countered facetiously.

"But I'll bet you do a terrific Haka!" Alan tried again.

She poked out her tongue in Maori fashion, rolled her eyes with right arm upraised in a threatening gesture, tapping her elbow with the finger-tips of her left hand as she gave a small jump into the air. Alan and Joe laughed. Her eyes sparkled and a half smile played mischievously around the corners of her mouth.

"You know," Joe confided. "It gave me quite a start this evening when I first saw you. You're the living image of my late wife, and she was a Nursing Sister and a Kiwi as well! When I first met her, she and my elder sister were Army nurses in Egypt and I was a Trooper in the Light Horse. She came from Wellington and her maiden name was Smithfield. I'll bet you're related! The resemblance is remarkable!"

Stefanie shook her head, "It must be just a coincidence. I'm from Auckland and the first and only Kiwi in my line. My mother is English and my father was an Australian, but he was killed in Vietnam before I was born."

"I'm sorry about your Dad. I lost a son in New Guinea in World War Two and a grandson in Vietnam. Both were aircrew."

Stefanie nodded, then said, "Mum was very bitter about the Vietnam war, particularly because of how it turned out, with all that sacrifice in vain! I feel much the same."

"Yes. Especially for the ones who were conscripted," Joe sympathised.

"Thankfully, he wasn't. He was a regular and a flyer, like your boys. I think Mum would have cracked up if he'd been conscripted as well," Stefanie told him. She didn't mention that although her father was an Australian, he was USN; that would have made a simple statement appear more complicated. Also, because Joe had lost a son and a grandson, she had somehow assumed that they were father and son, both named Merriton. She hadn't expected any family connection with them. Indeed, there seemed no reason why she should, given that from what she knew of her own background, her supposed resemblance to Joe's World War One nurse would have been a mere coincidence.

"War is always a waste of human life," Joe said. "During my lifetime, this country has been involved in six or seven foreign wars. I'll admit, as a young fellow, I was keen enough to go to the Great War, the war to end all wars, we were told. Looking back now, at all the death, destruction and suffering, I don't think we Australians and New Zealanders had any right to become involved in any except for the Second World War. I can't see how we could have avoided that one! Even then, our leaders threw away men's lives needlessly in 1944 and 1945, yet nowadays, our wheeler-dealers are happy to auction off the country to the very people who tried to take it from us then." Alan and Stefanie were in sober agreement with the old man's sentiments, but, embarrassed by his own philosophising, Joe steered the conversation away from doom and gloom.

"Anyway, Sister, how long have you been working here and how do you like the place?" he asked.

"Six weeks and I love it. I've felt quite at home, despite the heat and the dryness. This little hospital is a nice change from the big city hospitals that I'm used to; everyone is so informal and friendly. Some are a bit too informal and friendly!" she said, pointedly looking at Alan and waving her index finger in mock reproof.

"Ah, come off it, Stef! Good sorts like you just thrive on a bit of attention! Besides, I really would leave home for you," Alan baited her. "That would be a wasted journey," she smiled, consulting her watch and rising to her feet.

Including outpatients' clinic, administration clerk, doctor, matron, nurses and domestics, full and part-time staff totalled around two dozen. Currently, there were eleven patients distributed among four wards of the tiny hospital. The nurses' office, centrally located between two partitioned wings, allowing the duty Sister adequate supervision of all. Stefanie noticed Joe in a dressing gown, heading in the direction of the male toilets late in the evening. Most of the lights were already out, most of the patients already asleep, though both Alan and Bert were still reading beneath their respective bed lamps in the semi-darkened ward. Stefanie checked the time; a quarter to ten. With the junior nurse, she was commencing another quick inspection of the wards and would switch off all but essential night lighting. The muted buzzer of the telephone recalled her to her office as Joe walked back towards his bed. All after-hours' calls were diverted to the duty Sister, though calls were rare enough at this time of night.

"Wilga Creek Hospital, Sister Zietarski speaking," she answered.

"Oh, hello!" a well-spoken female voice with a slight North American accent introduced herself, "I'm Rosemary Clarke, Joe Merriton's daughter. I am sorry to call at this late hour, but it's not yet seven a.m. here in Michigan. My Aunt phoned last night to tell me my father has had an accident and I'm anxious to know of his progress!"

"Your father is progressing very well, Mrs. Clarke! He is able to walk about. In fact, he just passed me on his way back to bed a few moments ago. If you'd like, I'll call him to the 'phone, provided you keep it short and sweet. I'm sure he'd love to hear your voice," Stefanie replied.

"Oh, that would be swell! I do hope that it won't cause you any bother," Rosemary sounded relieved.

"It's not the usual procedure, but I'm sure I can bend the rules just this once since you're calling from so far away! Hold the line while I fetch him," Stefanie said.

She escorted Joe to the telephone, with the request to keep it brief and quiet, and then resumed her rounds.

"Hello, Rosie! Now, don't worry, I'm nearly as good as new! Jenny got a bit of a scare when it happened but I'm fine now. I should be out of hospital in a day or two," Joe told his daughter.

"That's great news, Dad! You sure gave us a fright! We are trying to book on an earlier airplane, but it all depends on cancellations. We have our visas already, so with luck, we may see you sometime around the weekend. That nurse sure is a sweetie to bring you to the 'phone!"

"Yes, Love, she is. By coincidence, she is a Kiwi and the spitting image of your mother in her early twenties. She gave me quite a start when I first saw her, I can tell you!"

"Perhaps she is a relative," Rosie ventured.

"No, she doesn't know your mother's family. She says she is the first of her family to be born in New Zealand. Her name is Polish, her mum is English and her dad was an Australian. He was a pilot, killed in Vietnam, so there's another coincidence."

"How extraordinary! I promised her I wouldn't tie up the line for long, so 'bye for now, Dad. Take care and we'll see you soon!"

86

The following day, a Wednesday, Ted was deemed well enough to travel. His wife and daughter came to collect him, and Doc Rogensen wrote a letter of referral to a specialist physician in Brisbane. Earlier that morning, a further patient, a sixteen-year-old lad was admitted for an emergency appendectomy that Rogensen had performed. Bert, the postmaster, was given the O.K. to go home, a net reduction of one in the male ward population.

"When do I get the nod, Doctor? I'm feeling pretty fit; I might as well be at home as here," Joe made his own bid.

"I think you've pulled up very well, Mr. Merriton, but how about we give it another day, then we ought to be on firmer ground?" Rogensen proposed.

Joan Kirkyard smiled tolerantly at the old bushman's impatience, "I don't know why you're in such a hurry to leave us! You will still have to take things easy for quite a while, you know. No more cattle work for a few weeks until you are fully recovered," she gently admonished.

"Old fellows, like old dogs and old horses, get pretty set in our ways, Matron. You've all been very good to me, but there's no place like home," Joe replied.

Doc Rogensen was firmly insistent, "I'll feel a lot more confident if we give it another day or so!" He glanced at his watch with a weary smile and said to nobody in particular, "I'd better go home and have my breakfast."

Around noon, Stefanie split the day shift, substituting for a few hours to allow Sister Abrams to keep a personal business appointment elsewhere. Afternoon visiting hours saw a brief visit to Alan from his grazier employer, while the younger lad, Ian, still drowsy from the morning operation, brightened somewhat with a visit from his mother. Joe also received a very welcome lift as Jenny arrived with an escort. It was Billy!

"Good day, Bill! My word, it's great to see you again!" Joe responded warmly, "Jenny was worried, but I'm right as rain; should be home tomorrow! It was good of you to come, though! I really appreciate it, it must be what; a five-hour car trip?"

"Oh, that's nothing, Joe! You and Mrs. Merriton were like a second father and mother to me when I was a youngster. If it hadn't been for you and Sergeant Thompson, there's no telling what would have become of me!"

The speaker was a fine-looking man, an Aboriginal whose open-necked safari jacket bore a cross on each lapel; a form of dress frequently preferred instead of the "dog collar" by clergymen of the north and the hot dry inland areas. He was tall, erect, with grey hair and strong but compassionate facial features. He'd probably be in his sixties, Stefanie guessed. She had completed her tasks and was leaving the ward as Joe replied.

"You'd have made the grade, no matter what! Everything you've achieved has been by your own efforts and studies, Bill! I've always been very proud of you, as much as if you were my own son!"

It was a sincere, emotional moment. Stefanie was out of earshot by the time Bill spoke again.

"Speaking of Mrs. Merriton, Joe, that young Sister bears an amazing resemblance to her!"

"Yes, that is what I thought on the night Joe was admitted!" Jenny agreed, "I thought my imagination must have been running away with me at the time, I was so worried about Joe."

"She is very much like Diana, even down to being a New Zealander," Joe informed them. "We had a bit of a talk last night and that appears to be just a coincidence. By the way, Rosie phoned last night! She hopes to arrive over here around the weekend."

They yarned about old times for almost an hour, then Bill announced that he'd better make tracks to return to his parish that evening. Jenny and Joe reminded him that there was always a bed for him at their place, but he declined gracefully.

"I realise that, and thanks, but I do have other duties. A parson doesn't merely work only on Sundays, you know!" his eyes twinkled good-humouredly. Alan's visitor had left also. Alan and Joe were talking horses and cattle when Stefanie returned to the ward. Alan glanced at her, his brain racing to conjure up a witty, flirtatious greeting, but she had anticipated his intention. Mischievously, she took the thermometer from its receptacle above his head and placed it beneath his tongue. She gave Joe an impish, Diana-like wink and irreverently remarked, "This cowboy business must be pretty dangerous stuff if you pair of crocks are anything to go by!"

Joe's smile was nostalgic. Stefanie and the young ringer reminded him so much of another young nurse and her cheeky Light Horseman, in another hospital, in Cairo, seventy years earlier.

Stefanie returned his smile. She felt a very warm feeling towards this old man. The thought suddenly entered her head that he might know something of the Roxton family. After all, he obviously knew the district intimately. She had mailed her request to the Registrar of Births late in the previous week and didn't know how soon she might expect a reply.

"Mr. Merriton," she started to ask, "have you ever known anyone around here na-"

Her question was interrupted by a junior nurse in the doorway, with the urgent news. "Stefanie, Mrs. Wilson has just fallen out of bed!"

The next morning, Thursday, Joe persuaded Doctor Rogensen to discharge him.

"Tell you what, I'm going back to town at eleven; I might as well give you a lift," the genial medico offered.

Rogensen delivered Joe home to a grateful Jenny, with some advice. "Try to keep old Skuthorpe here, in the house as much as you can; although it's probably a losing battle!" the doctor admitted.

362

He turned to Joe and gently cautioned, "You're not a spring chicken anymore, remember! Give yourself time to recuperate".

Joe fully understood the medico's concern. The mere effort of returning home had weakened him noticeably, after the few days of relative immobility at the hospital, yet by late afternoon, he was bored. He walked down to the yards while his sister fussed about him like a mother hen with an errant chick. Joe poked around for a while, venturing into the small adjoining paddock to satisfy himself that his young weaners were, all present and correct.

An aged brown mare lifted her head from a sweet patch of short grass and whinnied a friendly greeting. She trotted up and nuzzled Joe affectionately, his last remaining horse on the place; they enjoyed the mutual bond between them. She had missed his presence these past few days. "Hello, old girl!" he rubbed her poll then reached into his coat pocket to produce a slice of bread that he had smuggled from the kitchen for her.

For once, Jenny overlooked the misdemeanour and the resultant crumbs it would leave in the pocket. "Dolly had sensed there was something amiss during your spell in hospital. She was quite frantic at times!" Jenny told him.

Well, I'm home now," Joe assured them both.

87

Joe slept well that night, in the comfort of his own bed again. He rose at first light, quietly lit a fire in the old wood stove, filled the kettle and put it on the stove. By the time Jenny came into the kitchen, he'd brewed the tea. There was no logical reason as to why they still required such an early start to the day, but life-long habits do not change easily.

"I'll stay on for a few days after Rosemary and Cliff arrive, then I'll go on down to Tom and Jill before the really hot weather sets in," Jenny told him.

Cliff and Rosie were now expected to arrive at Wilga Creek late Sunday. Bob and Kate were also due sometime over the weekend; there was plenty of room for all in the big old house and it promised to be a happy family reunion. No doubt, Jenny would give Rosie some firm advice to persuade her father to toe the line, Joe mused, but he'd cope with that when the time came.

"Thanks again for everything, Sis," he said, "I'm sorry it all had to fall on your shoulders when I had my buster"

Joe busied himself with light duties during the day. He fetched some firewood into the house and noted the diminishing pile in the backyard. He would let Bob cut and split to replenish the stock when his son arrived. It went against Joe's grain to be dependent, but he realised that it could be some time yet before he felt up to that particular task.

In the relative coolness of late afternoon, to his sister's chagrin, she found him saddling old Dolly. Joe hadn't previously realised that his old Barcoo Poley could feel so heavy. Winded by the exertion, he sat and rested for a few minutes. Dolly was not a tall mare; she was only 14.2 hands high, but the old man had to lead her beside an old tree stump before he could mount up this time. Once in the saddle, he felt right as rain.

"Now don't get yourself all worked up, Sis. There isn't a gate on the place that I can't open from a horse's back!"

It was true; having good, well-maintained gates had always been a matter on which Joe had prided himself. Jenny watched him ride off, every bit one of those legendary Australian kings on a leather throne.

"Roll on next week! He can be Rosemary's worry then," Jenny told herself in exasperation.

Joe returned around sunset, physically tired but mentally pleased. He unbridled Dolly and gave her a small ration of grain and chaff in a nose-bag. After unsaddling, he brushed her back then replaced the saddle on its rail in the shed before turning the mare out into the small paddock.

He returned to the house as darkness fell. Jenny was preparing dinner when he walked into the kitchen. She was still a little peeved and moody. Joe hugged her gently in silence with a brotherly kiss to her forehead, then walked through to the lounge and promptly fell asleep in an arm-chair. Jenny woke him shortly for dinner. Afterward, he dried the dishes for her, listened to the radio for about an hour, and then retired to bed.

What he called indigestion woke him around 3 am. He'd had a few bouts of "indigestion" in recent years, and occasional shortness of breath, but had never disclosed this to Dr. Rogensen. Joe's blood pressure had always seemed quite good considering his age. His shortness of breath he had attributed to his old age or, as on the previous evening, a temporary lack of fitness. On this occasion though, the attack of "indigestion" seemed particularly sharp and of long duration. The sun was well above the horizon when Jenny came into his room.

"You don't look at all well!" she informed her brother.

"I'll be alright, it's only indigestion," Joe insisted.

"Indigestion, my foot!" Jenny exclaimed. She went straight to the telephone and called the doctor.

Stefanie strolled across from the nurses' quarters to commence her

Saturday evening shift. The previous day's mail had brought an air letter from her mother, but nothing from the Registrar of Births. Oh well, perhaps on Monday, she hoped. She looked forward to Monday for a further reason, too. From the end of Monday's shift, she would have a full four days' break! If the copy of her father's birth certificate arrived in time, she might be able to progress with tracking down her Queensland origins during those four days. The small, separate intensive care area which faced the nurses' office now contained an occupied bed. With a start, she realised that it was Joe Merriton, back so soon! Susan briefed her while the old man slept in apparent unconcern.

When he next awoke, Joe seemed his old self and insisted he didn't know what all the fuss was about.

"I'm sure it was only a bad attack of indigestion," he again insisted.

"We think you may have had a mild coronary occlusion, so we've put you right next to my window, so that I can keep an eye on you," Stefanie smiled tactfully, trying not to alarm him.

A few hours later, the monitor audio alert sounded as Joe suddenly convulsed in sharp pain. He gave a little involuntary shout as a nurse dashed to his bedside, signalling her workmate to summon the Sister.

The pain ceased as suddenly as it had begun and Joe felt himself drifting into a peaceful, darkening void. The urgent, insistent alarm buzzer became fainter as he heard it receding into some distant background. Stefanie joined the nurse and worked urgently, efficiently, trying to restore normality. Temporarily her efforts appeared to promise a slight improvement. She addressed him by his Christian name as she sought to stop his drift into unconsciousness, attempting to motivate him to not give up the struggle.

"Joe? Joe? Answer me!" she said loudly, "Joe!"

The old man's countenance took on a tender, loving and contented expression. Almost inaudibly, he answered her with his very last breath.

"Diana."